MJ Raco, author of the fantasy/adventure series *Realm Travellers,* is an orthoptist by day, a novelist by night. Her debut novel, *The Ancient Gateway*, is the first in the series, followed by *A Parallel Dimension* and the sequel *The Forbidden Passage.*

MJ lives in Sydney, Australia, has three adult children and two grandkids she adores. She has two exceptionally large ginger rescue tabbies she's allergic to, but wouldn't part with for anything.

The daughter of a great storyteller, songwriter and poet, she grew up surrounded by mythology and parables from the scriptures. Her love affair with fantasy began when she was gifted her first Enid Blyton book at the age of seven. Escaping into a world of endless imagination was her happy place, and she hasn't stopped venturing there since.

When she isn't saving sight, babysitting or tucked away tapping on her archaic laptop, MJ spends her time reading, cooking and making plans to see the world—especially ancient worlds!

REALM TRAVELLERS

THE FORBIDDEN PASSAGE

M.J. RACO

AIA PUBLISHING

Realm Travellers—The Forbidden Passage
M.J. Raco
Copyright © 2022
Published by AIA Publishing, Australia
ABN: 32736122056
http://www.aiapublishing.com

ISBN: 978-1-922329-39-4
Book Design by K. Rose Kreative
Original silhouette art by Michael Raco

To all the awesome readers of Realm Travellers, remember this:
'Self-confidence is a superpower; believe in yourself and watch the magic start to happen!'
—Anonymous

1

WELCOME HOME

JACK

It's Monday morning and the class is abuzz with excitement. Three weeks have passed since Jack and the gang returned from the depths of an unknown world—The Ancient Realm—and it's the first day back at school.

Mr McPhee, the roll-call teacher, rubs his temples, stands at his desk, loosens his necktie, then attempts once again to get the students' attention. He raises his voice to be heard over the throng. 'Now settle down, class; the bell has already gone. Everyone, please take your seats.'

Peanut jumps up, holding his chair in front of him. 'Where to, sir?'

His question momentarily stumps their teacher; he frowns.

Peanut turns to Jack and gives him a wink. 'So where do ya want us to take our seats?'

Mr McPhee's lip curls. 'Nice try, Mr Brown. I see your stint in the vast unknown hasn't dampened your sense of humour.'

The class chuckles.

'Welcome back, Realm Travellers,' Mr McPhee continues. 'I must say, you've had a lot of media attention these past few weeks, and I'll confess I've been just as intrigued with your experiences as the next person, but right now we need to take the roll.'

'Where to, sir?' Peanut lowers his face to hide a smirk.

Suddenly the red-headed larrikin is bombarded by a myriad of projectiles—notepads, pencil cases, balled up bits of paper, a half-eaten apple, someone's sacrificed vegemite sandwich—anything that the students can get their hands on. Peanut deflects and dodges with the skill of a hotshot hockey player.

Jack ducks to avoid being caught in the crossfire. 'Remind me again why I bother sitting next to you!'

'Why? Because we're mates, and because I saved your butt. And not just once, I might add, but that many times I've lost count. So you owe me … big time!'

Jack splutters. '*You* saved *me?*'

Peanut glares at him. 'You're kidding me, right?'

He shakes his head. 'You, my friend, have got a pretty selective memory when it suits ya. Tell me something; who was the genius behind smuggling fireworks to camp? Those fireworks saved your life, buddy. And what about the time—'

'Hey!' Jack stops him. 'Using fireworks was Kenny's idea. Yeah, you might've brought them in, but the genius behind it wasn't exactly you now, was it?'

Peanut's hazel eyes darken. 'Now hang on a sec …'

'Fireworks? At camp?' Mr McPhee approaches and stands before them, hands on hips. 'You do realise that fireworks are illegal, don't you? Especially a minor in possession of such prohibited items.' He peers down his nose at them. 'So … they were *your* fireworks, Mr Brown?'

Jack snorts. The class sniggers.

Peanut cringes. His freckles blend into the flush of his face. He sinks into his seat until only the wavy ginger tresses on the top of his head show.

Jack holds back from chuckling. 'Who says we've lost our superpowers? Won't be long before you've completely disappeared under that desk.'

The class erupts with laughter, and Jack can't hold back either. He turns and winks at Max, sitting in the back corner of the classroom. Ruby sits next to her, arms crossed, clearly not amused … not by a long shot. Her glare is enough to make Jack thankful he's not the focus of that scowl. He turns to high-five Kenny, who sits in the seat behind him. The gang is solid.

A loud knock at the door gets everyone's attention.

'Yes?' Mr McPhee calls out.

The door opens. A stout, older woman enters, flushed and flustered, her neatly plaited grey hair plastered to her sweaty brow.

'Annie?' Max sits higher in her seat.

Jack blinks a few times. Annie—Annuska—is Max's housekeeper, and the last person he would've expected to see here. She juggles multiple overladen shopping bags and almost topples over.

Their teacher eyes her with curiosity. 'Madam, can I help you?'

'*Koszonom* … oh, I mean, tank you,' she says in her thick Hungarian accent. 'Dat is so good of you. Just take dis heavy one from me, please.'

Mr McPhee frowns. 'I mean is there something I can do for you?'

Annuska stops short. 'Yes … you can take de food.' She gazes around the room, and her demeanour changes to a smile as she looks upon the students' happy faces. 'I make it plenty—someting for everyone!' Annuska turns back to Mr McPhee, then takes a moment to look him up and down. 'You eat too; you are too shkinny. I could shnap you like a chicken bone!'

Jack splutters. *That's my Annie!* He pauses on that thought. Annuska has always been *Max's* Annie, but since their return, he considers her just as much *his* Annie now. He'll be the first to confess that he's developed a soft spot for her—well, *soft spot* is probably an understatement—the fact is she's become pivotal in Jack's readjustment to life. So much so at times he finds it hard to share her … even with Max.

Annuska's motherly warmth and ability to comfort and shepherd them through the nightmare they survived had everyone vying for her attention. Her own life experiences, a survivor from post-war Hungary, stood her in good stead to help with their healing.

Since their return from the realm, Annuska had been in her element, clucking and fussing over each and every one of them—the South African kids included. Annie was an instant hit and soon became everyone's favourite *oma*. And now, selfishly, since Ryker, Edra and the twins returned home, Jack has relished Annie's extra attention—although at times he feels the need to hog-tie and gag Peanut to stop him from monopolising her.

'Annie, what are you doing here?' Max is clearly happy to see her but a little surprised, as Jack is, at her visit.

Annie spots Max. 'Ah, my sveetheart.' She blows her a kiss, then shrugs. 'I bring it food!' She says this as if her presence this morning is nothing out of the ordinary.

'But Mrs, ah ...' Mr McPhee begins.

'Miss!' she corrects him. 'Miss Annuska Hedtke—I never married.' She takes a moment to eye him up and down again, this time taking a closer look.

Jack snorts.

'Okay, Miss Hedtke—' Mr McPhee attempts to continue.

'Vell, it vas Peanut, really,' Annuska interrupts their teacher again, then stops to look around the room for him. 'Oh, dhere you are!' She laughs, spotting the top of his head. 'Vell, Peanut asked for me to do *Home Delivery*, but I tink *School Delivery* is much better idea. Yes?'

Annie sees Jack. 'Oh, and dhere's Max's Jack! Hello, Jack.' Her chubby fingers wiggle in a wave. She gives him a special smile, her twinkling eyes disappearing in her scrunched-up face. She turns to their teacher. 'Such a handsome boy and, you know, so brave too!'

Jack grins. *Yep, that's right—Max's Jack!* He turns in his seat to smile at his girl.

'And Kenny,' Annie continues. 'You know someting?' She tells Mr McPhee in a lowered voice, 'dhat boy is a *genius*.' Annie searches the classroom again and spots Ruby. 'Ah, and my beautiful Ruby.' She waves to each of them. 'Dis is good you are all here. Come, eat! I make em *Rantott sajt, Kifli* and *wiener schnitzel*. And after, you eat *Dobos* cake … dhere's plenty for everyone.'

Mr McPhee smacks his forehead, then falls into his seat.

And then a mischievous voice calls out from under the desk. 'Hey, Annie, did you bring any *Retesek*? Man, have I got a hankering for some right now!'

'Peanut!' Max and Ruby both cry out, mortified.

Peanut sits higher in his seat and twists to face them. 'What? I can't help it, I'm starving!'

2

THREE MONTHS LATER

RYKER

Ryker shakes the small brown parcel, curious to know what's inside. Its contents sound like marbles. The delivery came late this afternoon, sent from Max. He rips open the package, too eager to guess any longer. Inside he finds a bright coloured wrapped box with a flattened bow on top.

'Argh, crazy girl! What's this all about?' He smiles at the thought of his best friend's eccentric indulgences. Taped to the present is a birthday-card-sized envelope. A letter falls out when he opens it. He snatches it up to read what's written.

Since his return from Australia, he's kept in touch with all his Aussie mates, but with Max it's different—

there's a bond there that can't be explained. And a hand-written letter from her is just on another level. Call him old-fashioned, but there's something about it that makes it super special.

> *Dear Ryker,*
> *I know you said that turning 22 is just 'meh', but sorry, I'm going to have to disagree with you on that one. Each and every birthday is as special as the one before. Having survived, what we have makes every day worth celebrating. And because you're so far away, and I can't be there to tell you, I've sent you something that'll remind you every day just how special you are … to me, anyway :)*
> *Love you heaps, Max xoxox*

Ryker smiles, then tears at the layers. The sound of the rolling balls is driving him nuts; he needs to find out what it is.

'Finally!' Inside he discovers a container filled with hundreds of small candy-covered chocolates in every colour imaginable. He runs his hand over his blonde buzz cut a few times and frowns. 'I don't get it …' He stops when he realises that every candy has

something written on it. He looks closer and reads
Max's hidden messages:

> *You're the best.*
> *You're my hero.*
> *You're amazing.*
> *You're kind.*
> *You're generous.*
> *You're thoughtful …*

'What the …?' He blinks a few times. Each candy
bears a different message. Overwhelmed by a sudden
need to see her, he grabs his cell phone to FaceTime
her. After several tones he hears a sleepy voice on the
other end of the line.

'H'llo.'

'Awe crap!' He smacks his forehead; it's the middle
of the night in Australia.

'Ryker, is that you? What's wrong? Are you okay?'

'Yeah, sorry, Max, it's me. Don't panic, everything's
good, I'm just an idiot, that's all. I didn't think of the
time difference—my bad.'

He struggles to see anything. 'Hey, turn on the
light so I can see you.'

'See me?'

He chuckles. 'Yeah, I'm FaceTiming you, and all
I see at the moment is your ear, I think.'

She takes the phone away from her ear and glares at him. 'Ryker! You can't be serious. I just woke up! And I'm in my pyjamas, for crying out loud!'

'Hey, I've seen you in worse,' he teases. 'Come on, I want to see you properly; turn on the light.'

He hears a growl before the light comes on. 'Happy now?' She squints in the sudden brightness and shields her eyes. 'This had better be good!'

'There's my girl. Hi, gorgeous. Hey, I received something in the mail today.'

She squeals. 'Oh my God! You've got it already?'

He laughs at her transformation—one second, she looks like the living dead, the next, her whole face lights up like a beacon.

'Stop laughing at me and tell me what you think.'

'You're the best, Max. I love it.'

The image on the screen goes out of focus as she shakes the phone in her excitement. 'Yay! I knew you would.'

Her happiness uplifts his spirits, and he smiles. 'Candy-covered chocolates with personalised messages on them—that's totally awesome.'

'Hey, you'd better appreciate it. Try coming up with 365 ways to pay someone a compliment—I'll tell you, it's not that easy.' She smiles. 'Happy birthday, you big softie.'

He can't help but smile—her friendship means

the world to him. 'Thanks, buddy.'

She's quiet for a moment.

'Hey, I miss you guys,' she says in a soft voice. 'How are the gang? How's Edra? Is she getting better?'

'Edra's doing okay, considering. She's still getting therapy, of course, but we're starting to see signs of the old Edra returning. Having to relive Jae's death was tough on us all. The group counselling was something, though; it helped me understand my barbaric behaviour. I'm a different person now because of it—and of course thanks to Annie and you, Max.'

'Me?'

'Come on, Max, you know it is. Me getting better began the day you saved my life. You're my angel, you know that, right?'

Ryker watches her squirm as he tells her this. She tugs at her fringe, trying to disappear behind it— something she does often. He smiles, surprised that he knows her so well already.

He notices her hair is slowly growing back. He smiles, knowing how upset she was when it was hacked off—even though the pixie-look Aelianna gave her suits her.

He shakes his head, annoyed at his distraction.

For a while now, he's wanted to tell Max how much it means to him—her saving his life—but each time he tries, his tongue gets tied in a knot. What he had said earlier, he meant—she truly is his angel. He knows that his behaviour back in the realm was nothing short of a nightmare. He'd evolved into a monster and reached a point of no return. But Max was patient and, with time, had learned to forgive him.

He shifts in his seat. 'Um, Max … I've never really thanked you properly, and I think it's well overdue.' He clears his throat. 'You know I'd do anything for you, right? You're everything to me, Max, and I'm ashamed of what happened … I'm sorry for what I did to you back then.'

Max lowers her gaze to hide further behind her fringe. She discretely swipes at a tear then clears a lump in her throat. 'Hey, you saved me too, don't forget, so we're even. Okay?' She sniffs then runs the back of her hand across her nose. 'Um, so what's the plan? Are you catching up with the others to celebrate your birthday?'

Ryker smiles at her familiar sidestepping tactic. He decides to leave it at that. 'Hey, I wish you guys were here … we could celebrate together.'

It still surprises him how quickly he became attached to his Aussie friends. Although having spent such a short time together, what they experienced back in the realm somehow has forged a bond he knows will never be broken.

'So how's it going with Jack? You two still good?' He smiles, knowing this is a topic Max won't shy away from, and he's not disappointed; Max's big brown eyes light up at the mention of Jack's name.

'Jack's amazing!'

'He'd better be.' He laughs. 'Tell him to look after my girl or he'll have me to answer to.'

Ryker's smile wanes. His thoughts go to Aelianna—if only he could have what Max and Jack have. He reaches for the book on his bedside table that conceals within its pages a small red flower … given to him by Aelianna. With care, he plucks it out and twirls the dried stem between his fingers. The moment he clamped eyes on the beautiful village girl, he knew he was a goner. But sadly, what he thought he had with Aelianna was clearly a figment of his imagination.

'You're thinking about her again, aren't you?' Max's teasing voice snaps him back to the present.

He can't hold back a grin.

'It's not that hard to guess, Ryker, it's written all over your face. You're an open book when it comes to her.'

'Can't I hide anything from you?'

Max giggles. 'Nope.'

He sighs. 'She was something else though, wasn't

she? Cute, smart … and she had a heart of gold too—you saw yourself what sacrifices she made for her family.'

'Oh, Ryker …'

Max's pitiful look makes him squirm. 'You know what though; I'm glad we were able to help her before we left. I feel better knowing her life will be easier thanks to your father. By the way, how's the prof?'

Max smiles. 'He's great … more to the point, *we're* great. He's had counselling and is slowly learning to deal with things. In fact, now at times he can be a little too overbearing—doing *way* too much to make up for what happened.' She laughs, then her expression changes as her thoughts become sombre. 'I don't think he'll ever really forgive himself for all the years he missed having me in his life.' She sighs. 'I've forgiven him, of course, but he's still battling with those demons.' She pauses, then smiles. 'Overall, we're good. I love having him back in my life. We've both come to terms with the fact that we'll never be the Three Musketeers again, but we're getting there.'

'More like Hans Solo and Chewbacca, huh?' He laughs.

'Hey! Who are you calling Chewbacca?'

'Hey, yourself! Geez, talk about having a complex. Who said anything about *you* looking like Chewbacca?' He struggles to hold back from laughing. 'Well, to be honest, you've kind of got this hair-everywhere-in-your-face look happening there.'

'Ryker! I just woke up … remember?'

He chuckles. 'Relax, I was kidding. But really, I'm stoked—for you and your dad that is. It's hard to imagine the person you were before I met you. Emo? Really? I hope you're letting Annie pretty you up a little now.'

She looks at him sideways and grins. 'Let's just say it's a work in progress.'

'You'd better not be giving my Annie any grief!'

'*Your* Annie?'

He laughs at her possessiveness. 'Well, you do realise you have to share her now. Annie's like a clucking mother hen, checking in on us most days to see if we're okay and posting all this positive stuff on social media. Where she only had you to fuss over, now she has *nine babies!* Ryker mimics Annie's voice.

They both chuckle.

Ryker adores Annuska. From the moment they returned from the nightmare they were imprisoned in for four years, Annie was there, ready to step up and become everyone's surrogate grandmother. She couldn't do enough—she brought food and treats to the hospital every day and made sure that every one of them felt safe. Most of the time she just sat there and listened … really listened. And those hugs!

Man, if you could bottle those hugs! Ryker smiles. In all honesty, a lot of his healing was thanks to his one-on-one talks with Annie. Annie was there for him at a time when he felt confused and needed to talk. Somehow, she just got him, better than anyone ever could have. He came to realise very quickly why Max loves her the way she does. *She's definitely no longer just Max's Annie; that's for sure.*

'Hey, I'm looking forward to Annie's visit next month—we all are,' he tells her. 'I've really missed her cooking. I'm hanging out for one of her home-made apple strudels.'

'Oh my God, tell me about it! She's been going on and on about this trip … *Vat vill I cook for my babies? Maybe I makem Goulash and Toltott Kaposzta. Den I makem Dobos cake. Dat Ryker, he love it, my Dobos cake.*'

They both laugh at Max's impersonation.

'Seriously, though,' Max says, 'she'll be ecstatic when I tell her that you're craving her apple strudel. Annie's been in her element since we've come back— she hasn't stopped cooking. I think Peanut's moved in—he's here every time he has the tiniest twinge of a hunger pain. And I swear he's put on ten kilos since you saw him … you wouldn't recognise him!'

Ryker laughs. Max paints a colourful picture with her over-the-top description. He won't lie, he's not the least bit sorry that he woke her—well, maybe a little—but he'll never regret moments like these. 'So tell me what else is happening.'

'Ryker! It's the middle of the night! And I've got school tomorrow.' She glares at him, then softens. 'Look, I promise to ring you in a few days, and we can catch up some more. Okay?'

He realises how selfish he's been. 'Sure; sorry, Max. Thanks; that'll be great.' He forces a smile. 'Goodnight. Love you.'

Max smiles in return. 'Love you too. And happy birthday again, you great big hunk of marshmallow. Ryker …' she calls out before he hangs up.

'Yeah?'

'I'm glad you rang.'

The silence after the call ends remains a while before he puts down his phone.

God, I miss her!

3

FRICTION

JACK

The school day is about to begin; the gang are at roll call. Jack sits on his desk, his feet on his seat, while Peanut hovers uneasily around him. They're deep in conversation about an afternoon detention Peanut got for skipping hockey training again—well, at least Peanut is. Jack's attention is diverted elsewhere, to Max on the other side of the room giggling at something Ruby has just said. Peanut frowns and steps deliberately to block his view.

'Hey, shove over, chubs.' Jack tugs him aside. The girls are up to something and he knows it. Just at that moment, the sound of loud belly-splitting laughter echoes across the room, their mischief now unmistakable. Jack can't help but smile.

'For crying out loud, will ya get a grip?' Peanut

smacks Jack on the back of the head. 'It beats me how your brain turns to mush every time Max is anywhere near you. And who the heck are ya calling *chubs*, anyway?'

Jack's smile disappears—it's crunch time. He knew this conversation was coming, and he's been dreading it. There's no dodging it any longer. He stops to choose his words carefully. 'Look, you're hearing this from me because we're mates. Right?'

Peanut snorts. 'O-kay, hit me with it. I'm a big boy; I can handle it.'

Jack shakes his head. For once he wishes Peanut would quit being the clown. 'Hey, I'm serious.'

'Yeah, yeah, yeah; come on, spit it out.' Peanut plonks himself down, leans back in his chair, balancing on its two hind legs. 'I'm all ears. What's eating ya?'

Jack sighs. 'D'ya want it straight? Or do I sugar-coat it?'

The rocking stops. 'Oi, this looks serious.' His chair lands on all fours with a thud.

Jack runs his fingers through his hair. 'Mate, what the heck's going on?' He turns to face him straight on. 'Look, you barely made the cut for the team this year—did ya know that? And d'ya wanna know why? That extra weight you're carrying from you skipping training all the time is slowing you down. The thing is, Johnno's gunning for your position, and I won't be surprised if he gets it.'

Peanut sits up in his seat. 'Johnno! You've got to be kidding me, right? He's got two left feet!'

'Says you, but lately he's faster *and*, I might add, more committed than you are. I think he's only trailing you by one goal already, and the season has just begun. Your goal average will soon need CPR if you don't get your act together. I hate to say it, mate, but you're losing form.'

'Who's losing form?' Ruby asks as she approaches with Max. The boys clam up, then look away. Ruby nudges Peanut with her knee.

'No one. Forget it,' Peanut snaps.

Ruby leans over from behind and wraps her arms around his shoulders, nestling her cheek against his. 'Hey, what's up, butterball?'

Peanut turns and glares at her. 'Ruby!'

Jack and Max share a look, then lower their gaze. Peanut jumps to his feet and shakes his finger at them. 'Great friends you turned out to be!'

Jack holds his hands up defensively. 'Hey, what did we do?'

Peanut snatches Ruby by the hand and stomps away. Jack leaps out of his chair to go after him, but decides against it. He turns to Max and groans.

She takes his hand. 'So … I gather you told him.'

'Yeah, but it didn't go down too well, did it?' He rubs his face. 'He's right, you know; I'm not much of a mate, am I?'

Max gives his hand a gentle squeeze.

Jack's shoulders slump. 'But what was I supposed to do? The guys in the team are talking behind his back—they're staging a mutiny. Let's face it, we won't get anywhere near the finals this year if he keeps this crap up.'

'Well, we both know where he's going when he ditches training.' Max groans. 'It's Annie … she needs to stop encouraging him! It's no secret what Peanut's appetite's like, and God love her, she'll do anything to keep him happy.' She reaches up on her tip-toes to kiss his cheek. 'Look, leave it with me; I'll have a word with her.'

Jack pulls her in for a hug. 'Thanks, babe, you're the best.'

'Don't worry, we'll tackle this thing together. Okay?'

Man, how did I get so lucky? Peanut's right, and Jack knows it; when it comes to Max, his brain turns to mush—she's the best thing that's ever happened to him. It's hard to believe there was a time she didn't come close to registering on his radar. He shakes his head … *and she's been here the whole time!* In all fairness, the Max of today is a very different person to the Max back then. Gone are the black clothes and her dark attitude. She hasn't ventured to wearing florals and dresses yet—to Annie's disappointment—but you'd be hard up finding a stick of mascara or eyeliner in her makeup case now. She's even stopped dying her hair. You wouldn't think she was the same girl.

Jack rests his chin on the top of her head—she's so tiny she fits perfectly there.

The school bell rings.

'No public displays of affection during class, Mr Braden,' Mr McPhee warns as he enters the room. 'Everyone, settle down; the bell has gone. Please take your seats.'

Jack is disappointed when Peanut's classic comeback doesn't come.

Their teacher notices it too and frowns. He watches Peanut approach his seat without comment. 'Um, is everything all right, Mr Brown?'

Peanut throws himself into his seat. 'Never better,' he grumbles. He reaches into his bag for his pencil case and diary, then unzips the case, pulls out a pen and slams it down before sitting back in his seat with his arms crossed.

'Mate …' Jack starts.

'Just let it go, will ya?' Peanut grabs his pen and fidgets with it, clicking it on and off repeatedly. He stops, puts it down and turns to face him. 'Look, I kinda get it; it's no biggie.' He shifts in his seat. 'I reckon I had it coming, anyway.'

Jack says nothing.

'The truth stings a bit, that's all.' Peanut lowers his gaze.

Jack nudges him. 'Are you okay?'

Peanut shrugs. 'I'll live.'

Jack sighs, then tries to lighten the mood by telling a joke. 'Hey, listen, did you hear the one about the two bulls in the field?'

Peanut's head snaps up. 'What do you think you're doing?'

Jack sits back and shrugs.

Peanut turns side-on to face him. 'I'm warning ya, don't even think about it.'

Geez, what's gone and ticked him off this time?

'Mate, it's *cows* in the field, not *bulls*, you twit! If you're gonna tell me one of my own jokes, you've gotta get it right—otherwise you'll kill the punchline. It's *Mad COW'S Disease* ... Duh!' He glares at Jack and shakes his head. 'Pfft, amateur! Leave the gags to me, all right?'

That earns Jack a whack to the back of his head. He rubs at the sting then whacks him back. Both boys chuckle, then wrestle each other before getting a warning look from their teacher.

4

The Cat's Out of the Bag

MAX

Max groans. She has just spent the last twenty minutes sitting in the kitchen explaining the situation with Peanut to Annie and getting nowhere. Even over a soothing cup of camomile tea, Max is struggling to keep her cool. 'Annie, I know how much you love to fuss, but you've got to stop encouraging him. You're not doing him any favours by cooking up a feast every time he drops in to see you—and lately that seems to be every day.'

Annuska slaps her hands on her hips. 'Vhat, now I cannot feed dhe poor boy?' She clicks her tongue. 'But he is alvays so hungry. Maxy, please, he is too shkinny, Annuska must be cooking.'

'But that's just the point,' Max grumbles, 'he's not too *shkinny* anymore. In just three-and-a-half months you've managed to fix that.'

Annuska shrugs. 'So?'

'Don't get me wrong, he's looking good, but the thing is he's skipping training to be here, and because of that he's going to be cut from the team.'

'Vhat! Dhey cannot do dhat! Dhis is terrible! I vill go talk to dhat nice teacher, Mr McPhee. He love it, my Dobos cake … maybe I take him some.' She looks at Max with earnest. 'Vhat you tink?'

Max slaps her forehead. As much as she loves Annie, she's finding it near impossible to keep it together at the moment. She stops, then counts to ten. 'Annie, you know you don't have to feed the *whole* school, don't you?'

But oblivious to Max's torment, Annuska trails off in her own thoughts. 'You tink it he is married?' Her eyes light up. 'Maybe I take some wiener schnitzel too. I make it good wiener schnitzel, no?'

Max bangs her head on the kitchen benchtop. 'Yes, Annie, your wiener schnitzels are the best … we all love your wiener schnitzel, but can you *please* stop for a minute and focus on what I'm saying?'

Annuska claps her hands to her bosom. 'Maxy, sveetheart, I upset you, no?' Annie totters off her stool, hobbles to the other side of the bench and pulls Max into a warm embrace, giving her a hearty squeeze. 'My poor Maxy. Annuska vill be quiet now.'

Annie strokes Max's hair and looks down at her, smiling. 'Okay, next time I see Peanut, I vill talk to him and make it deal. I tell him he must be going to training or Annuska vill stop feeding him. Yes?'

Max breathes out a sigh of relief.

'Come, sveetheart, it break it my heart, seeing my Maxy upset.' Annuska gives her another motherly squeeze. 'Soon, I be going; ve must not be fighting.'

'Oh, I nearly forgot; I spoke to Ryker the other day. He can't wait for your visit, and he's craving your apple strudel.'

'Ryker? Vhen? Oh, such a good boy, dhat one. I do miss him.' Annuska claps her hand to her chest and settles on her stool again. 'And I miss Edra and dhe tvins too. Poor babies, my heart break it vhen I tink how much dhey suffer for so long.' Annuska reaches over to pat Max's hand. 'Don't vorry, I vill cook for dhem.'

Max rolls her eyes. But Annie chuckles, leans in to pinch her cheeks, and winks. Max laughs at her attempt at a joke.

'So you talk it vid Ryker?' Annie asks. 'How is his poor mamma? Has she started her treatment?'

Max sits back in her seat. 'Treatment? What treatment?'

Annuska slaps her hand to her mouth.

Max's eyes narrow. 'Annie, what's wrong with Ryker's mum?'

Annuska realises her mistake too late. She fidgets with her apron and doesn't know where to look.

Max leans in closer. 'Annie, tell me! *What* treatment?'

Annie bites her lip, then mumbles something under her breath. '*O, ne*, I tell someting not for my Maxy's ears.'

Max frowns. Usually they share everything, so whatever she's keeping from her must be serious. Determined to find out, Max sits back, crosses her arms, forces a smile and waits. She'll get to the bottom of this whether Annie likes it or not.

Annuska's gaze darts to the door. 'Please, Maxy, I make it promise not to tell. Your papa vill be angry.'

'What, Dad knows?' Max can't sit there any longer; she hops off her stool and stands before her, her hands fisted on her hips. 'Annie?'

Annuska scrambles to get away and makes a beeline to the pantry. 'Oh, look at dhe time!' she calls out over her shoulder. 'Your papa vill be home soon; he vill vant his dinner to be ready.' She disappears in the small room off the kitchen, clanging and banging in search of what she needs. Then there's silence. Moments later she returns empty handed, her shoulders slumped, her face lowered. 'Maxy, I cannot.'

Max grits her teeth; this is getting her nowhere. 'Then I'll ring Ryker and ask him myself. It must be bad if you're keeping it from me. Is it cancer?'

Annuska's head whips around; her eyes almost pop out of her head. Her lips clamp shut, and the colour drains from her face.

Max crosses her arms, glares at her through narrowed eyes and waits for Annie to crumble.

'Oh, Maxy, no!'

But Max is relentless, using her famous death stare on full throttle.

Finally, Annuska's shoulders slump. 'Fine, I vill tell you … and only because you guessed it.' She sighs, then begins. 'Igen, Ryker's mamma has got dhe cancer. The doctors vant to start chemo soon, and Annuska vill go to help. Your papa is good; he make it I go.'

Max stumbles backwards, the stool stopping her fall. 'Cancer?' The word is a whisper on Max's lips.

Annuska totters to her side and takes Max's hands in hers.

Max shakes her head. 'But … but can't they operate? Where is it?'

Annuska studies her face, clearly battling with how much to tell her. 'She has breast cancer, but your papa says dhey cannot operate again.'

'Again!' Max tugs her hands free. 'So she's had surgery already? Why didn't I know this?'

Annuska slaps her hand to her mouth.

'Annie!' Max gives her another *tell me now* look.

Annie lets out her breath. 'Igen, she has already one operation, but dhe cancer, it is spreading. I tink your papa said level four.'

'You mean *stage four*?' Max falls onto her stool.

Annuska frowns, then mutters something under her breath. 'Igen, someting like dat. Your papa told me, but Annuska doesn't understand his big words.'

Just then Max's father enters the kitchen. 'What big words? What stories have you been telling my little girl, Annie?' he teases.

Max dives off her stool and runs to him. 'Dad, you didn't tell me Isebel is sick.'

Edward Rutherford's smile vanishes. He turns to glare at Annuska. Annie looks away, her face flushed.

Max takes her father's hand in hers and squeezes it, silently pleading for him to explain.

He hesitates a moment, contemplating what to say, then places his hands firmly on her shoulders. 'Honey, Ryker didn't want to upset you, so he asked me not to say anything.' He tilts her chin up. 'You've got to believe me—we were only keeping this from you for your own good. It was Annie who found out after talking with Isebel. The fact is, Mrs Engelbrecht was diagnosed with breast cancer nearly three years ago. She underwent treatment then, but the cancer has returned and has metastasised … it's now in her liver. I'm sorry, Max, but it's not looking good.'

Max can't move, her father's final words echoing in her ears. Her mouth dries, her throat clamps tight. *Poor Isebel … Oh God, poor Ryker!* She knows only too well what it's like to lose a mother. Her head starts spinning. She can't think straight. She needs to help Ryker … but how?

'Honey, are you okay?'

Max looks up at her father. 'Dad, we need to do something.' Her eyes search his. 'It's not fair, they've only just found each other—four years … they've lost four years!' Her vision blurs from the threat of tears. 'No … not now! Why her? Why them?' She clings to her father, then lets the tears fall.

Edward tightens his hold. She feels trapped. Her heart pounds, and a dense fog clutters her thinking. She sees her mother before her, and for a moment relives the pain of her loss … and, just like an old friend, she welcomes it. But then she jerks out of his arms. She won't let this drag her back to that dark place—the place she thought she'd bricked up and buried. *No! This is NOT happening! Not today, not EVER!*

'Dad, we have to help!'

'Honey, we *are* helping—we're sending Annie. She'll be a tremendous support during Isebel's treatment.'

But Max isn't listening. With the rush of adrenaline coursing through her veins, her every heartbeat booms in her ears. 'Hey, wait a minute. I'll go with Annie. I can help. Ryker will need me.'

'Whoa! Sweetheart, slow down. Let's think this through.' Edward stops to take in a breath. 'Look, how about we see how Isebel goes with the chemo first. Annie will let us know when it's a good time to visit. What do you say to that?'

But Max is too wound up to listen to reason. 'I've got the term break coming up; it makes sense to go now. Don't you see? Please, Dad.' Her eyes are wide with hope. 'I promise I won't get in the way.'

Edward shakes his head. 'Max, stop and think about it for a minute. Chemo makes most patients quite ill, so Isebel won't be in the right frame of mind to focus on her recovery with you there.' He frowns. 'Honey, I don't think it's a good idea.'

Max's shoulders slump. She can see the sense in what her father's saying, but she also feels the need to be there for Ryker. She's torn.

Edward squeezes her shoulder. 'I promise we'll go as soon as Isebel is feeling a little better. Okay?'

Cancer. Such a horrible word. She struggles to get her head around it. *But surely doctors are having success with their treatments these days, right? There's always something on the news about medical breakthroughs: new drugs, new procedures and life-saving treatments.*

She groans. *If only I had a magic wand …*

And then from out of nowhere a thought comes to her and strikes her like a lightning bolt. Suddenly several ideas bombard her at once—they're coming at her so fast she needs to grab hold of her father to steady herself.

Annuska gasps and clutches at her chest.

Her father's eyes widen. 'Max, honey, are you okay?'

Max closes her eyes to slow her thoughts. She remembers to breathe. Bit by bit her ideas start to take shape in the form of a plan. She looks from Annie to her father, contemplating her next words. She knows her father's reaction to what she's about to say before she even says it, but she needs to take this leap of faith for Isebel. She draws in a deep breath. 'Dad, please hear me out before you say anything. Okay?'

His eyes narrow.

'What if we take Isebel back into the realm? You could take away the cancer—you could heal her!'

Annuska fumbles for the stool to sit on.

Edward's eyes widen. 'Max, you can't be serious?'

He shakes his head. 'Look, sweetheart, you're in shock. I know you want what's best for Isebel—I understand that, but honey, think about it.'

'No, Dad, *you* think about it! Why not? Imagine if it was Mum, you'd do it for her. I know you would.'

Edward stiffens. Nearly four years on and the pain of losing the love of his life to a drink-driving accident still haunts him.

Max shrinks away; she may have gone too far this time. But she needs him to listen, to really hear what she's saying. She holds her breath as she watches her father's thought process play out before her. At first there's shock, then sadness, followed by conflict, and eventually his eyes soften when it's clear that he envisages his darling Grace. When he looks back at Max, there's a hint of hope in his expression.

Max's eyes light up.

Annuska jumps to her feet, gripping the bench to steady herself. 'Dr Rudherford! No! You cannot be tinking dis is a good idea?'

But it would seem that Edward Rutherford can't bring himself to agree. He reaches for Max's hand and gives her a crooked smile. 'Max, I'm not promising anything ...'

Max can't believe it—he's actually considering it. She lets out a squeal. 'Really! You'll do it?'

'Now let's not get ahead of ourselves,' he warns.

'There are so many things to consider, so many obstacles.' He pauses. 'For instance, will Isebel be well enough to travel here? Once her treatment starts, she may not be fit to leave South Africa. Who knows how she'll respond to the chemo? And even if she was able to, will the authorities allow it? Getting approval for this kind of thing might be impossible, and if by some miracle they listen and show compassion, how soon can we do this? With all the typical red tape, it might take ages for us to get clearance. Do we have that kind of time? And let's not mention the danger—we've seen what's on the other side. Is it just too risky?' He runs his hand through his hair, reflecting on his words.

Max needs to fix this. That cloud of doubt hampering her father's earlier enthusiasm needs to get shut down, and fast. She needs to come up with viable solutions before he changes his mind. She takes a moment to calm her thinking. 'Dad, what if we get Isebel here before she starts her treatment? The trip would be doable then, wouldn't it? As for the red tape, maybe your friends at ASIO can fast track a decision for us. And the dangers ... what has the realm got that the task force can't handle?'

Max has her fingers crossed behind her back. She holds her breath, waiting for her father to consider her argument. 'Dad, they can't *not* help. And remember, we've got friends on the other side. Medwin and the forest people are there for us, like they've been before.'

Edward rubs at his chin and paces back and forth with indecision.

Max waits.

After a while, he stops. 'Honey, I know you want what's best for Isebel—we all do—but there are so many uncertainties. Yes, there's a chance we could get rid of the cancer, but will she remain well when we come back? We don't know the power of these healings.'

'But, Dad, look at Jack and Peanut,' she challenges. 'The doctors said they couldn't believe they'd recovered so well from their injuries.'

Edward groans.

Max remains silent, allowing a few moments for her argument to take hold. Her crossed fingers behind her back are ready to snap from the strain. She looks across to Annie for reassurance, but Annie, with her white-knuckle grip on the benchtop, looks like she's about to pass out.

A long period of silence passes, her father lost in thought. He then looks up; the deep furrow of his brow softens, and there's an unmistakable gleam in his eyes.

Max's heart skips a beat.

Annuska wavers, her hand clutching her bosom.

'Dr Rudherford, vhat you be tinking?' She reaches back blindly, seeking the stool to sit again.

Edward's smile doesn't falter. His eyes glaze over. 'Do you realise what this could mean? My God, we could be onto something epic here; the possibilities are endless.'

Max is beyond ecstatic. She needs to tell Ryker. She turns to race upstairs, but her father calls out. 'Max, wait. Let me think on it a bit more before we say anything to Ryker.'

'But, how did you know ...'

'I wasn't born yesterday.' He laughs at her surprised look. 'I know that's where you're headed. Look, just let me run it by Gerard Thompson first and see what he has to say. We don't want to elevate everyone's hopes unnecessarily. Agreed?'

'But ...'

'No buts about it, Max, please. I know you're excited, but don't go against me on this one. Okay?'

How she's going to hold back from telling Ryker is beyond her. *Excited* is an understatement; she's just about ready to burst with the news. But Max knows her father is right. 'Okay, Dad, I'll wait until you've spoken to Deputy Thompson. So can you call him now?'

'Now? No, I don't want to make any rash decisions. Like I said, there's a lot to consider. I'll ring in the morning and ask him what he thinks is the right thing to do. Look, at this stage I can't promise you more than that. But I'll tell you one thing, I'll be doing all I can to get him to see what this could potentially mean. Can you imagine what would happen if we get the all-clear on this? There's no end to what this will do for the medical world.'

Annuska jumps up and grabs Max by the hand, eager to take her from the room. She looks at Edward as if he's lost his mind and mutters something unintelligible under her breath. 'Okay, Maxy, you heard your papa. Now come, help me pick some peas and tomatoes from dhe greenhouse. Ve make gombapaprikas for dinner. Dr Rudherford, we eat soon. Go finish your vork. I vill call vhen it is ready.'

Max's mind boggles with what the future holds. Surely Deputy Thompson will see the benefits of revisiting the Ancient Realm … *and not just for Isebel!*

Later at dinner, Max wolfs down her meal, tasting nothing of it and asks to be excused from the table only minutes after they've sat down to eat.

'Max, remember, not a word to Ryker yet. Okay?' Edward warns.

'Not a word, I promise.'

Max climbs the sweeping staircase to her bedroom, taking the stairs two at a time with the enthusiasm of a kid on Christmas morning. The long corridor to her room suddenly seems never ending. She breaks into a sprint, thinking of what she's going to tell him as she pulls her mobile phone from the back pocket of her jeans. She slams the door shut behind her, dives on her bed, presses number *one* on her favourites and holds for the connection. As she waits, she tries to get comfortable by plumping up the zillion pillows Annie insists on arranging meticulously every morning. She rolls her eyes at the flowery, beaded one Annie smuggled in among the plain ones and tosses it aside. 'Nice try, Annie, but it's not going to happen!'

Come on! Where is he? She chews on her lower lip.

'Hey, Max! How's my girl?'

She sits up, too excited to lay down. 'Jack, you're not gonna believe what's happened! Isebel's got cancer, and we're going back into the realm to make her better!'

She says it so fast, her words run into each other, and Jack struggles to understand any of it. 'Whoa, slow down. What was that about the realm?'

'Jack!' Max groans. 'Don't you get it? She'll die if we don't do anything!'

'Max, you're not making any sense!' He pauses. 'Hang on; did you say Isebel has cancer? What, you're not thinking to …? Nah, you can't be serious? Are you *nuts*? Wait right there; I'm coming over.'

She jumps to her feet. 'NO!'

'What? Why not?'

'Because you can't. I promised Dad not to say anything. And if you turn up, he'll know.' She pauses as a thought comes to her. 'But hold on … technically he told me not to say anything to *Ryker*, so I guess you don't count.'

'Geez, thanks, talk about a low blow!'

'Oh shoot! Sorry, Jack. It's not that you don't *count*, count, but you're not Ryker … so I can tell you. Right?'

Jack groans. 'Max, you're starting to sound a lot like Peanut, and right now, I don't think I can handle two of you.' He sighs. 'Okay, so let's have it again. Back it up, slow it down and tell me what you're *not* supposed to tell.'

Max takes a deep breath, starts from the beginning and fills Jack in on the details. 'In a nutshell, we'll know by tomorrow if we'll be able to help poor Isebel.'

For a long while, Max hears nothing but silence on the other end of the line. She tugs at her fringe. 'Jack? Hey, are you still there?'

'Yeah, Max. Just give me a sec.'

Max chews at her lower lip. 'Jack, I know that's a lot to take in. Are you okay?'

'Yeah, Max. Just wait,' he repeats, sounding distant.

Max worries her lip again.

'If only they could locate the other gateway—the one they fell through back in South Africa,' Jack mutters, as if to himself. 'Isebel wouldn't need to come here.'

Max's eyes light up. 'But of course! Jack, you're a genius.' Jack's way of thinking has her mind racing. It makes perfect sense to locate the other portal. But before getting too excited, she recalls Ryker telling her they spent weeks looking for it when they first returned home, and the search was fruitless. Too much time had passed, and Ryker's recollection of the activities leading up to their disappearance was a little vague. Even with his father's extensive experience, they had no success in finding it. As far as Max knows, the taskforce set up to locate the portal in South Africa was still out there searching.

Her enthusiasm fizzles. 'I don't think they've got time to keep looking. Isebel needs our help now.'

Silence on the other side of the phone.

'Jack, what if they won't listen?' She says in a barely heard whisper. 'What do we do then?'

'Hey, how could they *not*? Max, it's a no-brainer. Of course, they'll listen. Look, I've got a good feeling about this. You watch; everything will work out. Trust me.'

Jack's confidence gives her sudden hope. Her

spirits skyrocket, and she suppresses a squeal.

'After what we've been through, anything's possible.' He chuckles.

She giggles. 'You can say that again!'

5

Planting a Seed

Jack falls back on his pillow, a knot forming in his stomach. He stares at the ceiling, rethinking the conversation he'd just had with Max. He jerks upright, sits cross-legged, smacks his forehead and groans. '*Trust me?* What the hell was I thinking!' He'd just about promised Max they'd have Isebel cancer free in no time. He rubs at his brow and groans again. 'I've gone and done a classic *Peanut*—blurting out stuff the moment it's popped into my head.' He squeezes his eyes shut. 'Me and my big mouth.'

He wraps his arms around his head. *What's wrong with me? Why do I keep doing this?* It's been a common thread lately. Against all logic his thinking becomes scrambled every time Max needs rescuing—whether it's life-threatening or not. Something primal and instinctive just kicks in and takes over from his normally sensible self.

He jumps to his feet and paces back and forth in his small, cluttered bedroom, thinking of a way to undo this. *There's no way in the world this is gonna happen.* He stops. *Or is there?* He takes a few minutes to consider it, to really weigh up the possibility of taking something like this on, and actually doing it. The more he mulls it over, the quicker his strides and the faster his pulse. *What's stopping us? Why not do it?*

Jack dives on his bed, rests against the headboard and hugs his knees. 'Okay, so what have we got so far? The prof. doesn't reckon Isebel is strong enough to travel, so the clear option is the other portal. And since they've had no luck finding it, maybe the odds would be better if we enter the portal here, then hunt down the other one from the inside.' His eyes light up. 'Yeah, I reckon that'll work!'

A plan starts to take shape. Jack feels good.

But enough for now; he's got maths homework he needs to finish. He'll work on the idea some more in the morning. But he soon finds he can't focus on anything but the plan. His rational numbers are suddenly irrational; his x and y's aren't adding up, and Pythagoras's theorem is no longer making sense. He groans, slams shut his laptop and calls it a night.

While lying in his bed, his mind ticks over with

various plots. He tosses and turns for a long while, unable to sleep. That earlier knot in his stomach is gone, replaced by butterflies. He throws off his covers, jumps out of bed and grabs his mobile, yanking it free from the charger plugged in at his desk. In his hurry he fumbles with the text he sends to Peanut. He hopes he's still up.

In no time his phone pings with a return message. *'S'up?'*

Jack doesn't bother messaging back. He needs to talk. He makes the call.

'Are you freakin' out of your mind?' Peanut yells into the phone after hearing Jack's strategy. 'Tell me you're joking because, mate, you *cannot* be serious!'

Jack dives under the covers. 'Shhhh! Keep it down, will ya! D'ya want everyone in the street to hear? Anyway, it's just a thought at this stage. I was gonna bounce some ideas off you first.'

'If any are like that one, I'll tell ya right now, your ideas stink! Look, I'm coming over. I can't do this over the phone. And I really need to knock some sense into that noggin of yours.'

Peanut lives two streets from Jack, so he's over on his bike before Jack's had a chance to take offence.

He lets Peanut in through the back door. Peanut makes a beeline for the pantry, grabs a jumbo-sized packet of cheese puffs, then follows Jack upstairs to his bedroom. They both avoid stepping on the floorboards that creak. Having to explain Peanut's visit at this time of the night is something they can both do without.

Jack dives onto his bed, crosses his legs at the ankles and waits for the fallout he knows is coming.

Peanut straddles Jack's desk chair and digs straight into the cheese puffs. He then looks at Jack sideways. 'You're dead-set serious, aren't you? Even after all we've been through.' He shakes his head. 'You're *nuts!* You know that?'

Jack looks at his feet and shrugs.

'So what exactly is the plan, genius?' But before Jack has a chance to start, Peanut's hand shoots out to stop him. 'And I don't want you telling me anything that's half-baked; give me details—you know, the nitty-gritty. I want dates, times, locations, names— you and whose army? And before you even think about it, count me out. O.U.T. Out! There's no way in hell I'm going back in there.' He shakes his head again. 'Man, either you've got a death wish, or you've got rocks for brains.'

Put like that, Jack questions his earlier enthusiasm.

Peanut stuffs his mouth full of cheese puffs and waits.

Admittedly, Jack hadn't given much thought to the *hows* and *whens*. He'd only considered the *whys*.

His thoughts were for Isebel. He imagined if *his* mother had cancer. Knowing how hard it was for Max when her mother died made him all the more determined to fix this. Jack takes a breath, then runs his ideas by Peanut.

'C'mon, Jack, don't tell me you can't see the cracks in this plan of yours?'

Jack frowns. 'You make it sound like it's a stupid idea. I reckon I can pull it off.'

Peanut jumps up, grabs Jack by the shoulders and looks him in the eye. 'Look, I get it. You can't help yourself; you're Mr Fix-it. But let's break it down together so you can see what I'm seeing here.' He holds up his fisted hand with his thumb extended. 'One,' he begins, 'you've got a snowflake's chance in hell if you think Deputy Gerard Thompson will ever allow it. His allegiance is to the Australian government, not you.' He pauses to continue his argument. 'Then there's point two; even if by some miracle you get Thompson onside, and you somehow manage to get past the goons protecting the portal, how the hell are you supposed to find the other one? Man, you've got Buckley's chance at finding it in that huge forest. Do you even remember how near impossible it is to see these portals in the first place?'

'But I could get the forest people to help,' Jack argues, surprised that he hadn't thought of their friends earlier. 'With Medwin's freaky knack of seeing the future, I bet he already knows I'm coming.' He grins, suddenly very pleased with himself, his spirits once again high.

Peanut's eyes narrow. 'Mate, Medwin owes you nothing. What makes you think the forest people will be happy to see your dumb arse again? If anything, they'd be running the other way after the mess we left them with.'

Jack grits his teeth to bite back saying something he'll regret. 'Okay, then, *you* think of something. We can't do *nothing*.'

To Jack's surprise, Peanut stops to take up the challenge. He's silent for a long while, his brow furrowed, deep in thought. Eventually his face lights up. 'Hey, I think I've got it.'

Jack sits taller on his bed, crosses his arms and waits. *This'll be interesting.* 'Yeah? So come on, Einstein, let's have it.'

Peanut smiles a crooked smile. 'I've just got one word for ya—Ryker.'

Jack's attention spikes. 'Ryker?'

'Yeah. Isn't it obvious?' Peanut snorts. 'No offence, mate, but I don't rate *your* chances. Sending Ryker in, on the other hand; well, that's a different ball game. You know what? I reckon I'd have better luck finding it than you.' He laughs. 'Sorry, but hey, it's true. At least I can make myself invisible. You? You'd get caught before you knew it.'

Jack rolls his eyes. 'So basically, you're saying my so-called *stupid* ideas don't stink that bad after all.'

Peanut chuckles. 'Jack, I reckon you were halfway there. But you've gotta agree, if we go with your way of thinking, you'd get shut down the second you opened your mouth and blabbed your ideas to Thompson.'

Jack frowns. Surprisingly, Peanut makes sense.

'Just think about it,' Peanut explains. 'The secret is not letting anyone know what we're planning, especially the olds.' He stops to consider something. 'Well, maybe with the exception of the prof., of course. But I'm telling ya, getting Thompson on board is your biggest mistake—he's gonna say *no*, guaranteed! And then what'll happen? I'll tell ya what; security will tighten to stop us trying to sneak in, and before you know it, your dumb-arse attempt to help Isebel goes straight down the gurgler.

'Now with Ryker's freaky military training,' he hurries to continue, 'he's a shoo-in to get past Thompson's security, as well as deal with the goons on the other side. Not to mention the fact that Medwin and Ryker have got some kind of allegiance. No offence, Jack, but if Medwin was gonna help anyone, he'd help Ryker.

'And remember,' he adds, 'Ryker knows the forest

better than anyone. So with him in and the other portal found, then, and only then, do we call on Max's dad. Although to be honest, I reckon Max could do it herself.' He pauses to consider this. 'Hmm, maybe we should keep *him* out of it too. What d'ya think?'

What do I think? Jack blinks several times. His mind boggles—never in a million years would he have guessed that Peanut could've come up with such a viable solution to his not-so-doable plan. 'I *think* you've been invaded by aliens. Who the hell are you? And what have you done with my best friend?'

Peanut chuckles, but then his triumphant smile wanes. 'Look,' he says in all seriousness, 'Ryker's the better fit this time—even you can see that. And you know what? It doesn't have to be you who sticks his neck out all the time. Let someone else have a turn. Okay?'

And that, right there, is what *mates* are all about.

Peanut straddles the chair again and tilts his chin up. 'So what do ya reckon? How about we fill Ryker in on these brilliant ideas of mine? What time's it in Johannesburg?'

Jack splutters. *His* ideas? 'You're unbelievable; you know that?'

Peanut shrugs and smiles his characteristic crooked smile. 'What can I say? You've either got it or you don't.'

Jack gets up and smacks him on the back of his head. 'Mate, that wasn't exactly a compliment.' He ducks to avoid Peanut's payback, then grabs his laptop to Skype their buddy on the other side of the world.

Soon a strategy is put in place. Ryker is to fly to Australia, re-enter the realm, find the other portal then get out. Simple, according to Ryker. And then, somewhere in all the toing and froing with the plan making (and Jack's head is still spinning from it), Peanut sticks his hand up to go too. *(What the …!)* Whether it was the thrill of the adventure that lured him to do it, or perhaps the way Ryker downplayed the assignment—either way Peanut was hooked, and there was no way in the world Jack could talk him out of it.

Now it's well past midnight, and Jack falls exhausted on his bed. The wheels are set to be in motion as early as the morning. The only foreseeable obstacle to the success of this operation is going to be Max's dad. And getting that right, Jack knows, sits wholly and solely on his shoulders.

Great … no pressure!

6

BLINDSIDE

JACK

It's 5 am, and Jack rubs his eyes to get them to open. Sleep evaded him last night, the plan they devised on constant replay in his head. But now it's time to get the ball rolling. Max is his first call. He skims over the details with her—enough to get her on board with what needs to be done next. And the success of that pivots on how she deals with his instructions right at this very moment. But having just woken, she struggles to concentrate on what he's asked her to do.

'What? Hang on a sec; I don't get it. So when did this happen?'

Jack runs his hand through his hair. 'Max, right now, I need for you to focus. I'll explain everything later, I promise. Just trust me. Okay?'

'But why aren't we talking about this with the others?'

'Max, please, just do it! You said your dad's in the shower now, right? So that means we've only got a matter of minutes before he's out. This needs to be done before he leaves for work, before he contacts Deputy Thompson.'

'But, Jack!'

As much as he's crazy about her, right now she's stretching his limits. 'Max, it's now or never—we either do this or we don't; it's your call.'

'Argh! Okay, I'll do it. But you'd better not be making me do something I'll regret. Stay on the phone; I'll be back in a sec.' The line goes quiet.

For the fiftieth time this morning, Jack stops to consider if what they're doing is right. His gut tells him they are, albeit a little underhanded. He shakes it off. His focus turns to Max and the real possibility of her getting caught in the act.

He paces back and forth. The seconds feel agonisingly like minutes. 'Geez, what's taking her so long?' He strains to hear what's happening at the Darcy-Rutherford household. The silence is killing him.

Max's sudden voice on the other end of the line makes him jump and almost drop the phone. 'Okay, it's done.'

'So you didn't have any problems?'

'Nope.'

'And you did it like we said?'

'Um, duh!'

Jack can almost hear the eye roll on the other side of the line. He takes a breath. 'Sorry, Max, of course you did. So how did you know his access code?'

'Too easy, 47223. G.R.A.C.E. He uses Mum's name for all his passcodes.' She laughs. 'I really need to talk to him about that.'

'And you remembered to save the number before you changed it?'

Max groans. '*Of course*, I did. You asked me to, didn't you? Jack, give me some credit; I'm not stupid!'

And now he's gone and ticked her off. He gives himself a mental kick. He can just picture her on the other side of the phone, brow furrowed, eyes shooting daggers, something he hasn't seen for a long while. 'I know you're not, Max, but I'm losing my shit here. I've gotta get this bang on from the get-go. All right?'

She draws in a deep breath. 'Okay. So tell me again what you three got up to last night. Why am I switching these numbers?'

He glances at the time—there's too much to explain. 'Look, can I fill you in at school? I've got to get Ruby on board before your dad rings her. This could turn pear-shaped real quick if he gets to her before I do.'

'Ruby? But why's he going to call Ruby?'

He tugs at his hair and groans.

'Look, never mind,' she says. 'You told me to trust you, Jack, so I will. I'll see you at school. Hey, I'll send a text to everyone to meet in class before roll call, say around 8 am?'

He relaxes his fist and lets out a haggard breath. 'Sounds like a plan. I'll see you at eight.' He ends the call, already drained, then braces himself for what needs to be done next. Getting Ruby onside with all this is going to be no easy feat. His finger hovers a moment over the phone before he presses it to connect.

'H'llo?' a sleepy voice says on the other end.

'Ruby, it's Jack. Look, I don't have time to explain, but I need you to do something for me. I need an academy award-winning performance. Are you up for it?'

'Huh? What?' She yawns. 'What time is it? Jack, it's 5:20 in the morning! This had better be good!'

Jack can't help but smile. *Someone's definitely not a morning person!*

Before Ruby has a chance to go on with her tirade, Jack stops her short. 'Isebel's got cancer and needs our help.'

'Say what?'

And with that grim, six-letter word, Jack has her complete and undivided attention. He fills her in briefly before telling her how she can help. They end the call sometime later and agree to meet at school before roll call.

Jack jumps into the shower and prepares for school. So far, so good; things are running to plan. He can't wait to meet up with the others and fill them in on what's happening. What they're doing feels right. He only hopes they feel the same.

With a spring in his step, Jack hurries his brothers and sisters out the door, gives his mum a peck on the cheek, then races to make it in time to catch the bus. Once on, he spots Peanut at the back and dives into the seat next to him. With hushed voices and heads down, they waste no time going over the plan once again.

Jack's mind races. He can't stay seated. He's up and waiting at the door of the bus a whole block before their stop. He stares out the window, seeing nothing of it, his thoughts consumed by what's ahead of him and how it's going to pan out.

As the bus comes to a stop, Peanut and Jack jostle to exit first, then there's a mad dash to get to the pre-roll-call meeting. Peanut beats Jack by a whisker. It's 7:40 am, and they're the first to arrive. They look at each other, shrug, then plonk themselves in their seats and wait.

But too agitated to sit, Jack is up within seconds, pacing. 'Man, what are we doing here? Does this feel right to you?'

Peanut chews on his nails, his eyes focused on a bit of fluff on the floor like it's a crucial element in their discussion. He shrugs.

They remain silent, each lost in their own thoughts.

Eventually the others turn up, with Kenny being the last to arrive. 'Hi, guys! So what's happening?'

Jack pounces to shut the door. 'Great, I'm glad you're all here. We haven't got much time, so I'll cut to the chase.' He dives into his seat.

Ten minutes later, they've all been informed about Isebel's situation and the plan for both Ryker and Peanut to re-enter the portal.

Max and Ruby exchange a look. Kenny remains quiet.

Jack turns to Max, clasps her hands in his and prepares to drop the bombshell he's about to hit her with. 'Um, Max, there's something I didn't tell you this morning.' Max sits taller and looks at him. He shifts in his seat; she's been quiet, perhaps too quiet. And what he has to say next might not sit well with her. 'So this is the thing; after talking to Ryker, the three of us agree that keeping this a secret is crucial if it's going to work.'

Max's posture doesn't change. 'I would've thought that's a given. But what's that got to do with me?' She takes back her hands.

Jack frowns. *Something's ticked her off already.* He shakes it off. 'What I mean is that we don't involve anyone—not even your dad.'

Max blinks a few times. 'But how's that a good thing? Don't we need Dad to help Isebel?'

'Well, that's the thing,' Peanut interrupts. 'Who needs your dad when we've got you?'

Max's eyes widen. 'Me?'

'Sure, why not?' Peanut laughs. 'You were awesome back there. I'd say you're just as good as your dad, maybe even better.'

Max jumps out of her seat and paces back and forth a few times, mumbling something under her breath.

'Look,' Peanut continues before she has a chance to object, 'as soon as the olds get a whiff of what we're doing, they'll be on us like a dung beetle on a cow pat.'

Max stops and folds her arms. Her lips press into a thin line. She turns, firstly to Peanut, then to Jack. 'So the three of you nutted out some kind of plan without asking what we think about it. I'm sure Kenny and Ruby would've liked to have had a say. I know *I* would've.' She juts out her chin. 'So you're going to hear it now. Isebel's cancer is aggressive; I can't do it. We *need* Dad on board.' Suddenly her eyes widen. 'Crap, he's ringing Thompson today!'

Just then the melodic tune of Destiny's Child's, *Survivor*, plays from Ruby's phone. Jack and Peanut exchange a worried look before whipping around to face Ruby.

Ruby looks down at the caller ID. She glances at Max, pauses for the shortest moment, then looks at Jack. 'It's Professor Rutherford.'

Peanut crouches by her side, his hand on her thigh. 'You can do this, Rubes.'

Ruby glares at him. 'I know I can *do it*, Charlie, it's a question of whether I *want* to!'

Peanut draws back.

Ruby grins; there's a glint in her eye. 'All of a sudden, it looks like I've got the upper hand.' She clicks her tongue. 'Well, I'm sorry, boys, but I'm with Max on this one—we're meant to be a team.' She turns her attention to Jack. 'And this morning, you never mentioned anything about Peanut going in. Why is that, Jack?'

Jack flinches.

Ruby looks down at the ringing phone in her lap, then back to Jack. 'So if you want me to put on an *award-winning performance*, Jack, you need to agree to one or two of *my* terms; the first one being, if Peanut goes, I go.' She sits back, folds her arms and raises her brow, waiting.

Jack and Peanut exchange a worried look. Ruby has them well and truly backed into a corner. The colour drains from Peanut's face. His eyes ping-pong from Ruby's phone to Jack. 'Just agree to it, will ya!'

Jack knows they may not get another chance to do this. The ball's rolling—Ryker is on his way—and right now, Ruby needs to take that call. Jack has no choice but to agree.

Ruby smiles, pulls a scrunched-up bit of paper from her pocket and flattens it on her lap. She straightens in her seat, draws in a deep breath and forces a smile before answering the call. 'You have reached the voicemail of Gerard Thompson, Deputy Director-General of Security, ASIO,' Ruby begins in an efficient, authoritative voice. 'Deputy Thompson is currently on leave and will be unreachable until the end of the month. You may leave a message after the tone, and he will get back to you at his earliest convenience. Matters of emergency should be dealt with by contacting emergency services on zero, zero, zero. I repeat, for emergencies, please phone zero, zero, zero. Thank you for your call.' Ruby relaxes back in her seat, but jolts forward again when she realises that the caller is waiting for a tone to leave a message.

Peanut is quick to help. He leans into the phone

and simulates the high-pitched electronic beep that typically follows.

There's complete silence in the room as they wait to hear the caller's response.

'Oh, um, hello, Gerard, this is Edward Rutherford. I hope you and your family are well. I'm calling to ask a favour—there's a matter regarding the portal I'd like to discuss with you. If you could get back to me, I'd appreciate it. Cheers.'

Ruby ends the call, then throws the phone to Peanut as if it's about to explode. Peanut grabs her in a hug and swings her around, her feet dangling. 'You were great, Rubes! I'm sure the prof. didn't suspect a thing.' He turns to Max. 'That right?'

But Max, left dumbfounded after the blindside, says nothing.

Jack cringes; he knows he has a lot of explaining—*and some grovelling*—to do. But right now, he can only grin that the plan worked.

Kenny blinks a few times. 'Hold on a minute. What just happened? How is it that Professor Rutherford called Ruby? And why did he think he rang Gerard Thompson?'

Jack chuckles—the look on Kenny's face is priceless.

'Hang on ... did you just ...? But why?' Jack watches Kenny's thought process as he works it out.

'Oh ... wow, cool! Whose brilliant idea was that?'

'That stroke of *brilliance* would be Jack's,' Max growls, clearly not impressed. She turns on Jack, her face flushed. 'You told me to trust you, and like an idiot, I did!'

Jack's smile vanishes. Max's glare has him shifting in his seat.

'So between the three of you knucklehead geniuses, you've come up with a plan—a stupid plan that doesn't involve my father. And now the pressure to help Isebel sits with *me*, and I don't think that's fair.'

Jack needs to save this. 'But, Max, it's not your dad we're worried about, it's the risk of the whole thing being shut down once Thompson gets wind of it. I'm sorry, I didn't have time to explain this to you this morning, but Ryker was adamant that no one else was to be involved, and to a degree, I agree with him. This was the best way to do it.'

Her expression darkens. Colour flushes her cheeks. 'Says you! What about the rest of us? Don't our opinions matter? And just for the record, helping Isebel was my idea. It burns me that you've run off with it and used me to help you do it. Jack, you used *me and* you used *Ruby*! And that's pretty low. Kudos to Ruby for sticking up for herself. I'm surprised you didn't drag Kenny into the mix.' She storms out of the room, the door slamming shut behind her.

Jack considers going after her, but knows, given time, Max will realise it had to be this way. And right now, he needs to redirect his mindset and focus on Ruby's unexpected bombshell. Like it or not, plans have changed—and he has no one else to blame for it but himself.

7

THE DUMMY-SPIT

MAX

Max slams the door behind her and takes off down the corridor to get as far from Jack as she can. She's so dirty with him at the moment, she can hardly breath. She soon finds herself down at the oval where she can stop and think for a few minutes alone.

Of all the pig-headed, idiotic, selfish, hare-brained decisions to make! We already had Dad on board—he was prepared to stick his neck out and risk everything to do this! So why did they have to change it?

She paces back and forth. *'Sure, why not?'* she mimics Peanut. *'You're just as good as your dad ... maybe even better!'* Max can't believe it. 'How did those three numbskulls come up with that? How could I possibly be better than someone medically trained with years of experience?' She mutters a few expletives under her breath.

'And so the *decision* was made. *Of course*, Max will do it!' she continues. 'But did anyone bother to think to ask me first? No! *Me man, you woman. Man, hunt and make decision; woman, clean and cook … grunt, grunt.* Just who do they think they are?'

She lets out a frustrated growl. Birds in a nearby tree flee at the sound. Her shoulders slump. 'What if I can't do it? It's cancer, for crying out loud!' Max rubs at the tension forming at the back of her neck. 'This is *so* not fair.

'And to think that it was my idea to help Isebel in the first place! Of all the arrogance! It should be me calling the shots, not them. Aargh!' She takes off at a run again, blind to where she's headed and too distraught to care. '*Trust me*, he says! Huh! What an *idiot* I am!'

After a while she stops running, plonks herself on the ground and pulls her knees to her chest. 'He's such a control freak!'

But then Max recalls her phone call to him last night—her cry for help. She groans. 'Me and my pathetic moment of weakness!' She shakes her head. *But can't I just vent without him feeling the need to take over and fix things?* Max hugs her knees closer, then reflects on that thought for a moment. She shrugs.

But that's just Jack—he really can't help it. She takes a moment to let that sink in, then realises her fault in all this. She shuts her eyes and groans. *God, I've got to stop falling apart in front of him!*

Max looks at the green that surrounds her—she's made her way to the middle of the oval without realising it. She stops to take it in, then looks up at the cloudless sky. The breeze kisses her heated cheeks, and the warmth of the sun seeps deep into her bones, calming her senses. She draws in a deep breath. The freshness of the morning, imbued with the scent of newly cut grass, eases the tension and wards off a doozy of a headache that was threatening to explode.

She sighs again. She can't be angry with Jack—his protectiveness is one of the things she loves about him. Yes, she's a strong, independent female, but there's a small part of her that melts when he treats her like she's his everything and he'd do anything for her.

She shakes her head, then smiles. *You can't have it both ways, Darcy-Rutherford!*

Calm now, Max reflects on what happened earlier at the meeting and comes to terms with the fact that Jack was probably right—telling Gerard Thompson could jeopardise everything. *If they keep it simple—go in, find the other portal and get out—then it's not such a bad idea to keep everyone in the dark. And now that Ruby's volunteered to go with them, how could they go wrong?* She smiles at Ruby's daring. 'One hundred percent for thinking, girlfriend!'

Inspired, Max makes a promise to herself to keep an open mind about what's to come but not hold back on being heard. After all, it doesn't matter who comes up with an idea, so long as they've all had a say.

The bell for the start of roll call sounds. Max makes her way back to class, where she knows Jack will be waiting to reassure her that everything will be okay.

And when she gets there, he is.

8

Wheels in Motion

RYKER

Ryker is with Edra and the twins, catching up for a coffee. They're in down-town Johannesburg, sitting in a booth at the back of a bustling café. He fidgets in his seat, toying with the sugar dispenser, his eyes diverted from the stares he's getting from his friends—he's just revealed he's going back into the Ancient Realm. The temperature suddenly feels like it's shot up a few degrees, and beads of sweat form on his brow and upper lip. With Banji blocking his exit, he feels trapped.

Edra sits on a chair at the head of the booth. Her amber eyes narrow at the news. 'You're *what?* Are you *insane?*'

Ryker isn't surprised by Edra's reaction. He ignores the attack and distracts himself by focusing on

68

the many patrons nattering in the busy coffee shop. The tiny air-conditioned room is bursting from the amount of people crammed in there trying to escape the blistering heat outside. It's noisy, and exactly how Ryker had hoped it would be. He draws in a breath, then braces himself for the fallout. 'Like I said, I'm going back.'

From across the table, Ulan grips his forearm, her eyes wide, her caramel-coloured skin suddenly paler. 'Oh, my God, I thought you were joking! Ryker, you can't be serious!'

Banji stares at him. 'What's going on? You wouldn't be going back unless you had to.'

What he's about to tell them will test their friendship, especially Edra's. But his decision to go has been made, and what he has to do needs to be done. He shifts in his seat, interlocks his fingers, his knuckles white, and lets out an unsteady breath. 'Mum has cancer.'

And just like that, hearing it spoken out loud makes it suddenly all too real. A knot forms in his throat. Tears prickle his senses. His vision blurs. The surrounding noise becomes distant. A high-pitched ringing deafens his ears.

He clears his throat, then chances a look at their reaction. They're speechless. He should've told them sooner; he knows that now.

But they had their own crap to deal with.

He shakes his head. Who's he kidding? Deep down, he knows why he kept it from them—it was denial. In his own twisted and tormented head, he believed that if he didn't think about the cancer, it would just go away.

But now he needs to face reality. 'So Mum was diagnosed with it nearly three years ago, soon after we went missing. She's had surgery and chemo, but it's come back in a bad way. The doctors … well, they, um, don't hold much hope.'

Ulan smacks her hand to her mouth.

Ryker stops a moment to compose himself. 'Anyway, I figure a bit of superhuman intervention is what she needs.' Ryker can't bear to look at them; he lowers his gaze. Heat flushes his face.

Their silence is freaking him out. 'And so'—he pushes through the emotions clogging his throat—'that explains *why* I'm returning. As for the *how* … well, I'm going back to Oz, entering the realm from there and hoping to find the portal we fell through all those years ago. Then we'll get Mum the help she needs without her having to trek across to the other side of the globe for it.' He runs his hand back and forth over his clipped hair and sighs. 'God knows we've had no luck finding it from here.'

Ryker looks up. Their stunned expressions speak

volumes. He shifts in his seat. 'I reckon we should give it a go—Mum has suffered enough.'

Banji sits higher, his green eyes darkening. 'So when do we leave? I'm ready when you are.'

Ulan reaches for Ryker's hand. Her eyes, green like her brother's, fill with tears. She sniffs them back. 'Banj, if you're in, I'm in too. There's no way you're going without me.'

Edra says nothing. Her posture remains rigid, her lips pursed.

Ryker rubs at his sweaty brow. 'Guys, wow, um, thanks, really, but I didn't mean to drag you into all of this; I just thought I'd tell you, that's all. I fly out tomorrow.'

'Tomorrow?' Edra jumps to her feet, knocking over her seat. She swipes away the wisp of auburn hair that's escaped her ponytail and glares at him.

Banji reaches for the chair to set it right, then indicates for her to sit again. 'Edra, let's hear him out.' His tone is calm and gentle, but Ryker can tell he's just as uneasy about this as Edra. Banji runs his fingers through his tight dark curls. 'Why does it have to be tomorrow? You only made the decision to go last night, right? Surely your father needs a bit more time to prepare for this.'

Ryker gulps. Things are about to turn ugly. 'Dad doesn't know.' His hands shoot up to stop Banji from countering. 'And I'd prefer that we keep it that way. We don't have time. I need to act before the authorities back in Sydney become wise to my movements.' Ryker stops, suddenly conscious of the implication of his words.

And Edra doesn't miss the meaning. Her eyes widen. 'You mean to tell us that you're doing this without *any* backup? Not your dad, not the taskforce, not anything?'

Ryker scans the crowd, seeking the quickest way to exit the café, but with Banji at his side, he's cornered. Choosing the booth to sit at was a bad idea. He tugs at the neckline of his T-shirt and shifts in his seat—their glare is making him squirm. 'Look,' he tries to explain, 'it's best we keep it simple—you know, get in, find the missing gateway, then get out. Jack, Peanut and the gang are helping me get in, and once inside, I'll have Medwin and the forest people. If all goes to plan, we'll have Mum better in no time.'

'Ryker, you *cannot* be serious!' Edra's eyes turn dark. 'You're freaking mental! And I thought *I* had problems.' She shakes her head. 'You're delusional if you think you can do this on your own.'

Ryker stiffens. His breathing accelerates. He struggles to hold back from reacting, but for Edra's sake, he needs to. *She's got enough on her plate already.* 'Look, Edra, I know what you're saying, but involving parents and the authorities means red tape, which means unnecessary loss of time, and time is something we can't afford to waste. Mum needs help *now*. I've made up my mind; I'm doing this. No one else needs to get involved. All right?'

Edra snorts, tucks a wayward strand of her hair behind her ear, then leans in closer, with one brow raised. 'And what about Max's father? Surely, *he* needs to know about this, after all, *he's* the doctor!'

Ryker bites back from saying something he'll regret. He looks away, counts to ten, then lets out a held breath. 'Look, he doesn't need to know at this stage. I'm only going in to find the portal, that's all. And the truth is we can do this without him. We've got Max; she can do it.'

Edra slaps her hand on the table and laughs. 'You're kidding me, right? Max? Ryker, we're talking about cancer here, not a few broken bones.'

Ryker clenches his teeth. Her attack makes him question his decision, and that irks him. He crosses his arms. 'Yeah, Max! What's wrong with that? You've seen what she can do. Christ, she's managed to bring me back from the brink of death a few times already. And not just me. I think we can all thank her for surviving that nightmare of a place to some degree. Don't you?' He juts out his chin. 'Edra, you don't know the half of it. With everything she's gone through, I'll back Max, one hundred percent.'

With sudden clarity, Ryker realises that in trying to convince Edra, he's managed to reassure himself at the same time. The cloud of doubt evaporates.

Edra falls back in her seat. Her shoulders slump. She rubs at her temples. 'Look, Ryker, I really don't want us to fight.' She draws in a deep breath, then reaches for his hand. 'You've kind of surprised us, that's all.' Her head lowers. 'I guess I overreacted.' She peeks up at him from under her fringe. 'I'm sorry, okay.'

Ryker clamps his massive hand over hers and gives it a gentle squeeze. He knows she's been battling with everything *realm*-related lately, so it shouldn't have come as a surprise that she'd be the one struggling most with his decision.

'And if it means anything, you're right about Max. I shouldn't have said anything. I know Max has it in her to do it.'

Ryker breathes easier. Edra's support means everything to him.

'Wow, I can't believe you're going back,' Ulan says, almost to herself.

'Yeah. Who would've ever imagined it?' Banji says. 'But I'm behind you all the way on this, Ryker. I think we all are.'

Ryker smiles. Banji's words give him strength.

'So are you sure you don't want us to come?' Banji asks. 'The offer still stands.' He chances a look at Edra. 'Well, from me, anyway.'

'It's all good, Banj. I know I didn't mention it earlier, but I won't be on my own. Peanut has offered to come with me.'

'Well, thank God!' Edra flops into her chair and laughs. 'Finally, I'm seeing some sense in this plan of yours.'

The mood shifts, Ryker smiles. 'Yeah, we figured he might be useful. And you all know Peanut; he's only too happy to get up to some mischief.'

'As long as he keeps focused.' Ulan giggles, her tiny nose scrunching up. 'I've never met anyone so distractable.'

Edra rolls her eyes. 'Yeah, good luck with that. He's like an excitable puppy.'

They all laugh.

'So what can we do? Is there anything you need?' Banji asks him.

Ryker sits higher in his seat. 'Look, all I need from you guys is to cover for me. I'll be gone for a few days, and I don't want Mum and Dad worrying.'

'So how long are we talking?' Edra asks. 'I mean, when do we send in the search party?' She winks at Ulan and smiles at her own joke.

Ryker nudges Edra with his knee. 'Hey, thanks

for nothing. Nice knowing what you really think of my chances.' They laugh. 'Seriously though, we've worked it out. Jack's going to call you the moment Peanut and I have passed through the portal. After that we're allowing seventy-two hours to locate the other gateway. If you don't hear back from either Jack or me in that time, give my father this.' He hands Edra a sealed envelope. 'It explains everything he'll need to know.'

Edra looks down at the letter for a while, tapping it on the table, deep in thought. 'So what's your alibi? What are you telling your parents?'

Ryker had been toying with a few ideas but hadn't come up with anything solid. He looks at his friends. 'Any suggestions?'

Edra shifts in her seat. 'Um, so you could tell them I needed to get away—you know, sort some stuff out—and I asked you to come.' She shrugs, then lowers her gaze. 'I guess it needs to be believable, and we all know how screwed up I am.' She laughs. 'So it wouldn't come as a surprise.'

Ryker's heart sinks. Edra's attempt to make light of her suffering cuts him deep. He knows it's taken a lot of guts for her to suggest this. He reaches for her hand to give it a squeeze.

Banji and Ulan sit silent.

Edra's shoulders lift, and she's quick to laugh it

off. 'Ryker, don't look so worried. Like I said, you can't fake what really is.'

He lets out a shaky breath, leans over and pulls her into an awkward hug. 'Thanks, Edra, you're the best. Did you know that?'

9

Get Me Out of Here!

Edra

Edra's face warms. She's Ryker's alibi. Her ears feel as if they're on fire. Suddenly the confines of the small coffee shop overwhelm her—her pulse races; her chest tightens. She needs to get out of there, and fast, but she doesn't want to make a scene by pulling out of Ryker's embrace.

She draws in a few deep breaths.

Of course, it's believable. Blind Freddie can see she's struggling with reality. They've been back for three months, and she's been in therapy all that time, but still she feels like she's drowning—spiralling downwards, out of control.

The doctors agreed that she wasn't well and

holding onto Jaeger's memory wasn't healthy. 'Let him go, and get on with your life. Allow yourself to find someone new,' they said.

Yeah, right! Like that's ever going to happen.

So they prescribed medication. But the little white pills didn't help—in fact she felt worse. They made her drowsy, and all she wanted to do was sleep. So she stopped taking them, and then at every appointment after that, she plastered a plastic smile on her face and told them what they wanted to hear—that she was feeling great, thinking more positively and seeing herself getting better. Of course, the doctors bought it, and after that the sessions became less intense and eventually bearable.

But Edra is a long way from being okay. Flashbacks of that day consume most of her waking thoughts, and in her sleep, nightmares plague her. Over and over again her subconscious replays the horror scenes—the lions, the stalking, the attack … and then Jaeger's blood-curdling screams.

She truly believed she'd dealt with it all back in the realm, but now she knows she only managed to bury it, and bury it so deep that, when it resurfaced, it came back with a vengeance. The tragic retelling of what happened only opened those deeply embedded wounds.

Jaeger was her heart, her one and only. A huge

piece of her died that day. How is she to move on from that?

Her eyes squeeze tight as she tries to hold back the tears. She then clears her throat and frees herself from Ryker's embrace. 'Okay, enough with the sappy hugs. So you think three days are enough?'

'Should be,' Ryker says. 'Whether we find the other portal or not, after seventy-two hours, we're out of there. Mum will get the treatment either way. It'd just be easier if she could get it without leaving South Africa.'

'And your mum?' Ulan asks. 'She'll be okay with keeping all of this from your dad?'

Ryker scratches his head. 'Look, we'll regroup when I get back and work out how to get her on board with this. If Dad gets wind of it, we can expect nothing less than a full-scale military intervention, nothing like the half-baked attempt we're making now.'

Edra's eyes pop wide open. *Half-baked? He can't be serious!* An overwhelming tightness in her chest sends her into a tailspin. All her familiar anxieties come crashing down on her. Her palms sweat; her breathing accelerates. She needs to escape. Her eyes dart to the exit, and she prepares to leave. 'Well, it sounds like you've got it all worked out. I'll head off then and let my parents know I'm going *camping,*' she half-heartedly jokes. 'I'll just race home, grab some gear, then head out.' She turns to him. 'So what time should I meet you?'

Too quickly, Ulan jumps up to stop her. 'Edra, wait, I'm coming too. You shouldn't do this on your own.'

'What? No!' Edra blinks several times. 'I mean, you don't have to do that. I'll be fine.'

'I'll come too,' Banji offers.

What! Now they're all coming? She rubs her clammy palms on her jeans. *Why can't they just leave me alone?*

'Great, then we'll all go,' Ulan says. 'To tell you the truth, I've been feeling a little down lately. This might do me good, do us all some good. What do you think?'

Edra stops. She can see what her friends are doing. Something inside her starts to thaw. She smiles. 'Sure. Why not? I'll pack a picnic basket.'

And so the pace is set for the 'short trip away with Ryker'.

10

DETENTION

JACK

Jack shoots Ryker a look, trying to convey the reason for the change in plans without stirring his father's suspicions. They're at the airport. Ryker has just cleared customs, and Jack can tell by the look on Ryker's face that he's not too happy to see his dad there instead of their red-headed, freckle-faced friend. The original idea was that he and Peanut would pick Ryker up from the airport and head straight down the coast to start their assignment. Of course, the shift in the situation has thrown him, and the knot in Jack's stomach tightens when he thinks of the other dilemma they need to address—Ruby coming too. He's not looking forward to seeing Ryker's reaction to that.

Jack tries to keep it casual but struggles to keep

his voice composed. 'It's good to see you, mate. Good flight?'

Ryker gives Jack a severe look. He turns to greet his dad instead. 'Hey, Mr Braden. I wasn't expecting a welcoming party.'

'Ryker, how are you, son? You look worried. Is everything okay?' Daniel Braden pulls Ryker into a fatherly hug.

Jack blinks a few times. He doesn't remember Ryker being so big. Although his dad is quite tall, Ryker towers over him. And if he's not mistaken, he's filled out quite a bit since they last saw him, dwarfing his father in comparison.

Ryker looks at him over his father's shoulder and frowns. He pulls out of the embrace and slaps Daniel on the back. 'Ah, just a bit of a headache, that's all, Mr B. I didn't sleep much on the plane. I'll be fine.'

'Jack only mentioned yesterday that you were coming. Bit of a surprise, really. Don't get me wrong, we're happy to have you. I'm looking forward to catching up on what's been happening.' He looks down at his watch. 'But we'd better make tracks, Trish will be wondering what's keeping us. Dinner should just about be ready.'

Ryker's eyebrows rise at the word *dinner*.

Jack flounders, unable to find anything to say that'll reassure Ryker that things are okay. He resorts to giving him a thumbs-up sign, hoping that's enough.

Ryker frowns, then runs his hand through his bristly hair. 'I was expecting to see Peanut.' He looks at Jack.

Jack shakes his head. 'Yeah, about that, the bloody idiot got an arvo, so he couldn't make it. I know we planned to head off once you got here, but there's been a change of plans. We'll head off first thing tomorrow instead. Okay?'

Ryker stops midstride. 'Tomorrow?' He turns away and rubs the back of his neck. Jack can tell he's not happy hearing that.

Ryker hoists his backpack over his shoulders and adjusts the straps. 'Look, how about you drop me off at the train station, and I'll make my way down there now. You and Peanut can meet up with me later tonight once you've got yourselves sorted out.'

Jack's father frowns. 'Hey, there'll be none of that. You've just had a long flight, and you said yourself you didn't get much sleep. Stay tonight, then head off in the morning. I'll drive you boys down there myself. Anyhow, everyone's dying to see you, so I'd better bring you home if I know what's good for me.' He laughs.

'I can't ask you to do that, Mr B. What about your work?'

'It's all good,' Jack assures him. 'It's Saturday

tomorrow. Dad's going to drop us off first thing in the morning, then meet up with a few of his mates for a golfing weekend. And because it's a public holiday on Monday, he'll pick us up Monday afternoon once we're done. That's if it's okay with you.' Jack tries to gauge if Ryker's happy to hear all this or not. 'Will that be enough time to do what you need to do?'

Ryker visibly relaxes. 'Plenty. Thanks for doing that, Mr B, much appreciated.'

Jack breathes a little easier.

On the drive home, they chat about the purpose of Ryker's visit. Jack's father cranes his neck to look at Ryker in his rear-vision mirror. 'I'm surprised you picked Blue Ridge for your thesis, Ryker. Of all the national parks in the world to compare, you picked that one. Strange, but I would've thought you'd had enough of that place.'

Jack turns in his seat to face Ryker. They expected there'd be some suspicion from his father about his visit, and they'd prepared for it.

'Mind you, I'm no expert on the matter,' his father continues, 'but I wouldn't have thought you'd see too many similarities with the national parks back your way.'

Jack knows what's coming; they rehearsed it last night.

Ryker clears his throat. 'Well, it's not so much

the similarities but the differences that were obvious to me when I first saw them,' he says convincingly. 'Unfortunately, under the circumstances I didn't get a chance to appreciate it back then. It just so happens that our thesis requires us to compare two *dissimilar* environments. And since I was missing my Aussie friends so much, what better way to kill two birds with one stone? And don't worry about us stumbling across the portal; we'll be avoiding that particular area like the plague. After what we've been through, there's no way in hell we'll be going anywhere near it.' He laughs, then gives Jack a wink.

Jack relaxes. Ryker's performance was convincing enough.

'Anyway, I'm planning on being here for a few days before accompanying Miss Hedtke back home with me,' he continues. 'Father doesn't approve of her travelling alone. You may have heard that Annie is coming over to help Mum. She's about to start treatment for cancer.'

Jack's father clicks his tongue and shakes his head. 'Yes, terrible news, Ryker; I'm sorry to hear it. And this is her second time? Jack said she had treatment a couple of years ago. I pray that she beats it this time.'

'Oh, I've every faith that she'll pull through, Mr B, every faith in the world.'

'That's the spirit. I've always said that despite

whatever challenges life throws you, you need to keep optimistic. All that positive energy you put out in the universe somehow comes back in the form of good luck—must be the Irish in me; I don't know.' He chuckles. 'Take a half-filled glass of water, for example; I always say to my kids to look at it as a glass half full, not a glass half empty. Your perception of life greatly influences your attitude and ultimately your outcome. Do you get what I mean?'

'Absolutely. I completely agree. My father adopts the same approach in life.'

'By the way, how *is* Denvon? This must be a trying time for you all.'

'He's keeping a positive outlook. In fact, it was Dad who insisted that we continue living our lives as normally as possible. When I told him I was thinking of visiting you guys for my research, he was the first to encourage that I do.'

Jack's eyes widen. Ryker's doing a pretty good job of lying. He seems to have thought of everything and come prepared to cover all angles.

They eventually arrive at the Braden household, and the gang, minus Peanut, meet them in the driveway. Max flies from the back of the group to give Ryker his first welcome hug. Jack cringes, but stops and tells himself to be okay with that—like it or not, Ryker is special to her. What happened to them in the realm forged a strong connection. In the end, Ryker saved her life and brought her home, and that's what he needs to keep reminding himself.

Ryker's face lights up. 'Max!' He picks her up and spins her around in a big bear hug. She giggles. 'Ryker, it's great to see you, but boy, you need to ease up a bit; you're squeezing the life out of me.'

He laughs and puts her down.

'Wow, have you been working out or something?' She eyes him up and down, blinking a few times.

Jack has a quick look at his own trim form, puffs his chest out, then inwardly moans—there's no way he can compete with that.

Ryker smiles awkwardly. 'Hey, sorry, my bad, but you know how much I've missed you. It's so good to see you.' He turns to the others. 'All of you.' He hugs them in turn.

'So a thesis on the comparison of two dissimilar national parks?' Kenny asks, his brow raised. 'Should make for an interesting read.'

Ryker winks at him. 'You can be the first to read it, my gifted friend.'

'It's good to see you, Ryker,' Ruby says. 'Sorry about Peanut.' She looks up the driveway and frowns. 'I can't imagine what's keeping him. The twit should've been here by now.'

Ryker chuckles, then turns to Jack's mother.

'Thanks for putting me up for the night, Mrs Braden. A good feed, a comfy bed and a good night's sleep— exactly what we need to take on a weekend of hiking.'

Trish Braden places a motherly kiss on his cheek. 'Think nothing of it; we're happy to have you. Come on in before dinner gets cold.'

'Did someone mention dinner?'

They turn to see Peanut making his way towards them, his backpack slung off one of his shoulders. 'Awesome, I'm famished! I couldn't have timed it better if I tried.'

'Peanut! My man!' Ryker pulls him into a man-hug and pats him on the back. 'Hey, so what's with the detention, dude?'

Peanut shoves his hands in his cargo-pants' pockets and shrugs. 'Ah, just something stupid. Hey, I'm sorry I stuffed up our plans. We could've been on our way by now.'

'Just as well,' Max says with a pout. 'I'd be spitting chips if you came all this way and didn't drop in to say g'day.'

'Spitting chips?' Ryker chuckles. 'Now that's a new one. I take it that it means you wouldn't be happy?'

Peanut slaps Ryker on his back. '*Now* you're getting the hang of it! We'll have you Aussiefied in no time.'

Ryker laughs, then turns to Jack. 'I'm glad you're coming, my friend, otherwise I'd need to bring an Aussie urban dictionary to get my head around half the stuff Peanut comes out with.'

Jack half-heartedly laughs. Little does Ryker know that he'll have Ruby with him to help as well. Ruby clears her throat to get Jack's attention, but he avoids looking at her. He'll spring that particular news on him when the time's right.

Ryker places his arm over Peanut's shoulders, and they make their way inside. Kenny and Max follow. Ruby catches up to Jack and elbows him in the ribs. He clenches his teeth. 'Not now, Ruby!'

Her amber eyes darken; her chin juts out, and she clears her throat again, this time a little louder. 'So, Ryker, did Jack happen to mention that I was coming too?'

Ruby turns to Jack and smiles sweetly.

Jack groans.

Ryker whips around so fast, Jack dives for cover.

Peanut grins and gives Ryker a slap on the back. 'Hey, what can I say, you've either got it or you don't. It's a curse, sometimes; the poor girl can't live without me.'

Jack feels Ruby stiffen by his side. He can only imagine what she's thinking, and he'd put money on it that it's got something to do with wiping that smug look off Peanut's face with her power-packed shield once they've entered the realm.

Ryker and Jack exchange a look. Jack tries to reassure him with another thumbs-up sign, but Ryker's frown says it all. He turns to enter the house.

Apart from that little hurdle, the night passes well. Everyone's on a high. It's good to see Ryker and hear how their friends are doing back in Johannesburg. Soon it's time for Max and Kenny to leave.

'Right, so I'll just set up a bed on the floor in the girl's room, will I?' Jack's mother asks Ruby. 'There's plenty of room in there, and Katie and Meara are bursting to have you sleep over. And as for the boys, they can bunk down in Jack's room.' She leaves to prepare the beds.

Jack scratches his head, sighs, then looks at Ryker. He has a lot of explaining to do. He can't imagine they'll get much sleep tonight.

They see Kenny and Max off. Halfway up the driveway, Max runs back with a grin on her face. 'Kenny and I are meeting up with you tomorrow,' she whispers in his ear, her eyes twinkling. 'Not fair you being out there on your own.' She winks at him, then races off, laughing. Jack stares after her.

'And no arguments. Okay?' She calls out over her shoulder.

He can't hold back a smile. *Arguments? Nope,*

no arguments here! 'Hey, has anyone ever told you you're pushy?'

She turns and pulls a face.

Jack laughs. *God, I love that girl!*

II

Ghosts From the Past

Jack

The following morning comes around fast enough. Last night's curveball was a shock to Ryker initially, but it didn't take too much to convince him that having Ruby on board was a good thing. In the end he was all for it and grateful for her support. Having spent most of the night making plans and going over strategies, a quick breakfast of cereal, tea and toast recharges their energy levels. Although a little weary-eyed, Jack is ready to go. With backpacks filled to the brim with *necessary* supplies—according to Ryker—some of which make Jack a little nervous, they jump into the Land Cruiser and begin their journey down the coast to Blue Ridge National Park.

It's 4:30 am and still dark as they head out of Sydney. Ryker, Ruby and Peanut huddle in the back seat exchanging ideas in whispered tones and scribbled notes, while Jack does his best to distract his father with idle conversation. The roads are quiet this time of the morning, so the run down there takes them a little under three hours.

Jack jerks awake as the car comes to a halt. He turns in his seat to see his friends yawning and stretching. He rubs his eyes, eager to get going.

'You lot must've been up all night catching up.' Jack's father chuckles. 'All four of you were dead to the world. It was a snoring symphony. Oh, all except you, Ruby.' He smiles at her in the rear-vision mirror. 'I don't know how you coped, you poor girl.'

Ruby pulls some rolled-up bits of tissue out from her ears and grins. Daniel laughs.

The reserve is peaceful, and the air is fresh when they arrive at the carpark. Jack throws on a jumper, then takes a moment to appreciate the calmness surrounding them. He closes his eyes, draws in the crisp air and allows the early morning sun filtering through the trees to warm his face. He listens to the birds twittering their excitement at the new day.

Peanut joins him, throwing the hood of his sweater over his head. He blows warm air into his clasped hands, then rubs at his arms, trying to stir up some warmth, while shifting his weight from one foot to the other. 'Man, it's cold!' He sees Ruby zipping up her puffer jacket. 'Hey, Rubes, come here; I can warm you up.'

She rolls her eyes and adjusts her hair under her beanie. 'I'm good, thanks.'

Ryker wastes no time. He grabs his backpack from the boot of the SUV and hoists it over his shoulders ready to go. He slaps Jack's father on the back. 'Mr B, you're a saint. We really appreciate you driving us. But we'd better not keep you any longer. Weren't you meeting up with some friends?'

Jack's father hustles. 'Oh, right. The Country Club. Tee off's at 8:00 am. I'd better not keep them waiting.' He looks down at his watch. 'Geez, is that the time?' He hops back into the car and fumbles with the seatbelt. 'Will you kids be okay if I just drop and run? I might make it in time if I leave now. Look, I won't be far if you need me for anything. Okay?'

Jack closes the door for him. 'No worries, you go. We're good. And Dad, I'll ring you Monday afternoon when we're ready. Don't worry if you haven't heard from us before then; reception can be non-existent in some parts of the park.'

'Stay safe, guys, and I know I don't need to remind you, but stay clear of trouble.' He waves them goodbye.

'No worries, Mr B,' Ryker calls back. 'Thanks again. See you Monday.'

The car disappears from view, and they collectively breathe out a sigh of relief.

'Piece of cake.' Peanut laughs. 'I don't know what you guys were stressing about.' Ruby smacks him on the back of the head, then finishes tightening her backpack around her waist.

'Okay, let's go.' Ryker readjusts his kit, then gestures for them to make the first move.

Jack leads the way. They walk along a well-established track that takes them to the entrance of the wooded forest. Small animals scurry in the underbrush, their early morning routines disturbed. Birds twitter in the treetops, oblivious to their presence. Jack pauses to take it all in. Everything seems so peaceful, totally opposite to how he's beginning to feel. He leads them towards a small wooden bridge that crosses over a shallow rambling stream. From there they climb up a ravine using saplings to haul themselves up the steep slope, then follow the course of the creek.

They're off any discernible path now. And as they venture further, they enter into thicker vegetation, slowing their progress. Ryker unsheathes a sizeable black hunting knife from the inside of his boot and offers it to Jack. It's huge, one side a smooth blade, the other, a jagged edge. The formidable cold metal sits heavily in his hand. But time is ticking. He shrugs, then puts the blade to use, and they soldier on.

Less than an hour later, they're back on some kind of track and come across the first indicator that they're getting close. Warning signs have been set up along the walking trail.

KEEP TO THE PATH —
DANGEROUS CREVASSES

DANGER—UNSTABLE CLIFF EDGE

As they venture a little nearer, the signs become somewhat more foreboding.

DANGER OF DEATH—KEEP OUT!

Ruby stops to eye each sign, then turns to look at Jack. Her expression mirrors what he's feeling. Ryker rushes past them to take the lead. 'Great. This is looking good.'

Peanut's brow furrows. 'How d'ya figure that? It looks pretty creepy to me.'

Ryker chuckles. 'All these signs indicate they haven't had any luck destroying the portal. It's still out there.'

Jack blinks a few times. The possibility of not accessing the portal hadn't crossed his mind, but clearly it had Ryker's. They pick up the pace.

As they get nearer, the warnings become more and more ominous. And although Jack knows the signs are there to deter bushwalkers from stumbling across the portal, the reality of what they're doing—the real risk—floods him with a deluge of doubt. Images of their last encounter overwhelm him. And from the look on Ruby and Peanut's faces, he's not the only one reliving it. Jack stops and squats on his haunches to control his breathing.

'Hey, are you okay?' Ruby rests her hand on his shoulder.

He reaches up to reassure her.

Peanut plunks down next to him. 'Man, it's getting to you too, huh?'

Jack hangs his head.

Peanut clutches his chest. 'Don't know 'bout you lot, but I think I'm having a heart attack here.'

'I know what you mean.' Jack looks around at the daunting signs. 'Geez, just look at this place, will ya?' His earlier enthusiasm hits a brick wall. *What the hell are we doing here?*

Ruby turns her back on Ryker. 'Guys, we can turn back if you're not one hundred percent into this. It's not too late. I'm good with whatever you decide.'

She peeks over her shoulder where Ryker has stopped to see what the holdup is. His hands sit firm on his hips, his lips pressed in a thin line.

Jack ignores him and looks at each of his friends. 'Guys, it's your decision. You're the ones sticking your necks out.'

Peanut focuses on a blade of grass he's toying with and says nothing. Ruby stares vacantly at the warning signs.

'Hey, what's the hold-up?' Ryker calls out, his tone impatient.

Peanut runs his fingers through his shaggy mane. 'Hold ya horses, will ya? Just give us a sec.' He blows out a breath, looks at Ruby for a good while, then back at Jack.

Jack remains silent. Whatever Peanut decides to do now will affect what happens next. Either they're all in or Ryker goes it alone. Jack is prepared to back Peanut, no matter what.

Ruby squats by Peanut's side, takes his hand in hers and smiles. 'Hey, like I said, I'm game if you are.' She gives his hand a squeeze. 'We can do this; I know we can, but don't let me be the reason for any second thoughts. Make your decision on what *you* need to do. Okay?'

Peanut hangs his head. 'Guys, I can't explain it, but somehow I feel I've gotta do this.' He pauses to look around. 'I never said anything before, 'cause I felt stupid, but since we've been back, I've kinda lost my mojo. You know, I'm all over the shop. My head's all messed up or someth'n. S'pose that's why I've been mucking up at school.' Peanut gives them a sheepish look. 'I know I said I'd never go back in there, but what we're doing here, well, somehow it kinda feels right. D'ya get what I'm saying?'

Jack says nothing. He looks at Ruby, then considers Ryker, waiting impatiently down the track. He sighs. 'Yeah, mate, I think I do.' He looks back at his friends, his respect for them heightened. 'You know something, what you guys are doing takes guts; I'm proud of you. But promise me something; don't do anything stupid. Okay?' He juts his chin towards Ryker. 'Just listen to him, and do exactly what he tells ya. Stick to him like glue. All right? As much as he can be a pain in the neck, I trust him. I saw what he did for Max.'

Ryker backtracks and stops, arms crossed, before them. 'Guys, are we doing this or what?'

'Yeah, we're doing this,' Jack reassures him. 'Just got a bit spooked, that's all.'

Peanut pulls himself up and dusts his pants. 'C'mon, it's not that much further.' He takes Ruby by the hand, and powers on.

Ryker follows, and Jack trails along behind.

They continue in silence, and soon the gateway is just beyond the crest of the ravine. Ryker gestures for them to slow down and silence their movements. He drops to the ground and crawls on all fours, commando style.

Jack stops short, eyes widening. *What the …? Is this guy for real?* He almost laughs out loud, but Ryker's seriousness sobers him, and he scans the space around them, suddenly wary. Without further thought, he throws himself to the ground and imitates Ryker. Peanut and Ruby do the same.

Closer to the edge of the gully, Ryker rolls onto his back and shuffles the rest of the way. From his vest pockets, he pulls gadgets that rival those on any *Bourne* movie. He inserts tiny wireless earphones into his ears, then blue-tooths them to a small satellite dish before adjusting its position in search of reception. Once he seems satisfied with the set-up, he pulls out a small rectangular mirror and attaches it to a telescopic handle that extends to overlook the ravine.

Peanut's eyes bulge, and Ruby blinks several times. Jack slaps his hand to his mouth to smother a chuckle.

'The area is heavily sectioned off with yellow warning tape,' Ryker whispers in all seriousness. 'There are signs everywhere cautioning of radiation exposure. Anyone in their right mind would steer clear of this place.' He takes a moment to tune into the sonic device, which whistles and crackles.

Jack holds his breath to listen.

After a thorough surveillance, Ryker confirms they're the only ones there. 'Okay, so we're good to go. All we need to do now is check for traps.'

'What, booby traps?' Peanut's eyes widen. 'Mate, they wouldn't go that far, would they?'

Ryker shakes his head. 'I don't know. They wouldn't risk anyone getting hurt, but we shouldn't drop our guard. Come on, let's get down there. I'll scout the area before we enter.'

A surge of adrenaline courses through Jack's body as they make their way down the slope, his eyes and ears peeled, ready for anything.

Sure enough, a mass of yellow tape sections off the area at the bottom of the ravine, and daunting messages are nailed on every other tree.

DANGER—KEEP OUT—
HIGH RADIATION AREA

WARNING—DO NOT ENTER—
NUCLEAR HAZARD

AUTHORISED PERSONNEL ONLY

Before entering, Ryker begins his investigations of the outer area.

'Wow, he's thorough; I'll give you that much,' Ruby says, her eyes wide. 'I've never really seen him in action. And I won't lie, what I'm seeing is pretty hot.' She fans herself, then turns to Peanut and gives him a wink. Peanut scowls.

Jack shakes his head and laughs. *Poor guy. If nothing, the next couple of days will definitely be interesting.*

Jack quickly sobers when he catches a glimpse of the wispy gossamer veil beyond the tangle of tape and warning signs.

Peanut shudders next to him. 'Sends a shiver down my spine, that does—real creepy if you ask me. No matter how many times I see it, that *thing* still spins me out.'

Jack can't help but stare at it. 'I can't even begin to imagine what you must've thought the first time you saw it.'

'I honestly thought I was going nuts. One second the four of you were tumbling down the slope, the next you all vanished into thin air.'

Ruby reaches for Peanut's hand and moves in closer.

Peanut looks around, then scratches his head. 'So what's the go? How come they haven't destroyed it yet?'

Jack shrugs. 'Maybe they haven't figured how.'

'Looks like they've tried,' Ryker answers as he approaches. He points to the area around the gateway, which is charred and ravaged from what looks like an attempt to burn it or blow it up. 'I've had a quick look around the perimeter and can't find anything that resembles a trap. I think it's safe to enter.'

Knowing this is the prompt to make a move, Jack turns to Peanut and raises his brow, silently offering him a final chance to change his mind.

Peanut gives Jack a reassuring pat on the back. 'Hey, just be ready for us when we get back. Okay?'

Heat rushes up Jack's neck; his palms sweat. 'So this is it. No turning back.'

'Just stick to the plan, Jack. Okay?' Ryker is all seriousness.

Jack's lips press in a thin line. 'You too. And don't do anything stupid.'

'Oi!' Peanut cries out in mock offence. 'You looked at me when you said that!'

This earns him a smack at the back of his head from Ruby.

Jack isn't seeing the funny side of things either. 'I mean it, Peanut. Quit mucking around! Just find the portal and get out.'

Peanut's hands shoot out in front of him. 'Geez,

relax, bro. It was just a joke!'

Ryker looks from Peanut to Jack. 'Jack, don't worry; there'll be no room for *stupid*. We can't afford there to be. And we'll be back before you know it.' He forges ahead, prying apart the weave of tape, forcing an entry into the forbidden space. He stops to scour the area, then with calculated precision, inches closer towards the portal. Once there, he turns and gestures for Peanut and Ruby to follow.

Peanut holds the tape apart for Ruby to enter, then gives Jack a thumbs-up sign before ducking between the tape and walking to the gateway.

Jack holds his breath.

Ryker, Ruby and Peanut stop before the shimmering, gauzy curtain, turn to Jack, smile, and then, without a second thought, they plunge into its depths.

And just like that, they're gone.

12

This is Totally Insane

Ruby

Ruby questions what they're doing. Although putting on a convincing mask of bravado, inside, she's anything but heroic—in fact, she's very close to falling apart. But she won't let that happen—the show must go on. So, with a smile plastered on her face, she stays the course and gives her audience the performance of her life. There's no way she's letting Peanut do this without her.

Ruby keeps herself distracted by riling him up. As much as she's mad about him, she can't help but pick on him—he's such an easy target. She thinks back to the first time she met him: he'd stood there with his mouth gaping, struggling to find something impressive to say but only managing to send her running. He came across as a complete loony. She remembers that slap she gave him and rolls her eyes. *Such a drama queen!*

But that was then, when her whole world was falling apart—she'd just spent a month in hospital recovering from the beating her so-called friends gave her. After that, she was forced to change schools. Traumatised by the whole experience, she lost confidence and became petrified of what this fresh start would bring. But what lay ahead was her saving grace. She'd learned to trust again, not only in others, but more importantly in herself—although at the moment that confidence is questionable.

They're about to enter the Ancient Realm. She stops to remind herself that she can do this. She has Peanut by her side, which comforts her to no end. He's her rock, her constant. She knows without a doubt that if things turn ugly, Peanut will be there for her. She remembers the time she nearly gave up, when she had nothing left to give, but it was Peanut, steadfast in his belief in her, that pulled her through. 'I've got faith in you, Ruby. You're not the weakest link,' he'd said. His softly spoken words still bring a tear to her eye.

Ruby shakes off that memory and reinforces her resolve. They're in this together, no matter what. She takes Peanut by the hand, closes her eyes, searches for that heroine within, then plunges feet first.

13

THE COUNTDOWN BEGINS

RYKER

Ryker has his guard up the moment they land. He waits for Peanut to vanish and Ruby to produce her shield, then searches the area for any threat. They're in luck; the portal is unmanned. But that won't be the case for long. The place will be swarming with guards soon enough. Their intrusion will trigger some kind of alarm to alert them—he knows this from past experience. And sure enough, within minutes he catches the sound of thundering feet and whipped vegetation. Someone, or something, is coming at them with speed. He grabs Ruby's hand and takes off into the forest, looking for temporary refuge. He hears Peanut follow.

Ryker knows this area well. He ducks around trees, weaving his way through the forest with confidence, and soon finds them the perfect cover. He dives deep into a mesh of tangled vines, followed by the others, and there they settle under the protection of Ruby's bubble. They're safe with Ruby there, but he can't risk their presence being known—they can do without having a target on their back. It takes him a moment to calm his breathing.

'Piece of cake,' Peanut whispers between deep gasps.

Ryker puts his hand up to silence him, then closes his eyes to intensify his senses. In the distance he hears them: guards, now at a stop, panting from the sprint. One voice bellows orders, dominating the others. Herodus.

'They cannot have gotten far. Artemius, head north; Dareios, south; Miltiades, east and Kallius, west. I will remain and guard the gateway.'

Several feet hit the ground at once as they scatter in search of intruders. Within seconds one of them passes mere metres in front of them. Ryker hears him pause, as though picking up on their trail. Ruby grabs his arm. Ryker prepares to pounce, adrenaline pumping through his veins. But in moments, the guard powers on past them. They wait until the footsteps fade into the distance and quiet returns to the forest.

Ryker crouches motionless until the pins and needles in his legs force him to move. He shifts, then stops to listen: birds twitter in the treetops, small animals scurry unseen in the undergrowth—all is as it should be. He allows himself to breathe a little easier. The freshness of the morning cools his beaded brow.

In the distance he hears the guards return to the portal. 'Have you found anything?' Herodus asks.

'No, sir,' one of them reports, out of breath.

The other two state the same, but the fourth thinks he saw something. 'There was a disturbance in the shrub yonder, but on inspection I found it came to naught.'

'Are you certain?' Herodus's interest is peaked. 'Did you search the area thoroughly?'

The guard hesitates. Ryker knows he hadn't. They're in trouble.

Herodus mutters something unintelligible under his breath, then growls. 'Miltiades, answer me! Must we investigate?'

Ryker looks at Ruby. Her eyes are wide, pupils dilated. They're both ready.

'No, I exhausted the search.'

There's a pause. Ryker waits.

'Then we shall return to the fortress and report our findings.'

Ryker listens as they retreat, then allows himself to breathe. The tightness in his chest subsides. 'That was too bloody close.'

'You can say that again,' Peanut whispers. 'I nearly crapped my pants.'

Ryker chuckles, but then his ears prick up at the sound of movement nearby, and his hand shoots up, warning the others. Once again his senses sharpen.

A twig cracks under the strain of a weighted foot. Ryker braces himself, ready to respond.

'Friends, it is I, Medwin. You are safe to reveal yourselves.'

Ruby shoots him a questioning look. Ryker nods, and the shield retracts. In his eagerness to see Medwin, he dives from their hiding place, startling the smaller man, who falls to the ground.

'Sorry, old friend,' Ryker laughs as he helps him to his feet. 'It's good to see you.'

Medwin dusts the twigs and leaves from the hessian sack he's wearing, then pulls Ryker into a friendly embrace. 'And me, you.' The forest dweller pulls out of the hold. 'We have been anticipating your arrival.' He looks at Ruby, scratches his head, then searches the scrub. 'Although, I must have miscalculated, for I predicted you would arrive with two others.'

Peanut materialises. 'Hey, Medwin, how's it

going?' He shakes their friend's hand with exaggerated eagerness. 'Man, you nearly gave us a heart attack. We thought we were goners!'

Medwin smiles and smacks his forehead. 'Ah, but of course—the invisible one. I should have known, for I am very rarely wrong in these matters, you understand. It is also a pleasure to see *you* again, Peanut.'

Ryker chuckles. 'Medwin, your power of foresight is second to none, my friend.'

'Hey, have you met Ruby?' Peanut takes her by the hand to introduce her. 'She's wicked. What with *my girl* and her awesome forcefield, I reckon we'll be safe as houses.'

Medwin frowns and turns to Ryker for an interpretation.

Ryker laughs. 'What he means is that Ruby's got the power to produce a shield, and it's formidable. Nothing can penetrate it.'

Medwin's eyes widen. He looks at Ruby with obvious admiration, then bows his head in respect.

Just then, from behind the bushes, several other forest men emerge, eager to welcome the visitors, and among them is Molan, Aelianna's father. Ryker's mouth goes dry. He shakes his head. *Man, get a grip! Focus on what we're here for!*

Molan steps forward to greet them. 'We have

been awaiting your visit, curious to know what brings you back to our forest.'

Ryker is quick to tell them the purpose of their return and what they're looking for.

Medwin strokes his long, bushy beard as he listens. 'Explain it to me, Ryker, for I must be mistaken. You have powerful healers in your world, have you not? This we have all witnessed. Alger and Molan's return to health is a testimony to this. So the purpose of your return—to heal your mother's illness—makes very little sense to me.'

Ryker rubs his brow, unsure how to explain.

Ruby steps forward. 'You're right; we do have powerful healers, but there are some illnesses that can't be healed using anything less than a superpower. Can you understand that?'

Medwin frowns.

But there's no time to elaborate. Ruby's explanation will just have to do. Ryker presses further. 'So does anyone know of the other gateway?'

The men become lively, keen to assist and clearly undeterred by the consequences of helping. Going by their previous involvement, Ryker can only assume they're only too happy to rebel against the autocratic system. And who can blame them? The nobles live in the lap of luxury, while the village people struggle to survive.

Ryker watches as they chatter among themselves, but not one of them has anything significant to offer.

Medwin turns to their chief hunter. 'Molan, surely from your vast travels you have come upon something.'

Molan scratches his head.

Ryker had banked on the forest people coming up with a lead to locate the other portal, but now, with so little to go by, he realises the gamble they're taking is a huge one. He searches their eager faces. 'Perhaps one of you may have seen something out of the ordinary—maybe even noticed the gatekeepers somewhere you normally wouldn't expect to see them.'

'The gatekeepers … out of the ordinary, you say?' Molan asks, tapping his chin, his focus elsewhere. 'I do vaguely recall, a few years ago, something rather peculiar.'

Ryker watches as Molan struggles to retrieve the memory and wills him to remember.

'I was returning from a hunt,' Molan begins, his gaze fixed ahead. 'And as I recall, it was late in the morning. I was anxious to return home for I had ventured deep into the forest, well beyond my customary travels, and had lost track of the time. In my haste, I collided with a guard. He appeared agitated and somewhat surprised to see me.'

'What do you mean, agitated?' Ryker hopes this

is a lead.

'He became hostile and ordered me to leave. While doing so, he repeatedly glanced over his shoulder, as though concealing something. I turned to see what held his interest, but this angered him further, and he drew his blade. As I fled, he shouted for me to never return to this part of the forest again.' Molan blinks a few times. 'I must admit, his threat only heightened my curiosity, so I swore to return on the morrow to see what mystery he was secreting.'

Ryker's excitement escalates. 'And did you return?'

Molan shakes his head. 'No, and I cannot recall why, but I feel it may have been at the time of my hunting mishap.' He taps his chin in thought. 'Yes, that must have been it. I could not return due to my injury.'

Ryker's enthusiasm intensifies. They may have stumbled onto something significant. 'Molan, would you be able to find this place again?'

'Perhaps,' he answers. Then his eyes widen. 'Yes, I believe it is possible.'

Time is of the essence. 'Could you take us there now?'

Molan looks up at the sun and frowns. 'If we are to avoid crossing paths with those of The Dark Forest, we must leave immediately, otherwise we must wait 'til the morn.'

'But Molan, what of the feast?' Medwin reminds him.

Ryker stiffens. *Feast? What feast?*

'Food? Cool!' Peanut says with a grin. 'Yeah, I reckon I could eat.'

'Peanut!' Ruby gives him a pointed look.

Molan throws his head back and laughs. He slaps Ryker on the back. 'I am afraid our arrangements will have to wait, my son.'

What? No! Ryker looks from one man to the other—there might be a lead, and they're thinking of food? *Not now! Search first, eat later!* He whips around to glare at Peanut, but, oblivious to the threat, Peanut is ready and raring to go.

The men begin the trek to the village. Medwin leads with Molan close behind. They retrace a familiar path, winding through the dense vegetation. A multitude of massive trees create a canopy high above. Filtered rays of sunlight create pockets of well-lit areas, but mostly the density of the forest conceals their journey.

Ryker catches up to Molan in an attempt to steer the conversation back to finding the missing portal. 'So these people of The Dark Forest, who exactly are they?'

'There is a village of people beyond our lands who are best avoided,' Molan tells him as he blocks a huge palm leaf from smacking them in the face. 'They are exiles, or descendants of exiles, as we are,' he continues. 'But unlike us, they choose to live idle lives. They drink and feast to excess until the early hours of the morn, then slumber the remainder of the day. They are indolent and do not provide for themselves. They survive by pillaging the surrounding villages. What they don't need, they trade for favours with the fortress guards.'

'So you think now's a good time to head that way?' Ryker asks, hoping to incite them into action.

Medwin stops, looks at Molan and frowns. 'Not now. We can leave at first light on the morrow. Come, Ryker, we must celebrate your return. We have prepared quite the feast, and I am certain Aelianna has set aside a jug of wine for such an occasion as this. She is most anxious to see you again.' He smiles, then gives him a wink.

Behind him, Peanut snickers.

Ryker growls and turns to Ruby for help.

She shrugs. 'Ryker, they've mentioned food. There's no stopping him now.'

Ryker curses. The clock is ticking. They're wasting time, and he can't do anything about it. Resigned, he continues to trail Medwin as he leads them to the feast.

Ryker's thoughts turn to Aelianna. His face warms,

and suddenly he's off-kilter. But then he remembers the reason for his return—his mother—and like a slap in the face, he's instantly grounded. And then to drive the message home, he reminds himself of the last time he saw Aelianna—the time he'd asked her to come back with him, and she'd turned him down. The truth hurts.

Focus on the mission!

Ryker tugs at the neck of his T-shirt, then slows his thoughts to properly think things through. Whatever Molan came across in the woods that time might have nothing to do with what they're looking for. In which case, tomorrow's scheduled journey, like the feast, could be a complete waste of time. All of a sudden, the seventy-two hours he allocated for the mission feel way too few. He silently blasts himself for not being better prepared for something like this.

Once again Ryker considers baling out of this get-together, but realises he can't afford to offend his new friends. They've proven to be pivotal in their escape in the past and may turn out to be their greatest ally in the days to come. And then he spots Aelianna, and all thoughts of his inner turmoil fall to the wayside. He pulls Peanut aside. 'Hey, we're not staying, okay? We eat; we go.'

Ruby nods. 'Fine by me.'

Peanut frowns. 'What? Why?'

Ryker clenches his teeth. 'We haven't got time for this!'

'What's your problem? A few minutes won't hurt. We've got'—Peanut looks at his watch and pauses to think—'like seventy-one hours and twenty-two minutes left. Plus, they're our mates, and real mates don't let their mates down—well, not in my book anyway. Besides, we need to eat at some stage, right?'

Ryker rubs his temples. It's done; there's no way out of it. He reconciles himself with the decision and prepares for the inevitable.

14

The Phone Call

Jack braces himself as he witnesses his friends getting swallowed up into thin air. He stares at the gauzy curtain for a long while, unable to do anything. It's all too surreal. No amount of psyching can prepare anyone for what he just witnessed.

Finally, he pulls out his phone, checks for reception, then presses one of his contacts. The phone rings once. 'Edra, they're in.'

'Thank God. Is everything okay?'

Jack lets out a shaky breath. 'Yeah, all good. You know Ruby's with them, right?'

'Ryker messaged last night. Thank God. At least they've got her to protect them.'

Edra's relief at hearing that reassures him somewhat. 'Yeah, true. Look, I'll get back to you if anything happens my end. You do the same.'

'Of course. Good luck.'

'You too.' Jack ends the call, thankful that the conversation was short. He squats on his haunches and hangs his head. His mind races. *God, I hope they made it okay.*

He draws in a few deep breaths, then looks up and around. He needs to do something to stop his thoughts wandering. *Hey, Max will be here soon!* He jumps to his feet, and with that in mind, readies the campsite. Firstly, he prepares an area just inside the cordoned-off section, a few metres from the portal. It's a little flatter there, better suited for setting up the tent, and also within his view of the wavering curtain. Jack clears the space of any large rocks and small shrubs, then pulls out the tent and has it up in no time. He then gathers material for the fire they'll light later. To keep his thoughts from straying, he invests all his energy in the preparation. The rocks he dug up earlier, he uses to border the fireplace, and the dry wood he gathers is more than enough—sufficient to start a huge bonfire, let alone a humble campfire.

Jack stops when he hears someone approaching. He swipes the sweat from his brow and, shielding his eyes from the sun, looks to the top of the ravine. He spots Max, and by her side is Kenny. He smiles.

'Hey, Jack, how did it go?' Max calls down to him.

'Hey, yourself. As you can see, I'm here on my own, so I guess that means everything went to plan. You guys made good time. I wasn't expecting you so soon.'

'Just in time for lunch.' Max chuckles. 'Hungry?'

Right on cue, Jack's stomach growls. 'I wasn't until you mentioned it. Did you bring me anything decent? These nut bars aren't quite hitting the spot.' And that's the truth. Jack's gut has been so tied up in knots, the protein bars have tasted like cardboard.

They begin the descent. Max stumbles with the heavy weight of her kit, but Kenny scrambles to her rescue. 'Geez, Max, what've you got in here?'

She groans. 'Well, you know Annie!'

Enough said. Jack laughs. 'Well, thank God for Annie is all I'm gonna say.' He takes the few steps it takes to meet them, then pries the tape open for them to enter, taking their backpacks to help.

'We're lucky Peanut isn't here,' Kenny says with a chuckle, 'otherwise we'd have to hog-tie him to stop him from devouring the whole lot.' He snorts. 'Boy, can that kid eat!'

'So, Kenny, how did you get away?' Jack knows how overprotective Kenny's parents have been since their return. He has stricter curfews, and his older brother, Leonard, accompanies him everywhere he goes.

Kenny shrugs. 'Len's kinda sick of babysitting me, so we've made a pact: he gives me some space, and I promise not to tell our olds that he's got a girlfriend.'

Max frowns. 'What's wrong with him having a girlfriend?'

'Well, the thing is, Ming, our neighbour, isn't even sixteen yet, which in our culture is considered way too young to be dating—*school first!* If our families caught a whiff of what they're up to, the *you-know-what* will hit the fan.' Kenny laughs, his face colouring.

'Well, I for one am glad you're both here,' Jack says, monopolising Max's backpack to rummage through it.

Max's eyes narrow. 'Hey!'

She tries to push him aside, but her efforts are almost laughable. He grabs her around the waist and moves her out of his way.

Max huffs and turns to Kenny. 'And who said Peanut wasn't here?'

Jack laughs, then digs around until he finds what he wants—Annie's famous schnitzel rolls. He takes one, hands one to Max, then motions to Kenny to help himself.

Max shakes her head. 'Un-be-lievable!'

Kenny chuckles, grabs another roll, then settles on a nearby rock to eat. 'So I gather you guys didn't have any trouble?'

'Nope, the place is completely unprotected,' Jack says between chews. 'You can see for yourselves; there's nothing but warning signs and tape.'

'Yeah.' Kenny laughs. 'They must've had a sale at Bunnings or something. How come there's so much of it?'

'We figured it's just scare tactics to put off bushwalkers from entering.' Jack points out the charred area at the foot of the portal. 'Because they didn't have much luck in destroying it.'

'And you've rung Edra?' Max asks.

'Yep, all done.'

Kenny looks about them. 'And now, I guess we wait.'

'Yeah. And now we wait.'

15

THE WAITING GAME

EDRA

Edra ends the call to Jack, blinks a few times, then lets out the breath she'd been holding. The twins stand beside her, both anxious for the news. 'Okay, they're in,' she tells them, then turns away and stares vacantly at the campsites within the reserve, her own state of calm questionable. She tries to block the negative thoughts that threaten to bombard her. Her single-minded focus now is what surrounds her. She notes the ratio of tents to cabins, the sparseness of the trees, the dryness of the land, thinking of anything other than what might be happening this very moment in the realm. But it's useless. She paces back and forth, imagining the worst. Knowing they've got Ruby to protect them isn't enough to ease the nagging feeling she has that something will go wrong.

Edra catches a look shared between brother and sister. Neither say a word. She grits her teeth. They've been walking on eggshells around her since their arrival, and it's so obvious, it's driving her nuts.

The heat of the day is stifling, the sun's rays unforgiving. Suddenly Edra needs to put some distance between them. She walks to the other side of the unlit firepit and takes a moment to concentrate on her breathing—something her therapist suggested she do when things become too much for her. And by the time she's counted ten rounds of inhalations and exhalations, she's feeling a little more composed.

'So that's it, then, our ridiculous friends have set off on their journey.' And that's how Edra needs to look at it—a journey. *Not a mission, not a poorly formed covert operation, nor a half-baked military assignment, a journey!*

A familiar tightness in her chest sends her in a spin, and she turns away. She can't let the twins see her like this. *Breathe in; breathe out; breathe in; breathe out …*

Ulan steps towards her, her approach guarded. 'They'll be okay, Edra. You watch, they'll be back in no time.'

'Yeah, straight in, find the portal and then back out,' Banji reassures her. 'Just as planned.'

Edra whips around to glare at him. *Yeah, right!*

Like that's going to happen! As brilliant as Ryker is, Edra can't help but feel cynical. She tries to remember the last time Ryker stuck to a plan, and for the life of her, she can't. Maybe once upon a time before the madness of the realm, yes. But since? Well, let's just say nothing comes to mind.

Banji folds his arms and shifts uncomfortably. 'Um, so what did Jack say?'

Edra clamps her lips, then takes a moment to collect herself. She forces a smile. 'Banj, you saw how short the conversation was; there's nothing more to it.'

Banji shares another one of those worried looks with his sister, and Edra sees it. She needs to step away before she says something she'll regret. 'I'm going to stretch my legs.' Edra takes off at a run, weaving aimlessly between the scattered tents and cabins enclosed within the gated compound until she's well away from their sympathetic glances.

When far enough away, she slows, then rests on a sheltered bench to settle her thoughts. A soft breeze tickles her heated cheeks. She breathes easier, then closes her eyes and basks in the welcome silence. A sparrow tweets happily nearby, and in the distance, she hears children at the playground laughing. Her mind strays to the last time they were here, four-and-a-half years ago when she was an excited teenager on a geography field assignment—excited because she was about to spend three days with Jaeger.

Was that really four years ago? It seems like another lifetime.

Jaeger, Ulan and Banji had been friends since forever—both their families knew each other from way back. Edra met Ulan in high school, and through her, she met Jaeger. The four became inseparable—they even enrolled in the same course in college.

Edra fell hard for Jaeger, but she kept her feelings a secret. Unfortunately, half the female population on campus shared her crush. *And why not? He had the dreamiest dark brown eyes and a smile that could melt you into a puddle.* But those were the superficial things that most girls fell for—and they did. A queue of them vied for his attention.

But to Edra he was so much more than that. She smiles, remembering the time he jumped out of his car in the pouring rain to offer her his coat and a ride home—she'd forgotten her umbrella and was soaked to the bone. And the time he stepped in to protect her from Dumi Abrahams who was hassling her for a date that he somehow thought he was entitled to.

Edra was as giddy as a schoolgirl the day she and Jaeger were placed in the same group for their field trip—three fabulous days studying the wildlife of the Kruger National Park; three whole days to spend time together.

He was keen on her; that much she was almost sure of. So many times he'd looked like he was going to ask her out, but each time he got spooked and backed out at the last second. That awkward shyness is what endeared her to him the most.

But once they were thrown into the hell of the ancient world, life suddenly became very serious—too serious for such nonsense.

Edra swipes at a runaway tear as her thoughts return to the present. She stops to look about her and blinks. Her wandering has taken her to the boundaries of the enclosed compound. She pauses to look out into the vast wilderness of the Kruger National Park. The sound of distant trumpeting reaches her ears. The elephants are protected and happy, and this knowledge somehow brings her peace. She sighs; this is her home, and here within the gated campsite, she is safe.

And somewhere out there is the lost gateway, and on the other side of that elusive portal, she prays, is Ryker, working towards coming safely back home.

Edra draws in a deep breath, then tries to do what her doctors have urged her to do—confront her demons. *Well, this is just about as confronting as it gets—standing here, reliving the horrors of the past.*

If only they'd located the portal they'd fallen

through all those years ago, she wouldn't be standing here now. She thinks of Ryker and the countless hours he and his father spent trying to find it—scouring the reserve, retracing their steps, reliving the days just before they lost their way. They were on a mission to find and destroy it.

And now Ryker's on a different mission. To save his dying mother. Her eyes squeeze tight. *Who am I to judge? If it were me, I'd do the same.* And with that profound declaration, a newfound understanding and respect for the man awakens.

Edra takes a moment to let it sink in. She's been wallowing in her own self-pity for so long, she's been oblivious to anything outside her tormented bubble. With that realisation comes a clearer perspective of the goings-on around her. *Okay, so Jae is gone—and there's nothing I can do about that. And I'm here—I survived. So the thing is, I should be living my life … for both of us.*

Feeling strengthened by this new resolution, she turns to make her way back to the campsite. She suddenly stops and smiles. 'Hey, those doctors might be onto something there.'

16

Ryker's Return

Aelianna

Aelianna steels herself for Ryker's arrival, but the thought of him coming has her heart racing. She looks down at the smock she's wearing and regrets not wearing her green one. The brown one she has on is newer, but it isn't as pretty. She checks her hair again, securing it in a tight bun, then considers letting it down or braiding it. She stops suddenly, closes her eyes and exhales sharply. 'Enough with this nonsense! He is but a guest, so I will greet him like any other acquaintance—completely unaffected.'

When she hears the men approaching, Aelianna looks up from preparing the feast table and wavers at the sight of him. She shakes her head, then laughs at herself. 'Perhaps not *completely* unaffected.'

She can't believe he's here. Has he come back for

her? She lowers her face to sneak a peek at him. Her heart flutters. He's just as handsome as she remembers, perhaps, if at all possible, even more so—now with his clipped hair and clean-shaven face. She bites her bottom lip to stop from grinning. *Soon all will be revealed—for it is his eyes that will speak his heart.*

At that moment, their eyes meet, but too quickly he looks away. Her breath catches, and a pain, sharper than anything she has ever felt, sears through her chest. She sees that he hasn't forgiven her for rejecting him. She is not the reason for his return. Aelianna chokes back the tears. She has her answer. And now she must move on.

There is a feast to prepare, and she will do it. He is their guest; therefore, she must wait on him. She clears her throat. 'Mamma, what more can I do to help?'

Her mother frowns. 'Where is your head, child? Fill the cups with wine and offer them to our guests.'

Aelianna turns away, not yet ready to face him. She busies herself with anything but the offering of the wine.

'Aelianna!' Her mother gestures for her to make a move.

Aelianna can no longer delay the inevitable. She forces a smile and prepares to be the perfect hostess. She manages to fill the cups without spilling too much of the precious wine, then draws in a few deep breaths, balances her tray and approaches her visitors.

Aelianna first makes eye contact with Peanut, and his welcoming smile puts her raw nerves at ease. She focuses all her attention on that smile. 'I am ever so pleased to see you again,' she says, a little out of breath. She turns her gaze to Ruby, and her eyes widen at how exquisite she is with her golden eyes and long mane of sunset-coloured hair—never has she seen such beauty. Her heart sinks further as she wonders if Ryker ever saw anything in her at all— next to Ruby she must appear very plain. Aelianna straightens her smock, lifts her chin and shakes off her reflections. 'Um, I have not yet had the pleasure of meeting you; I am Aelianna.' She clears her throat. 'I must ask, how is our good friend, Max? Has she recovered well?'

Ruby's face lights up. 'I've heard so much about you, Aelianna.' She gives Ryker a sideward glance, then turns her attention back to Aelianna. 'I'm happy to finally meet you. Max told us how you stuck your neck out for her—you really saved her life. She's great by the way, and she told me to tell you that all's forgiven—you know, that issue with that famous haircut.'

Comprehending her meaning, Aelianna laughs and tries to ignore the burning stare she's getting from Ryker. She lowers her eyes.

'Oh, that reminds me,' Ruby says, diving into her bag, 'Max gave me something to give to you.' She takes a moment, rummaging to find it.

There's an uncomfortable pause as Aelianna waits. Her instinct is to turn her gaze to Ryker, but she resists and keeps her eyes focused on the ground.

'Hello, Aelianna; it's good to see you.'

The sound of his deep voice so close makes her jump. She commands herself to look at him and deliver the speech she had prepared. But what she sees in the depths of his eyes silences her—the look of pain and sorrow mixed with a tenderness she's never seen puts a stop to any words she had earlier rehearsed.

'Got it!' Ruby's unexpected outburst diverts her attention. Ruby retrieves a small parcel and hands it to her. Ryker takes the tray, freeing Aelianna to open Max's gift.

Giddy with excitement, Aelianna unties the twine and wrapping to reveal a small box. Inside the box, protected ever so carefully with a cloth of gossamer, is a glass ball filled with water. And floating in the water are white flakes. She holds the sphere a little closer and looks upon it with reverence. Never in her life has she seen anything so beautiful.

17

I Hear You, Loud & Clear

RYKER

Ryker can't take his eyes off Aelianna as she watches the white flakes fall to the base of the snow dome to reveal two tiny figures embracing in dance—one, a pretty girl with long dark hair wearing a gown of gold, and the other a beast. 'Beauty and the beast,' he mutters under his breath.

Aelianna turns up her heart-shaped face and looks at him with her deep dark eyes, a question lingering on her lips. She's so beautiful it makes his heart ache.

Ryker clears his throat. 'Er, um, perhaps I'll tell you the story behind it another time.' He turns to leave. 'Because now I need to catch some fish for the feast. Your father is waiting.'

'Will you not take some wine?' Aelianna asks after him.

Ryker stops, turns, takes one of the cups and gulps it down. He then stomps away, calling out his thanks as he heads towards the stream, his face heating. 'Best friend or not, I'm going to kill Max next time I see her!'

Peanut runs after him. 'Oi! What was that all about?'

Ryker doesn't stop. 'What was what?'

'Mate, I've never seen you like that. And your face is the colour of a tomato.'

'Must be the wine.'

'Mate, you were red before the wine.'

They catch up to the men by the stream.

'Medwin, hand me the stick. I've a sudden need to spear something.' Ryker snatches the weapon from the grasp of his surprised friend, then perches on a rock, ready to kill. He spends the next half hour spearing everything and anything that dares cross his path, driving his wayward thoughts from the dark-haired, dark-eyed beauty sitting by the stream chatting to Ruby and giggling at Peanut's ridiculous jokes. The breeze off the water soon cools his mood, and in no time he's ready to face his friends once more.

The women of the forest have prepared a wonderful banquet. The table, stretched out for several metres, overflows with culinary delights. Among the fish Ryker provided is wild boar, pheasant and spatchcock along with various fruits, cheeses and breads. Ryker knows food like this is an extravagance and is humbled by their efforts.

He takes his place next to Aelianna's father at the table. 'Molan, we're very grateful for your hospitality. Thank you.'

Molan shakes his head. 'It is *I* who should be thanking *you*, and of course, your friends. If it had not been for our chance meeting, I would still be bedridden and of no use to our people. Now I am well and able to be productive once again. With Aelianna's mother's health returned to her, she too can continue with her duties, freeing Aelianna of the burden to provide for us.'

They look at Aelianna sitting further down the table with her new friends, laughing hard at something Peanut has told her, her eyes glistening with tears.

Molan reaches for the jug of wine. 'She is a good girl, Ryker. The weight she has carried for her family has been heavy, especially for someone so slight. It fills my heart with joy to hear her laugh and see her cheerful.' He sighs, then turns to face Ryker, his look stern. 'Ryker, she deserves to be happy.'

Ryker frowns. There's a hidden message in

Molan's meaning—he's certain of that—but what that message is, he has no idea. *Was it a warning?*

Molan's countenance changes. He holds up his cup and smiles. 'Come, drink with me as I toast your health.' Ryker blinks a few times before accepting the wine. Molan then stands to make the toast, and as one, the men raise their cups to their guests and repeat his words, 'To your health.'

Later, as they leave the celebrations to make their way to the treehouse, Ryker tries to make sense of Molan's private speech. Was there something to it? His gut tells him there was. Molan's words echo in his mind—*she deserves to be happy*. He can't help but wonder if she would've been unhappy leaving her family to be with him when he'd asked her that time. Was Molan telling him that Aelianna is happiest with her family, living a life she knows?

'Earth to Ryker. Come in, Ryker,' Peanut teases from behind.

Ryker's thoughts snap back to the present. 'What?' He stops to look at his companions. Both wear apprehensive looks on their faces.

Peanut chuckles. 'Man, you're miles away. What's going on in that head of yours?'

Without a word, Ryker turns and forges ahead, slashing his hunting blade through the leafy scrub.

Peanut persists. 'Mate, you can tell me to mind

my own business, but—'

'Then mind your own business.'

Peanut grabs Ryker by the arm and swings him around to face him. 'Will ya hold up a sec? Let me say what I need to say first.'

'Peanut, don't.' Ruby tugs at his shirt.

Ryker turns away, staring ahead, his gaze fixed.

'Look,' Peanut begins, 'a wise man once warned that *emotions can be the cause of many a downfall.*' Peanut scratches his head, then frowns. 'Or something like that.'

Ryker pulls a face, not getting his meaning.

'So,' Peanut continues, 'do I need to worry about that being the case with you? Mate, your head's been in the clouds since you clapped eyes on Aelianna. And don't tell me I'm wrong, 'cause I'm not.' Peanut looks at him sideways. 'You know that's come straight out of left field, that has. I had no idea you had a thing for her.'

Ryker looks at Ruby, but she looks away and says nothing. Clearly the girls have been careful with who they share his secrets. He can at least be thankful for that.

'Seriously, I didn't realise you two even knew each other that well.'

Ruby tugs at his shirt again. 'Peanut, let it go.'

Ryker turns to leave. 'You've got nothing to

worry about.'

Peanut clicks his tongue. 'Come off it!'

Ryker sighs. 'So who's this wise man you're talking about, anyway?'

'Who?' Peanut laughs. 'You, ya twit! Don't ya remember?'

This surprises him. 'When did you ever hear me say anything like that?'

Peanut's lip twitches. 'That time you and Ulan were spying on us in the garden, and you realised that Jack had a thing for Max. You said then that our *emotional immaturity* would be our *downfall*. Your words exactly.'

Ryker's eyes widen. 'Hey, I remember that. But how did you ...?' He chuckles, quick to put two and two together. 'So you were spying on us while we were spying on you, and we had no idea. Clever, real clever.' Then Ryker realises something. 'But wait a minute, you guys beat us in the end, so emotions didn't get in the way of you winning, did they?'

Peanut snorts. 'Oh, how quickly you forget, my friend,' he teases. 'You *do* remember that you and Max were left behind while the rest of us made our escape, don't ya?' He turns to wink at Ruby. 'Jack was so busy ogling Max that he forgot about that arrow sticking out of his chest. That *distraction,* my friend, nearly cost you your lives.'

Ryker chuckles at the memory.

'Ah, you laugh now, but you won't be laughing if we stuff up because you keep tripping over that tongue of yours. Man, tuck it in, we're drowning in your drool here!'

Ryker's smile disappears, Molan's warning echoing in his ears. 'Listen, like I said, there's nothing to worry about; there's nothing there,' he lies. 'And even if there was, her father has already laid down the law. It wouldn't happen even if I wanted it to.'

Ruby exchanges a look with Peanut. 'You're kidding? Where were we when that happened?'

Ryker shakes his head, turns and forges ahead. 'That's beside the point. I'm not that into her anyway, so it really doesn't matter, does it? So that's the end of it. I don't want to hear about it anymore.' He chances a look at Ruby, knowing she's a lot more clued up on how things really are. But at the moment he couldn't care less what they think. The sooner they stop talking about it, the quicker they can get back to the mission.

After a few more hushed words muttered under their breaths, Ryker doesn't hear another peep from them, and he knows he has Ruby to thank for that.

18

Searching for the Elusive Gateway

After visiting the treehouse and establishing that it's still a viable option to stay in, Ryker suggests that they make the most of what daylight is left and search their immediate surrounds. They scour the area, re-familiarising themselves with the various nooks and crannies, and look out for anything that might point them in the direction of the other portal.

After a few hours of fruitless searching, Peanut plonks himself on a nearby rock, looking defeated. 'Mate, I'll tell ya one thing, we've definitely bitten off more than we can chew. This place is huge! It's like looking for a needle in a haystack. There has to be a better way of doing this.'

Ryker stops and runs his fingers through his hair. Peanut's right. They've essentially given themselves three days to comb acres of forestland looking for a transparent gateway. He lets out a long breath and takes a moment to re-evaluate the situation.

'Hey, I've got an idea,' Ruby offers. 'What if we go back to the portal and trigger the alarm to attract the guards. Once they've realised it's another false alarm, Peanut could follow them, and who knows, they might lead him to the other one.'

Ryker shakes his head. 'More likely they'll lead him back to the fortress. No, it's better we keep them out of the forest as much as we can while we're here.'

'Ruby might have a point,' Peanut argues, looking hopeful. 'You never know; stranger things have happened.'

Ryker chuckles. 'Look, we'll give Molan's suggestion a go first, and if that fails to bring up any leads, we'll try Ruby's idea. Okay?'

Peanut gives Ruby a wink, then asks Ryker, 'So what d'ya reckon about those forest people Molan mentioned? I don't know about you, but I'd like to steer clear of those guys if we can help it.'

Ryker barks out a laugh and slaps Peanut on the back.

'Hey, what did I say?'

'Peanut, you crack me up; you keep forgetting

one significant detail. You know you can disappear, right? I really don't think you've got anything to worry about.'

Peanut shakes his head. 'Mate, you surprise me. Don't let these people fool ya. That first time I took off into the forest, I got snared like a rabbit, and then speared in the foot by one of them, while, I might add, I was invisible.'

'Don't remind me,' Ruby cries out. 'That was when you nearly got yourself killed. It was Medwin, wasn't it? The guy we met earlier?'

'Yeah, sharpshooter Medwin.' Peanut chuckles.

Ryker sighs. 'Peanut, you've got a point there. Never underestimate the enemy …'

'Vigilant at all times,' they all say together.

'Alright already!' Peanut teases. 'Stop ramming it down our throats; we get it!'

Ryker can't help but laugh. If nothing else, Peanut will definitely keep him on his toes while they're here. He sobers. 'Hey, I'm glad you guys are here; it means a lot to me.'

Peanut grins. 'What are friends for? Besides, from the looks of it, you kinda need us. What with your head stuck in the clouds with girl trouble, and now your memory goin' in your old age, how the heck did you expect to do this on your own?'

Ryker chuckles. *Nope, never a dull moment!*

They've wandered a fair way into the forest, and Ryker stops when he realises he's leading them in the direction of Aelianna's home. He turns to take them back the way they came but stops suddenly when he hears someone singing in the near distance, a girl.

'Wow!' Ruby says in a whisper.

Peanut's eyes glaze over. 'That voice! It's mesmerising.'

It captivates Ryker as well.

Peanut and Ruby float in the direction of the singing, as if they're in some kind of trance state. But Ryker's senses prickle—something's not right. He shakes off the hypnotic control reeling him in and grabs the others to stop them going further. 'We need to go back.'

Peanut shrugs off his hold. 'No, I've gotta see who it is.'

And he's not the only one. Movement in the bushes alerts Ryker to another presence, a young man, close to his own age, at a guess, but much smaller in build and height. Not unlike the other forest dwellers, his clothes are worn, his appearance scruffy. But somehow this guy is different. This one Ryker instinctively doesn't trust. There's something evil in his steely look. Ryker grabs Ruby and Peanut, muzzles their mouths to stifle their protests, then dives for cover.

Ruby snaps out of her daze and summons her shield. With that done, the spell breaks. The singing continues, but its hold on them dissipates.

With a quick and deliberate look, Ryker alerts them to the looming threat. They huddle deeper into the undergrowth and watch. The stranger isn't alone. Three others are with him. His friends are huge—closer to Ryker's size—and they all move towards the voice as if spellbound.

The singing suddenly stops.

Ryker cranes his neck to catch a glimpse of the girl.

'Do not stop,' the first stranger urges. 'Your voice is a gift sent straight from the gods. Please, Aelianna, go on.'

AELIANNA! Ryker almost chokes on a gasp.

'Why is it that I have not heard you sing before?' the stranger asks. 'After all this time, and I had no idea. It rivals that of an angel and is more beautiful than a song bird's.'

There's something in this guy's tone that has Ryker's hair at the back of his neck stand on end. Every ounce of his being cries out warnings.

'I must confess,' the stranger continues, 'after hearing your alluring voice, our future together is even more attractive to me. Come, Aelianna, you cannot deny it, we were meant to be.'

The three goons at his side laugh.

Suddenly, stars flicker before Ryker's eyes. He wavers, threatening to topple from his squatting position. Peanut steadies him, then turns to Ruby. They silently convey an understanding. The shield dissolves, and Peanut vanishes.

19

WULF

PEANUT

Peanut inches closer. He can see Aelianna—and her fear. Her eyes dart from the stranger to the forest, clearly looking for a means of escape. This stranger is no friend.

Aelianna backs away with her hands raised. 'Wulf, you cannot be here, please leave. Father is nearby and will return at any moment.'

Wulf smiles. 'By all means, call him,' he challenges, 'for I wish to see him.' He cups his hand and calls out to the forest. 'Molan, come forth so we may speak. I am certain, by this stage, you know of my *intentions*.'

Wulf smirks. His goons snigger. All four circle her. She's trapped. Peanut needs to do something, and fast.

Aelianna snatches a nearby broken tree branch

and readies herself.

Peanut dives out of the bushes and onto the nearest goon, knocking him to the ground. He then grabs the second thug by the arm, swings him in circles and uses him as a battering ram to send the third guy flying. The three goons scramble to their feet, comb the forest in search of the invisible threat, then take off, yelling.

Peanut turns to take on the ringleader, but Ruby, in all her glory, is in the throes of taking care of that threat. Using the force of her shield, she propels Wulf head first into the bushes. And before Peanut can make a move to help, Ryker leaps out of his hiding place and pounces on the bully. Wulf doesn't stand a chance. Ryker is all over him, his attack relentless. Peanut needs to stop him before he kills the guy. He runs towards the fight and throws his weight into the men to break the assault. Ryker falls to the ground, his fists bloodied, chest heaving.

Peanut materialises. 'What the hell do you think you're doing?'

Ryker pushes past Peanut to get to Aelianna. He takes her hands in his. 'Aelianna, are you all right?'

She nods and smiles. 'I thank you for your help. There has been no harm.'

Peanut looks down at the unconscious body before them, then scans the woods. 'Let's go before those thugs come back.'

The journey back to Aelianna's home is a silent one. And although burning to say something, Peanut doesn't utter a word. Once within the safety of the small mudbrick house, he tells Aelianna's parents what happened.

Molan paces back and forth in the tiny home, shaking his head as he listens. When Peanut has finished his story, Molan slams his fist on the small dining table. They all jump. 'Wulf! I will destroy him!'

Peanut scowls at Ryker. 'I reckon our friend here just about did!'

Molan frowns at his daughter, then turns to face Ryker. 'You have saved Aelianna from unquestionable harm. I thank you for your courage.' He looks at his wife and other three children. 'By the grace of the gods, she is safe.'

Ryker peers outside the small window near the front door. 'Molan, who is this guy? And what does he want with Aelianna?'

Father and daughter exchange a worried look.

Ryker frowns. 'He's threatened your family before, hasn't he?' he asks, his voice low, almost a growl.

Aelianna inhales sharply.

Ruby steps to Aelianna's side, her lips pressed into a thin line. 'Stop it, will you! You're scaring her!'

'Nice one, mate. Ease up on the testosterone, will ya?'

Ryker turns away from Peanut's reproachful glare and curses under his breath, then he softens his voice and says, 'Please, Aelianna, I'm sorry, but I need to know. What's going on?'

Molan rubs at his brow. 'Ryker, he and his henchmen frequent our village. He wishes to court Aelianna.'

Peanut splutters. 'You're kidding me, right?' He looks from Molan to Aelianna, then frowns. 'Let me get this straight; he wants to *marry* her?'

Molan takes Aelianna by the hand and pulls her to his side. He lowers his gaze and shrugs.

Peanut's eyes widen. 'Man, he sure has a weird way of showing he's keen on her. Bad move, Romeo.'

Ryker frowns. 'But I don't get it; he was about to hurt her.'

'He has asked for her hand several times,' Molan tells them. 'Aelianna has refused him, and I support her in her decision, but he continues to seek her. And after hearing what tragedy could have befallen today, I feel that his patience has come to an end.'

He turns to his daughter. 'I cannot understand your actions, Aelianna. Tell me, why is it that he found you in the forest on your own? I have warned you of this before.'

Aelianna lowers her flushed face. 'Father, forgive me. He … he must have been drawn in by … by'—she gulps—'by my singing.'

'Your singing!' Molan's eyes widen in alarm. 'Aelianna, you know the power of your voice. What possessed you?'

Aelianna turns away from her father's penetrating stare and clears her throat. ''Twas a mistake, and I am truly sorry for it.' She glances at Ryker. 'But when I feel happiness such as I do, tis beyond my power to contain it.'

Peanut's eyebrows shoot up. *Wow! Ryker might not be 'that into her', but she's definitely got the hots for him.*

Ryker's gaze darts to the door.

Peanut chuckles to himself. *Planning a quick getaway, are we?* He turns to Aelianna. 'So you couldn't *contain your happiness*, huh?'

Ryker gives Peanut a murderous look before turning to Molan. 'Well, he'll never come near any of you again. I'll make sure of that.'

Aelianna lowers her eyes. 'The fault lies with me,' she says in a small voice. 'I should never have befriended him that time in the fortress. I should have kept to my tasks, as was my duty, and refused to speak to him.' She looks up and her eyes soften. 'But he was different then; he was gentle and kind.'

Gentle and kind! Peanut snorts. 'Hey, are we talking about the same guy here?'

Her brown eyes fix on Peanut. 'Do not misunderstand me; there was a time when he was most agreeable. But what they did to him changed him.' Aelianna looks from Peanut to Ryker. 'You see, Wulf is the son of Beowulf. And for reasons unknown, the Ancients banished him and his mother to the forest following his father's death. At the time, Wulf volunteered to stand in for his father as an Invincible—he, too, having the ability to talk to animals—but Herodus chose you, Ryker, over him. Remember?'

Ryker's head snaps up.

'He and his mother were taken in by the people of The Dark Forest,' she continues. 'Wulf's bitterness soon became all-consuming, altering his character. So now he and his henchmen cause havoc among the good people of the forest—stealing, terrorising and instilling unrest.'

''Tis true, he is a tyrant,' Molan tells them. 'There is talk that his own men fear him. No one dares oppose him.'

Peanut groans. 'Do ya realise what this means?'

The colour drains from Ruby's face. 'What have we done!'

Ryker turns away and runs his hand through his

hair. 'We've just gone and made ourselves a target.'

'Ya reckon!' Peanut curses under his breath. 'So much for keeping a low profile, *mate!*

Ryker's jaw tightens, and Peanut puffs out his chest. Ruby steps between them. 'Hey, back down! What's done is done. We can't change that.'

After a few moments of them eyeballing each other, Ryker steps away and draws in a deep breath. 'Look, it just means we need to watch our backs, now more than ever. All right?'

Peanut snorts. 'No kidding. How did ya come up with that, Einstein? First, we killed the jerk's father, then we had his family exiled into a forest full of savages, and now we've beaten the crap out of him. He's gonna *butcher* us!'

Molan places a firm hand on Peanut. 'Calm yourself. I agree the situation is not favourable, but let us think on this for a moment.' He rubs his chin. 'Since it is clear that your journey will continue, this is what I propose. We will travel as they do, in packs, and only venture out in the early hours of the morning when we are less likely to cross them.'

'Sounds like a plan.' Ryker prepares to leave. 'We'll go now and return before first light.' He stops. 'Unless you need us to stay.'

Molan shakes his head, then walks them to the door. 'Your presence at Aelianna's time of need is more than enough. I do not think we will be visited by Wulf and his men again tonight.'

While Ryker leads them back to the treehouse, Peanut can't help but stew on their predicament. 'So what the heck possessed you? Couldn't you see I had it in the bag? They didn't have a clue what hit 'em. But no, you had to lose your shit and pulverise the jerk. And now he knows you're back. It'll be a miracle if he doesn't come gunning for ya.'

Ryker says nothing, just ploughs ahead, slashing at the underbrush.

Ruby pulls at Peanut's shirt to shut him up. But Peanut can't let it go. 'You know what, you really need to keep those psycho emotions of yours under better control, mate. It was gonna be hard enough as it was, and now ...'

Ryker suddenly stops and turns on him, his eyes reduced to slits. 'And *now* we're going to move on. Okay? So I stuffed up. I'll own it. Just back off, will ya!'

With a hundred-plus-kilos of pure rage aimed at him, Peanut rethinks his actions.

Ruby steps between them. 'Do I need my shield here, or what?' Her lips press into a thin line. 'What the hell's gotten into you two? Whose side are you on? And as for you'—she glares at Peanut—'just shut your trap, otherwise, so help me God, I'll let him thump you.'

Peanut and Ryker exchange a look; not another word is spoken. They continue in an uncomfortable silence, Ryker slashing a path before them. Soon the intensity of his strikes lessens, he stops and his shoulders slump.

Peanut hangs back, not sure what to expect.

Ryker turns to face him. 'You're right. I've really screwed things up.' He lets out a haggard breath. 'And now I'm really worried. Not so much for us— I'm sure we can handle these guys—but for Aelianna and her family.'

Peanut says nothing.

Ryker runs his hand over the top of his head, then turns away. 'Argh! I wish we had more time! I don't think we can do this properly. We can't commit a hundred percent to the mission knowing Aelianna could be in trouble. We've only got two days to do this—just two! What the hell was I thinking!'

Peanut regrets saying so much; he can see Ryker losing his nerve. Somehow he needs to fix this. 'Hey, what if we leave Ruby with Aelianna and her family? She can look out for them.'

Ryker's eyes light up.

Peanut turns to Ruby, happy that he's come up with a viable plan. 'What d'ya reckon?'

Ruby's eyes darken. 'What do I *reckon*? I *reckon*

that's a *brilliant* idea! Why not leave the *little lady* at home while the *men* go on with the hunt!'

Both boys shrink back.

Ruby's face floods with colour. 'You arrogant Neanderthals! I haven't risked my neck coming here just to pick up the crap you guys leave behind. I came here with a focus, and finding the portal *is* that focus.' She stops only to draw breath. 'It might come as a complete surprise to you two *numbskulls,* but these people have survived in the forest for hundreds of years without the help of interfering teenagers from the twenty-first century. So what's changed?' She waits, her hands fisted on her hips. 'Whether you realise it or not, you two need me more than they do. At this rate, I'd be surprised if you make it through the day without killing each other!'

She slows her heavy breathing. 'Look, maybe I overreacted, but can't you see we need to stick together on this? Once we've located the other gateway and helped Isebel, then, and only then, do we hunt down that creep and make him wish he'd never laid eyes on Aelianna. Okay?'

Ryker looks at Peanut sideways. He nudges him. 'Brains as well as beauty! It beats me how you got so lucky. Sorry, Ruby. You're right—enough with the crap. Let's do this.'

With that said, the rift is mended and

they continue.

The sun starts to set, daylight fading. They pick up the pace and make it back to the treehouse just on dark. Ryker does his impressive lumberjack-climb up the tree to retrieve the braided rope before climbing down and landing at their feet. He does it so effortlessly, Ruby's jaw drops. Peanut groans. How's he supposed to compete with the likes of that? He stops to remind himself that while his superpower is invisibility, Ryker's is strength.

But when Ryker offers Ruby a piggyback ride up the tree, Peanut arcs up. 'Oi! I'll take it from here! Move over, *muscles*.' He steps between them and offers Ruby his back. 'Hop on, Rubes.'

Ruby's lip twitches. She steps to one side, takes the plait from Ryker and begins the climb on her own, leaving Peanut with his mouth gaping. Once she's reached the top, she drops the rope, looks over the floor of the treehouse and grins. 'Did I tell you I did nine years of gymnastics before playing hockey, *Charlie*?'

Ryker chuckles. Peanut groans.

Red-faced and put in his place, Peanut begins the climb. Ryker is quick to follow. And without another word they roll out their sleeping bags to settle for the night.

They're warm, they're dry and they're safe, and

that's what Peanut focuses on as he tries to find sleep. Ruby reaches over to hold his hand, and she's soon dead to the world. But his other roomie isn't as considerate—Ryker disturbs Peanut's calm with his incessant tossing and turning. The sounds of the night animals scurrying beneath in search of a meal aren't threatening. The cricket symphony is comforting. The stars twinkling through the treetops are soothing … so why can't he unwind?

Peanut rolls over, trying to get comfortable. Ryker shifts again, this time muttering something unintelligible under his breath. Then there's a groan, followed by the sound of gnashing teeth. He can practically hear Ryker's thought process, and this has his own mind reeling.

Far out, Ryker!

Peanut clamps his lips tight, pulls his beanie over his ears and tries to focus on all the positives that've come from today. As far as he can tell, they're on track—there's a plan, and if that fails, they've got a Plan B. With those reassuring thoughts, Peanut finally drifts off to sleep.

20

ON THE PROWL

Ryker can't sleep. His mind's racing—they've wasted too much time already. He wishes he could somehow turn back the clock and change the way they've tackled this whole messed-up situation. But it's useless wishing for the impossible. Tossing and turning, he begs for sleep, but he's too wired to get any. Then a thought comes to him like a lightning strike: *Why the hell am I wasting time lying here?* He reaches for his backpack, rummages through the things he packed and pulls out his thermal-imaging goggles. His heart skips a beat at what he's about to do.

With adrenaline pumping through his veins, he flies down the rope, confident that Peanut and Ruby will be okay on their own for a while. He coils up the rope, tosses it back up and, after hearing it land safely, he pulls on the goggles and is instantly immersed in a world of nocturnal activities. *Now that's more like it!* With the ability to amplify small traces of residual light, the goggles enable improved visibility in the dark. He curses himself for not thinking about venturing out earlier.

Who needs sleep?

With compass in hand, he heads back towards the known gateway. He's not sure what to expect regarding security at this time of night, but he takes a chance that the portal won't be manned. *Herodus would be an idiot to risk leaving his men in the forest all night.*

Ryker's got a hunch that he needs to test, and if his theory's right, the goggles might come in handy when it comes to finding the elusive gateway. Moving at speed but with caution, he focuses on the task at hand. He's done with the never-ending distractions they've been thrown lately—distractions that he's finding near impossible to avoid. If they're to save his mother, he really does need to keep his mind on the mission.

Ruby is right, we can deal with that creep later! With that in mind, Ryker concentrates on making his way through the darkness.

He reaches the portal in no time and without any

difficulties, thanks to the goggles. He stands before it, shielding his eyes from the glow, and grins—his theory was right—the gateway emits heat.

Ryker's confidence skyrockets. But now's not the time to revel in it; he's got to keep going. He decides to scour the forest in the hope of finding more hidden gems. As he goes, he leaves a trail, snapping twigs in his path and scuffing the ground with his boot.

After a long and gruelling trek, he ventures into an unfamiliar area. And in the far distance, he hears what sounds like boisterous celebrations. He moves in closer to inspect, suspecting that he may have stumbled across the people of The Dark Forest. His senses peak. *Expect the unexpected ... vigilant at all times!*

Ryker approaches, beads of sweat dripping from his brow. He's so close now. The smell of charred meat on an open flame rouses his senses. He inches nearer until he has a visual. The camp is a mess of activity. There's loud singing, laughter and an occasional drunkard yelling as brawls break out. A dog yelps, caught in the crossfire. The settlement looks nothing like Medwin's little village. The homes appear makeshift, and if he had to liken their lifestyle to anything, he'd compare it to a band of gypsies. Around the fire, which is central to the festivities, lie several people, strewn haphazardly in an overindulgent coma. He tries to estimate the numbers—there must be at least fifty of them—and scours the area looking for Wulf. He doesn't really expect to see him after the beating he got today, but he's curious just the same.

Just beyond the fire, he notices a dark, sunken area, several metres long and just as many metres wide. Its depth is anyone's guess. He can't imagine why they'd have dug up such a large space.

A twig cracks nearby. He freezes. Suddenly feeling very exposed, he squats lower, wishing he had Ruby with him. His body prepares for battle, ears pricked, eyes searching around him. But the goggles detect no glow. He gets out of there while he can, keen to leave the people of The Dark Forest behind.

As he retraces his way back, his thoughts go to his friends. He's taken longer than he'd anticipated, and it'll soon be morning. He picks up the pace.

21

PUZZLE PIECES

RYKER

Ryker nudges Ruby awake.

She jumps up, arms swinging and lands a punch on his chin.

He grabs her hands to curb the attack. 'Whoa! Settle down, tiger; it's me.'

She blinks. It takes her a moment to realise where she is.

He lets go of her hand and laughs. 'Hey, nice right hook.'

Ruby rubs her eyes, stretches, then peers into the darkness. 'What time is it?'

'Time to get going.'

He prods Peanut a few times with his boot, then reaches for his backpack. But Peanut doesn't stir. Ryker frowns. 'Unbelievable. This guy could sleep through an earthquake.' He crouches by his side and shakes him. 'Hey, sleeping beauty, time to get up.' But Peanut is out to the world. It takes Ryker a few less-than-subtle jabs to make an impact.

Peanut swipes at him. 'Will you wrack off! Far out. Just go to sleep!' He rolls over, grumbles something unintelligible under his breath and is asleep in seconds.

Ryker tries again. This time he gives him a firm slap on the back of the head.

Peanut jolts upright. 'For crying out loud! What's your problem?' He rubs at the offensive sting and looks around. 'What the hell, Ryker, it's the middle of the night!'

Ryker chuckles. 'I've got news for you. The sun's about to come up, and we've got stacks to do. I couldn't sleep, so I checked out a few things, and I've come up with a few ideas ...'

Peanut frowns. 'What? You've been out there already? On your own? Are you insane?' He groans. 'Did ya miss the memo or somethin'? Molan said to stick together. What part of that didn't you get?'

Ryker shrugs. 'Like I said, I couldn't sleep, so I started our search. I managed to cover quite an area too. I got as far as The Dark Forest.'

Ruby whips around to face him. 'Tell me you're kidding! The Dark Forest?'

'Well, I can't be sure, but going by what Molan told us about them, I'm guessing it was them.'

Peanut curses. 'Look, if you were that desperate to go, why didn't you just wake us? We would've come with you.'

Ryker shrugs and gets to his feet. 'Look, once I got it in my head to go, I had to do it. And I'm glad I did, because I've learned a lot—they really *are* party animals. So now's the time to make a move. There's just too much forest out there and not enough time for us to search it all. I was thinking we should leave now to meet up with the others and on our way have another poke around. We might find something. You coming?'

Peanut gives him a stink-eye, but Ryker laughs it off. 'Come on, you can sleep all you want once we've found the portal.'

Ruby crosses her arms and shakes her head. 'You're fricking nuts. What if you got caught? Did you stop and think about that?' Her raised voice echoes into the darkness of the forest.

Peanut shushes her. 'For crying out loud, Rubes, keep it down, will ya!'

They stop to listen. The forest remains silent.

Ryker lets out a deep breath. 'Look, I didn't get caught, did I? And right now, I'm wide awake and ready to go again. So what do you say? Are you with me?'

Peanut rubs his eyes. 'Yeah, yeah, keep your shirt on. My eyelids haven't caught up with the rest of me yet.'

Ryker chuckles. 'Suck it up, buddy; we've got stacks to do and less than fifty-one hours to get it done.' He throws Peanut a protein bar. 'Here, eat up. I know how *hangry* you get.'

Peanut looks down at the snack and frowns. 'You'd better make it two, because I'm pretty ticked off with you right now.'

Ryker chuckles, hands Ruby a bar, then another to Peanut. With breakfast taken care of, they clamber down the rope to begin their trek.

Ryker powers ahead through the darkness, goggles firmly in place, oblivious of Ruby and Peanut's struggle to keep up. Behind him they stumble and fall behind.

After landing on his face for the third time, Peanut cries out for him to stop. 'I don't know about this bright idea of yours, mate! How the heck are we supposed to see where we're going?'

His whining stops when Ryker reaches into his backpack and hands him a spare pair of glasses. Peanut's eyes light up. Ryker grins. 'Sorry, I forgot I had extras. They're thermal-imaging goggles—might be useful.'

Ruby and Peanut look at each other. Ruby rolls her eyes. 'You think?'

Peanut is quick to slip them on. He gasps, then spins around in circles. 'Whoa! Rubes, you've gotta check it out! This is so cool.' But Peanut isn't quite ready to give them up, and Ruby fights him for a turn. In the end she jabs him hard in the ribs to claim them.

Ryker pulls a drawstring bag from his backpack and hands it to them. 'And here, before I forget, put this in one of your kits.'

Peanut snatches it and fumbles with the tie. 'What's this? More goodies?'

'Look, I'll explain what's in there later. Just keep it in your backpack—it might come in handy. Right now, we need to keep moving.'

Ruby takes the bag and stows it away. Peanut retrieves the goggles, and they're off.

'Back to the goggles,' Ryker says as they continue, 'I went for a test-run earlier—trekking back to the portal on a hunch that it might give off thermal energy. It does. These life-savers picked up the glow from the portal without any trouble.'

'Unreal!' But Peanut isn't listening; he's too engrossed in what he's experiencing with the goggles.

Ryker, unaware of Peanut's inattention, continues. 'I know, right? With the amount of energy the gateways give off, we'll find the missing one in no time.'

'That's great, Ryker,' Ruby says. 'Maybe that earlier gamble of yours wasn't such a dumb idea after all.'

'Man, I love your life!'

Ryker stops to look over his shoulder.

Ruby shakes her head. 'Amazing how focused he can be when he wants to.'

Ryker laughs.

They watch Peanut hunt around, happily picking up random things to study. 'Some kids have all the luck. Why couldn't *my* old man send me to some fancy-schmancy military school?' He stops, then turns to Ryker. 'You know something, I think you're my new hero.'

Ryker chuckles.

'*New* hero? Who was your *old* one?' Ruby asks.

Peanut rubs his chin. 'Well, in the beginning it was Jack, and then for a while it was a toss-up between you, Kenny and Max.' He gives Ruby a crooked smile. 'Girl, that shield of yours is hot! But in the end, Max tipped the scales. Sorry, babe.'

'I know what you mean; she's my hero too,' Ryker tells him.

Peanut sighs. 'Yeah, I reckon if it wasn't for Max, we'd all be screwed—she's the best.'

Ryker looks into the distance and smiles. 'That she is, mate. That she is.'

Peanut frowns, then exchanges a questioning look with Ruby. 'Um, Ryker, can I ask you something? There's nothing going on between you two, is there? I mean, you don't have a thing for Max, do ya?'

Ryker stops short to look at him.

'I mean, the way you two carry on sometimes,' Peanut continues, 'well, let's just say I'm not the only one who's noticed. Jack doesn't say much, but I've seen the way he is when you and Max are together.'

Ruby jabs Peanut in the ribs and glares at him.

'Hey! What did I say? I'm just telling it the way it is.'

Ryker's face heats up. He's not quite sure how to answer. There was a time when he thought he did have a thing for Max, but since meeting Aelianna, he knows what he felt for Max is nothing like what he feels for Aelianna. But that's something for him to get his head around later, not now. He shakes his head, angry for even contemplating answering. *Vigilant at all times!* 'Don't be stupid; she's my best friend. Come on, let's just find this frigging gateway and get the hell out of here.'

They plough ahead, their destination, Molan's little mudbrick house. Every now and then, they veer off the path to investigate further, going deeper into the woods. Thermal detection here and there sends them on wild goose chases as forest animals scurry to escape them.

'Ryker?' Ruby asks. 'Precisely what happened that first time you guys fell through the portal?'

Ruby's question is unexpected. Ryker turns to face her. 'Why do you ask?'

'I don't know. I was thinking maybe if you talk about it, it might trigger something.' She looks at Peanut as if contemplating her next words. 'I say this, because I, um, hit my head last year and ended up in hospital with concussion and amnesia. I couldn't remember a thing about how I ended up there. The doctors said my memory could return, bit by bit, or it might never come back. For me, most of it did.' She shrugs. 'But you know, sometimes the most random things come to you when you least expect it.'

Ryker sighs—he's done this so many times already. Although he doubts whether it'll help, he pauses to think back to the time they were caught. If only he could recognise something discernible that might jog his memory: a landmark, a gully, a stream, anything. 'Okay,' he says with a shrug, 'let's give it another go.' He draws in a deep breath. 'So, somehow, we suddenly found ourselves in this forest with these massive trees. We had no idea what was happening. It was so *not* what we were used to seeing.

It completely disorientated us. Our safety became my first priority. My inner radar kicked in, and I scoped the area for any threat. Sure enough, moments later, six huge Viking-looking dudes ambushed us from out of nowhere. I remember thinking it must be a joke or a bad dream. Anyway, the three guys—me, Jae and Banj—surrounded the girls to protect them, but the guards were ruthless and broke our pathetic stronghold in a matter of seconds. When they grabbed the girls by the hair, I lost it. I jumped on the biggest one and started pounding his head.' The memory makes Ryker anxious. He remembers it as clear as day. The guard was huge, so it surprised him to find that he could hold his own. He didn't know he had superpowers at that stage. 'But then he grabbed me in a chokehold and slammed me—' Ryker stops suddenly. 'Oh my God!'

Peanut spontaneously disappears into the darkness. Ruby activates her shield.

Ryker chuckles. 'Shit, sorry, guys.' He laughs some more. 'Hey, it's okay. Peanut; where did you go? It's all good. I just remembered something, that's all. And it's a *big* something! Man, I can't believe I clear forgot about it.'

Ruby relaxes; the shield vanishes. Peanut reappears, breathing heavily, his hand on his chest.

Ryker slaps Peanut on the back. 'Hey, good

reflexes, guys.'

Ruby raises an eyebrow.

Peanut's eyes narrow. 'What the hell's going on, man? I nearly crapped my pants!'

Ryker struggles to hide a grin, but then sobers with what he's about to tell them. 'Look, I remembered something really important.' He cranks his neck to look up and about them, but the darkness conceals what he's looking for. 'We need to find a huge rock formation. I remember being thrown up against it.'

He pulls Ruby into a hug and plants a kiss on the top of her head. 'Ruby, you're a genius!' He shakes his head. 'I can't believe I'd erased it from my memory. Look, if we can find that outcrop, there's every chance I can get us to the other portal.'

Peanut's eyes light up. 'Awesome! That shouldn't be too hard to find. It's not like it's something you'd easily miss. We should ask the guys.'

Ryker can't believe how randomly that vital bit of information just popped into his head—just like Ruby said it would. 'Come on; let's go. I can't wait to see if this means anything to them.'

The sun's first rays of light filter through the tree canopy as they reach the village. All is quiet in the small, tight-knit hamlet. The flickering glow from fireplaces within hint that all is well with those tucked away in their tiny, unassuming mudbrick homes. A rooster crows, signalling the start of the day.

Molan stands at the entrance of his home in deep discussion with Medwin. A scruffy black dog approaches out of the darkness and sits by Molan's side. He bends to pat it, then looks up and smiles when they arrive. 'Ah, good morn to you. Enthusiastic to begin our journey, I see.'

'Molan, I remembered something this morning,' Ryker says, breathless from running, 'something that might help find the other gateway. Tell me, is there a large rock formation somewhere in the woods? One with a passageway with sides almost as tall as the fortress walls?'

Molan's smile disappears. He and Medwin exchange a wary look.

Ryker's excitement escalates. 'You know what I'm talking about, don't you?' The two men remain grave. 'But going by the expressions on your faces, this might not be such a good thing. Why?'

'Ryker, this place you speak of …' Molan hesitates and glances at Medwin before looking back, then he shakes his head. 'We cannot take you there.'

'What?' Ruby starts, her fists curled on her hips. 'You're kidding! But you have to.'

Molan raises his hands to calm her. 'I understand that we vowed to help, but this is one promise we must break. I am truly sorry.'

Peanut crosses his arms. 'Guys, come on. What's the go?'

'Peanut, please understand, The Forbidden Passage is a place no one dares visit,' Molan begins. 'There are tales of strange occurrences there, entities that defy explanation.'

Ryker frowns. 'Strange occurrences? What kind of strange occurrences?'

Medwin's eyes widen. 'The old people used to say those who venture through the passage never return.'

Peanut's hands shoot up in front of him. 'Whoa! Back it up a bit. Suddenly I'm not liking the sound of this.'

But in contrast, Ryker's face lights up. 'Peanut, can't you see what I'm seeing? This is it. We've found it!' He turns to Medwin. 'You're right; people who go there disappear because they fall through the portal, the one we're looking for. You've got to take us there.'

The colour drains from Molan's face. 'No, you are wrong. Anyone entering will face certain death! Ryker, please, you must reconsider.'

Ryker can't believe it. Why aren't they listening to reason? This is it—he's sure of it. 'Molan, I'll never ask for anything again. Please!'

'But how can you be certain that this is the place that you seek?' Medwin challenges.

Ruby crosses her arms; her chin juts out. 'Yeah,

Ryker, what makes you so sure? I mean, they're spooked for a reason. Just look at their terrified faces; they really believe we're going to die!'

Ryker looks at Ruby and Peanut's worried faces. He needs to come up with something credible. Then he remembers Molan's encounter with the guard. 'Tell me something, Molan, is the place you were planning to take us to today anywhere near this *Forbidden Passage*?'

Molan frowns, and for a long moment his thoughts appear elsewhere, then he nods. 'Yes, I recall it is nearby.'

Ryker's stomach does a flip. They've virtually found the missing portal! 'Guys, if that doesn't convince you, nothing will. All this can't be a coincidence.'

'He's got a point,' Ruby says to Peanut. 'What do you think?'

Peanut remains silent.

But if they're to go anywhere near this passage, it's the men Ryker needs to convince first. 'Look, if I could just see this place for myself, I'll know for sure. You won't need to take us all the way, just point us in the right direction. Okay?'

Peanut rubs his chin. 'So, Ryker, what you're saying is if you've got doubts about the place, we don't go in?'

Ryker grins. 'Peanut, I promise you, so much as a whiff of doubt, and we're out of there.'

Ruby places her hand on Peanut's arm. 'It won't hurt to have a look. Right?'

Peanut turns from Ruby's hopeful expression to look Ryker in the eye. 'I mean it, Ryker, I'm not waiting for it to be a *stench*; a *whiff* and I'm gone. Okay?'

Ryker slaps him on the back and chuckles.

Peanut peers into the darkened forest, readjusts his backpack and shrugs. 'So let's make tracks. The sooner we get going, the less chance of us coming across the forest ferals!'

Ryker won't argue with that—time is wasting. He turns to lead, but stops when he notices the older men not following. 'Guys, what's up?'

Both men exchange a look, then Molan steps forward. 'Ryker, you cannot be seriously considering going ahead with this?' He pauses. 'No, I stand firm, and I think I speak for Medwin when I tell you we will not go further with this.'

Medwin shakes his head. 'Ryker, this was never to be an easy task, and I had foreseen complications but was willing to accept them in order to assist you. But I had not anticipated *this*! You must heed our warning.'

Complications? Ryker stops. Medwin's predictions

are often spot on. So is this a risk he's prepared to take? And it's not only his life he's playing with. He looks from Ruby to Peanut, takes a moment to think it through and decides that it is. *We've come this far, and Mum's life depends upon us taking a chance!* He's determined—they need to finish this. 'Medwin, I beg you. We can't do this without you.'

Both men remain silent. Ryker prays for hope.

'Then I shall take you.'

Ryker turns to see Aelianna at the door of the small cottage, armed with a sheathed blade in a leather holster and sheer determination on her face. She straps the holster around her waist. 'Father, you surprise me—after all that Ryker and his friends have done for our family.' She turns to Molan. 'And yours. Do you forget the glut of fish Ryker provided your family when they were ill and starving? 'Twas the time father was unable to hunt and provide for us all.' She turns her gaze to Ryker. 'I will take you.' She looks over her shoulder at her father as she turns to lead the way.

'Aelianna, I forbid it!'

She stops. 'Father, give me one good reason why I must not defy you!'

Her father takes her hands in his. 'My daughter, I will not consent. Are you not listening? They seek the passage of death!'

'But could we be wrong and Ryker be right?'

'Look, guys, Ryker's got a point,' Peanut says to them. 'I'll admit it sounded a bit iffy to me at the beginning too, but it can't all be a fluke—the dodgy guard Molan came across, the spooky stories, Ryker remembering the passage. Let's face it, it all adds up. This could be it.'

Molan shakes his head. 'I make no sense of your words, Peanut, but I can see that you are all determined to continue on your quest, no matter the consequences.' He turns to his friend. Medwin, although stern in his looks, lowers his chin. 'Very well, we will go but only under renewed terms. We will accompany you as far as we deem safe, no further. This is our final word.'

Ryker grins. 'That's good enough for me!'

Aelianna just saved their butts, and he knows it. He could kiss her right now, but instead, he tightens the reins on his emotions and shows his gratitude to her by way of a smile and a nod.

As they follow the older men into the forest, Ryker can't help but feel giddy knowing that their mission to find the missing gateway is finally within their grasp.

22

THE FORBIDDEN PASSAGE

Aelianna listens, frozen on the spot as her father and friends argue outside the window. Tucked out of view, she has overheard every single word of their plan and doesn't know what to do. Her mind races. Who does she believe? She, like all forest children, was brought up on the terrifying tales of The Forbidden Passage. These stories gave her nightmares for years. And although she knows of its whereabouts, she has never ventured there, nor has she ever had the inclination to do so, until now. Listening to Ryker, and hearing his reason for dismissing these tales as stories without substance, makes her question everything she's ever been told. *If indeed he has passed through the passage before, then the myths are untrue.*

Her mind is made up. Ryker must see the passage to be certain. He needs her help. She draws in a deep breath. *And now to convince Father to take them.* Her mind ticks over with a scheme of her own. She grabs one of her father's hunting blades, then exits. A convincing performance follows. Of course, her father would never allow her to accompany her new friends alone, especially to a place deemed to be perilous. Her cheeks burn. It's beneath her to shame her father so publicly, but under the circumstances, she has no choice.

And now the journey begins. Her father leads, with Molan and Ryker following close behind. Aelianna is content to trail along with Peanut and Ruby.

She breathes in the freshness of the morning. The woods are at peace at this early hour. She feels safe. But having Ryker so close unsettles her composure. She does her best to ignore the way her body reacts to him. Earlier, their eyes met, and he conveyed his gratitude with a slight tilt of the head and a guarded smile, and just that alone threw her off-kilter.

She shakes off the memory and makes an effort to divert her gaze as they walk. But how can she avoid him? His impressive form is there in front of her at every turn. If only she could keep herself distracted with idle conversation with her friends, but she must remain silent. She forges ahead, her attention focused on anything but the man who has plagued her dreams from the moment she first laid eyes on him.

23

THE COMMAND

RYKER

They're making good time. Molan leads the way to The Forbidden Passage with Medwin and Ryker close behind. The pace has been unremitting, and Ryker is thankful for that. His focus is honed. He observes the master hunter, Molan, manoeuvre through the undefined forest paths with experience, hardly disturbing a leaf, barely making a sound. Ryker mirrors his moves in an attempt to refine his skill.

Vigilant at all times! Ryker can't afford to think of anything but the mission—their goal is within their grasp. But try as he may, his attention keeps diverting to what's happening behind him. Her every movement, every breath, every sigh are all amplified to his highly tuned ears. When it comes to Aelianna, he knows he's a goner. She has, once again, well and truly bewitched him—not only with her beauty but also by her wits. He can't believe what she did for them back there. He was losing hope of ever seeing The Forbidden Passage, and then, with her quick and clever thinking, she managed to turn the tide.

His chest could burst with pride. But now more than ever, he needs to keep his head out of the clouds and stay focused. Too many times he's stuffed things up because of the loss of it. He's determined to do this, and do it right. They soldier on.

The sun sits higher in the sky by the time Molan slows their approach. He stops, crouches, then turns to inform them that they're nearing an area not far from The Dark Forest, and they must remain alert. Ryker looks about them to orientate himself. The woods during the day appear different from last night.

They continue in silence.

A little further on, Molan stops again. Beads of sweat trickle from his brow. He pauses to consider his bearings, then points to a clearing up ahead. 'There lies the place I spoke of—the incident with the guard.'

Medwin scans the area. Eyes widening, he grips Molan by the shoulder and indicates into the distance. 'And just beyond the thicket lies The Forbidden Passage.'

Ryker's eyes light up. This is it; they're only minutes from finding the rockface he came across all those years ago, and more importantly, moments away from finding the missing portal. He glances at Ruby and Peanut; their excitement mirrors his.

Molan's expression turns grave. 'Ryker, we venture no further. The place you seek is within your grasp. You need only look for the rock formation, and there, within its walls, lies the passage. I pray that it is the passage to life, as you say, and not to your death.'

'Thank you for bringing us here.' Ryker says. 'We really appreciate it.'

Just then, barking resounds in the far distance, and the older men become restless. 'We must go,' Molan warns. 'There are savage dogs in the forest.'

'Dogs?' Ruby gulps; her eyes grow wide.

Molan reaches out to Ruby. 'Do not fear, my friend, your shield will protect you. We, on the other hand, must make haste.' He turns to his daughter. 'Come, Aelianna!'

Ryker looks at Aelianna for the first time since leaving the village and sees indecision in her eyes. He goes to her and takes her hand in his. 'It's okay; we can find it from here. Now go.' He gives her hand a gentle squeeze. 'And thank you.'

She hesitates a moment, her eyes searching his. Then she turns to go.

He swallows hard. This might be the last time he sees her. And then he remembers his promise. 'Aelianna,' he calls out after her.

She turns, her look hopeful.

His breath hitches, and for a moment he forgets what he was going to say. After a pause, he remembers. 'I swore to take Wulf down, and I will. Your family will be safe; I'll make sure of it.'

The transformation in her expression confuses him. The sparkle of anticipation he saw in her eyes clouds over.

'Oi, Romeo, let's get going!'

Peanut's snickering breaks his thoughts. And as much as he wants to keep gazing into those deep, dark-chocolate eyes to understand the hidden meaning there, now's not the time. Aelianna turns from him, and the moment is gone. He watches as she disappears into the woods.

'I'm out of here! You coming?' Ruby takes off like she's seen a ghost.

Peanut and Ryker race to keep up.

Ryker can't help but smile. They're on the verge of locating what they've come for. *Let's hope I'm right about this!* He shakes the doubt from his mind as quickly as it entered. He needs to believe that The Forbidden Passage *is* the missing portal.

The thicket Medwin mentioned proves to be a challenge. They struggle to weave their way through the tangle of vines, bushes and exposed tree roots. Ruby appears frantic in her efforts to reach the rocky outcrop.

'Hey, Rubes, take it easy,' Peanut calls out after her.

Ryker watches her battle with the web of the forest and frowns. 'He's right, you'll hurt yourself at this rate.'

Suddenly she stops and motions for them to be quiet.

And that's when he hears it—the sound of barking dogs taking chase. And then someone screams. Ryker's blood runs cold. 'Aelianna!' Without a second thought, he unsheathes his knife and takes off to save her.

'Ryker, wait!' Ruby yells after him.

But Ryker doesn't stop. Somewhere in his head a switch has flicked. He ploughs ahead; his sole focus, reaching Aelianna before the dogs do. As he closes in on the chase, he hears Molan cry out for help. He pushes harder. Ryker prays that he can get there in time, but from the sounds of it, the beasts are zeroing in on them faster than he can. He digs deeper.

And then he spots them: Aelianna has fallen and Molan stands protectively between her and their three attackers. Medwin is nowhere to be seen. Ryker quickly evaluates the situation. These dogs are nothing like he's ever come across. They're enormous, and ready to kill. Jaws snap, saliva flies. With a plan of action decided on, Ryker races towards them, scooping up a large stone and hurling it at the bigger of the three. He hits his target with great accuracy. The beast yelps and falls back. The other two stop and redirect their focus. Ryker reinforces his hold on his blade. He needs to keep their attention to give Aelianna and her father a chance to escape. His breathing deepens; his nostrils flare. 'COME ON!'

The dogs begin their dance, circling their newest prey. Those black eyes and bared teeth have Ryker's undivided attention. From the corner of his eye, he sees Molan help Aelianna to her feet. They brace themselves, each with a weapon firm in hand.

'I've got this,' he reassures his friends. 'So go. Back. Away. Slowly.'

They waver.

'Go now!'

They hesitate once more before turning to make their escape.

Ryker cries out to draw the dogs' attention from them. 'You want a piece of me? LET'S GO. Three against one!'

The animals close in on Ryker, their interest whetted, their growls low and guttural. He's ready. But movement from the corner of his eye catches his attention. His gut clenches; the situation has just taken a turn for the worse. It's Wulf, and he's not alone.

The three goons laugh. Wulf sneers. 'Well, well, look at what we have here. Such a twist of fate—my attacker, trapped by my trusted companions, awaiting my command.' His eyes narrow. 'My vengeance will be sweet.'

Ryker braces himself—seven against one. *Bring it on!*

'Blade, Menace, Savage … ATTACK!'

24

ʙLOODBATH

Oblivious to Ruby's protest, Ryker races off to help their friends. Peanut swears under his breath, turns to Ruby, then makes the decision to go after him. Ruby curses, but follows him. There's a commotion in the distance. Molan cries out. Peanut needs to get to them. He sprints, flying over fallen trees, dodging boulders and fending off the scrub as he charges through it. He chances a glance over his shoulder, sees Ruby struggling to keep up, then hears Ryker's ominous taunt, and a shiver runs down his spine.

He's nearly there, but then a sudden yelp from behind changes everything. Peanut turns to see Ruby clawing at the ground, trying to save herself from falling into a deep hole.

'Ruby!'

'I … I can't hold on!'

Peanut dives to get to her, but as their fingers touch, she slips from his grasp, screaming, and is swallowed by the blackness of the pit.

And then there's silence.

'RUBY!' Peanut throws himself forward, stopping short of falling in after her. He stops, but sees and hears nothing. 'No, no, no, no! Ruby!' The echo of his voice fades into the darkness. He jumps to his feet in search of something to help get to her—perhaps a long vine. Then he hears her coughing and spluttering, trying to catch her breath. 'Rubes, can you hear me? Are you okay?'

She struggles to reply.

'Rubes?'

'I … I think I'm okay,' she says between coughs. 'Just winded.'

His eyes squeeze shut. *Thank God!* 'Hey, you scared the crap out of me—you weren't answering.'

'I must've blacked out. My head hurts like crazy.'

Peanut suddenly hears something in the distance that fills him with dread—a dog attack, and from the sounds of it, it's a bloodbath. A surge of adrenaline courses through his veins. He looks down the pit, then into the woods. *What the hell do I do?* 'Rubes, I've gotta go—those dogs have got someone, and they're being massacred.'

'Get me out first. You'll need me!'

There's not enough time to get Ruby out safely *and* go to help. 'Sorry, but I can't.' He vanishes, then takes off. Ruby's growl of infuriation isn't missed, but he figures she'll be safe while she's stuck down there.

It doesn't take him long to reach the affray. A quick scan sees Ryker in the throes of defending himself against what appear to be three massive black dogs. Wulf and his goons watch from the outskirts. And there's no sign of their forest friends.

Peanut doesn't think twice. He grabs the nearest broken tree branch, charges towards the tangled mess of human, beast and blood, and lashes out, sending the dogs scurrying in confusion.

Wulf stumbles back. 'What is this?' His eyes dart from the scene in front of him to his fleeing dogs. 'Savage, Blade, Menace; you will not defy me. Come back!' But the deserters have bolted. He turns to his men. 'Cato, Galen, Titus, get him!'

Ryker staggers to his feet and prepares to take on the new threat. In no time they're on him. And with the skill of a seasoned fighter, Ryker defends himself, kicking and punching like nothing Peanut has ever seen. He's a muscle-bound, power-packed fighting machine, deflecting his attackers in every direction.

But then the attack stops. The goons regroup

and, as one, tackle Ryker to the ground. With three against one, Ryker needs help. Peanut reinforces his grip on his makeshift weapon, flies at Ryker's attackers and slams them. They scramble to get upright, then prepare to take on this unseen threat. Peanut stands ready.

Ryker battles to get upright. 'Watch out behind you!'

Peanut turns in time, Wulf's blade missing him by centimetres.

'Get out of here!' Ryker calls out the warning before being taken down again by Wulf's goons.

Wulf lashes out at Peanut in a rage, but his strikes miss the invisible target. Soon his attack weakens, and he pauses to catch his breath. Peanut sees his chance and kicks the blade from Wulf's hand into the bushes. Wulf reaches over his shoulder and pulls a baton from a holster fastened there.

Just at that moment, Ryker cries out in pain, distracting Peanut from the baton coming at him … the impact throws him hard up against a tree. Peanut collapses in a heap, gasping for air, clutching at his chest, each breath agonising.

Wulf doesn't need to see Peanut now to know where he is. He raises his stick ready to deliver another blow. Peanut can barely move without a stabbing pain searing through his chest, but he musters everything he has to dive out of its path in time. If the pain was bad before, it's unbearable now. But he can't afford to give himself away again, he bites back from crying out.

Wulf hovers over him, listening for movement, ready to strike, but an urgent cry from one of his goons sends him scurrying to help.

It's four against one. Ryker doesn't stand a chance on his own. Pain or no pain, Peanut needs to do something. But what? And how? And then, conveniently, Wulf staggers back from the brawl, wounded. Now's his chance. Peanut crawls towards the broken branch he used earlier, grabs it, pulls himself upright, then takes the few steps it takes to reach Wulf. He readies himself and swings, but at that moment, Wulf re-enters the fray. Peanut misses and falls to the ground, writhing in indescribable pain.

The situation is hopeless. He can't do a thing to help. He thinks of Ruby and curses himself for not listening to her earlier.

His head drops; his eyes squeeze tight. Sickened by what he's about to do, he blocks out the sounds of the scene behind him and focuses his efforts into getting back to Ruby. His decision to abandon their friend is the hardest one he's ever had to make. His retreat is painfully slow—each step unbearable, each breath a stab in the chest. But Ruby needs him, and knowing this drives him to find the strength to go on.

'Enough!' Wulf cries out unexpectedly.

Peanut stops. It's all over. His heart sinks. A tightness in his throat makes it hard to breath.

'Now bind his hands and feet. We can finish this in the arena.'

Arena?

And then there's hope.

Wulf's goons laugh. There's excitement in their voices as they talk about a challenge of some kind. Peanut struggles to hear what's said. Soon he hears what sounds like Ryker's body being dragged away. Eventually the voices fade into the distance, and then they're gone.

Peanut rests against a tree, sinks to the ground, blinks a few times, then swipes away the moisture in his eyes.

Ryker is still alive!

25

Just You Wait!

Ruby listens to Peanut's footfalls fade. He's abandoning her to run after Ryker. She drops on the floor of the animal trap with a thud, grits her teeth and curses under her breath. *The twit. We could've tackled this together!* But then the thought of having to face Wulf's beasts sends her into a tailspin—beads of sweat form on her brow, and she battles to control her erratic breathing. She jumps up, panicked, and claws at the dirt in a manic attempt to escape—until she remembers. *There aren't any dogs here!* She stops, rests her head on the wall of the pit, shuts her eyes tight and reminds herself that she's safe. *There aren't any dogs down here.* She repeats this over and over again until logic kicks in. Ruby's intense fear of dogs is real—the doctors call it cynophobia. For her to voluntarily go anywhere near a dog would be a first.

Ever since a neighbour's dog attacked her, her reaction to dogs has been irrational. Big or small, cute or ugly, they all produce the same response—complete and utter terror. Even the sound of a dog barking in the distance has her pulse racing. Once she nearly ran in the path of an oncoming car just to avoid one ambling towards her. She shudders, remembering the incident. Fortunately for her, she was yanked to safety by a mother who knows her too well.

Ruby takes a deep breath and straightens her shoulders. *Suck it up!* She won't allow another senseless reaction to cloud what needs to be done now—and that is, finding a way out of this hole. But at the moment, thinking hurts too much. She has a whopper of a headache coming. She runs her hand over the lump on the side of her head and groans.

She looks up. It's a long way to the top. If she hadn't activated the shield when she did, it could've been a lot worse than just a bump to the head. That fall could've killed her.

'So what's next?' There's very little light at the bottom of the pit, but she can see some tree roots jutting out from the walls. Maybe she can climb out. *Can't be that different from rock climbing. Right?*

And so she begins her effort to escape. Every step

of the climb, Ruby checks and rechecks her handgrips and footholds, tugging and putting weight on each protruding root before elevating to the next level. In this way, she eventually reaches the top. The final haul is the hardest. Dragging herself out of the hole takes a few grunts and grumbles, but she makes it.

She flops in a heap and takes a moment to catch her breath, then smiles. *Men! Who needs them!*

But now's not the time to gloat. She gets to her feet and stops to listen. *Thank God, no dogs!* But then in the distance, she hears laughter, and it's not from anyone she knows. She takes off at a run, not knowing what she's about to come across, but ready to put her shield to work. As she goes, Ruby remembers to mark her path—a forest this big can look the same at every turn, and she can't afford to get lost. She smiles, knowing how far she's come from being that insecure, guarded sixteen-year-old. That girl is gone. *Yeah, mess with me, and I'll kick your butt!*

Ruby activates her shield, slows her approach and conceals herself behind a large rock. By her estimation, she should be very close. Again, she stops to listen. The forest is as it should be—birds squawk in the treetops; small animals scurry in the underbrush. A soft breeze tickles the foliage and cools her sweaty brow. But something doesn't feel right. She inches forward and enters an area where the vegetation has been disturbed. Ruby scans the space and soon notices a puddle of blood and scattered tufts of black fur. She squats to investigate, but movement behind her makes her jump. She whips around, senses intensified, and hears a moan from deep within the bush. Someone's hurt.

Her voice shakes. 'Peanut?'

'Rubes, is that you?'

Ruby races to find him in a crumpled mess, doubled over in pain, all colour drained from his face. She falls to his side and encircles him within her shield.

'Hey!' He struggles to breathe.

'Hey, yourself. What happened? You don't look so good.'

He groans and shakes his head. 'So how d'ya get out?'

'Yeah, thanks for ditching me, you creep.'

He chuckles, then flinches.

'What happened?' she asks again.

Peanut takes his time going through the details, stopping now and then to catch his breath, occasionally diverting from the topic in his typical fashion, but quick to refocus each time Ruby purses her lips and glowers at him.

She takes a moment to consider what they need to do. Peanut's in a mess, so it won't be easy, no matter what. But decisions need to be made, and as far as she can see, they've come to a crossroads. Yes, Ryker needs help, but what use are they with Peanut in this state? And she can't leave Peanut to go after Ryker. He needs Max's help! *But the portal is kilometres away!* Then Ruby considers the other portal and their South African friends waiting on the other side of it. *At least I can get Peanut some help from there!* 'Peanut, our best bet is to find the other gateway and get you fixed up. We were so close before.'

'But what about Ryker? They'll kill him. We've gotta do something.'

Ruby crosses her arms. 'Like what? As far as I can see, we don't have a choice! You're not much use like this.'

Her glare makes him cower. 'Man, have you been getting lessons from Max or someth'n?'

Ruby's lip twitches. *Yeah, be scared. Be very, very scared!* 'Come on, let's make tracks.'

Peanut struggles to get upright. Ruby grabs him around the waist to support him and slings his arm over her shoulder, and they set off. The journey is gruelling—Peanut moans and flinches with every step. They can't go on like this. She stops. 'There's got to be a better way.' She considers her shield for a moment. 'Hang on a sec.'

Ruby retracts the sphere encircling them, plays

around with the form of it for a few minutes, shaping and reshaping it until she's created a stretcher. Pleased with the final attempt, she scoops Peanut up in it and smirks.

Peanut relaxes into it and grins. 'Hey, not bad.'

Her brow knits. 'Not bad? It's bloody brilliant!' She giggles with excitement. 'Who knew I could do that?'

'You're right, Rubes; it *is* bloody brilliant—*you're* brilliant!'

So begins the trek back through the forest to find the missing gateway.

With some effort, Ruby navigates the stretcher over tree roots and boulders, and then through dense forest vegetation, retracing her footsteps back towards where they were before Ryker took off. When they reach the animal trap Ruby had fallen into, she stops to consider the next step.

'Hey, Rubes, I was thinking,' Peanut says. 'It'd be easier if we could see where this rock formation is.'

She frowns. 'Um, duh!'

'No, listen.' He chuckles. 'How high d'ya reckon you can raise the stretcher? Maybe you can get me high enough to see over the treetops.'

Surprised by his thinking, Ruby stops to consider this. What's stopping her turning her shield into a cherry picker? Giddy with the idea of it, she takes a moment to channel her inner strength. With all thoughts focused on conjuring such a thing, her shield transforms from a flat stretcher to a chair shape, and soon she has Peanut elevated above the canopy to where he has a clear view.

Peanut fidgets with excitement and gestures for her to lower him. 'Awesome! I know exactly where it is.'

Ruby wastes no time getting them moving, and soon they have their goal in sight.

26

SPOOKED

PEANUT

They've made it. They've reached the escarpment Medwin had alluded to. And somewhere within its crevices, they hope, lies the passage to the elusive portal to South Africa. Ruby lowers Peanut to his feet, then transforms her shield to enclose them protectively within the bubble. Peanut stops a moment to take in the ominous, tall-walled rocky outcrop, then hobbles towards it, each step a stab in his side. Together they traverse its perimeter, searching for the corridor of rock Ryker had described. And then they see it, a wide split in the formation—The Forbidden Passage. Peanut stops. Images of their forest friends' terrified faces come to mind. He draws in a quick breath, then shakes it off. *Get a grip! You're not gonna die. And Ryker needs help!*

They inch closer, his pulse flying, uncertainty killing his confidence. *Ryker had better be right about this!* He turns to Ruby to see if she's freaking out like he is, but she seems unfazed by it. She gives him a reassuring smile.

At the entrance, he hesitates; beads of sweat form on his upper lip. He leans to peer inside. A sudden cold draft brushes past him, and he falls back, stepping on Ruby's toes. She grits her teeth and growls.

'Sorry, Rubes.'

Her lips purse. 'What's with you?'

'Look, how do we know this is the right place? What if it's a death trap, like the locals think it is?'

Ruby's eyes narrow. 'Of course it's the right place—it's exactly how Ryker described it.'

But Peanut's not convinced. His gaze pings back and forth from the passageway to the woods. He's ready to bail out. The sound of something approaching from the forest freezes them both on the spot. Without thinking, Peanut grabs Ruby and dives for cover in the nearby bushes. This he instantly regrets. *Son of a …!* Tears sting his eyes, and he bites down on his tongue to stop from crying out. The pain in his side is nothing compared to the look he gets from Ruby though.

But there's no time to go back—whatever's coming is coming fast. They crouch down low, safe within the shield, and wait. Ruby gestures, suggesting they make a run for it. She starts to stand, but he tugs her back and shakes his head. The window of opportunity to enter the passage is closing.

Then out of the woods, three beefy guards appear. Peanut shrinks lower and studies them. Two look familiar. He frowns, trying to place them, and then remembers they're the guards that chased them into the Blue Ridge National Park that time. Ruby's expression tells him she recognises them too.

She indicates that they could use the shield to get past them. Peanut considers Ruby's idea for a moment but decides against it, remembering Ryker's advice to keep a low profile. They need to come back this way later, so the less attention they bring to themselves now the better. He shakes his head.

'Marcus, search the area and look for any disturbance,' the bigger of the three commands. 'Lucius, you are to inspect the passage. Make certain the gateway is safe.'

Gateway? Peanut's heart skips a beat hearing it confirmed. He turns to Ruby. Her lips are pursed; her brow raised.

The guard asked to inspect the passage, Lucius, curses under his breath. The one giving the orders scowls. 'Do you have a problem with that?'

Lucius juts out his chin. 'Only that I did it the

time before, Atticus. Why not send Marcus?'

Atticus steps up to the smaller guard, puffs out his chest and stands taller than his already impressive height. 'You dare question my authority?' Lucius falls back, and Atticus sneers. 'I thought not. Now go! Marcus and I will survey the surrounding forest.'

With that said, the two men depart, leaving Lucius to follow through with the command. But the dejected guard paces at the entrance of the passage for several moments, apparently reluctant to enter. Peanut's eyes narrow. He watches with renewed interest. *Will ya look at that; the guy's spooked! Man, those stories even have the big boys freaking out!*

This gives Peanut an idea. He gathers some stones, stashes them in his rolled-up T-shirt and gestures for Ruby to do the same. She shrugs but follows his lead. Once they've collected a few, he braces himself for what he needs to do. The opportunity for them to get past the guard is now while the other two are gone— and time is ticking. They need to get to that portal.

Peanut stands from his crouched position, ready to act. He cranes his neck to check on the guard— Lucius has stopped pacing and is looking very much like he's contemplating entering. Peanut gestures for Ruby to take down the shield, which she does. He tosses one of the stones into the passageway, and Lucius jumps so high, it's almost comical. Seeing the big brawny guard reduced to a quivering mess has Peanut struggling to hold back from laughing. Ruby covers her mouth to restrain a giggle.

Lucius takes a moment to compose himself before peering into the passage to investigate. Peanut pitches a few more stones—this time with a little too much enthusiasm—and instantly regrets it.

The guard leaps clear of the entrance.

Ruby lobs her stones in a rapid-fire. The guard yelps, jumps further back, then high-tails it out of there as though running from the devil himself.

Their passageway is clear. With Ruby's help, Peanut staggers the short distance to the entrance, then stops, Molan's foreboding echoing in his ears. *'I pray that it is the passage to life, as you say, and not to your death!'* Ruby yanks at him. He shakes off the memory and inches closer.

Once within the passageway walls, Peanut struggles to see more than a few metres ahead. It takes a moment for his eyes to adjust to the darkness. What lurks in the shadows is anyone's guess. The temperature drops several degrees; nevertheless, sweat trickles from his brow. Peanut stops again, looks out the way they came, then decides *there's no turning back.* Placing one step after the other, they continue until they come around a slight bend in the path. Peanut stiffens at the vision before them. A familiar translucent floating curtain waves at them out of the dim light. Peanut is torn between relief at seeing it and terror that he's about to test Molan's archaic belief. His breathing quickens; his head becomes light. He presses against the wall to steady himself.

Ruby grits her teeth. 'What's gotten into you? Let's do this—Ryker needs us!'

'Back off for a sec, will ya?' He takes a moment to psych himself up. 'Look, I'll go first. Okay?'

She frowns.

He shrugs, and his lip curls. 'I guess there's no point in both of us dying. Right?'

Ruby groans. 'Just do it!'

'Rubes, as much as I'm nuts about ya, right now you're ticking me off!' He stops again, takes a breath, then turns to her, wagging his finger. 'So no matter what happens—'

Ruby curses, and without warning shoves him forward, and then they're gone.

27

THE OTHER SIDE

PEANUT

Peanut stumbles through the portal and lands with a thud. Ruby falls next to him. He holds back from screaming in pain. It's pitch black. He can't see a thing. And when he tries to vanish and can't; he knows they're back in the real world. Exactly where, he can't be sure. *Hopefully somewhere near Edra and the twins.* And then a sudden thought hits him; *crap, we could be anywhere … in any time-zone!*

The notion of the portal misdirecting them had never entered his mind until now. He struggles to focus on anything that might give him a clue as to where they are. A chorus of nocturnal animals and insects floods the air. The sound of something scurrying nearby makes him jump, but the searing pain in his side reminds him that he shouldn't make any sudden moves. The scampering animal runs from them. Peanut takes a deep breath.

'Are you okay?' Ruby grabs his hand, and at once he feels better.

He pulls her to his side. 'Where the hell are we? Can you see anything?'

'Well, at least we're not *dead*!' She teases.

Peanut ignores the dig. Slowly his eyes begin to adapt to the darkness. He can see the silhouette of a distant mountain against the night sky, and the outline of a few huge trees thinly scattered on fairly flat land. These upside-down trees with their bulbous trunks and root-like branches are something he's only seen on documentaries and, if he's not mistaken, found only in certain regions of the world, *like Africa!* Seeing them gives him hope.

And then, way out in the distance, he hears something that makes the hairs on the back of his neck stand on end, and confirms that they're where they should be. He hears it again—the lazy yawn of a lion carried on the slight breeze. The yip and squeal of a distant hyena fight makes their location suddenly all too real.

Ruby squeezes his hand.

'We need to get out of here.' Peanut knows that Edra and the twins are at a nearby campsite waiting to hear from them, and Ryker estimated that the camp was within a three-to-five-kilometre radius of the portal. All they need to do now is make contact. He pulls out the walkie-talkie Ryker had given him, tuned at the same frequency as Edra's, and turns it on. 'Testing, testing … Peanut to base. Are you there, Edra?'

Static fills the silence as they wait for a response. He almost drops the device when Banji's voice comes through loud and clear.

'Peanut! You guys made it! Hey, where are you?'

'Mate, I don't have time to explain, but you'd better get your butts out here ASAP.' After a moment of what sounds like a tug-of-war between the twins over the walkie-talkie, Peanut describes, as best he can, where they are.

'We're coming,' Ulan says. 'We'll just grab Edra— she's gone for a walk. Hey, listen, have you got a torch or something? It might help us find you.'

Peanut shakes his head, knowing he hadn't packed one, but then remembers the kit Ryker gave them that morning. He reaches into Ruby's backpack, finds the kit, then rummages through it, using the glow from the light on the walkie-talkie. He comes across something that feels like a torch. *God, let it be a torch!* He flicks a switch, and sure enough, there's instant light. 'Hey, I've got one!'

'Great, we'll look out for you. Are you somewhere

safe? Never mind, I guess Ryker's onto that already.'

Peanut groans. *If only Ryker WAS onto it!* He ends the call and looks about them—they're sitting ducks out here. All sorts of wild animals could be surrounding them, lining them up as their next meal.

Ruby wraps her arm around his waist. 'Come on, let's get out of here. We'll find somewhere protected. I could help you up a tree.'

A rustling sound in the nearby tall grasses makes Peanut nearly jump out of his skin. He cries out in pain, and his breathing accelerates—there's no way he can outrun anything in his condition, and climbing a tree doesn't appeal either. If only he could see what's out there. *But it's so bloody dark!* And then he remembers the goggles. 'Geez, I'm an idiot!'

'What is it?'

He dives into his backpack, throws on the goggles, scans the tall grass and lets out an unsteady breath. 'It's okay; there's nothing there.'

He turns to check the area around them and almost falls on his butt when he sees the glow coming from the portal. He lowers the goggles and sees nothing, then puts them on and is once again shocked at the amount of energy coming from it. 'Shit, will ya get a load of that!'

Ruby snatches the goggles to look. 'Oh my God! Ryker was right.'

Peanut frowns, then vaguely recalls Ryker explaining something about the goggles that morning. *Man, I should've paid more attention.*

Ruby finds a tree that looks climbable, but Peanut can't manage it, even with her help. His chest hurts like nothing else. So they settle for squeezing themselves into a cleft between the cluster of rocks beneath it. With rock on three sides, he relaxes, his breathing slowing, and the pain soon becomes bearable.

Ruby takes the torch, switches it on, then waves it about. They wait.

But Peanut, being Peanut, can't sit still for long. 'Hey, I wonder what else is in that bag of goodies Ryker gave us.' He snatches back the torch, wedges it under his armpit and begins to explore: there's a box of matches, a compass, some bandages, a rope, a reflective space blanket, a zip-lock baggie full of gooey cotton balls *(what the?)*, a canteen, a whistle, a laser pointer, a Swiss army knife, a bright red gun and cartridges in a clear plastic bag …

'Whoa! A flare gun! Cool. Check it out!'

Ruby frowns. 'Yeah it's cool, but have you ever fired one?'

'Nah, but it should be a piece of cake.' He doesn't waste time reading the instruction leaflet and safety warnings. The illustration on the side of the flare tells him which end of the cartridge to ram down the barrel. He stands and steps out of their hiding place. 'Can't be that hard … just load and shoot. Right?' He fires the flare. It shoots off with a bang—and gets caught in the branches of the tree above.

'PEANUT!'

He shields his eyes from the blinding glare. 'Well, they can't miss us now! Beats a torch any day.'

But then things rapidly turn pear-shaped. The tree catches alight, and the risk of starting a wildfire is suddenly very real. 'OH, CRAAAP!'

They need to do something, and fast. Ruby grabs Peanut's backpack, clambers up the tree to the branch on fire and whacks the flames with it until there's no longer a glow. She falls back exhausted. 'Got any more *bright ideas*, genius?' she asks as she makes her way back down the tree.

In the far distance, Peanut hears what sounds like a car engine revving. 'Hey, did ya hear that?' He peers into the darkness but sees nothing, then remembers the walkie-talkie. 'Rubes, quick, pass me my backpack.' He dives in to retrieve the walkie-talkie and gasps. It's shattered—the pieces fall through his fingers. 'Argh! Ruby! What the hell have you done?'

Ruby scowls. 'Don't start playing the blame game with *me*, Charlie!'

He stops to listen for the car … nothing. He just

about convinces himself that what he heard earlier was a figment of his imagination, when he spots two headlights moving their way. He gulps, not quite sure what to feel—the way their luck's been lately, this might not be such a good thing. If it's a park ranger, they're in big trouble—how are they supposed to explain how they got there? On the other hand, if it's Banji and the girls, their prayers have been answered.

Just to be on the safe side, they return to their place in the rocks and squat low, hiding from view. As the vehicle approaches, the driver throws on the high-beam, then angles the car to light up the tree before coming to a stop. Peanut hears the door open and shut. Footfalls on the gravel draw nearer. He holds his breath.

'Hey, guys, where are you?'

It's Edra. Peanut sighs.

They stand and show themselves. Peanut shields his eyes from the floodlights now blinding them. 'Hey, cut the lights, will ya.'

The lights die, revealing Edra and a caged safari jeep out of which jump the twins.

'I can't believe you're here!' Ulan laughs. 'That's awesome; you found the missing portal.' She looks around, and her smile vanishes. 'But where's Ryker?'

Peanut doesn't know where to begin. The whole situation has turned into a nightmare.

'Um, guys. He's not with us,' Ruby tells them.

Edra curses. 'Why am I *not* surprised? We're talking about *Ryker*, for crying out loud. What the hell has he done now?'

Ulan reaches for Ruby's hand. 'What's happened?'

'Not now, Ulan,' her brother tells her. 'We need to get out of here; it's not safe.'

Edra watches Ruby help Peanut to the jeep. Again she curses. 'And, *of course*, you're injured!' Her lips press in a thin line. 'I knew it! This was always going to be a bad idea! No plan, no backup, no fricking nothing! Bloody idiot!'

Banji shares a look with his sister as he helps Peanut into the jeep.

Edra throws herself behind the wheel, slams the door shut, then speeds off, kicking up gravel in a cloud of dust. The drive to a gated camping ground nearby is a bumpy and reckless one. Peanut bites back from saying anything, knowing it would only add to the obvious tension.

Once settled in a small cabin there, Ruby runs through the details of what's happened in the last twenty-four hours.

Ulan's eyes are wide, her grip on Ruby vice-like. 'Poor Ryker!'

Banji frowns. 'But you think he's still alive. Right?'

'Yeah, I heard Wulf say something about an

arena,' Peanut tells them. 'But God help him if Wulf's thinking of handing him over to Herodus again. After what happened last time, he won't stand a chance—they'll kill him!'

Edra stumbles back. The colour drains from her face. Ulan is there to steady her, then helps her to a chair. Brother and sister share another look. Peanut frowns. The vacant expression on Edra's face makes him wonder what the heck's going on. He heard she had some issues, but he didn't think she was this bad.

Ulan gives a nervous laugh. 'Well, we all know Ryker—mister unstoppable—lands on his feet every time.'

It's hard not to miss the friction in the room. Peanut looks at Ruby. She frowns and shrugs. And Ulan's comment does nothing to pacify Edra.

She's up like a shot, pacing back and forth within the confined space, fists clenched. 'What a fricking mess! I told him this was a bad idea!' She turns to the twins. 'But did he listen? No! *Ryker* does what *Ryker* wants—be damned the rest of us. And now they're going to *kill* him—just like they *killed* Jae!' Her eyes fill with tears; she turns away and swipes at them.

'Whoa, Edra, hold your horses!' Peanut says. 'We're not gonna let that happen. We'll come up with a way to get him out, okay?' Peanut doesn't get it. He's never seen Edra like this—she's usually so together.

'Mess or no mess,' Banji says, 'we need to come up with a plan, and fast. Any ideas?'

Banji's determination to act quickly snaps Peanut back to the situation. 'Yeah, so in theory, it should be me going back in, since I'm the only one that can get past the guards. But as you can see'—he shifts uneasily on the camp bed—'I'm pretty useless like this.'

Ruby gets to her feet. 'The thing is, we need Max.'

So between them, a plan is hatched. Ulan will remain to tend to their patient as best she can, while Ruby, Banji and Edra return to the Ancient Realm and go back to the other portal for Max.

But the way Edra is at the moment, Peanut doubts she'll be of use to anyone. He would argue it, but Banji seems determined that she should come with them, saying that her superhuman speed could prove more valuable than the telepathy he shares with his sister.

In any case, Peanut isn't in any fit state to argue, and based on the vacant expression on Edra's face, it would appear that neither is Edra.

28

FOG

EDRA

If Edra was to think about what they're about to do, she'd probably turn around and walk away—well, no, not walk, run! And she'd urge the others to do the same. But she's not thinking. Her brain is in a fog. And since Banji has taken the reins, she numbly follows his lead, content to remain oblivious under that blanket of nothingness that's protecting her right now.

It's still dark. They've just left the safety of the compound and, with the help of the thermal-imaging goggles, have driven back to the glowing portal near the charred boab tree ready to re-enter the Ancient Realm.

Edra stares vacantly at the floating veil waving at her, beckoning her to pass. Then suddenly her protective bubble pops. She snaps out of her stupor and looks around, frantic—the nightmare she was having is no dream; it's a reality. A knot twists her insides, her palms sweat. Somehow, she needs to stop this from happening—stop herself from plunging into the hell she despises so much.

Banji takes her hand. 'How about you sit for a minute?' He squats by her side. 'Edra, look at me.'

His voice sounds distant. And the darkness engulfing her is somewhat comforting.

'Edra,' he repeats.

She snaps back to what's happening and searches his eyes. He looks worried.

'We're in this thing together,' he tells her. 'And not just for Ryker, but for you too. Okay? If you can't do this, that's all right—I can drive you back. Ruby and I will do it. Right, Ruby?'

Ruby stands speechless.

Edra blinks a few times. It takes a moment for Banji's words to sink in. She gets to her feet and steps away. 'Just give me a minute.' Deep down, she knows what to do—life would be too unbearable if something happened to Ryker and she hadn't lifted a finger to help.

She silently curses him to hell and back for making her do this again. And then the threat of tears prickles at her senses. *I can't lose Ryker too.* The dread of that engulfs her, and then, predictably, her unrelenting demons return to taunt her. This time she lets them. In a haze of blankness, she loses herself in their familiarity. The numbness she feels is comforting; they're nothing new, nothing unexpected—they're constant.

If she can remain in the fog and keep herself cocooned in this oblivion, she might just survive the hell they're about to enter, and somehow get through to the other side.

29

SIXTH SENSE

MAX

Max tosses and turns in her sleeping bag, trying to get comfortable, then looks at her phone for the zillionth time—it's just after midnight. To help her settle, she focuses her attention on the sounds outside their tent—the night animals scurry and the campfire crackles. But the whispered voices next to her are keeping her awake. Clearly Jack and Kenny are finding it hard to switch off too. Once again her thoughts drift to what might be happening on the other side of the portal, and she questions whether they've made the right decision not involving the adults.

She rolls over and buries her head deeper under the covers. The voices stop, and eventually she drifts off into a restless sleep.

Several hours later, Max wakes in a confused panic.

Jack is wiping her hair off her sweaty brow. 'Hey, it's okay, you're just having a bad dream.'

She sits up and looks around, disorientated, then realises where she is.

He frowns. 'I thought you were done with those.'

She rests her head against him, relieved that what she saw wasn't real. But the disturbing images are vivid in her mind. She squeezes her eyes tight trying to block them out.

'I made you some breakfast. You hungry?' He gets up to go and holds his hand out for her.

But Max hasn't the stomach for food; her gut tells her something's gone wrong on the other side. She saw it in the dream. Blood, lots of it. And her ears still ring from the scream—someone's been attacked by a wild animal. *A wolf?* Her chest tightens.

Quit it! It was only a dream!

Or was it? A shiver runs up her spine. She's never had a premonition before, but she bets it feels exactly like this. She looks up at Jack. Does she tell him? But how can she? *He'll think I'm a complete freak!*

Jack frowns.

She shakes her head. *No way!* She'll keep this one to herself.

So Max pastes a smile on her face, takes his hand

and follows him out to get on with the day.

The morning passes slowly. There's little to occupy her thoughts, so the images from her nightmare plague her. She stares at the flickering campfire flames, recalling them.

'Hey, what's up?' Kenny asks.

She blinks a few times, considers telling him about the premonition, but decides against it. She forces a smile. 'Me? Nothing; just a little tired, I guess.'

Suddenly alarmed, Kenny jumps up and points at something behind her. 'Guys, something's coming!'

Max turns to see the portal oscillating with energy. She dives for her trusted baseball bat, thankful she thought to bring it.

Jack races to shield her, wielding a hockey stick. 'Quick, get behind me!'

Kenny grabs the nearest fallen tree branch, but before they've had time to assemble, Banji appears from out of nowhere, a compass in hand and some weird goggles around his neck. Ruby and Edra stumble through after him.

'I don't believe it!' Jack drops his stick and runs to them. He hugs the girls and fist bumps Banji.

'Man, you guys had us going there for a second.' Kenny throws aside the branch and laughs. 'So you've found the other portal? That's awesome!'

But Max is seeing things differently. She grabs

Ruby's arm. 'What's happened? Where are the boys?' Ruby pauses, and Max's gut churns. She knows something's gone wrong. 'They're in trouble. Aren't they?'

'What? Come on, Max,' Jack laughs. 'Where did that come from?' He turns to their friends, but from the expression on their faces, it's clear Max is right. His smile vanishes.

Banji runs his hand through his short, dark curls and looks from Jack to Kenny, then Max. 'Guys, they need Max's help.'

Before Banji finishes, Max is up collecting her things. Jack grabs her by the arm. 'Whoa! Hey, what do you think you're doing?'

Max looks down at his grip, grits her teeth and tugs her arm free. 'I'm going with them.'

Kenny steps between them. 'Max, you can't just take off. Let's at least hear what's happened.'

Max knows what's happened—she saw it in her dream. But does she tell them that? She presses her lips together to stop from saying something she knows she'll regret.

Jack scowls. 'Don't be stupid.'

STUPID!

That does it—Max can't hold back any longer. 'Okay, here it is, *Jack*, that nightmare I had, it wasn't just a dream, it was a premonition. Call me a freak, call me anything you like,' she turns to Ruby, 'but Ryker's hurt, and he's in a bad way, isn't he?'

Ruby says nothing; the expression on her face tells Max all she needs to know. 'He was attacked by a wolf, wasn't he?' She asks this, dreading to hear the answer.

Ruby's eyes widen. 'But, how …?'

'It doesn't matter how, Ruby,' Max cries out, 'the thing is, Ryker is hurt. He's lost a lot of blood; he's in trouble, and there's more to come—I've seen it. So we don't have much time. We need to go now!' Her insides twist in a knot. What she saw in her dream was true.

Her friends stare at her, their mouths gaping. Heat rises to colour her cheeks. But what they think of her at the moment shouldn't be the issue. Ryker needs help. She stands taller and fortifies her resolve. *Yeah, so I'm a freak! Get over it!* 'What are we waiting for?'

'Max, it's not just Ryker,' Edra tells her. 'Peanut is hurt too.'

Max doesn't need to hear any more, she grabs her backpack and shoves her things into it. Jack yanks the bag from her. 'Will you quit it!' Max snatches it back. *What's with him? Was he even listening?*

They stare at each other for a long while, both unwavering. And then Jack's eyes soften. He sighs. 'Look, we'll all go, *but,*' he emphasises, 'we talk about this first. All right? I'm not going back in there with any half-baked ideas. Okay?'

'And that's how it should've been in the first place,' Edra says, her face flushed. 'We wouldn't be in this mess if Ryker had thought things through before diving in. I'm done with all this crap. From now on, we either do it right or we don't do it at all! Call in the taskforce, or get Ryker's dad on board, but I'm not going back in there without a set plan.'

'Edra's right,' Kenny begins. 'We're way out of our depth. It was meant to be simple—get in, find the portal and get out. What the hell happened?' He stops to look at his friends. 'Guys, we need help.'

Jack paces back and forth. 'But, Kenny, there's no time. Remember how long it took before anything happened last time? It took forever. I reckon we can do it—with a good plan and Ruby's shield, we'll be unstoppable.'

Max—arms crossed, anxiety bubbling over—listens to the conversation toing and froing. Ryker and Peanut are hurt, and this standing around doing nothing is killing her. 'Look, I'm done biting my tongue about this crap. I vote we move ahead. Like Jack said, we've got Ruby, so let's agree on a damn plan so we can get the hell going.'

Max's outburst surprises everyone, herself included. All this angst has been gurgling inside her since having the premonition—it's exhausting holding it in. Her friends stare at her, and she doesn't know where to look. She particularly can't bring herself to make eye contact with Jack. *God, he must think I'm a complete whack job!*

But she shakes it off, straightens her shoulders and turns to Ruby. 'So Ruby, you would have the best idea on what we should do, so let's hear it.'

Ruby blinks a few times. 'Well, um, I guess we can't just race back in there, security's tight.'

'And we need to pass through two guarded portals now,' Banji reminds them. 'We were lucky to get past the three goons on the other side of this one by distracting them, but I think they suspected something, so their guard will be up.'

'I know we've got my shield to fall back on,' Ruby adds, 'but we need to keep a low profile—the less they know of our being there, the better our chances.'

'Tell them about the other portal,' Edra says.

'Oh yeah,' Ruby continues. 'And as for the guards at the other gateway, well, there's a way of getting past them—it was Peanut's brilliant idea, actually— they're all spooked by some old ghost stories.'

Max, Jack and Kenny listen as Ruby, Edra and Banji fill them in with the details. Plans are made. There's no time to waste. The campsite is abuzz with activity. Jack and Kenny collect their things; Banji and Edra put out the fire; Ruby helps Max finish packing.

Geared up and eager to get going, Ruby leads, ready to activate her shield the moment they enter the Ancient Realm.

Max breathes a little easier.

30

ᴴURRY

MAX

Max, Jack, Kenny, Ruby, Banji and Edra enter the Ancient Realm without a hitch thanks to Ruby and her magnificent shield. As expected, they were ambushed. Three brawny guards wielding machetes and axes came at them from every direction. But Ruby was ready and surprised them all by transforming her shield into the shape of a huge meaty fist, and then, with the finesse of a seasoned boxer, took them out single-handedly, so to speak. And now with the guards out for the count, the team get busy gagging, hog-tying and disposing of their victim's unconscious bodies—dragging them deep into the forest to ensure they won't be troubled by them again.

But for Max, nothing's moving fast enough,

and her patience is wearing thin. They need to get to Ryker, fast. She chews on her lower lip, waiting for the boys to return from dumping the guards. She prays that Ryker is still alive and groans thinking of all the holdups already: first they needed to come up with a plan, then they spent ages going over it. *And now it's getting dark!* Just like a bad dream, each step is agonisingly slow, as if weighted down with lead, and each turn shrouded with complications. She feels trapped—her pacing quickens.

The boys finally arrive. She lets out a sigh of relief, and their journey begins.

Banji and Ruby lead the way. Max, Edra and Kenny follow, and Jack trails at the rear. To Max's relief they go in silence, focused on their objective.

But it doesn't take long before the quiet is broken. 'So, Banji, how come you know which way to go?' A question from Jack, as innocent as that, has Max ready to turn on him and snap. *For crying out loud! Less talk, more action. Keep walking!*

Banji stops, turns and gives her a look. 'Um, yeah, about that. I guess we're a lot wiser now, and we can thank Kenny for that.'

Kenny's eyes go wide. 'Me?'

Banji chuckles. 'We've left a trail, and so far, so good.' As they continue, he points out the whitish pebbles on the ground. 'See these moonstones; they're showing us the way.'

This casual conversation infuriates Max. *Ryker could be dying, and they choose NOW to talk about rocks?* She bites her tongue and counts to ten to stop from saying something she'll regret.

Again, Banji stops to glare at her. Max draws back—his repeated stare unsettles her. *Geez, what's with the weird looks?* She shakes her head and scowls. *So okay, it's official; I'm the local freak. Build a bridge and get over it!*

Banji frowns.

It's only then that it dawns on Max that her thoughts haven't been her own—Banji has been copping all her inner turmoil. Her cheeks heat. She looks away, mortified.

Kenny then asks Banji about the military-looking headgear he's wearing. He pauses to answer. 'Um, yeah. They're heat-detecting goggles—they're Ryker's. Look, how about we keep going? We can talk later.' He catches Max's eye, raises his brow in silent acknowledgment, and they forge ahead.

'Wow, I've read about those,' Kenny says excitedly, oblivious to the exchange. 'You know, the science behind the way they work is so cool …'

Max moans but says nothing and concentrates on keeping her thoughts to herself.

'… they convert light energy into electrical

energy, or electrons,' Kenny continues, insensible to the tension he's creating. 'These electrons pass through a small disc the size of a ten-cent piece that contains over ten million channels. As the electrons travel through and strike the walls of the channels …' He pauses when he realises Edra has stopped and is staring at him, her mouth gaping.

'I'm with you, Edra.' Banji laughs. 'I've been in his head and seen what goes on in there—it's mind-boggling.'

Jack pats Kenny on the back. 'Welcome back to the realm, Kenny.'

Kenny smacks his forehead and laughs at himself.

Ruby chuckles. 'You'll soon get used to him breaking out in *Google-talk*.'

'Hey! You know I can't help it!' Kenny tells them. 'It just happens.'

'And we wouldn't have it any other way,' Ruby says.

Max can't bring herself to give in to this idle chatter—it's time-wasting. Again, she holds back from saying anything. She won't allow herself to relax until she's seen how bad Peanut and Ryker are. She rubs at the tightness in her chest. They continue.

'So get this,' Ruby tells them excitedly. 'By using the goggles, Ryker worked out that the gateway gives off heat, and that's how we've been able to find the portals so easily. Pretty cool, huh? We'll be with Ulan and Peanut before you know it.' She sighs. 'Poor Peanut, he really copped it in that brawl.'

'So how about we quit with the crap and pick up the pace?' Max snaps before barging past them, ignoring their shocked expressions.

'Max, stop,' Banji calls out. He races to catch up to her. 'Look, I get it, you're stressed about the guys—we all are—but don't take it out on your friends. They're just trying to cope with this mess the only way they know how. I know you think a lot of what's going to happen next rests on your shoulders, but you're not alone; we're going to deal with this together. Okay?'

Banji's words are comforting. Max glances at Jack and wishes *he* could read her mind, so he can see how much this has been eating at her. But the frown and look of disappointment she sees cuts her to the bone. Tears threaten to fall. But now's not the time for this. She shakes it off. She needs to focus on what has to be done once they reach Peanut. If only she had the power to teleport herself to him right now, she would. But healing is her thing, she reminds herself, and she wouldn't, even at this very moment, trade that for anything.

Caught up in her thoughts, Max doesn't register Banji's warning until he yanks her back behind him. Before Max has a chance to protest, he raises his hand to indicate something's wrong. Ruby is quick to activate her shield.

Banji throws on the night goggles and points ahead at something. He then lets out a shaky breath. 'It's okay; it's someone you know, Max, and she's got news on Ryker.'

Max struggles to see anything in the near darkness, but then a tiny figure appears from behind a tree. *Aelianna!* 'Ruby, take down the shield.' The barrier vanishes, and Max rushes to her. Aelianna's eyes are wide, and her appearance ashen. 'Oh my God! What's happened, are we too late?'

Aelianna grabs Max's hands and crushes them in hers. 'Medwin foresaw your arrival. I have been most anxious to see you. Max, they have Ryker. I beg you, do something to save him.' She turns to the others. 'Please, help him escape The Dark Forest, or Wulf will kill him!'

Max steps back, but Jack is there to steady her. She turns to look at him and immediately feels the effect of his calm.

'Father and Medwin believe Ryker to be alive, but we must take him from there, for these cruel games they play will most certainly destroy him.'

It's the barbaric arena challenges all over again.

'Aelianna, Peanut is hurt too,' Jack tells her. 'We're on our way to him now. Our friends Banji and Edra are taking us. But we need to go to him first—he's our best hope to save Ryker.'

Aelianna nods. 'I beg you, make haste, for there is little time. And now I must leave. If Father were to learn of me being here, there will be trouble. But before I go, I have something of Ryker's.' She runs to a tree and returns with Ryker's backpack. 'Jack, my father came across this in the forest; there may be something of use in there.'

Jack takes it from her. 'You're right, there is. Now go home and leave everything to us. Will you be okay getting back?'

She clutches the dagger at her side, nods, then disappears into the forest as quickly as she'd appeared.

To Max's relief they don't waste another moment. Banji picks up a relentless pace. No one objects, and this time no one utters a single word.

31

DOUBT

JACK

They plough through the forest in silence. Aelianna's news has Jack's mind racing with what needs to be done. Once they've got Peanut back onboard, things will need to move quickly. He hopes Peanut's injuries aren't too bad. But whatever the case, he knows Max will have him up and running in no time.

Thinking of Max reminds him of what happened just before they ran into Aelianna—Max's outburst. He saw a coolness in her eyes that scared the crap out of him. It was the same look she gave him earlier at the campsite.

What's gotten into her?

Jack gets it; she's worried about Ryker. But the looks she's been giving him lately makes him question just how important Ryker is to her. He can't help but think that Max's connection with Ryker is more than just friendship. *It's like nothing else matters but him!* Jack's not blind. He's seen the way her face lights up whenever he's around. *And Ryker's just as bad.*

Jack watches Max forge ahead, dreading to think what's going on in her head. She's dirty with him, and he knows it. She hasn't spoken a word to him since that last incident.

But now's not the time or place for a suspicious mindset. He makes an effort to focus on what needs to be done. Once Max has helped Peanut, they'll put together a plan that'll get Ryker out of the mess he's got himself into.

And what a fricking mess! A familiar anger surfaces. *The plan was to go in, find the missing gateway and get out. Simple. But no, Ryker couldn't leave it at that; he had to go one better and play the hero! What was he thinking? And now he's gone and stuffed things up for everyone!*

Jack's breathing becomes heavy, and without intending to, he begins to recall the challenges in the arena when Ryker was the enemy. He tries to shake it off, but his thoughts keep going back there, and it starts to scare him.

This mess of emotions is driving him nuts. He needs to get his head straight, and the only way he can do that is by talking to Max. The first chance he gets, he'll ask her outright where he stands in all of this. And whatever the outcome, he'll deal with it. *And then I can focus on what needs to be done, so we can get the hell out of here.*

Banji stops abruptly, turns and frowns. Jack draws back. *What's wrong with Banj?* Banji rolls his eyes, and Jack realises his thoughts have gone public. His face heats. He turns away, then silently apologises to him. Banji shakes his head, then gestures for everyone to lie low after pointing out the huge rock formation ahead.

They've reached their destination. Jack looks up at the impressive entrance to The Forbidden Passage, and his breath catches—it's as large as it is ominous. And at the end of the passage is the other portal. *Let's do this!*

Jack scans the area for guards. At this time of night he's hoping, and half expecting, not to have any encounters with them. But it's clear Banji isn't going to take any chances. He gestures for them all to be ready, searches the ground for some stones, then tosses one into the passage. Jack figures it's to see if it triggers a reaction. They wait, but nothing happens.

Banji nods. 'Okay, it's safe. Let's go.'

They move forward, but it's so dark inside that they need a torch to see where they're going. Once they've reached the end of the passage, Banji takes off the goggles and hands them around to show the others the portal. When it's Jack's turn, he gasps— the glow coming off it is enough to light up a small village.

Ruby doesn't wait, she pushes past them and steps through. Max is next, with the others following close behind.

On the other side it's not so dark. Jack trails as they run across the arid parkland towards a small thicket of bushes camouflaging an old jeep. One by one they hop in. Edra wastes no time; she starts the engine and takes off, leaving a cloud of dust behind them.

Jack's thoughts turn to Max again. He noticed she was quick to tuck herself as far away from him as possible. Ruby is by her side, their arms entwined, neither one saying a word, both staring into the distance.

Kenny nudges him, distracting him from his thoughts. 'Will you check it out, look where we are!'

Jack blinks. It suddenly dawns on him exactly where they are. It's hard to believe—one minute they're in a national park on the coast south of Sydney, the next they've entered an ancient forest in a medieval world, and now they're in the middle of a nature reserve in present day South Africa—a place full of wild animals he's only seen at the zoo or on the internet. Despite the potential dangers surrounding them, he smiles. 'It's surreal, isn't it?'

Banji, sitting beside him, beams with pride.

Jack looks across to Max to see if she's experiencing the same exhilaration, but her expression hasn't changed—her posture is rigid, gaze fixed, eyes empty. Ruby throws her arm over Max's shoulder and gives her a squeeze. Their heads gently bump, again not a word is spoken.

'She's got a lot on her plate, Jack, maybe cut her some slack.'

Banji's words are like a jab in the gut. Jack groans. *How could I've been so stupid?* It's suddenly so clear— Max has been in a world of torment, worried about their friends. The weight to heal them sits on her shoulders.

But why's she doubting herself? She's awesome! But the reality of it is, for whatever reason, she's lost confidence and is feeling fragile. He blasts himself for not seeing it earlier. He turns to look at her again. He needs to fix this, and he will.

The jeep rolls up to a gated enclosure. Banji jumps out to unlock the entry, then locks it again behind them. They pull into a firelit campsite, get out, then head to a small cabin.

Max and Ruby enter first. They find Peanut lying on a low bunk, motionless, with Ulan by his side.

Ruby rushes to him.

'He's just sleeping,' Ulan tells her. 'I've dosed him up on painkillers.'

Ruby noticeably relaxes, then brings his hand to her cheek. 'Wake up, babe. Max is here; you're going to be okay.'

32

SAYING YES

Aelianna has left her friends. She races through the woods to get back to the safety of her home before her father becomes suspicious. If he knew what she was up to he would string her alive. She knows it was a risk to come out on her own, but she couldn't do nothing. Only by chance had she overheard the conversation between her father and Medwin and learned of Medwin's prophecy about Ryker's friends returning with Max. It provided the incentive she was looking for to do something to help—her father had possession of Ryker's bag, and although its contents baffled her, she knew she needed to get it to them. How could she not do this after all Ryker had done for her family? Now, with her mission accomplished, all that was left to do was pray that Max and her friends get to Peanut quickly. The sooner they reached him, the sooner they could do something for Ryker. The thought of Ryker suffering at the hands of Wulf cuts her to the core.

She cannot fathom it. Wulf's transformation still astounds her—the circumstances of his life have turned him into a monster. From the stories her father has told her of the games he plays, Wulf is no better than the realm's Nobles—taking pleasure from the cruelty of brutal challenges.

But she can't worry about that now. It's darkening, and she needs to get back while she can still see her way. She clutches her father's dagger closer to her chest and wishes for the hundredth time that Shadow, her brother's dog, was with her for added protection.

The sound of something scurrying in the near distance makes her jump. Her hand tightens on the dagger. She listens, but all she hears are the tranquil sounds of the forest. Suddenly a chill runs down her spine—something's wrong. She senses she's not alone. Her instinct is to run, so she does. She takes off at a sprint as adrenaline courses through her veins. Her gaze darts in every direction, looking for what's out there. And then she hears it—something's after her, and it's coming fast.

It's closing in on her. The trees become a blur as she runs. A root trips her, and she stumbles, slowing her escape. A glance over her shoulder, trying to catch a glimpse of what she's up against, reveals nothing. She urges herself to keep moving and soon approaches the clearing by the river—a place with which she's familiar. At least here, she can draw out her pursuer. She might have a chance if she knows what she's facing.

Within the open space, she turns to face the hunter, her weapon raised. But her heart sinks—it's no animal; it's Wulf's thug Titus. She looks from his battle-scarred face to her dagger, psyching herself to use it. Titus is a freak of nature, huge and powerful, and by the look in his eyes, determined to get her, no matter what.

Aelianna darts back into the forest, where her small frame may have an advantage over his massive one. Titus gives chase. She needs to escape him. Her life depends upon it; whether Titus finishes her off there in the middle of the woods or takes her back to Wulf, she's done for either way.

As she ducks and weaves through the forest she scans the surrounding trees, briefly considering them as an option for escape but decides against it. Titus would be up after her in no time. She'd be trapped and up for the taking. She keeps running.

A thicket provides her with a chance to hide. Thorns and branches tear at her skin as she worms her way deep within it, but that doesn't stop her. And when she has buried herself as far as she can go, she urges herself to burrow deeper.

She then stops and slows her breathing to listen—all is quiet. Could she have lost him? Her eyes sting. This temporary refuge may have saved her. She remains motionless, curled up in a tight ball, trying hard to remain invisible from him.

After a long period of stillness, the peaceful sounds of the night lull her senses. Her eyelids grow heavy, and she fights to stay awake. To ward off sleep, she calls on happy thoughts. She thinks of Ryker and imagines a future with him—in his mysterious world. A smile twists on her lips.

But then she remembers the look in his eyes when they exchanged glances at the feast. It seemed he had not forgiven her for refusing him. Her smile vanishes. Her chance has passed. But at the time, how could she have gone with him? Her duty to her family was too deeply ingrained—leaving then was never an option. But it was the hardest decision she had to make ... and now, one that she'll forever regret.

She wipes away a runaway tear and steels herself to the problem at hand. If she makes it through the night, then all is not lost. With Ryker's friends here to save him, she may get another chance to escape the dangers of this place. And this time, if he happens to ask again, she won't hesitate in saying yes.

With that thought warming her from the chill of the night, Aelianna finally gives in to sleep.

༄

The sound of the forest animals waking tickles Aelianna's consciousness. She opens one eye, reluctant to wake, but the reality of where she is and how she got there jerks her from her dream-like state. She tightens her grip on the dagger.

She listens for anything out of the ordinary, but all is as it should be—birds peeping, lizards scurrying, and frogs croaking in the distance. She grins. *I made it!*

Slowly and carefully, she disentangles her cramped-up self and crawls out from her hiding place. It surprises her how far into the thicket's web she managed to burrow. It takes her a good while to reach a point where she can finally stand. And when she does, she takes a moment to stretch the tightness from her stiff limbs.

A force from above suddenly slams Aelianna to the ground. Her weapon flies from her grasp.

'Got you, wench!' Titus pins her beneath his weight, leaving her no room to breathe, let alone move.

Aelianna struggles to throw him off, but Titus seizes her by the hair and yanks her up. Aelianna cries out in pain, tears stinging her eyes. Desperate to escape, she tries to kick and claw at him, but he's too far out of reach.

He laughs at her attempts. 'So you thought you could evade me, my spirited imp?' He leans in closer. His amber eyes darken; his breathing deepens. 'And I can see you have been worth the wait.'

Aelianna yanks against his hold, leaving only a clump of her hair in his clenched fist, then dives for her dagger, now in reach. She grabs it, turns and slashes at him, drawing blood with every strike. Titus stumbles back. She runs, but doesn't get far before the brute tackles her to the ground and within seconds has her pinned under his weight, again weaponless. She thrashes about to free herself. He only laughs, his nauseating breath turning her stomach.

And then the load lifts, and Titus jerks her to her feet. 'Wulf will be eager to hear of our chance meet, Aelianna. Your return will please him, I am sure— for I am certain he has designs for you.' He takes a moment to regard the bloody wounds her blade has made. 'And I am keen to see *exactly* what those designs are.'

Aelianna lashes out with feet and fists, fighting to get away, but Titus has a firm grip on her. She screams, but his filthy hand over her mouth stifles her efforts.

No one hears her. No one can help her now. She's doomed.

33

ᴛRANSFIGURATION

PEANUT

After a restful sleep, Peanut feels fantastic. Max the super-medico has once again woven her magic. Of course, for Max to do this, they needed to revisit the realm briefly—her diagnosis was a punctured lung from a splintered rib. She said he was lucky it wasn't worse. What that meant, he has no idea, but by the look she gave Jack, he imagines it was pretty bad. He remembers Jack's incident with Vyvian's arrow—Max said he could've died from that injury.

And now he's fighting fit.

The eight friends are back together, safe within the gated campsite in South Africa, ready to come up with a cohesive plan to get Ryker back safely. The heat of the morning is stifling, and the already crowded small cabin suddenly seems smaller still. Peanut grabs Ryker's backpack—the one Aelianna gave them yesterday—and takes it outside to rummage through it. The others follow.

Before leaving for this adventure, Ryker had packed his kit with some pretty nifty military gadgets. And from what Peanut remembers, a lot of it's comparable to the gear Ryker's dad had passed onto his son that day he blew up the fortress wall. Peanut grins.

He lets out a long whistle as he picks through the assortment. How Ryker got all of this through customs is beyond him—not that he's complaining. There's enough in there to keep him amused for a very long time. 'Man, I reckon with all the gear in here, we should just go in and blast the lot of them to smithereens.'

Ruby looks at him with her brow raised. 'Don't get too excited, *007!* Do you even know what to do with the stuff in there?' Her hand shoots out to stop him. 'And before you answer, just remember, your track record kinda speaks for itself.'

Peanut glares at her.

She giggles. *'Can't be that hard, just load and shoot. Right?'*

They all laugh, having heard the story of the flare.

Peanut groans. 'Give it a rest, will ya?'

'I would've paid to see that.' Kenny chuckles with the rest of them, then sobers. 'Okay, guys, we need to knuckle down and work out what to do here. Any thoughts?'

Eager to give directions, Jack says, 'We'll put together a team, arm ourselves with some of Ryker's gadgets and sus this place out.' He paces back and forth in thought. 'I reckon it's a given that Ruby goes, Peanut too. And I'm willing to give it a crack.' He looks at the others. 'Anyone else?'

Kenny clears his throat. 'Um … I can see where you're going with that, Jack, but sorry, I don't agree. I think our best bet is to send Peanut on his own.' He turns to Peanut. 'But only if you're okay with that. Peanut's got one up on all of us. One, he's got a fair idea where this Dark Forest is, and two, his invisibility is crucial—we can't afford to draw attention to ourselves. If they know we're there, they'll tighten up security, and we definitely don't want that.' He turns to Jack. 'You can see that, right?'

Peanut is only too happy that Kenny's pulling rank on this one. Jack's mind has been elsewhere lately—*distracted by Max, no doubt*—so any decision-making by him could be a gamble, and Peanut's not prepared to take any chances.

He looks from Jack to Max, and frowns. He's not sure what's going on there, but it's clear the power-duo have lost their *mojo*.

Jack draws back. Peanut can see he's taken offence. He nudges him. 'Hey, Kenny's right, you know; it's better I go alone.' He turns to the others. 'And yeah, I'm okay with that.'

He then begins to fill his pockets with some of the gear from Ryker's kit, but Kenny is quick to stop him. 'Hold your horses, Peanut. Like Ruby said, your past performance hasn't exactly been that crash hot, buddy. So how about we do a little research first? Whatever we can't figure out between us, we'll google. There's no point you going back and not having the foggiest idea on how to use these things. Agreed?'

Peanut steps back, crosses his arms and pouts.

Kenny clicks his tongue. 'Always in a hurry.' He turns to the others. 'And before we do anything, I'd like to hear what everyone else thinks.'

Ulan has been quiet. She looks at Banji sideways—clearly the siblings are at loggerheads over something. She turns to her friends, her hands deep in her jeans' pockets. 'Look, I think you're right, Kenny, sending Peanut on his own is the way to go, but as far as I'm concerned, as much as I want to be part of this for Ryker's sake, I'm bowing out—I can't do this anymore.' She sighs and glances at her brother. 'And Banj, you need to promise me you'll back out of it too. You know it nearly killed Mum and Dad when we went missing the first time. I don't want to risk that happening again.' She looks at her friends. 'Guys, I thought I could cope with all of this, but I can't. Yesterday when Banj went back in, I couldn't handle it. I was a wreck the whole time he was gone.' Her big green eyes fill with tears. 'It was supposed to be a simple in-out assignment. I was okay with that, but now it's way out of control.' She crosses her arms. 'I'm okay to stay here for backup, but that's as far as it goes.' She gives her brother another sideways glance.

Banji tugs at his curls, then twirls a dark strand between his fingers. He lets out a breath, then pulls Ulan into a hug. 'Sorry, guys, from now on you're on your own.'

'At this stage, I guess we're all staying put,' Jack says. 'Kenny's right, we need to keep a low profile. Peanut is our best bet. But if we have to go back, count me in.'

Max's hand shoots up. 'Me too. Whatever it takes.'

'Me three,' Kenny says. 'I've come this far.'

Edra hesitates. Her gaze swings back and forth between the twins. She chews her lower lip for a moment, then groans. 'Okay, count me in too. But I mean it, Ryker's going to cop it from me the first chance I get. The bloody idiot! What was he thinking?'

Peanut chuckles. 'Hey, settle down, tiger. We're taking a vote on the plan, not asking you to donate a kidney.'

Edra's lip curls. She nudges Peanut, nearly knocking him to the ground, and laughs. 'Hey, it's your life.'

And so the decision is made. Together they formulate a strategy for Peanut to enter the realm. Kenny takes the lead, and with some help from the internet, they go over the gear in Ryker's kit, discovering what they are and how each one works. Kenny then adds a couple of interesting items of his own to the mix.

Peanut's face screws up as he holds up a small, brown-glass bottle labelled with a scientific name. His jaw drops after hearing what it is. 'Whoa, where the hell did you get that?'

Kenny smirks. 'Don't ask. The less you know, the better.' He slaps Peanut on the back and laughs.

Kenny's other item, his nunchaku, has Peanut itching to have a go. 'Wicked! I've seen these in action on the telly!' He steps aside to play with the martial arts weapon, flinging the chained wooden sticks back and forth, pretending to be a karate expert. Suddenly the momentum of his actions gets away from him; he loses control and whacks himself on the back of his head with it. Peanut blinks a few times, rubs at the spot, then is quick to put the nunchaku back. 'Oi, I hope you've got a permit for that thing.'

They all laugh. Jack applauds. 'That's gold! Who needs a forest full of guards? He'll knock himself out before anyone else gets a chance to.' He turns to the others. 'So are we sure about sending him in on his own?'

Peanut rolls his eyes. '*Jack*ass!'

And to add insult to injury, Kenny picks up the nunchaku and, with the confidence of a pro, shows them how it's done.

Max blinks several times. 'Kenny! Wow!'

Kenny smiles a crooked smile and shrugs. 'Nothing to it.'

Peanut looks at him sideways and nods with appreciation. 'Nice! With moves like that, maybe you should go in instead of me.' He scowls at Jack.

Kenny chuckles. 'Take no notice of Jack. You'll still kill it.' He pauses as a thought comes to him. 'Hey, listen, after watching Ruby transform her shield, I was thinking maybe you can do something with your superpower too. Do you want to try?'

Ruby claps her hands. 'Ooh, wouldn't that be cool? Give it a go, Peanut.'

Ruby's excitement spurs him on.

'Hey, wait a minute. Where was I when this happened?' Ulan asks.

'You should've seen her, Lanny,' Edra begins to explain. 'We'd just entered the realm; the guards were on us in seconds, and Ruby transfigured her shield into a huge fist. Boy, did those guards cop it! I nearly felt sorry for them. She was so amazing!'

'She wasn't *amazing*, Edra, she was *hot!* Banji rests his hand over his heart. 'I fell in love, right there and then.'

Peanut's head snaps around to look at him, his expression murderous.

Banji laughs and holds up his hands. 'Geez, if looks could kill …'

Peanut ignores Banji's taunting to focus on Kenny's idea, but his mind has drawn a blank. He shrugs. 'I've got nothin'. How are ya s'possed ta improve on *awesome*?'

Edra snorts. 'Someone's sure got tickets on themselves.'

Ruby groans. 'Welcome to *my* world!'

Peanut ignores them. 'So, Kenny, got any bright ideas?'

After much discussion and a few questionable suggestions, they decide to re-enter the realm to help Peanut reinvent himself. A small team is put together: Ruby to watch their backs, Jack for moral support and, of course, the genius of the group, Kenny, to bring inspiration.

Edra drives the four friends out of the compound and into the savannah of the national park. Within minutes, they've crossed the gossamer threshold. When they stumble through to the other side, the passage is shrouded in darkness, and Ruby is quick to activate her shield. They stop to listen for guards. The sound of daybreak filters into the passage; birds twitter high in the trees; all appears quiet.

Peanut gestures for Ruby to let down her shield so he can investigate. He vanishes. At this time of the day, he's half expecting to come across some security, but as it turns out, there's nothing. He races back to tell his friends, and on his way, he picks up some stones and stores them in his rolled-up T-shirt—they might come in handy later.

'Okay, the coast is clear.' He reappears before them and drops the stones to the ground.

Kenny studies the rocks for a moment, then his face light up. 'That gives me an idea.' He blinks a few times. 'Wow, I can't believe I didn't think of it earlier. Peanut, why do you reckon your clothes become invisible when you do?'

Peanut shrugs.

Kenny's eyes are wide. 'It's because you transfer your invisibility!'

Peanut frowns. 'O-kay …'

'Don't you get it?' Kenny laughs excitedly. 'I'll bet you ten bucks you can make other stuff vanish too.'

Peanut stops to consider this for a moment. He

knows he can make things disappear by tucking them under his clothes—like the time he took Ryker's backpack to him when he was holed up in the cell—but he's never considered transferring his invisibility to anything any other way. He bends to pick up one of the stones, places it in the flat of his hand, then vanishes. 'You guys can still see the rock, right?'

'Yeah, you're gone, but the rock is floating in mid-air,' Jack says.

The stone suddenly vanishes.

Ruby shrugs. Okay, you've stuck it under your T-shirt.'

'But I haven't,' Peanut tells them. 'It's still in my hand. I've transferred my power to it.'

Ruby whoops. Kenny and Jack grin and high-five each other.

Peanut pulls Ruby into an embrace. She yelps in surprise. He closes his eyes and magics her invisible.

Jack's jaw drops. 'What the hell?'

'She's gone!' Kenny says. 'Peanut, you're fricking amazing!'

They reappear. Ruby's eyes are wide, her grin infectious. Peanut laughs. 'No, Kenny, you are!'

34

SPECIAL OPS

PEANUT

Peanut's heart races with nervous anticipation—with a new plan set in place, he's ready and raring to go save Ryker. He waves goodbye to the team, throws his backpack over his shoulders, dives back into the realm and disappears. He shouldn't be this excited about what he's about to do, but he is. He's got enough stuff in the backpack and stored in his cargo-pants' pockets to get up to no good. He smiles as he envisages what he's about to do. But Kenny's words replay in his head: *Keep a low profile. Don't use any of this stuff unless you need to. Okay? Your job is to find out what you can and report back. That's all. So no mucking around. Stay focused!*

At the mouth of the passage, he spots three guards standing at a distance looking cagey, clearly hesitant to carry out the portal inspection. Peanut's eyes sparkle with mischief. He picks up a few stones ready to cause havoc but stops—*Keep a low profile!* He frowns, rethinks his actions and tosses the stones deep into the woods. While the guards' attention is diverted, he tip-toes past them to begin the task of locating The Dark Forest. He follows the path he and Ruby made the day before, finds the animal trap Ruby fell into and then locates the spot where he had the run-in with Wulf. From there, he adheres to Kenny's advice to follow the path Wulf and his henchmen would've created from dragging Ryker's unconscious body to their camp.

Peanut picks up the pace. So far, so good. Everything Kenny had anticipated would happen was panning out—the drag marks, the disturbed vegetation and the trail of blood. They all spur him on to complete his mission, but from the amount of blood he finds, he can only hope Ryker is still alive by the time he gets to him.

He pushes on, aware of the need to hurry. Through dense woodland, over rocks and shallow hollows, he eventually reaches the outskirts of the camp.

The sun is high, and all is quiet. Peanut takes a moment to take in what he's seeing: the villagers, strewn haphazardly around a smoking campfire, are yet to stir from their drunken slumber. Peanut scans the area before moving in closer to take a better look. The camp, tucked in the shadows of a few tall trees, is littered with several crudely assembled shacks that border a huge sunken area to one side. Peanut wonders what that's all about, and then a thought comes to him that instantly fills him with dread. *Is this the arena Wulf was talking about?*

He inches closer, approaching the sleeping horde, careful not to bring attention to himself. When he peers over the edge of the sunken cavity, he stiffens. What he sees is a bare, tall-walled arena with a crude ladder dangling down in one corner. By the looks of it, the space appears to have had a lot of action, and unlike the rest of the camp, it seems to be well kept. He thinks of Ryker and groans. *The poor guy's doomed!*

A huge flat stone in the centre of the arena catches his attention, and he goes to investigate. He uses the ladder to climb down to the arena floor, then makes his way to the stone. He pushes against it, but it doesn't budge. He can't imagine what it's used for. He shrugs and continues to look around. Another large stone sits hard up against the arena's wall. He goes to inspect it and puts his whole weight behind it, trying to move it, but it's too heavy for him to move.

And then a distant growl, scuffle and a yelp, diverts his attention. His eyes narrow—*Wulf's mongrels!*

Peanut runs to the ladder, climbs up and scans the area but doesn't see them. He can only hope they've taken their disputes elsewhere. Now's his chance to snoop a little further. He goes about the camp, sidestepping the fatalities of what looks like a bloodless battlefield. It's a symphony of snoring. He almost laughs at the sight of them, scattered randomly, hugging close to their chests, deflated pouches made of animal skins. Peanut imagines those sacs were earlier bulbous, filled with some kind of alcohol.

The sound of something moving in one of the shanties grabs his attention. The door is barred shut—*strange*—so he inches closer to investigate. A muffled grunt and then a moan come from inside. Someone's struggling. A small hole in the reed-thatched wall allows him to peer in. It takes a moment for his eyes to adjust to the darkness, and when they do, he pulls back, shaken.

But then a low, guttural sound at his back makes his blood freeze and his hair stand on end—it's one of Wulf's beasts. Even in his invisible state, Peanut doesn't dare take any chances. The dog may not be able to see him, but obviously it can sense his presence. Ever so slowly he turns. His heart just about stops—he's face to face with the monstrous beast. Peanut can't remember it being so big. It's nothing like anything in the real world, and seeing it this close, Peanut has to battle to keep it together—his basic instinct is to run. He squeezes his eyes tight and clenches his teeth to stop them from chattering.

How he's going to evade Wulf's brute of a dog *and* save Aelianna, he has no idea.

35

ᏢHEART SONG

AELIANNA

Aelianna struggles with the restraints, trying to work herself free. Since her capture earlier that morning, Wulf has had her imprisoned in one of his flea-bitten huts, tied to a large tree stump. How she's going to escape, she hasn't quite worked out, but while Wulf sleeps, she needs to at least try. If only she could break the binds. The rope snaked around her wrists bites into her skin, drawing blood, but this doesn't lessen her efforts.

She hears a growl at the door, and stops—one of Wulf's dogs has stirred. She prays that the commotion hasn't aroused its master. But its incessant growling soon attracts its companions, and between the three of them, it eventually does—Wulf cusses in the distance. The dogs whimper and scurry off but are quick to return. Something outside her door has their attention.

Their persistent fretting goads Wulf to investigate. He curses again, then staggers towards her hut. 'I will string you from the trees by your tongues! How is anyone to sleep with your infernal ruckus?' A dog yelps before fleeing. Sounds of the other two taking off follow.

Wulf checks the door. Aelianna throws herself to the floor, shuts her eyes and pretends to sleep. She hears him yawn, scratch at an itch, then stumble to the other side of the shanty to relieve himself. Moments later he's at the door again, fumbling with the bolt. The door opens, and the small room fills with sudden brightness.

'Get up!' He clutches his head and moans, instantly regretting his outcry. 'How you can continue to sleep with that damnable fuss at your door is beyond me.'

Aelianna shields her eyes to look at him. His dishevelled appearance and pallid colour makes her smile inwardly. She's seen the effect of over-indulgence before and has no pity. *Let him rot in Hades, for he is a beast and I loathe him!*

Earlier that morning following her capture, Wulf, in his drunken stupor, had boasted of his dominance over the little village and the games he plays. If he was hoping to impress her, he was sorely mistaken. All he achieved was to strengthen her hate for him.

How she ever thought him agreeable is beyond her. His self-righteousness and contempt for others shattered that image long ago, but hearing his barbaric plans for Ryker only deepened her revulsion. As he revealed his plot to destroy him, he had watched closely for her reaction, and this, she realised too late, was all he needed to validate his suspicion as to where her loyalty lies.

'I have a question for you,' he had said with a sinister look in his eye. 'That day I found you alone in the woods, who was it that begot a song to your lips and joy in your heart? Answer me honestly and I will spare you; lie and I will pour a vat of bubbling fat down the pit.'

Her guard had been down, and she'd gasped.

Wulf twitched with triumph. 'I fear your countenance has spoken for you, my dear.' But then, unexpectedly, his smile vanished and his eyes softened. 'It would seem your song and heart belong to another. Tell me once and for all, Aelianna, is there no hope for us?'

She'd just about spluttered; how could he even think it? Her head whipped around, eyes turned to slits. 'Never!' she'd hissed. 'Your kindness to me in the past is as lost to me as you are.'

His eyes darkened, a menacing growl resonated

from deep within, then he turned and stormed away, vowing that she would regret her words.

That was this morning. Now, Wulf stands before her, eyeing the blood seeping from her wrists. His lip curls. 'Are you planning on taking your leave, my love? Are you not to stay for this evening's entertainment? I assure you, the pit will provide an interesting distraction to while away the time.' His smile widens. 'Perhaps your *friend* may prove to be most amusing.'

Aelianna curses.

His grin vanishes, replaced by a scowl. 'You can forget any fanciful thoughts you may have, Aelianna! Make no mistake—he will never have you. With or without your consent, you *will* be mine!'

Bile rises to her mouth, the acid burning her throat. She spits at his feet. 'I would rather die!'

Wulf's nostrils flare; his lips press into a thin line. He leans in to her. 'Then so be it!'

She flinches. The venom in his eyes is palpable, and his malevolent glare penetrates to her soul. Never has she seen such hostility. She swallows hard. He leaves no doubt as to his intentions. Her fate is sealed.

A growl resonates from deep within his chest, and his dogs appear at once, ready to pounce at his command.

This is it. Her end has come. Her eyes close. If

these are to be her final moments, she wants to die happy. She thinks of Ryker and smiles. There can be no mistaking it, the tenderness she often saw in his eyes was love. If only she had said *yes* when she'd had the chance. She imagines the life they would've had in his faraway world, and the happiness they could've shared.

It's too much. Her heart is close to exploding from joy. And then it does. Her voice rises to the surface in a melody so pure it pierces Wulf to the core and has him falling to his knees.

Stunned at the power of her song, Aelianna blinks a few times, growing giddy with the knowledge of what she can do. She turns her attention to the dogs, but although disorientated by their master's submission, they remain unaffected, continuing to snap and growl at her. But then a disturbance from outside the hut distracts them. She watches on in disbelief as they turn tail and take chase.

With the singing stopped, the spell is broken and Wulf regains his senses. He staggers to his feet, exits the hut, slams the door and secures the bolt.

Aelianna stares ahead. How she managed to evade her seemingly inevitable demise is beyond her grasp at the moment. The only thing that's clear is that it's a miracle she's still alive.

36

RUN!

PEANUT

Peanut struggles to escape the spell of Aelianna's bewitching voice. With some major mental effort—focusing on reminding himself that it's just his friend singing—he manages it, and he immediately sees that her singing has no effect on Wulf's dogs. He needs to do something while they're disorientated by Wulf's dazed state. He looks around, finds some stones, then hurls them at them.

HOLY CRAP!!

Peanut runs for his life. His plan to distract the dogs worked, but now the beasts are hot on his heels. They may not be able to *see* him, but they can definitely *sense* him.

While he sprints to escape their snapping jaws, he searches for a tree bough low enough to save himself.

When he sees one, he leaps for it and hoists himself to safety, leaving the dogs in a mess of confusion below. Moments later a howl from their master sends them scurrying back to the camp.

With the threat gone and some time to think, Peanut tries to work out what he needs to do next. Somehow, he's got to get Aelianna out of there. Although safe from Wulf at the moment, she won't be for long. She made it clear she doesn't want anything to do with him, and the rejection cut deep. Wulf will want his revenge, and he'll get it—twofold.

What a bloody mess! First Ryker, and now Aelianna!

He takes a deep breath. At least he knows where Aelianna is, but where's Ryker? Where would Wulf keep him? He recalls Wulf talking about a pit. *But where the hell is this pit?* Could that large flat stone on the floor of the arena be a seal to a pit? *Yes! And in that pit is Ryker!*

The situation is fast getting out of control. Sweat drips from his brow, and his chest tightens. He can't do this on his own. He needs backup. But as he climbs down the tree to get it, movement from the bushes below changes everything.

37

WHAT HELL IS THIS?

RYKER

Ryker stirs, roused to consciousness. A pain like no other renders him helpless. He grabs his head and bites down hard on his lip. The slightest twitch feels like his skull's about to explode. He slows his breathing, then loosens his hold; his fingers come away wet. He traces the moisture down his face to his neck and finds his T-shirt drenched with the same tacky fluid.

It's pitch black. He can't see a thing, not even his hand in front of his face. Alarmed, he checks his eyes—although swollen, he should be able to see something, but he can't. *I'm blind!* His breathing accelerates. The smell of damp soil invades his senses. And then there's another smell, the stench of stale urine. *Where the hell am I?* Ryker tries to lift his head, but his gut twists into a knot from the pain. He can't take any more of this. He brings up the contents of his stomach, then blacks out.

♋

The cold from the ground beneath seeps deep into his bones. Ryker wakes shivering. The throbbing in his head intensifies with every movement. He blinks a few times. He still can't see. A foul stench surrounds him—vomit. He swipes the muck from his face.

How long have I been here? And how the hell am I going to get out of here?

Ryker struggles to get to his knees and feels a metal grid beneath him. He traces the bars and realises that they're not only under him but also above and to every side of him. He shakes the bars—trapped, like a caged animal.

The sound of his heartbeat throbs in his ears, but something moving nearby doesn't escape him. 'Who's there?'

No answer.

Ryker holds his breath to listen. Something or someone is lurking in the darkness. 'I know you're there. What do you want?' He hears it shift again. It's on the move, the sound receding. 'Please, you've got to help me. Come back!'

And then it's gone.

Unable to move, Ryker listens to the emptiness that surrounds him. Strangely, being confined within this restricted space comforts him; nothing can get at him. He's safe—for now. The silence lulls him. His eyelids grow heavy, and once again, he gives in to sleep.

❧

Ryker wakes to the sound of an animal panting above him. He jerks upright, hitting his head against the roof of the cage and stifles a cry. It's a dog, but it doesn't sound aggressive, unlike Wulf's giant mutts, just curious. Ryker remains still, listening to it sniff around him. Its humid, nauseating breath invades Ryker's confined space, bile rises from his stomach and burns his throat. After a few seconds, he hears the dog withdraw, and once again he's alone.

After what feels like hours of deathly silence, a sound, deafening to his sensitive ears, alerts him that, one way or another, he's about to face what's in store for him. High above him, something moves, grinding and screeching like stone on stone. A sliver of daylight enters the black hole. The sudden brightness blinds him, and he shields his eyes, tears streaming down his cheeks from the intensity of the light. Inch by inch, the heavy closure is dragged aside, revealing the magnitude of his confinement. He's alone at the bottom of a deep pit, possibly ten-to-fifteen metres deep and measuring roughly two metres square. A small low opening comes off it at ground level to his right.

All of a sudden, the surface beneath begins to fall from under him—*or is the cage elevating?* He realises it's the latter. Adrenaline pumps hard through his veins. The enclosure he's trapped in seesaws precariously in mid-air on a squeaky pulley, inching towards the opening above.

The sound of cheers and festivities bathe the pit as he rises higher. Ryker's unease accelerates. He looks down at his blood-drenched, mutilated body for the first time. In the dark, he could only imagine what the thugs and dogs had done to him, but now in the light of day, he can see the carnage.

He's got no idea what to expect, but whatever's about to happen, no matter how he looks at it, it can't end well.

The cage emerges from the ground, and the cheering escalates. Howls of approval flood his ears. Ryker examines the area around him—an arena of some sort. He groans. Seated around the large crater-like hole are dozens of loud, drunken people— the people of The Dark Forest. The cage is lifted high above ground level, then yanked to one side, suspended for all to see.

Movement at the mouth of the hole from which he came catches his attention. A rope, one end tied to a metal stake at the opening, dangles into the pit. And from the hollow emerges a man—a tall, gaunt, longhaired, threadbare man. He hauls himself up and out of the pit with an intensity that belies his battered, undernourished body.

The crowd cheers.

Above the excitement, Ryker hears enthusiastic barking. He scans the crowd, spots the beasts, then locks eyes with Wulf. And by his side, as expected, are his trusty henchmen. By the expression on their faces, Ryker's in trouble.

And then movement from behind Wulf grabs Ryker's attention. His stomach drops. *Aelianna!* Like a madman, Ryker struggles against the bars of the enclosure to free himself.

The crowd hoots and whistles, appreciating the spectacle.

Wulf stands and raises his hands to silence the crowd. He prepares to speak, but his excited mutts engage in a tussle. Wulf glares at them, and they cower and whimper to his unspoken command.

He turns once again to address the crowd. 'I had promised to entertain you, had I not? And as you can see, I have kept my word.'

The crowd applauds.

During the excitement, Aelianna relays to Ryker by way of gesture that she's unharmed. But the ties binding her wrists tell him she's not there willingly. And just as he's about to react to seeing this, her eyes widen, warning him to keep calm. He clenches his jaw and diverts his gaze—it takes every bit of his self-control to do it.

Oblivious to the exchange, Wulf continues. 'The swine caged before you,' he tells his people, 'has become the bane of my existence. His friends murdered my father, and he, himself, took from me my rightful place within the fortress alongside the glorified Invincibles.'

The crowd boo and hiss.

Wulf puffs out his chest and rests his hands on his hips. 'Let us trial him and bear witness to his *legendary* strength. We shall decide for ourselves his worth. Our very own Lazarus should prove to be a most adept opponent. What say ye?'

The crowd chants, 'Lazarus, Lazarus! Lazarus!'

'Release the cage!'

Wulf's command comes without warning, and Ryker is suddenly dropping. Everything becomes a blur as the cage rushes towards the ground. He braces himself, grabbing at the bars. The rusted pulley squeals under the strain of the rope slipping through, and then the cage crashes with a thud. Winded, Ryker struggles to catch his breath and chokes on the dust kicked up by the cage's landing. But if he's to somehow save Aelianna, he needs to make a move. He kicks at the cage, and after several attempts, frees himself. He gets to his feet and prepares for the assault. A cloud of dust obscures his vision, and he swipes at his eyes, trying to clear them.

Ryker hears his aggressor before he sees him. He turns in preparation and throws his arm out at the precise moment to knock Lazarus onto his back. The smaller man clutches at his throat, gasping for air and spluttering.

The crowd cheers, then chants, 'More, more, more …'

The dust settles. Lazarus gets to his feet. Ryker, now with a clear view of his opponent, notes that he stands a whole head taller than Lazarus and almost four times his size, but that doesn't seem to intimidate the smaller man. Lazarus lunges at Ryker, grabbing him by his shirtsleeves in an attempt to throw him, but Ryker, far too big for his efforts to make an impact, tosses him aside like a rag doll.

Lazarus picks himself up and, nostrils flared, prepares to go again, his resolve unwavering. He lets out a tremendous roar before charging. Ryker positions himself side-on, and, fist clenched, swings his arm in an uppercut that connects with his attacker's chin. Lazarus falls and whacks the back of his head on the solid ground with a thud.

He doesn't get up.

The crowd cheers.

Ryker staggers back. But he can't stop now. He needs to get to Aelianna and somehow take her from here. Searching for a way to escape, he scans the pit's high walls, but they're too tall to scale. He does, however, spot a makeshift rope ladder dangling into the arena, no more than a few metres away. He makes a run for it.

The crowd screams and scatters.

Ryker's at the ladder in no time, but in his rush to escape, he fumbles with the rungs. Once his hands find their grip, he clambers to the top, then freezes. Three pairs of familiar amber eyes stare down at him, bared fangs as long and sharp as kitchen knives, dripping with saliva are ready to devour him—his escape, blocked.

Ryker retreats, his eyes locked on theirs, careful not to provoke them. He waits, but surprisingly, they hold back from attacking, just remaining on guard.

A slow, solitary applause from above explains why. Wulf appears above him with a sneer fixed on his face, in total control. 'It would appear that you have run out of options, *my friend.*' He laughs. 'Yes, I agree, retreat would be your best option.'

Ryker has never hated anyone as much. If only he could get to him, he would rip Wulf to shreds, and that smile would be the first thing to go.

Wulf clicks his tongue. 'But why the rush to leave us? You are a *glorified Invincible*, are you not? And as a *champion*, is it not your duty to entertain?' Wulf's eyes narrow. 'But be warned, I have only just begun. I have vowed to amuse my people, so amuse them I shall.'

He turns to leave, but then stops. 'Oh, but where are my manners? I seem to have forgotten to introduce you to my betrothed.' He turns to the crowd and calls out. 'Aelianna, come to me, I have someone I wish for you to meet.'

One of Wulf's goons shoves Aelianna forward. She stumbles and falls to her knees. Ryker tries not to react. Wulf eyes him closely, then frowns as if deep in thought. 'But perhaps you are already well acquainted.' He raises his brow, and waits.

The response he was looking for, he doesn't get. Both Ryker and Aelianna remain impassive.

'Aelianna will soon be my bride, and I wish to impress her, as she has impressed me. For you see I challenged her with a riddle earlier today—one that has so often perplexed me—and would you credit it, my beloved was able to decipher it. Do you wish to know the riddle?'

Ryker keeps his face averted.

'Huh,' he scoffs, 'it would appear you have little interest in the matter. But I will tell you nonetheless, for I feel you may find it amusing. The riddle posed was this: What enchantment awakens such a happiness within to make one's heart sing?'

Ryker chances a look at Aelianna. Her face is lowered, eyes shut; a single tear escapes.

'You can imagine my surprise at my beloved knowing such things! And I am certain you would agree,' Wulf continues, 'such wisdom deserves rewarding, does it not?' He laughs. 'Come, you must be curious to know her response?'

'*I* am! Tell us her answer,' someone from the crowd cries out.

The crowd laughs.

Ryker remains silent.

Wulf sighs. 'Your indifference surprises me. But I shall reveal it, if only to indulge my audience. So it would appear that *you* have the power to enchant and make one's heart sing.' He leans in closer to study him, then turns away, repulsed. 'How this is possible is beyond me. But who am I to judge?'

The crowd laughs.

'Her wisdom is most inspiring, is it not?' Wulf

continues, enthused by the gathering. 'So in exchange for such a talent, I have fixed another challenge for you.'

The crowd claps and whistles, excited to learn of the new task. Wulf raises his hands to silence them. 'But I am afraid you will need to wait for the morrow, my friends, for I fear the day is nearing its end, and my thirst needs quenching. What say you? Is it time to feast?'

The people of The Dark Forest break out in boisterous agreement, then scatter to begin the festivities.

Wulf laughs as he turns to leave. 'You have entertained us sufficiently, *heartsong*. Now be a good captive and go back into the hole where you belong. Savage, Menace, Blade. Attack!'

The command comes without warning. Ryker makes a run for his only means of escape—the pit. He snatches the rope dangling into the shaft and dives in time to avoid the snapping jaws of the beasts above. His battered body is flung against the wall as he struggles to hold on.

The sound of the stone moving above to seal the pit has Ryker scrambling to get to safer ground before everything goes black. The light down the shaft starts to fade, and with the last sliver of daylight his feet make contact.

And then the rope, released from the top, falls to his feet, ending all hope of any means of escape.

Total darkness engulfs Ryker once again, but this time, he has no cage to protect him. His pulse races, and his senses come alive as he braces himself for whatever's down there with him. He knows he's not alone.

He finds the wall and runs his hands along it, feeling for the small, low opening he'd glimpsed earlier. Where does it lead to and what's concealed on the other side? Eventually, he finds it and crouches down on his hands and knees to crawl through. It's a tight fit, but he manages to squeeze through the narrow tunnel into another space. He gets to his feet and feels his way around it.

'GRRR!'

He freezes on the spot. That growl is hostile.

'Don't come any closer if you know what's good for ya!' a voice threatens.

Ryker jumps back, fists clenched, raised and ready to fight.

'Put down your hands, moron. You won't be able to takes us all on.' The voice laughs. 'Will ya get a load of that; he thinks he's Kostya Tszyu!'

From out of the darkness, a dog yips, as though laughing at him—this momentarily stumps him. But then he realises something more pivotal. 'Hey, you can see me?'

'Yeah, we can see ya, fathead. And man, ya sure as hell look like a dog's breakfast. Doesn't he, Connor?' The voice laughs, and again Ryker hears a yip as if in response.

'How many of you are down here?' Ryker asks.

The stranger scoffs. 'Ya reckon we're gonna tell ya that? Well, it's for us to know and for you to find out, *mate*. It's every man for himself down here.'

Ryker suddenly realises something else. 'Hey, you're Aussie!'

'Yeah, what of it?'

Ryker's excitement escalates. 'My best friends are Aussies; they helped me escape the realm last year.'

The voice barks out a laugh so hard he almost chokes. 'Escaped, did ya? Well, I've got news for you, Sunshine, you didn't escape anything. You're still here!'

The stranger hollers with laughter, and the dog howls, then yips several times.

'Yeah, I reckon, Connor, he's a few sandwiches short of a picnic, all right. Must be 'cause of those blows to his noggin. Man, I've never seen such an ugly mug.'

Ryker realises how ridiculous his statement must've sounded, but somehow, he needs to win them over and form an alliance with them. 'Look, I came back because I needed to save my mother. She's dying of cancer.'

The dog yips a few times again.

'Yep, like you said, Connor, a screw loose for sure. So how's that working for ya, Quasimodo?'

Ryker tries again. 'I know it sounds insane, and you can choose not to believe me, but I reckon we can help each other here. I've got friends in the forest, Molan and Medwin. They're good people. They've helped me before, and I'm sure they'll help you too. Hey, you might even know them.' At that, the dog growls. Ryker takes a step back.

'Yeah, you're right, Connor, we don't *know* anyone, and more to the point we don't *trust* anyone!' the voice snaps. 'We've been stuck in this hell-hole for years. The only reason we're still alive is 'cause we keep them entertained—we fight; they feed us; we live.'

'*Years!*' Ryker is horrified. 'How many?'

'How many?' The voice from the dark laughs. '*How many?*' he repeats, sounding hysterical. 'Will ya get a load of that, Connor, he wants to know how long we've been stuck down here. Hang on a sec, let me just check my calendar. Oh, that's right. Too bloody many, ya idiot! What a fricking stupid question!'

Ryker bites back from reacting. 'My point being, we can help each other here.'

Silence.

Ryker's ears ring—he hears nothing but that. This could turn pear-shaped really quickly. Either he's formed an alliance with this guy, or he's just dug himself into an early grave. He waits.

A whimper from the dog gives him hope.

38

$CHCl_3$

PEANUT

Peanut remains hidden in the outskirts of the arena watching the challenge and ready with a plan. When Ryker first appeared from the pit, Peanut was shocked to see the state he was in. Even from where he sat on the other side of the camp, he could see what Wulf's dogs had done to him. And then he watched as Ryker fought against his pain to free himself from the cage to get to Aelianna. And now there's the battle with Lazarus, the scrawny guy who'd climbed from the same hole. Ryker's challenger is a lightweight in comparison. Peanut almost laughs; *the poor bloke's got no chance. Ryker could beat him with one hand tied behind his back.* And Ryker proves him right within minutes.

He then watches Wulf goad Ryker and silently

begs Ryker not to react—those dogs will kill him. But Ryker doesn't rise to the bait and, thankfully, he makes it back to the pit before they get a chance to. Wulf's goons then re-seal the opening, and the festivities begin. The crowd becomes rowdy, excited from the earlier entertainment and eager to party hard. Loud singing and dancing begins.

'Titus, tie her to the tree stump!' Wulf calls out to one of his men. 'I'll deal with her later.'

A big, bald oaf drags Aelianna towards the shanty they'd imprisoned her in earlier. She puts up a fight, kicking and clawing at him.

It's now or never. In order for his plan to work, Peanut needs to get there before they do. He sprints. The window of opportunity is closing fast, and he's too far on the other side of the arena. He's not going to make it. He digs deeper, races on, and just as they get to the entrance, he leaps into the air and collides with Titus. They both topple to the ground inside the hut. Titus whips around and glares at Aelianna, set to retaliate.

Peanut needs to act before Titus strikes. He scampers to her side. 'Sing!'

Her breath hitches; her eyes widen and then the confusion in them turns to understanding. Her eyes close and a mesmerising smile warms her lips.

Peanut grabs the two Vaseline cotton balls he'd

stashed ready in one of his pockets and stuffs them in his ears.

Titus raises his hand and draws it back, preparing to strike.

Peanut is ready to intervene, but Aelianna does something that stops them both in their tracks. She sings, her voice cutting straight to the heart.

The brute's a goner in an instant. He falls to his knees before her, his eyes fixed adoringly on her face.

And if Peanut isn't careful, he'll be the same. He presses the balls deeper into his ears, and tells her to keep singing. (According to Kenny, the cotton-wool goop Ryker had packed was for starting a fire, but Peanut figured it'd work just as well as ear plugs.)

While Aelianna continues to sing, and Titus remains befuddled under her spell, Peanut dives into action. He kicks at the back wall of the shanty, which he'd weakened earlier with his knife, and creates a gap big enough to make good their getaway. He then takes a cloth and the little brown-glass bottle labelled $CHCl_3$ from his cargo-pants' pocket and smiles, knowing exactly what he's going to do with the contents. How Kenny happened to come by the chloroform, he has no idea, but does he really care? *Hell, no!*

Peanut plants an exaggerated kiss on the bottle, then, careful not to inhale the toxic fumes himself, dowses the cloth with the clear liquid before smashing it to the goon's face. As expected, Titus bucks at the assault, then falls limp once he's inhaled enough of the poison. Peanut then secures the chemically soaked rag over the brute's mouth using duct tape, thereby buying them some time—any attempt to call for help will only send him back to sleep. He then materialises.

Aelianna stops singing and dives on him. 'My rescuer!'

He laughs, then plucks the slimy balls from his ears. 'This stuff of Ryker's sure came in handy! Come on, let's getcha outta here.' He takes Aelianna by the hand and they both vanish. They then scramble through the opening at the back of the shack and run into the woods.

It could be a matter of minutes or several hours before Wulf finds out that Aelianna is gone, but Peanut doesn't stick around to find out. Giddy with excitement that everything has gone to plan, he races to meet up with his co-conspirator and the mastermind behind the scheme—Molan.

It was a godsend that their paths crossed earlier. After Wulf's dogs had chased Peanut up the tree, and while he was trying to work out what to do, Molan appeared out of the blue. He'd been searching for Aelianna, who'd gone missing the night before, and he was right in guessing she'd gotten herself into trouble with Wulf.

If it wasn't for Molan's clear, calm thinking, Peanut probably would've raced back to the others without any idea of a plan. But with father and daughter safely reunited and having witnessed what Ryker is to face in Wulf's arena, Peanut knows exactly what needs to be done.

39

Venatio

Ryker

Ryker wakes in darkness, disorientated. The grinding sound of the seal above being dragged open has his immediate attention. His knee-jerk reaction to jump up, he instantly regrets—every inch of him aches.

He shields his eyes from the sudden brightness that floods into the pit from above. 'What's going on?'

A mangy black dog comes out from the darkness and yips.

So this is Connor. Ryker scratches the dog's ears. 'Hey, boy. What's happening, buddy? Where's Mitch?'

Mitchell, the owner of the voice from the darkness last night, steps into the light, guarding his eyes. 'They're getting ready for another challenge.'

Ryker looks at the scrawny figure in front of him,

putting a face to the voice of his new ally for the first time. He sees a severely malnourished, unkempt young man, who he guesses is close to his own age—although it's difficult to tell. His dirty blonde hair is long and matted, his beard short and scraggly. He wears what appears to be a permanent scowl on his face with grime deeply embedded in the creases. And even with all that earlier trumped-up bravado, Ryker can see the vulnerability in his eyes.

Mitchell shields his eyes and looks upward. 'The bastards have started early tonight. This can't be good … for you, I mean.' He shakes his head. 'They've really got it in for ya, haven't they?'

'Hey, who knows, it might be my lucky day—they might call on someone else.'

Mitchell snorts. 'You've got Buckley's chance, mate.'

Although Ryker has no idea who Buckley is, Mitchell's meaning is clear. He groans. His body can't handle any more abuse. He's got aches in places he never knew he could have them.

The sound of drunken festivities seeps into the pit from above. One voice rises above the others. 'My friends, last night's presentation was entertaining, was it not?'

The crowd cheers and breaks out in appreciative applause.

Wulf continues. 'Are we eager for more?'

'Bring forth the lackey,' an excited voice cries out.

The crowd laughs.

'Who have you selected?' another asks.

Ryker closes his eyes, dreading that he'll hear his name.

'Who would you wish for me to summon?' Wulf calls out to the crowd.

The throng break out in a chant. 'RYKER, RYKER, RYKER!'

Ryker curses under his breath.

Wulf's laughter rises over the commotion. 'The people of The Dark Forest have spoken. *Heartsong*, present yourself. You have been chosen.'

The end of a rope drops down. Ryker watches it unravel. Do they really expect him to climb up it? They're up there, and he's down here; the way he sees it, nobody can make him to do anything. Right?

The chant continues. 'RYKER, RYKER, RYKER!'

Mitchell shoves Ryker towards the dangling rope. 'What are ya waiting for? Get up there!'

Ryker folds his arms and shakes his head. 'I'm not going anywhere.'

Mitchell's glare turns murderous. 'You're *going*, and you'd better hurry if you know what's good for ya!'

Ryker stands firm. 'Mitchell, how are they going

to make me?'

Connor growls and steps towards him, his hackles raised, teeth bared.

Mitchell's gaze darts from the pit opening to Ryker. 'Mate, you'd better start climbing otherwise we're all gonna cop it.'

'Cop it? What can they do to us from up there?'

Mitchell gulps. 'You don't wanna know.'

The mob become louder. 'RYKER, RYKER, RYKER!'

'Fetch the incentive!'

At Wulf's command, Mitchell turns a deathly shade of grey. He warns Connor to take cover, then grabs Ryker by his shirt. 'Get the hell up that rope! NOW!'

Alarmed by the desperation in Mitchell's eyes, Ryker dives for the rope and hauls his beaten body to the top.

The crowd greets him with a roar.

Ryker takes a moment to adjust to the glare, then scans the crowd. His eyes zero in on Wulf, his trusted mutts and goons at his side. *But where's Aelianna?*

'Well, it would appear that we have disrupted someone's slumber!' Wulf sniggers. 'Did you sleep well, my friend?'

The crowd laughs.

Ryker frantically searches the crowd for Aelianna,

but he doesn't see her. If Wulf's done anything to her, he'll kill him.

Wulf walks to the edge of the arena, his gaze hostile. 'I have another riddle, and this time it is for you. Answer me this: What is it that one seeks that can *never* be found?'

Ryker stiffens. Heat rises to his head so fast it feels like it's going to explode. His chest tightens and, with fists ready to pulverise, he races towards the ladder. The crowd screams and disperses. But Wulf, having predicted his reaction, positions his beasts once again ready to block his escape.

Wulf laughs and raises his hands to silence the crowd. 'Fear not, my friends, you are safe. And it will please you to know what I have in store for your entertainment this fine day.'

Ryker stops, takes a breath and studies Wulf closer. The rogue's lying about Aelianna—she's not dead. If he'd harmed her in any way, he'd be taunting him further, but he's not. And if Aelianna had escaped somehow, Wulf would be seeking his revenge, as he's doing now; his focus set on destroying him. Wulf's attempt to rattle him convinces Ryker that Aelianna is not only alive but also safe from this monster's clutches.

The crowd returns. Some sit on the edge of the arena, others hesitate to be so close.

Wulf paces along the lip of the arena, his hands clasped behind his back. 'Now, my friends, do you wish to see what lies in store for our challenger?'

The crowd cries out, eager to be entertained.

Ryker scans the arena, readying himself for what's coming.

Wulf stops. 'Then let us begin. For your amusement today, I have prepared an adaptation of the ancient Roman challenge Venatio.'

The crowd breaks out in excited cheering and whistling.

Ryker holds his breath. *Venatio? What the hell is that?*

The rest of the mob hurry to the edge of the arena, eyes gleaming in anticipation.

Wulf's dogs whimper.

'As we have observed in the past,' Wulf continues, 'Venatio entails the hunting and killing of innocent animals.'

The crowd boo and hiss.

Wulf plays wounded to the crowd. 'And, of course, I agree, my friends—those poor blameless creatures, such a waste. But as it is *my* choosing, a slight variation of the hunt would be most entertaining. What say you?'

His audience go wild with excitement. 'Wulf, Wulf, Wulf.'

Wulf grins, then motions for them to settle. 'Then I put it to you, my friends. What say we reverse the roles? Make the hunter, the hunted.'

Ryker frowns. That doesn't sound good.

Movement from the far side of the arena draws his attention. A stone seal set in the arena wall rolls aside, revealing a darkened cavity. Ryker struggles to see what's hidden in its depths.

Wulf lets out a haunting cat cry, and from out of the darkness emerges a creature, sleek and beautiful, but ever so deadly—a leopard.

The hair at the back of Ryker's neck stands on end. It's the final challenge all over again. Images of the animal attack on Jaeger flash before his eyes, diverting his attention from a more imminent threat. One of Wulf's goons comes up from behind, slashes Ryker's flesh with a dagger, then runs off laughing. Dumbfounded, Ryker gazes at the outpour of fresh blood. And then, with perfect clarity, he understands its meaning and knows exactly what's about to happen next.

He watches the goon climb the ladder and exit the arena, and notices that Wulf's dogs are no longer guarding it. Here's his chance, he makes a run for it. It will take only a second or two for the scent of his blood to reach his attacker—but enough time, he hopes, to get a head-start.

He clambers up the ladder's rungs, reaches the top, falls to his knees, then scrambles to get upright. Not slowing to look over his shoulder or think twice where to go or what to do next, Ryker runs for his life, taking off into the forest, trying to put as much distance between himself and the beast as possible.

Although challenged by the ladder, it takes the leopard only a few attempts to coordinate its escape and take chase. A cheer from the crowd alerts Ryker that the beast is coming.

Ryker's hasty decision to run without direction is a huge rookie mistake. He blasts himself for his stupidity, but is quick to switch modes. His entrenched, survivor mindset shifts into gear.

He analyses his options. There's no point climbing a tree; the beast will only follow—these cats are good climbers. He can't hide anywhere; the scent of his blood will inevitably lead it to him. What may slow its approach, though, is water—it will mask Ryker's scent. But where's the stream? Nothing's familiar. He's lost his bearings in the confusion to get away. But logic tells him that to find water he needs to reach lower ground. As it is, he's heading on a downward trajectory already, so he ploughs ahead, confident with his decision.

The adrenaline rush coursing through his veins heightens his senses. His eyes are peeled, his hearing focused. He stops to listen but can't pick up on any running water. What he does hear signals trouble; a fast-approaching thrashing sound suggests his attacker is closing in on him.

He takes off at a run, but an exposed tree root trips him up. He stumbles, and before he knows what's happening, he's rolling out of control down a steep slope, being whipped and battered with increasing severity as he picks up momentum. Images of the forest whoosh past him at a dizzying pace, and then the forest darkens. He stops abruptly when his already beaten body smacks into a tree trunk. Winded and disorientated, he pushes through the pain to get upward and mobile. But first he takes a crucial moment to listen out for his hunter. The mob shouts in the distance. He needs to get going.

A few metres further down the slope, a sudden, unnatural eeriness cloaks the darkened forest. His skin crawls, senses sizzling. Something's not right. He slows to inspect this unfamiliar area. The air around him becomes dense, making his breathing shallow. The temperature drops mysteriously, chilling him to the bone. The hair on the back of his neck stands on end in a way that he's never felt before. The air in his lungs expires, and he falls to his knees, groping blindly, gasping.

His head spins. Flickering lights twinkle before

his eyes—he's going to pass out. Something barely glimpsed whooshes high above, and then that *something* swoops down and stops only centimetres from him—studying him.

Ryker blinks a few times, not quite believing what he's seeing. He struggles to keep his focus. His eyelids are heavy, his head in a fog.

Jaeger?

He can't fight it any longer; everything goes black.

40

Was it a Dream?

Ryker

Ryker wakes shivering, frozen to the core. A dream lingers just beyond his subconscious. He closes his eyes, trying to remember it. It felt so real, so terrifyingly real. Scenes from the dream flash before him: Wulf, the arena, the leopard, the chase … *then Jaeger?*

He sits up with a jolt. *But this isn't the pit. And that wasn't a dream! Where the hell am I?* It's too dark to see much, but he looks around, stops and gasps. The glowing silhouette of a person sits nearby, watching him. He rubs at his eyes; he must be seeing things.

'Jae?'

The apparition gets up and floats a little closer. Ryker freezes. *This has to be a dream!*

'Yeah, Ryker, it's me.'

Ryker shakes his head. 'But, but … how's it possible?' And then in a panic, Ryker looks down at his own body and pats himself down. 'Am I dead? Did I just die?'

Jaeger half laughs. 'No, you're not dead, Ryker … only I am.'

Ryker can't find any words. He stares at his old friend, not trusting what he's seeing.

Jaeger smiles. 'It's good to see you, bro. I've missed you.'

Ryker struggles to understand what's happening. He searches the darkened forest, trying to make sense of this hallucination.

'No, you're not going nuts. I'm real,' Jaeger tells him dolefully. He points upwards. 'We all are.'

Ryker looks up, and his jaw drops. Dozens of transparent silhouettes float high above, drifting aimlessly in every direction, seemingly oblivious to his existence. Ryker looks back at Jaeger, dumbfounded.

'This is where the dead come—it's called *The Valley of Lost Souls*. It's supposed to be the passage to the other side,' Jaeger explains. 'The thing is, some of us have never found our way to it.'

Ryker shakes his head. 'So you're in some kind of limbo?'

Jaeger looks away and shrugs. 'I guess.'

Ryker's heart breaks a little—after all this time,

Jaeger is still suffering.

'You don't have to look at me like that. I'm kind of getting used to it now.'

'But how is it that you can't find your way?'

'I don't know. I've watched heaps of spirits come and go, and I still don't get it. Some leave as quickly as they come, while others like me and the ones floating above us, well, we hang around not knowing what we're supposed to do. I don't know, maybe we didn't get the memo or something.'

Ryker looks upward, wondering why so many souls are lost.

'How's Edra?'

Jaeger's question almost knocks the wind out of him—Ryker doesn't know how to answer.

Jaeger sighs. 'God, I miss her.'

Does Ryker tell him that she's a mess without him, that she hasn't been able to function since he's been gone? Or does he lie?

'She misses you too, Jae. We all do.'

Jaeger remains silent, deep in his thoughts. 'If only I could see her again, just once—maybe then I'd be able to bear this loneliness. You know, I never got a chance to tell her how much she meant to me. Things became a little crazy once we realised what this place was all about, and then we needed to focus on keeping ourselves alive. It's been my biggest regret

… not telling her, I mean.'

Ryker remains quiet, reliving that time.

'You'll tell her that for me, won't you?' Jaeger's eyes come alive for the first time.

How could Ryker refuse him? He forces a smile, but his heart breaks a bit more. 'Sure, buddy.' That's the least he could do for him. 'You know she felt the same, don't you?'

Jaeger's face lights up, like he's been given the most awesome gift ever.

Ryker smiles, but he wishes he could do more. Knowing that this is the extent of his friend's existence just about destroys him.

'Jae, what's it like? You know, being dead? I mean, do you feel pain?'

And just like that the spark in Jaeger's eyes disappears. 'Na, just emptiness—you know, like there's no purpose to anything anymore.'

Ryker doesn't know what to say. He can see the emptiness he's talking about by just looking at him. It's like the life's been sucked out of him, literally.

'So tell me, how did you find this place?'

Jaeger's question reminds Ryker of the sequence of events that brought him here. He looks about in a panic. 'Hey, how long have I been here?'

Jaeger shrugs. 'I've got no concept of time anymore, so I couldn't tell you.'

Ryker fills Jaeger in on what's been happening since that fateful final battle and ends by telling him how he'd just escaped the clutches of death.

Jaeger's eyes grow wide. 'What a fluke you stumbled into this place, because I'll tell you, nothing living willingly comes in here—it spooks them. That leopard would never have tracked you in here.'

Ryker knows how lucky he is, and escaping the leopard is only the half of it. He found Jaeger, and to him, that's worth more than words can say. 'You know something, Jae, there's not a day goes by that I don't think about what happened to you.' He notices the many deep gashes in Jaeger's silhouette and cringes. 'If I could somehow find a way to take you from this place, I would. You know that, right?'

Jaeger shrugs.

'Hey, wait a sec,' Ryker says as a thought comes to him. 'Maybe you haven't found your way to the other side because you never belonged here to begin with? What if you're meant to come back with us, back to our time?'

Jaeger's eyes come to life. 'You reckon that's possible?'

Ryker laughs. 'Man, anything's possible. Just look at what's happening here—I'm talking to a ghost, for crying out loud!'

Jaeger laughs with him.

'Look, Jae, I need to get going. I still need to find the way out of here.'

Jaeger's shoulders slump.

'Hey, but I'll come back for you, I promise,' Ryker adds quickly. 'I've gotta find that other portal, and when I do, we'll see if we can do something about getting you where you need to be.'

Jaeger's face lights up again.

'Hey, I owe you that much, buddy.'

Ryker gets up, ready to leave. He takes another look at the poor souls floating above and can't imagine spending the rest of eternity in this mindless state. Before leaving, he turns to Jaeger and sees a glimmer of hope in his eyes. The power of that hope will push Ryker to see this to the end. 'So I'll see you soon. Okay?'

Jaeger smiles. 'Hey, I've got nowhere else I need to be. I'll be waiting.'

41

THE ROCKY OUTCROP

RYKER

Ryker begins the uphill climb from The Valley of Lost Souls towards the brighter forest above, leaving Jaeger behind. He stops when there's enough light to see around him and looks for something with which to protect himself. He finds a sturdy broken tree branch and, by repeatedly rubbing it against a rock, sharpens one end to a point, transforming it into something that might just save his life. And he needs to prevent the scent of his blood—now crusting over the gash on his arm—from attracting the leopard again, or Wulf's dogs, for that matter. He uses his teeth to rip a strip off the bottom of his shirt and fashions a makeshift bandage over the wound.

That done, he braces himself for what he may be facing once he leaves the protection of the darkness. At the top he pauses to listen for any threat. He hears nothing but the peacefulness of the forest, but that means little. He's not in the clear yet.

With the stealth of a cat, he slips through the woods, trying to find familiar ground. His senses are on high alert, and he prays the leopard is long gone, having found itself another victim—with some luck the said victim would be Wulf!

Methodically, he marks his path every few metres by either snapping off a branch, scuffing up the earth or bundling up some twigs with pieces of vine. When the time comes, the trail he leaves will guide him back to Jaeger. He keeps a look out for any discernible landmarks and memorises them too.

After a good while, and endless markings, Ryker begins to feel a little better orientated. Things are starting to look familiar. He's found the path Molan took them on the other day in their search for The Forbidden Passage, which also means he's nearing The Dark Forest. He slows his approach, calms his breathing to listen, then plans his next move.

A rustling sound at a distance alerts him to someone or something coming up from behind. His hand tightens on his weapon. That 'something' is on his trail—he's almost sure of it. And then the movement towards him accelerates. Whatever's looming has picked up on his scent and is closing in on him. Cat or dog, he doesn't wait to see what's coming.

He picks up speed, but so does his assailant. Ryker races in the direction in which, he's almost certain, Medwin indicated they'd find The Forbidden Passage. If he can somehow find the rocky formation, he just might be able to save himself.

Ryker thrashes through the scrub, keeping up a relentless pace. A sudden guttural growl hot on his heels tell him his pursuer is one of Wulf's dogs. And the chances of it being alone is slim to none.

He searches for a clearing to give himself a fighting chance to take it on, and when he does, he stops and turns just in time to see the beast flying through the air at him, its teeth bared, saliva dripping. Ryker only has time to raise his stick to defend himself. The dog latches onto it, jerks his head, throwing Ryker onto the ground, and then releases the branch to go for Ryker's throat. Ryker manages to keep hold of the branch and bring it around quickly enough to whack the beast away, but before he can get fully to his feet, it comes back in full rage and pounces on top of him. While protecting his face and neck with his improvised weapon, Ryker brings a knee up with all the power he can muster and strikes the beast between its legs. The dog yelps and falls on its back.

Ryker leaps up and slams the stake into its chest. The dog falls motionless.

From the depths of the forest, Ryker hears its two companions fast approaching. His only escape will be if he can find the passage and the portal home before they're on him. He quickly scans the area and spots the rock formation he seeks jutting up to the heavens. It's not far, but can he make it there in time?

Ryker flies through the forest, the look of hope in Jaeger's eyes driving him to dig deeper and run faster. He's within reach, almost there, but so are the dogs. He glances back and sees the beasts in mid-flight, leaping towards him. He raises his weapon, but they knock him to the ground before he can get a strike in. He struggles in vain to stop them tearing at his flesh. One of them is at his arms, the other at his legs.

And then, when he feels there's no more hope, Wulf runs out of the woods, his goons not far behind, and orders his dogs to stop. Under protest, the beasts fall back.

Wulf, breathless from the run, shakes his head and laughs. 'Impressive.' He bends over, hands on knees, taking a moment to slow his breathing. 'How you evaded the cat is beyond me, but all is not lost. For you, *my friend*, will live to fight another day, and we will have the pleasure of being entertained once more.'

If only Ryker could have five minutes alone with Wulf, he'd tear him to shreds, and then all of his suffering would be worth it. But he's outnumbered, and Ryker is forced to remain submissive. His hands are bound, and once again he's dragged through the forest, away from the freedom that was within his grasp and towards the inevitable hell that awaits him.

42

DRUNK AS SKUNKS

RYKER

Ryker stirs from his sleep with a dream lingering playfully at his subconscious. He doesn't want to wake. For the first time in a long time, he feels happy. He rolls onto his side, trying to hold onto that feeling and ignore the pain in his head and his aching body, but what he can't ignore is the persistent poking in his side and the bright light in his face.

He covers his eyes with his arm and groans. 'Go away.'

The prodding persists. He swipes at it.

'Ryker, get up, mate. It's me.'

It's Peanut.

'What!' He jolts upright—big mistake. 'Argh, my head!' He bites on his fist to stop from screaming out again.

'Is everything okay down there?' Jack calls down quietly from the top of the pit.

'What the hell! Jack's here? What happened to Ruby?' His head feels like it's about to explode from the sudden rush of adrenaline. He moans.

'Hey, take it easy, mate. Geez, you don't look so good, do ya?' Peanut grimaces. He shakes his head and continues. 'Look, stacks has happened—I'll fill ya in later. But now, we've gotta getcha outta here.'

Ryker shields his eyes from the bright torch light. 'Will ya quit waving that thing in my face! My head's killing me, and it feels like you're stabbing two-inch needles into my eyeballs.'

Peanut redirects the light. 'Sorry. My bad.'

'So how did you get down here?' Ryker asks, looking up the darkened shaft. He notices the dangling rope. 'That seal must weigh a tonne.'

Peanut chuckles. 'Yeah, couldn't do it without Jack. He comes in handy sometimes. Come on, he's waiting to pull us up.'

Ryker remembers Wulf and his goons. 'So how did you get past security?'

'Mate, they're all as drunk as skunks up there. Look, we haven't got all day, or should I say, night? Anyway, Jack is literally hanging by a rope, waiting.'

'Wait, we can't go yet—'

'Yeah, yeah, yeah, we know all about your friends

down here, and don't worry, we've had time to talk things over. It's all sorted. Because there's so many of them down here, some will go tonight, the rest, tomorrow. Oi, Mitch,' Peanut calls out into the darkness, 'tell him we're good.'

Mitchell comes out from the darkness wearing a scowl on his face. Connor is by his side. 'You'd better come back for us!'

Connor raises his paw to him, and Ryker scratches his ears. 'Hey, boy. How're you doing?'

Peanut grins. 'So, *Connor*, are you ready, *boy*?'

Mitchell chuckles. Ryker frowns, not quite getting the joke.

The dog yips his response, then his body starts to quiver out of control. Ryker steps back. What happens next is beyond anything he could've imagined in his wildest imagination. The huddled-over body of the dog morphs into a thin, gaunt, young man.

Peanut blinks a few times. 'Whoa! You *did* warn me, Mitch, but I'll tell ya something for nothin', you've gotta see it to believe it.' He turns to look at Ryker and laughs. 'Man, you should see the look on your face—that's gold!'

Mitchell, in all seriousness, steps up to Ryker to poke him in the chest. 'Connor's coming with you, just in case you *forget* to come back for the rest of us. Got it?'

Ryker's brain is reeling from what just happened, but he needs to put it in the too-hard basket for now in order to focus on Mitchell's meaning. He frowns. '*The rest of us?* Why aren't we all leaving now?'

Mitchell shakes his head and clicks his tongue. 'Fill him in, Peanut.'

Peanut obliges. 'There's about a dozen or so guys down here—some, battle-worn but able, some not so good. It's too risky to all leave at once. With a few of them needing our help one way or another, someone's bound to catch us out, so we're sending up a few tonight, then, like I said before, we're coming back for the rest tomorrow.'

A dozen? Ryker had no idea there were so many.

Just then a string of men clamber through the small, ground-level opening, and into the pit. Some are tall, some short, some young, some old, but all are gaunt and to various degrees, wasted.

Ryker can't leave, not without helping these men out first. 'If that's the case, *I'll* stay; let one of them take my place.'

Peanut shakes his head. 'We need you to help them out tomorrow night, and you're useless to them like this. So first we visit the doc, and as soon as she's fixed you up, you're coming back before anyone notices you're gone.'

'Listen to him,' Mitchell tells him. 'Let 'em

patch you up, because you'll need it. They're gonna challenge you again tomorrow before the escape. You know that, right?'

Ryker groans—*of course they will.* And in this state, he doesn't think he could survive another battle.

Peanut reaches for the dangling rope, preparing to climb it then claps Ryker on the shoulder with his other hand. 'Sorry, mate, but that's the only way we can do this.'

'So make sure you come back,' Mitchell says. 'You don't want our blood on your hands.'

'Look, Mitchell, don't worry; it's as good as done. We'll deal with tomorrow together. Okay?'

'What the hell's taking you guys so long?' Jack cries out, his patience tested.

Peanut begins the climb up the rope then calls down when they're ready. And one by one, Jack and Peanut pull the men up and out of the pit through the narrow opening.

Ryker is the last to exit. Panting from the effort, he staggers to his feet to see the men trailing Peanut across the arena to the rope ladder. By his side, Jack also struggles to catch his breath. They look at each other—there's no time to lose, they take off after them. With some help from Jack, Ryker climbs out of the arena then watches Peanut and the men scatter into the forest. Just as they go to follow, Ryker hears, in the far distance, something that makes the hair on the back of his neck stand on end. Sure enough, he turns to see Wulf's dogs racing towards them.

Jack grabs him, and they make a beeline for the woods.

The beasts are fast approaching, and Ryker struggles to keep up. He yanks himself free. 'Jack, run! Save yourself!'

But Jack is determined to save them both. He throws Ryker over his shoulders, staggers unsteadily for a few steps, then makes a herculean effort to get away. But it's not enough. The dogs are soon upon them, their snapping jaws mere metres away.

Suddenly Connor runs from the forest, hollering and screaming. In an instant, he transforms into his canine self and takes off in the opposite direction.

Connor's obvious plan to divert the dogs' attention works. Wulf's beasts change course and take chase. Soon they've all disappeared into the darkness.

'Jack,' Ryker says, 'put me down; we need to help Connor!'

Jack does. He then runs his hand through his hair. 'Mate, what we *need* to do is keep going. Look, Connor had a good head-start. He should be all right.'

Ryker stares into the darkness and hopes Jack is right. He turns to see if the commotion of the chase has stirred Wulf and his goons. Apparently too drunk to stir, the camp remains quiet.

With Jack's support, Ryker hobbles onwards, and they meet up with the men from the pit, who are waiting for them as planned. *But where's Peanut?*

'That bloody idiot!' Jack has noticed him missing too. 'We haven't got time for this crap!' He paces back and forth a few times before making the decision to keep going.

They eventually make their way to the rocky outcrop. Ryker's heart skips a beat when he sees it. This time, he might just make it. But nothing's guaranteed. His senses heighten, and he looks out for guards. *Vigilant at all times; expect the unexpected!*

Jack looks at him and grins. 'Hey, don't look so worried, we've taken care of it. The six-foot brutes here don't like tasers just as much as the ones back home.' He chuckles. 'Thanks to you and your nifty gadgets, we're getting quite a collection of guards piling up in the woods.'

Ryker lets out a breath, then laughs.

In single file, they pass within the narrow walls of the passage towards the portal Ryker knows lies at the end. He stops only to listen out for Connor, but knows he won't be anywhere nearby. He can only hope he managed to escape—he owes him his life.

43

WHERE'S PEANUT?

MAX

Max waits, chewing her nails, at the foot of the portal in the depths of The Forbidden Passage with Ruby, Edra and Kenny. Jack and Peanut should be returning any moment with Ryker. And from what Peanut told them, Ryker was in a pretty bad way, so she's anxious to start his healing. Once done, they can go; they can finally leave this wretched place for good.

It seems like a lifetime ago since her premonition about Ryker, and it's killing her that it's taking so long to get to him. She stops to think about that dream: there was a fight, stacks of blood and a wolf. She shakes her head, baffled by it all. How could she have foreseen something like that? What forces in the universe create such a thing—for one person to see or feel what another is experiencing? She shrugs and puts it down to the strong psychic bond they share. How many times has Ryker popped into her thoughts just before the phone rings, only to find that it's him? Or how many times has he guessed what she's going to say before she says it? She can't explain it; it's like their minds are in sync. Does it stem from their shared past experience? Or have they somehow bonded as siblings? Could their lone upbringing do that? Ryker is more than a friend, he's the big brother she never had … he's blood.

She sighs. If only they would hurry. It's late, it's dark, and she's done with all this waiting. Although safe behind Ruby's shield, she's worried they'll be found before she's had a chance to do what she needs to do for Ryker. Guards at this time of the night would be uncommon, but the way they've been vanishing lately, she's sure Herodus will know something's going on—he's not stupid.

'Someone's coming!' Edra is up like a flash, braced and ready.

Max blinks—she forgot how quick Edra can be.

'I'm onto it!' Ruby reinforces her shield, then relaxes when she spots Jack. 'Thank God, they're back!'

She retracts the barrier, and Max runs to them but falls back when she spots several dishevelled men coming up at the rear. And then the surprise at seeing the strangers takes a back seat when Ryker comes into view. 'Oh, God! What have they done to you?'

Edra streaks to his side. 'Ryker! Are you all right?'

'Yeah, I'm good, Edra; don't fuss.' He looks over her shoulder. 'Hey, where are the twins?'

'They're back at the camp,' she tells him hurriedly. 'But, *Ryker*, just *look* at you!'

Ryker catches Kenny staring at him with wide eyes. He chuckles. 'That bad, huh? Hey, Max, I reckon I could do with some help here.'

Max splutters. 'You *think*?' Ryker is black and blue all over. His clothes are shredded and gashes cover his arms and face, the swelling so severe that his eyes are barely slits. The deep wound on his arm could be right to the bone, and every inch of him is covered in blood. He's a complete mess. Max bites her lip to stop it quivering.

Ruby takes a few steps to the mouth of the passage. 'Guys, where's Peanut?'

Max stops. Her head whips around to face Jack. He and Ryker exchange a worried look. *Oh, God, this can't be good.*

Ruby sees it too. She inhales sharply and her hands clench into tight fists.

Jack runs his hand through his hair. 'Honestly? We don't know. He came out of the pit with us, but after that … well, no one's seen him since.' He again glances at Ryker. Ryker shrugs. 'Look, Ruby,' Jack tells her, 'one of the guys from the pit took a detour, so I guess he went after him to help.'

Ruby turns away and curses. 'What the hell was he thinking? We were so close to going home, and now …' She waves her arms hopelessly.

Jack rubs the back of his neck, then lets out a frustrated sigh. 'Look, he'll turn up eventually; you know he will. He always does.'

Max can't believe it. Peanut's gone and done it again. She's about to say she'll tear him apart when she gets her hands on him, but the six men standing in the background start murmuring to each other, drawing her attention. She takes a moment to take them in—to really look at them. They're covered in grime, and the rags on their bodies scarcely conceal anything. Their filthy matted hair makes her shudder. *There's probably a whole ecosystem happening right there!*

To her embarrassment, Jack catches her reaction and struggles to hide a smirk.

She turns her attention to Ryker. 'You look terrible.'

'Yeah, so everyone keeps telling me.' He grins, but doesn't quite manage to hide a wince at the pain it causes. 'But really, I'm not that bad.'

Max almost laughs at how ridiculous that sounds. How he's even managing to remain vertical is beyond her. And just as she's thinking it, Ryker starts to waver. Max dives forward to steady him, and with Kenny's assistance, helps him to the ground. Ryker drops his head between his knees and slows his breathing.

Max squats by his side and rests her hand on his knee. He's in a pretty bad way, no matter what he says, but she won't let her emotions cloud her focus. There's work to be done. She begins his healing. The gashes to Ryker's body are numerous, some needing a lot of her attention. As her hands instinctively do the work, Max catches bits and pieces of the conversation going on around her. Jack fills everyone in on the plight of the extra men—now sitting with their backs against the rock wall.

'So there's still another half-a-dozen of them down there?' Edra asks.

'Yeah, can you believe it?' Ryker cuts in before Jack has a chance to answer. He turns to Max. 'So, Max, you need to fix me ASAP so I can go back. If Wulf finds that I've gone, there's no knowing what he'll do to Mitchell and the others.'

Max falls back. 'What? You're going back?'

Edra's head whips around. 'Are you *insane*? Ryker, they almost killed you!' She drops to his side; her eyes narrow. 'Will you just stop for a minute to think this through?'

'Edra, don't you think we have? Look, we can't

leave them; Wulf will kill them! The plan is to make the escape tomorrow night. Isn't that right, Jack?'

Jack looks at him sideways and nods reluctantly.

Edra gets to her feet, throws her hands in the air, then stomps off in a huff.

Max's eyes squeeze tight. She can't believe it—they were so close to going home.

Ryker then runs through what they've planned. The strategy seems solid, and Max feels it should work—she needs to trust that it will. She turns to Jack for reassurance and is surprised to see him standing away from the group with his arms crossed. It's clear something's bothering him—there's a tightness in his jaw she rarely sees. She wonders what's brought that on.

Jack steps up to Ryker and points his finger in his face. 'Just stick to the plan this time, okay? No more stuff-ups!'

Ryker gets to his feet and stands over him, frowning.

But Jack doesn't back down. 'And remember to look out for Connor and that idiot friend of ours on your way!'

Jack's behaviour and harsh tone surprises Max, and she's about to say so but is side-tracked by something Jack just said. She takes a moment to digest it, then shakes her head, a little addled by her sudden thinking. 'Hang on a sec, did you say Connor?'

Ryker stops glaring at Jack and looks at her. 'That's right. He saved my life.'

Her brow furrows deeper. 'And you said the other boy is Mitchell?'

Jack frowns. 'Yeah, why?'

Max's pulse quickens. *Nah, it couldn't be! Could it?* She sits taller. *What are the chances?* She jumps to her feet, excited. 'Are you guys seeing what I'm seeing?' She's met with questioning expressions. She just about laughs in her eagerness to tell them. 'Well, *Mitchell* and *Connor* aren't your typical ancient names, are they?'

'I guess not,' Ryker answers. 'What are you getting at?'

She turns to Edra. 'In the battles, you guys fought four Aussies, right?' Too excited to wait for a confirmation, Max focuses her attention on the six scruffy men sitting quietly in the background. 'Are any of you Aussies?'

The men look at each other, confused at her question.

And just like that, her enthusiasm fizzles. She sighs.

Kenny squeezes her shoulder. 'Max, I get it; for a moment I thought we'd found those missing kids too.'

Max shrugs, then forces a smile. So she got it wrong; it was a long shot after all. 'So who *are* you guys? I'm Max.'

One of the men hesitates before introducing himself as Flavius, then tells her the others are Vitus, Philo, Aetius, Homer and Orion.

Her shoulders slump. *Nope, not an Aussie among them.*

'Hang on,' Ryker says suddenly, 'Connor and Mitchell *are* Aussies!'

Max stumbles back.

Edra clicks her tongue. 'And you didn't think to ask if they were from our challenges? Didn't you at least recognise them?'

Ryker scratches his head. 'You'd think that I would've, but I didn't.'

'I guess four years in the bowels of the earth would change anyone,' Edra says grimly. 'Ryker, it may well be them.'

'But there were four kids,' Kenny reminds them.

'I do not believe you are talking about the same people,' the man called Flavius tells them, his brow knit in thought. 'Connor and Mitchell came from a place called Sydney.'

'Then it's them!' Ruby cries out. 'Oh my God, we've found them! But what happened to the other two?'

Flavius appears surprised to have given them information they're happy to hear—his excitement is obvious. 'Yes, this is true; originally there were four—I recall Mitchell saying so. He told of the time they had lost their way in a forest near Sydney and how they were captured by guards. After some time, they battled a strong team of five in the arena and lost. Soon after exile, one from his group died from hunger, and another was killed by a wild animal. The people of The Dark Forest found Mitchell and Connor, near death, and they've been fighting in the pit challenges ever since.'

Max feels sick to the stomach. She looks at the men sitting there and struggles to imagine the horrors they've lived through. 'God, I *hate* this place! We need to get these poor people out of here! Haven't they suffered enough?'

Jack jumps to his feet and snatches his kit. 'You're right. We've got to get the others out of there tonight. The sooner we go, the sooner we can get the hell out of here. Screw hanging around any longer than we have to.'

Max stops. She didn't mean for this to happen. 'What are you doing? We've got a plan. Why change things?' She turns to Ryker. 'It's too late to go tonight, right?' She looks back at Jack. 'And what about Peanut? We can't leave without him.'

Ryker squeezes her shoulder. 'Relax, Max. Jack's not going anywhere. Yeah, it's too late; we can't risk moving them tonight. We're sticking to the plan, Jack. Okay?'

Colour tracks up Jack's neck to flush his face. He looks away, curses under his breath, then flings his kit aside.

Max flinches at his reaction. She wonders what's gotten into him. To go out again tonight would be suicide—they all know it. She studies Jack from the corner of her eye. Why is he acting so weird? She figures it's got something to do with their missing invisible friend. She grits her teeth and growls under her breath, 'Bloody Peanut!'

But enough of that—Max needs to return her focus to Ryker's healing. She tells him to get his butt back down on the ground, and although her energy levels are just about sapped, she doesn't stop. Returning Ryker to full strength is the key to them doing this right.

A short time later, Max, Kenny and Edra watch Ryker prepare to leave. Jack continues to remain distant. Ryker packs his cargo-pants' pockets with some things he says 'might come in handy later', then heads down The Forbidden Passage to return to the pit.

As she sees him disappear around the bend in the path, Max prays that everything goes to plan, for a change.

44

It's Your Lucky Day, Connor

Peanut

Peanut can't believe it; Connor just saved Ryker's neck! After witnessing the dog man's heroic stunt, Peanut waits to make sure Jack, Ryker and the men from the pit are safe before taking off after him. With two massive wild dogs on his tail, Connor's chances aren't looking good, and being invisible gives Peanut the courage he needs to go in after him.

He follows Connor's trail deep into the woods, then stops to listen. Dogs bark in the distance, so he sprints towards the sound, praying he's not too late. But the darkness hampers his progress. Filtered light from the moon is all he has to light his way. He pushes on, the clamour from the dogs guiding him.

What he hears as he gets nearer gives him hope—
the hounds are clawing and whimpering. It sounds
like Connor is beyond their reach.

As Peanut approaches, he pulls a switch knife
from his cargo-pants' pocket, flicks it open, frowns,
then shrugs. *I guess it's better than nothing.* He spots
a good-sized rock that could come in handy, grabs it
and then braces himself for what he has to do.

Okay, let's do this!

He runs, shouting and screaming, in the dogs'
direction. They stand at the base of a tree, looking
his way, mute and cagey with confusion—stumped
by his invisibility. One of the mutts charges blindly,
but Peanut stops, standing ready, rock in hand. The
mutt slows and sniffs in confusion but continues its
approach. Now! Peanut whacks it hard on the temple
with the rock and knocks it out cold. He grins,
buoyed by his success.

The other dog, a huge black beast, growls and
bares its massive teeth.

'C'MON!' Peanut challenges. 'COME 'N GET
ME!' He grips his knife tighter, unsure how exactly
he's going to use it, but just as his attacker is set to leap,
Connor drops from the tree above, knocking it to the
ground. Quick as lightning, he snatches up a nearby
rock and smashes it into its head. The animal jerks
and twitches a few times before falling motionless.

Peanut materialises, and the boys high-five each other. 'Great job, Connor. I wasn't sure how I was gonna take them both on.' He holds up his knife and laughs. 'I reckon he would've taken a few chunks outta me before I did any damage with this pathetic excuse of a weapon.'

'So what do we do now?' Connor asks, looking down at the unconscious dogs. 'Do we, you know, just finish them off?'

Peanut shrugs. 'Dunno. I guess it'd be the smart thing to do, but to tell ya the truth, I don't think I could bring myself to do it. Pretty pathetic, huh?' He scratches his head. 'Do you wanna have a go?'

Connor's hands shoot out in front of him. 'Nah, I'm with you—couldn't do it even if you paid me. Must be the *dog* in me.'

Peanut laughs, slings his arm over Connor's shoulders, then pockets the knife. 'Come on, let's get outta here before we regret it.'

As they make tracks back towards the main path, Connor bounces around excitedly. 'You know, you had me stumped there for a minute. I could hear ya but couldn't see ya. I didn't know you could do that! Man, you've got the coolest power. I wish *I* could go invisible. D'ya wanna swap?' He scratches at his skin. 'I'm kinda getting sick of being a dog.'

Peanut chuckles. 'No way, you can keep it,

buddy—that *and* your fleas. You forget, I know how bad you stink.'

Connor laughs. 'Boy, that was a close one, though. Those dogs nearly had me.'

Peanut smiles. 'Hey, that was a pretty brave thing you did, saving Ryker like that.'

'You know, I didn't even think twice about it.' Connor shrugs. 'It just happened. You've got no idea what it feels like to have some freedom.'

Peanut grins. Actually, he's got a pretty good idea.

The sound of running water nearby prompts Peanut to look around. He smiles—he knows this place. 'Hey, talk about freedom,' he says with a smirk, 'how would ya like to come visit some friends of ours? I'm sure they'll take us in for the night. I reckon there's no point trying to find our way anywhere while it's dark. Besides, I've got a feeling that we might be needing their help later.'

Peanut's mind races. Somewhere in his head an idea has taken hold, and the more he thinks about it, the more confident he feels that it might just work. He smiles, picturing Ryker's face when he pulls it off.

They head in the direction of Molan's little village, but Peanut trips and fumbles in the dark. He curses when he takes another tumble and wonders if they'll ever make it there. 'Um, Connor, it sounded good on paper,' he confesses, 'but to tell ya the truth I'm having second thoughts about this brilliant idea of mine. It's as black as the ace of spades out here.'

Connor doubles over laughing.

Peanut frowns. 'What's the joke?'

'Mate, you crack me up. Just point me in the right direction, and I'll get you there. Dogs have got pretty awesome night vision.'

Peanut stops—he hadn't thought of that. 'Hey, yeah. Cool!'

Connor grins. 'So d'ya reckon we could swap powers now?'

'Nah, I'll keep mine and just sponge off Ryker when I need his night-vision goggles.'

Connor's cocky smile vanishes. Peanut slaps his arm around his shoulders and laughs. 'Man, you really don't know how bad you stink, do ya? C'mon, let's get out of here. The sooner we get you home, the quicker I can de-flea ya and hose you down.'

45

ᏗNDECISION

Ryker feels fantastic. Max, true to form, has worked her magic on him again, and he's ready to take on another round of whatever Wulf has in store for him. He heads off with his thermal-imaging goggles and a few choice necessities to re-join Mitchell and the remaining captives down the pit. The finish is near. He'll soon have the men from the pit home and safe. He smiles, his spirits high. If all goes to plan, he'll have accomplished something far greater than what he set out to do. Innocent lives will be spared, and his mother will get the treatment she deserves. She'll get well and their family will be whole again.

But right now, he needs to focus on the task at hand—there's a mission. *Vigilant at all times!*

He ploughs ahead with renewed determination.

It's well past midnight. Dawn will break soon; he needs to hurry. A guard encounter at this point will jeopardise everything. And just as he thinks it, his ears prick to the sound of something coming his way. He dives for cover. With his trusted goggles, he spots the glowing silhouette of three large figures approaching. He grimaces. But it doesn't surprise him—the recent disappearance of portal guards would be ringing alarm bells by now, and security would've tightened.

Crouching low, he watches as they pass and tries to pick up on their conversation.

'Stay alert,' one of them says. 'Herodus suspects intruders. Some of the men have failed to report back from duty.' He stops to look about them, peering into the darkness.

'Then let us not waste time,' says another, reinforcing his hold on his dagger. 'I am anxious to learn what awaits us now.'

They power on.

Ryker stops to consider what he should do. The guards will discover more men missing, which will prompt them to investigate or send for help. Does he try to stop them or does he follow through with the plan? He shakes his head; if they're to save Mitchell and the rest of the men, he has to get going.

He needs to trust that Jack will realise the danger and have the sense to return to South Africa.

There's no turning back now.

46

Ding, Ding, Ding

Ruby's eyes widen, her face brightens. 'Hey, everyone, someone's coming,' she whispers.

It could be Peanut. Max holds her breath and prays it is. But she notices, Jack isn't taking any chances. He arms himself with the stun gun, then presses a finger to his lips, reminding everyone to remain quiet. He glances from his friends to the men from the pit and then to her—something in his eyes disturbs her. She nods to reassure him that she's okay, but his expression doesn't soften. If only she knew what was going on in his head. Since that dream of Ryker, things have been strange between them—he's been distant. But she can't blame him for thinking she's a complete nut job. The experience of the premonition totally freaked her out, so she can only guess what it did to him.

But now's not the time for this line of thinking—Peanut might be coming. She squints to see down the passage and concentrates on listening. But it's too quiet to be him; Peanut would be making a racket. And then fragments of a whispered conversation drift towards them. *Guards!*

Ignoring Jack's directive to stay put, Ruby, secure within her protective bubble, inches closer to the head of the passage to investigate. Max presses her hands to her mouth to hold back from crying out.

Jack motions for Ruby to come back, but she indicates with a thumbs-up sign that it's safe, and then in mime reminds him that The Forbidden Passage generally spooks the people of the Realm. Ruby's comical impersonation of a ghost is so unexpected, Max almost laughs out loud. She looks at Kenny and sees him struggling to hold back a chuckle too. She gives him a wink. Edra just shakes her head. The men from the pit shrink back into the darkness.

Frustrated, Jack again gestures to Ruby to come back, but Kenny indicates to let her be. He holds up a roll of duct tape and some cable-tie fasteners, then shrugs. Max's eyes pop; clearly, he's suggesting they take out the guards. But then she realises Kenny has a point. The unprotected gateway will set off alarms and have the forest crawling with Herodus' men in no time. Overpowering this new threat will buy them the extra time they need.

Jack frowns, then looks at each of his friends. They all come to a silent agreement. Ruby nods and her eyes narrow in concentration; she's ready to dive into action. Jack reinforces his hold on the taser, and Kenny hands Edra the duct tape and ties before arming himself with his nunchaku. Max tightens her grip on her baseball bat and readies herself for the fallout.

Agitated voices at the mouth of the passage indicate it's now or never. Ruby grins, her shield evolves into a huge boxing glove, and before the guards know what's happening, Ruby knocks all three of them out for the count. *Ding, ding, ding.*

47

STICK FIGHT

After a spirited trek, Ryker reaches the outskirts of the arena, hesitating only a moment to scan the area for any activity before making a run for it. He reaches the open pit without detection, grabs the rope left there earlier and secures it around his waist before lowering himself a short way down and carefully replacing the weighty stone seal.

Once on the floor, he calls out to Mitchell, but is met with a deathly silence. A chill runs down his spine that has nothing to do with the temperature. He adjusts the night-vision goggles, squats low and searches the tunnel leading off the pit. 'Hey, is anyone here?' The thermal images he was hoping to see aren't there. 'Crap, they're gone!'

He hasn't a moment to spare. He needs to get out.

He clambers up the rope and, with his superhuman strength, hurls the stone closure aside. Shafts of light from the breaking day momentarily blind him, and what he hears next fills him with dread. He's too late.

Wulf's beasts are there, ready and waiting for him, and their incessant growling stirs their master to wake and investigate. Ryker can hear Wulf cursing the dogs as he approaches, so he lowers himself down the shaft a little to rethink the situation, but as soon as he catches sight of Wulf, all logic flies out the window and adrenaline kicks in. Ryker scrambles back up and pounces on Wulf, throwing him to the ground and jumping on top of him. He grabs Wulf's throat in a firm stranglehold with one hand and with the other delivers a barrage of punches. All his pent-up anger explodes. He's out of control.

Wulf doesn't get a chance to strike back, but his mutts pick up the slack. They latch onto Ryker's arms and legs with their razor-sharp teeth.

Ryker's rage spurs him to retaliate. Fur flies, bones crunch, yelps of pain fill the air. But he gets entangled by the rope around his waist, trips, stumbles and falls into the pit. The last thing he remembers is ricocheting off the walls like a rubber ball before whacking his head.

❧

Ryker wakes, choking on a metallic taste in his mouth. He spits out a mass of congealed blood from the back of his throat, followed by what seems to be a tooth. The seal to the pit is secured once again in its place, leaving him in complete darkness. The rope around his waist remains, but has been severed from above. He sits up and cringes at the pain. A fall like that could've killed him, but apart from a massive headache, a broken tooth and a few dog bites, he's good. And he needs to be, because he knows there's more coming.

With the time he has before the next challenge, he goes over strategies that could come in handy. He pats down his cargo-pants and breathes a sigh of relief; his MK3 navy knife is safe in its holster and his other gadgets are all there too.

The slow grinding sound of the heavy seal opening above alerts him that his time has run out. The shaft floods with daylight, and a rope lowers.

The crowd starts chanting, 'Ryker, Ryker, Ryker.'

Wulf's raspy voice can barely be heard over the commotion. Ryker shakes his head. He can't believe it; Wulf should be in a coma after the beating he gave him. Nevertheless, Ryker braces himself. Whatever Wulf has in store for him can't be good.

'But who shall we call upon to challenge him?' Wulf calls out feebly. 'Perhaps Mitchell?'

The crowd cheers.

Ryker freezes. *Mitchell? Crap!* He hadn't anticipated this. Of course, Wulf has no idea that no one is left for Ryker to battle.

'Mitchell, you have been chosen to take on the newcomer,' Wulf cries out. 'Come, enter the arena.'

There's nothing Ryker can do. He waits.

Wulf calls for Mitchell again.

Ryker prepares himself—something's coming. Mitchell's earlier warning echoes in his ears with every heartbeat.

'So suffer the consequences,' Wulf cries out suddenly. 'You have been warned!'

And then the repercussion of the no-show strikes. A huge, dark, writhing mass is dumped into the shaft. The anticipation of something terrible happening is nothing compared to Ryker's reaction when he realises exactly what the dark mass is. *SNAKES!*

Ryker dives for his only life-line, the dangling rope, and manages to save himself from the onslaught of hundreds of venomous fangs. Suspended above the angered vipers, he watches the black mass unravel, hiss and strike at each other. Some find escape routes and slither away.

He's safe for now but knows he won't be for long. And he's not mistaken; a gnawing at the rope from above alerts him that he has to move fast. Someone's about to make him into a meal for those snakes by cutting that life-line.

Ryker races up the rope and throws himself to safety on the ground above. He jumps to his feet, then circles to take in the situation, anticipating an attack. He sees one of Wulf's goons racing from the arena. It must've been him sawing at the rope. Ryker looks sharp, he's ready. But nothing comes.

The crowd, silent but eager, waits for others to surface, but of course no one does.

'Such a waste. I had hoped for a battle.'

Ryker locks eyes with Wulf. His face is swollen and bruised from the earlier beating, but that smug look on his face has Ryker ready to take him on again—and finish it this time.

Ryker scans the arena, looking for a means of escape. The rope ladder is there, but so too are Wulf's mutts. Not a good option.

'I know not how you happened to escape yesterday's threat,' Wulf begins. 'And your evasion cost me two valuable possessions. This displeases me.' Wulf limps to the rim of the arena. 'Perhaps another challenge may lighten my discontentment.' He turns to the crowd. 'What say you? For I feel you, too, have been denied.'

The crowd cheers.

'So shall we test brawn or endurance?' Wulf rubs

his chin. 'Personally, I feel every man has his breaking point, and it would give me great pleasure to test the extent of his.'

'Stick fighting!' Someone calls out from the crowd. This stirs them all to chant. 'Stick fight! Stick fight! Stick fight!'

Ryker stifles a smile—he knows stick fighting. He trained in it back home when he was a cadet. *Bring it on! One on one. I can do this!* He looks about, keen to meet his challenger. But who will it be?

Wulf smirks. 'So be it! My men against this filth.'

The crowd whistles and hoots their approval.

Ryker's confidence plummets when he sees all three of Wulf's goons enter the arena at the same time, each armed with a striking stick and a defending shield.

Wulf laughs at Ryker's unguarded reaction. 'As much as it would give me pleasure to have all three of my men take you on, I am no fool to wish the battle to end in haste. You will compete man-on-man.' He throws Ryker a stick and shield. 'And do not deceive yourself in thinking this will be an easy feat, for I assure you, before long, you will be begging for death.'

Wulf wants his revenge, that much is clear. Ryker grabs the gear thrown to him and takes a deep breath, preparing himself for what's coming.

'Galen,' Wulf calls out, 'proceed!'

One of the goons steps forward, grinning. Galen, although tall, is a head shorter than Ryker and definitely not in the same weight division.

Ryker smiles. *A lamb to the slaughter. I'll have this guy crying Mummy in no time!* He secures his grip on his weapons and locks eyes with his opponent. He's ready.

They begin the dance of circling one another.

The crowd watches in silence.

Ryker waits for the first strike, but nothing comes. After a few more turns, Ryker's patience wears thin. *Enough of this crap!* He raises his stick to strike, but Galen blocks it with surprising speed.

Galen smirks.

Ryker tries once more, but Galen blocks his strike again with the same swift reflex.

Now Galen laughs.

Ryker doesn't give him a moment to prepare for his next attack, but somehow Galen is ready, and he meets every strike with a faster block. Ryker's never seen such reflexes before—apart from Edra's, that is.

A sudden lightning-fast strike to the head from Galen makes Ryker see stars, and confirms his hunch—Galen's superfreak power is speed.

The crowd roars with laughter and applauds their champion.

Ryker draws away to collect himself, but Galen uses the opportunity to attack. Before Ryker knows what's hit him, Galen has delivered a dozen strikes. Ryker struggles to defend himself. Somehow he needs to break Galen's rapid attack. He fights back, swinging his baton in wild abandon, blocking and striking at every turn. His relentless retaliation has Galen on the back foot in no time.

Caught up in this enraged comeback, Ryker is momentarily disorientated when he realises that his strikes are no longer making contact. Galen has made a hasty retreat. Ryker takes chase, but Galen is faster and tags his teammate in moments.

Ryker falls back to catch his breath.

The bigger and more intimidating of the three men prepares to battle. Given his size, they're more evenly matched.

'Get him, Titus,' Galen calls after him.

Titus approaches, snorting like a bull, eager to charge.

Ryker takes a firm stance.

Titus lashes out as soon as he's within striking distance, but Ryker is ready, his shield up, blocking every blow. The impact is brutal, but Ryker takes it—and keeps on taking it.

Titus rages on, giving everything he has to coax a retaliation. But Ryker holds off, enduring the strikes.

Eventually, Titus tires—his blows weaken and the frequency of his strikes lessen.

Ryker waits, and then, at the crucial moment, delivers his one and only debilitating blow, straight between his bald-headed opponent's legs. Titus falls to the ground with a thud, clutching his groin and gasping for air.

The crowd flinches.

Ryker tosses aside his weapons, leaps onto his opponent and delivers several punches before Titus gets a chance to fight back. The two roll on the ground in an even battle, their fists bloodied, rage escalating.

Then Titus throws Ryker, and they get to their feet, eyeing each other. Titus lunges at Ryker and grabs him in a grapple hold, but Ryker sweeps his leg around and brings Titus crashing to the ground. Then he jumps on top of him and prepares to knock Titus out, but suddenly someone grabs him in a chokehold from behind, holding him back.

Ryker struggles against the vice-like grip as he's dragged to his feet. He stumbles backwards, but once stable, flips his second attacker, Galen, over his shoulder and delivers a punch to the back of his head, curbing the attack. Ryker plants his feet and prepares for Galen's comeback. Meanwhile, Titus lingers in the fringes to recover.

Ryker catches movement from out of the corner

of his eye; the third thug advances, keen to enter the battle. This guy is just as big as Titus. *Three against one, huh? So you want to play dirty? Okay, let's do this!* Ryker reaches down for the MK3 strapped to his calf, but as soon as he grasps the knife, Galen kicks it from his hand, and it flies across the arena and out of reach.

Galen dives onto Ryker's back, again locking him in a chokehold. He calls out to his friend for help. 'Quick, Cato, while I have him!'

Ryker waits for Cato's approach, and when he's within distance, Ryker headbutts Galen, hearing his nose break, and throws him over his shoulder to knock Cato off his feet.

Ryker staggers back, out of breath, and as his three attackers prepare to go again, he reaches into his cargo-pants' pocket, retrieves a canister of pepper spray and readies himself for the next assault.

Galen attacks first, but he doesn't get far—the chemical Ryker sprays in his face puts a stop to that. Galen falls back, shouting in pain and swiping at his eyes. Ryker grabs him in a chokehold and squeezes his throat with everything he has until Galen's body goes limp and falls to the ground.

Titus charges at Ryker and knocks him to the ground, but Ryker uses the pepper spray on him too. The man recoils, rubbing his eyes and cursing. Ryker discards the now-empty can and reaches into his other pocket to retrieve another life-saving device—his taser. He then scrambles to his feet and thrusts the device straight at his aggressor's neck. Titus doesn't stand a chance. While his attacker convulses from the electric shock, Ryker drops the one-shot taser, pulls back his arm and delivers a mighty blow to the man's head, knocking him into oblivion. With a blow like that, he won't be getting up again too soon.

Ryker doesn't get a chance to catch his breath. Cato is on him in seconds, delivering a series of punches to his face and head. Ryker stumbles backwards, struggling to remain upright. He tries to fight back, but the onslaught is relentless.

He's lost his knife, there's no more spray, and he's used the taser's single shot—Ryker has run out of options. He staggers backwards, trying to put some distance between them, but Cato is there at every turn, delivering punch after punch.

Ryker battles to strike back, but he won't give up—he can't. He thinks of his father, he thinks of his mother, and then he thinks of Aelianna. And from a strength found deep within, he channels the power he needs to charge Cato and knock him to the ground. Once on top, his arms fly, pounding like sledgehammers, his attack unrelenting, every ounce of his strength invested in each blow.

His muscles burn from the intensity of the

punches. He can't keep up the pace. He's weakening. His arms feel like lead weights.

NO!

Ryker fights the suffering, digging deeper, searching for the strength to finish this. But he can't; he has nothing left.

But Cato has. The brute pulls Ryker to his feet by the throat, tosses him like a rag doll, picks him up again and throws him once more. Ryker hits the dirt with a thud, winded. He needs to get up, but he can't. He lies there, fighting for breath, while Cato strolls up and stands over him, laughing. As bloodied and beaten as his face is, the man doesn't even look tired.

He's not human!

The crowd chants, 'Cato! Cato! Cato!'

Cato, relishing the attention, waves his muscle-clad arms in the air as though orchestrating a symphony, stirring them to chant louder. His toothless laugh brays like an excited mule.

A voice cries out from above. 'You may have succeeded in defeating Galen and Titus, but you will never match the endurance of Cato.'

Ryker scans the crowd to locate Wulf—the diminishing light renders it difficult—but then their eyes meet. Wulf stares him down, his dark eyes threatening, his smile sinister. 'And I am certain that Cato will be only too happy to go another round with you. What say you, Cato?'

Cato laughs stupidly, grabs Ryker by the scuff of the neck, pulls him to his feet, then turns to acknowledge the crowd.

They cheer.

Cato raises a meaty fist to deliver the final blow.

Ryker has only the strength to close his eyes and pray for a quick death.

Wulf triumphs; it's over.

48

ACHILLES HEEL

PEANUT

Well into the afternoon after a night spent with Molan and his family, Peanut and Connor make their way back to The Forbidden Passage. Peanut goes over their planned escape strategy, focused on what needs to be done later tonight. *We should be good to go. Ryker would've returned to the pit last night, and he'll be waiting with the rest of the guys.* He frowns, remembering that Mitchell told them Ryker would have to go through another challenge tonight. That could be problematic. He looks at the angle of the sun and realises they need to pick up the pace.

They've just increased their speed when Peanut hears something coming their way. Before he has the chance to tell Connor to hide, Connor morphs into his canine self and dives for cover. Peanut vanishes and waits to see what's approaching.

Connor yelps excitedly.

What the hell's he doing!

Peanut dives onto him to muzzle him, but Connor transforms back to his human self and throws him off. 'Quit it, you twit. It's Mitch!'

Peanut peers into the shadows and eventually spots Mitchell, four men trailing behind him.

Connor runs out to meet them. 'Man, you nearly gave us a heart attack!'

'Same!' Mitchell chuckles, clutching at his chest.

Peanut materialises before them, and Mitchell jumps back, startled. 'Hey, cool superpower!'

'Yeah, I know,' Connor grumbles, 'but don't ask him to swap; he won't.'

Mitchell chuckles. 'What are you guys doing here?'

'Us?' Peanut says. 'What about you? Ryker got you out already? That's awesome! So now we can get the hell out of here.' He stops and looks back along the path behind the men. 'Hang on a sec; where's Ryker? Why isn't he with you?'

Mitchell exchanges a look with the other men.

Peanut's eyes narrow. 'What the hell's going on, Mitch?'

Mitchell looks away and shrugs. 'Look, we saw the chance to get out last night after you guys left, so we took it. The pit was open; the rope was there. It was a no-brainer. We found a place to lie low, and now we're making tracks before it gets too dark again.'

Peanut can't believe it. 'But what about Ryker? He would've gone back to the pit last night. Remember the plan?' He rubs at his brow. 'God, I hope he realised you were gone and got out in time!' But his gut tells him, Ryker didn't—and the look on Mitchell's face doesn't give him any hope. Peanut bites back from yelling at him. 'Come on, let's get outta here; we need to get back to the arena. Ryker's bound to be in trouble.'

'Back?' one of the four men says. 'No, I am not going back. I am not going near The Dark Forest ever again.'

The other three men nod their agreement.

'We will leave you here,' the man says.

They say their goodbyes and scurry along the path towards Medwin's village.

Peanut turns to Mitchell and Connor 'What about you guys? Are you going to help me get him out or what?'

Mitchell has the decency to look somewhat ashamed. But he says nothing, just turns and strides back towards The Dark Forest and Wulf's arena. Peanut and Connor hurry after him.

A rumble from the heavens above signals a storm

brewing, and the light filtering through the forest canopy fades fast. With visibility now a challenge, Peanut struggles to keep up with the boys. Mitchell, on the other hand, doesn't appear to be having the same problem; he powers on.

Suddenly, in the distance, they hear a loud cheer. It sounds like a challenge. Peanut's stomach does a flip, and they sprint ahead, soon reaching the outskirts of the small, ramshackle village. Mitchell waves a hand, indicating for them to slow down and listen. But Peanut needs to get in closer. Ryker might need him. Before vanishing, he warns the others to stay put and be ready for anything. And then he's gone.

The sound of wood striking wood rings out—some kind of a stick battle, perhaps. Peanut makes his way to the arena and sees Ryker in combat with one of Wulf's goons—the tall skinnier one. And from the looks of it, the thug has got the upper hand, blocking Ryker's every strike and unyielding in his assault. Peanut pulls out his switch knife, looks down at it and frowns. Fortunately for both of them, Ryker finds the strength to retaliate, swinging at his aggressor with wild abandon, his offensive ruthless. He soon gains the upper hand, and Wulf's goon retreats to escape Ryker's onslaught, then tags his teammate for help. This new threat seems formidable. Although more evenly matched, there's something about this bald-headed guy's approach that makes Peanut draw back.

The situation quickly spirals downwards. Within seconds, Wulf's goon is dominating the attack. Strike after strike, the huge, bald brute hammers at Ryker's defence, and Ryker appears to be struggling to fight back. Peanut needs to do something. He considers whistling to Connor for help. But a sudden outcry from the crowd returns Peanut's attention back to the fight. Ryker's opponent falls, clutching his groin, gasping for air. Peanut flinches. *Ouch! Straight for the crown jewels.*

Ryker dives onto the goon and is set to take him out—*but what's this? The first guy's back! Hey! Not fair!* Peanut watches as the tall guy grabs Ryker in a chokehold from behind. And then the third challenger, lurking in the background, gears up to pounce. *Three against one? That's not gonna happen! Not if I can help it!*

Ryker reaches for something strapped to his calf, but the challenger is quick to disarm him—seemingly too quick. Peanut blinks a few times. If he hadn't seen it himself, he wouldn't have believed the speed with which that happened. There's no denying the inevitable—Ryker's in deep trouble. Peanut doesn't overthink it; he runs to the edge of the arena, searches for a means to get down there, remembers the ladder and races to it. But Wulf's mutts are guarding it, blocking his way. There's no time to lose. He flings a large stone at one of them, and the two break into a tussle, which allows him to fly down the ladder and dart in the direction of Ryker's discarded weapon.

Although gasps of shock and horror followed by cheers from the crowd threaten to distract him, Peanut doesn't stop. He scans the arena floor looking for it and spots it in the near distance. He races to get it, but draws back when he sees what it is. *Bloody hell! What am I s'posed to do with that!* He picks up the thirty-centimetre dagger with two fingers, then looks back at the fight. Wulf's third goon has Ryker by the scruff of the neck. He's laughing at Ryker, who dangles, seemingly lifeless before him. With a sense of victory in the air, the freak turns to the crowd, grins and, from what Peanut can see, is about to deliver a blow so fatal that Ryker will never see the light of day again.

NOOOOOOOOOO!

Peanut tears across the arena, dives at the feet of Ryker's attacker and, with a sure and swift motion of the blade, slashes the backs of the goon's heels in time to intercept that final blow. The giant collapses with a thud, crying out in agony.

Peanut doesn't give Wulf time to retaliate. With the knife clenched firmly between his teeth, he yanks Ryker up by his shirt and magics him invisible. The crowd gasps. Wulf staggers back.

Peanut struggles to keep Ryker upright. He half drags him to the ladder, then uses everything he has to push them both up and out of the arena. Ryker stumbles a few steps, then falls flat on his face, yanking Peanut forward. He reinforces his grip on Ryker's shirt to maintain contact—for this to work, they both need to remain invisible.

Wulf's dogs are there, sniffing and whimpering in confusion, and then as Peanut pushes Ryker towards the cover of the forest, they become wild with determination to ferret out their invisible targets.

At the forest's edge, Peanut turns to take them on, shoving Ryker behind him. With the knife in one hand and Ryker's shirt in the other, he waits, ready.

But then, Connor, in his dog form, runs out into the clearing and, once again, creates the diversion they need to avert an attack. Wulf's mutts race after him.

Peanut watches Connor vanish into the forest and makes the snap decision to go after him. He shoves Ryker in the direction he needs to go, trusting he'll somehow make his way on his own. 'Mate, get yourself to the portal—the others are there waiting. Connor needs back-up.'

Peanut takes off. But moments later, a commanding howl, echoing eerily throughout the forest, alters his course. He whips around and sees

Wulf, in silhouette, baying in the moonlight—those dogs will be back at any moment. He rushes back towards Ryker and sees him stumbling blindly in the wrong direction, heading for the other portal. Peanut sprints after him. But will he reach him in time?

Ryker vanishes into the forest, and Peanut runs in after him, but trips and stumbles in the darkness. It's hopeless going any further this way. He stops to listen for him, but hears nothing. *Where the hell did he go?* He contemplates going further but knows he'll only end up getting lost.

A rustling sound nearby draws his attention. He tightens his grip on the knife.

'Oi, Peanut, where are ya?'

It's Mitchell. Peanut materialises. 'Over here!'

Mitchell appears from the darkness, heaving from running. 'C'mon, let's go!' He turns to go. 'Wulf's got his dogs again, and they're about to go after Ryker. There's no way he'll make it without our help. We've gotta do a *Connor* and give them something else to chase. You ready?'

And so they take off to be that distraction, taking no care to mask their movement. Wulf and his dogs soon fall for the decoy.

With the hunters on their scent, Peanut and Mitchell need to hurry. But Peanut battles to see two feet in front of him. Thankfully, Mitchell doesn't appear to have the same problem, and so takes the lead. Together, with Peanut's guidance, they pick up the trail to the South African portal.

But the dogs are fast approaching; the sound of their snapping jaws is soon mere metres away. *Craaaap!* The hair on the back of Peanut's neck stands on end. Naturally faster than Mitchell, he struggles to stop himself from overtaking him. And then the huge rock formation is in his sights, and he can no longer hold back. He yanks Mitchell by the arm, magics them both invisible and powers ahead, dragging his surprised friend through the unguarded, narrow passageway. And with a rush rivalled to setting up the winning goal in a hockey grand final, Peanut hauls them both through the portal to exit the Ancient Realm.

And just like that, the threat of Wulf and his fast-approaching mongrels are left far, far behind.

49

WHAT A BUZZ!

MAX

Although The Forbidden Passage is now safe, thanks to Ruby's impressive assault, they decide to leave the realm and wait for Peanut and Connor on the other side of the portal. Max breathes a sigh of relief. The only hurdle is convincing the men from the pit to trust that they're not going to die once they pass through the ghostly barrier. And it's the threat of what waits for them in this savage world that tips the scales.

Wide-eyed and terrified, the men watch Edra and Ruby step forward and vanish through the rippling curtain. Ruby immediately reappears to assure them that she's not dead, and then, with a bit of coaxing from Max, they take that leap of faith themselves. On the other side, they're quick to jump to their feet to inspect, open-mouthed, the new world that surrounds them.

Then there's a struggle to get the men into the back of the jeep. Max almost laughs at their reaction to seeing what would appear to them to be an odd-looking, caged metal contraption. Once in, they huddle together, speechless, in the back corner.

Max stops to take it all in, seeing everything through their eyes. They would never have seen such a sight: arid land as opposed to the lush green of the woods, their view endless, as far as the eye can see. She sighs. Somehow the dangers lurking out there don't frighten her as they should; she's safe with her friends in the protection of the jeep. She closes her eyes and feels the warmth of the sun heating her cheeks. The tension she felt earlier fades. She could easily sleep—Ryker's healing having drained her energy levels earlier—but there's more to be done, and she's reminded of that when she hears Edra call back to base using the walkie-talkie.

Banji responds. 'Edra, is everything okay? Over.'

The pit men startle at hearing a voice coming from the small black box, and they shrink away from the oddity.

'Banji, can you and Lanny hire another jeep from the grounds and get over here? We've brought back a few extras. Oh, and bring all the food and water you can get your hands on. Don't ask; I'll explain when you get here. Over.'

'Extras? What? Look, never mind. We're a step ahead of you—we've got one already. We'll be there ASAP. Over and out.'

When the twins' jeep approaches, all six of their new friends look ready to run into the wilds of the reserve. It takes some convincing to get them to believe that they're not in any threat from the moving horseless chariot. Once they've settled the men with water and food, they all climb into the jeep with the twins to get down to business.

Jack fills Banji and Ulan in on the situation.

As they sit and listen, Max notices Ruby chewing her fingernails. She guesses she's anxious about Peanut. She links arms with her, closes her eyes and is asleep in moments.

She wakes a short time later with a jolt, breathing heavily. Alarmed, she searches for the danger she'd foreseen. But all is safe.

Jack, sitting beside her, squeezes her hands. 'You saw something?'

She studies his face. His gentle eyes and sincere tone just about has her in tears and forgetting the vision she had. She chokes them back. 'So ... you ... you don't think I'm a freak?'

The others watch on with interest, eager to hear

this new premonition.

Jack smiles a crooked smile. 'Hey, who am I to knock it? Yeah, it's weird, but what's *not* weird?' He snorts. 'Haven't you heard? *Weird* is the new *norm!* And just for the record, you were spot on last time, weren't you?' He shrugs. 'What's there to think about? It's a gift.'

Her eyes narrow. 'Seriously, you don't think I'm crazy?'

Jack smiles. 'Yeah, I think you're crazy, but awesome-crazy, not kooky-crazy.' He pulls her into a hug. 'When you think about it, it's not that weird; Medwin does it all the time.'

She pulls out of his hold to look at him. 'Yeah, but that's because of the realm, you know, magical powers and all'—she hesitates a moment—'and we're not in the realm now.'

Jack shrugs again.

She blinks and looks at her friends; they appear confused by her argument. Max can't believe it; she had it wrong all this time. They don't think she's a freak, and these premonitions she's getting aren't fazing them one bit. *So if Jack distancing himself has nothing to do with that, what has it got to do with?*

Kenny nudges her. 'So tell us, what did you see this time?' He shifts in his seat and leans in closer.

Max smiles at his eagerness, then turns her focus

on what needs to be done. With her eyes closed, she loses herself in what she saw in the dream. Her earlier anxiety returns. She sees Ryker, trapped somewhere and alone. Her pulse quickens. There's a challenge … a brutal, one-sided battle. Her eyes pop open. She turns to Jack. 'Ryker needs help. I don't know what's happened, but things have gone wrong.'

Edra curses and leaps out of the jeep, slamming the door shut. Colour courses up her neck and floods her cheeks. She kicks some stones, then turns to face them. 'This was a fricking stupid idea in the first place, and now it's becoming a complete disaster.'

The rest of the crew follow her out.

Ruby clings to Max's arm. 'What about Peanut? Did you see him in your dream? Is he in danger too?'

Max squeezes Ruby's hand and shakes her head. She prays Peanut *not* featuring in her dream is a good sign.

Jack suggests they make a plan to go back, but Kenny frowns. 'Mate, we've got nothing to go on, apart from Max's premonition. It's too risky—I vote we wait. Who knows, Peanut might be onto it already.' Kenny's suggestion makes sense, and so they decide to stay.

After several agonising hours sitting around waiting for something to happen, Max notices the portal oscillating with renewed energy. She scrambles to her feet. 'Guys, something's coming!'

Jack grabs his hockey stick. 'Quick, get behind me!'

Kenny stands at his side, nunchaku at the ready.

Edra arms herself with a tyre lever she finds in the back of the jeep.

Ruby searches frantically for something to arm herself with and grabs a steel coffee flask.

The twins have come prepared—Banji with a pocket knife; Ulan, a frypan.

Max snatches her baseball bat and joins the boys at the portal, standing ready. She won't let them face the threat alone.

'Get ready!' Jack cries out.

The portal spits out two figures. One, to her relief, is Peanut; the other, a boy Max can only guess is Connor. She scans them from head to toe, anxious to see if they're hurt.

Peanut scurries to his feet, then turns towards the portal, his face pale, his guard up. The other boy scampers back, away from the portal. Something must be coming after them. Max holds her breath waiting for it, but the gauzy curtain becomes tranquil.

'Woohoo! Man, what a buzz!'

Peanut's outburst startles her. She turns to scowl at him, not knowing whether to hug him or throttle him. And by the looks on everyone's faces, she's not alone.

'Where the hell have you been, you moron?' Jack asks.

Ruby pushes past everyone and shoves him. He stumbles. 'Charlie, I mean it, you pull a stunt like that again, and I'll have your guts for garters!'

Peanut's hands shoot up in front of him. He struggles to wipe the grin from his face.

Ruby rolls her eyes and shakes her head, but a smile tugs at the corner of her mouth.

Kenny steps between them. 'Peanut, have you seen Ryker? We were kinda hoping you were with him.' He looks at the new boy. 'And I guess this is Connor, the one that decoyed the dogs.'

Peanut cringes, then rubs his brow. 'Um, guys, this is Mitchell. And, mate, you're not gonna believe what just happened!'

'Mitchell?' Edra asks. 'But what happened to Connor? Weren't you supposed to be with Connor?'

'I was, but—'

'And if this is Mitchell,' Max interrupts, her pulse picking up speed, 'where's Ryker? Wasn't Ryker going back for Mitchell?' She isn't liking the sound of this—things aren't adding up. 'Look, before you answer, just tell us one thing: do you know if Ryker is all right?'

Peanut lets out a ragged breath and runs his hand through his tousled hair. 'My best guess is that he is.'

Max grits her teeth, but before she has a chance to say anything, his hand snaps out in front of him as if to fend off an attack. 'Geez, Max, give a guy a break, will ya! It's a long story, so let me catch my breath.'

Max holds back from losing it, any earlier concern for Peanut's wellbeing forgotten. She glares, first at Peanut, then at the new guy, Mitchell—who in her estimation of things can claim some ownership for this new stuff-up. Edra and Ruby stand either side of her; their impressive heights make for a more intimidating impact. Max smiles inwardly. 'Talk! And this had better be good!'

Max locks eyes with Mitchell. He cringes and takes a step back.

Peanut laughs. 'Yeah, I know, small but deadly! Never judge a book by its cover, my friend. That death stare is a superpower on its own. And watch out'—he looks from Ruby to Edra—'they've all mastered it.'

Peanut quickly explains what's happened in the last twenty-four hours, veering off on a tangent every now and then in his typical fashion, but a subtle reminder in triplicate soon has him back on course. Once finished, he settles on his haunches, shuts his eyes and holds his head.

Max can't believe what they've just been through, risking their lives to save Ryker. Peanut turns his gaze to her, and a flush of heat colours her cheeks. Riddled with remorse, she looks away—she'd judged Peanut, and to some extent, Mitchell, too soon.

'The thing is, Ryker got away, right?' Banji says.

Peanut turns to Banji and lets out a deep sigh. 'Yeah, but who knows where he's gone.' He pauses. 'He was pretty wasted, so hopefully he found somewhere safe to hide. But with Connor looking out for him, he should be okay.'

Should be?

Max squeezes her eyes shut.

50

Kicking Butts

Thanks to Mitchell, their objective has changed again. But Max can't blame him. He saw an opportunity to escape that hell-hole, and he took it. Unfortunately, the upshot of that decision wasn't good for Ryker. From what Peanut told them, Max has a fair idea where Ryker might be, so she figures they should start with that. She and Ryker have been through enough together for her to know him well, and the one constant in all their struggles has been the safety of the treehouse. It's well hidden and has good security. So if he or Connor are wounded and need somewhere safe to lie low, he might make his way there. In fact, something niggling within convinces her that he *is* there. With night fast approaching, it's time to step up, trust her gut instinct and start calling the shots.

'Look, Ryker and Connor might be anywhere,' she says, 'but after hearing that Ryker was last seen headed in the direction of the other portal, I've got a hunch he may've gone to the treehouse. And we can only hope that Conner has tracked him down and is with him. I suggest that Edra and the twins stay here, while the rest of us go back in and head for home. On the way, we'll check out the treehouse, and if they're not there, we'll exit the realm, then contact you from there. If neither of us have seen them by that stage, we'll call in Deputy Thompson and the taskforce.'

Max notices the look of apprehension on the faces of the men from the pit, who are listening at a distance. 'And as for our new friends, well, maybe they should come with us. Medwin will know what to do for them.' She looks at her friends, then shrugs. 'What do you think?'

Edra sits higher. 'I'm good with that. Enough with the stuff-ups; this situation is beyond us now.'

Mitchell shakes his head. 'I can't believe I'm about to say this, but if you're taking a vote on going back, you can count me in. As much as I'm relieved to be outta there, I'm not staying here, not without Connor.' He stops to look into the savannah. 'By the way, where the hell are we? Are we out bush?'

Peanut ruffles Mitchell's hair. 'Mate, welcome to

South Africa!' He chuckles. 'For what it's worth, we could be in as much strife here as we were on the other side of that portal.' Then, as if on cue, they hear a lion moan in the distance. Peanut chuckles some more. 'Thank God for these caged jeeps is all I'm saying.'

'So we're all good with this?' Max tries to gauge Jack's response. He seems to be taking everything in, but says nothing.

Peanut looks ready to put forward his thinking, but Kenny stops him. 'No. Whatever you've got to say, Peanut, drop it. Max is right, so let's start planning what we need to do from here on.'

Banji, eager to help in any way, suggests that his small group remain in the passage, in case Ryker and Connor show up and need help. If after a reasonable period of time they don't, they'll exit the realm and wait to hear from Jack.

Ulan whips around to glare at him.

Banji smiles and holds up a few of Ryker's gadgets. 'I've got us covered, sis. We'll be fine. Don't worry so much.'

Ruby laughs. 'Ulan, chillax. I'm planning on kicking every single butt out there—they'll all be TKO'd in no time. The guards won't know what's hit them.'

'Cool, I haven't seen the golden glove in action

yet, but I bet it's awesome!' Peanut turns to Mitchell, nudges him, then waggles his eyebrows. 'That's my girl, freaking Wonder Woman!'

Ruby shrugs, and Mitchell shoots her a grin.

'Remember, it's not just guards we need to look out for,' Kenny tells them. 'Don't forget Wulf and his dogs.'

Suddenly the colour drains from Ruby's face. 'Crap, the dogs!'

Mitchell shudders at the mention of them. 'Ya can't call them dogs, Kenny, they're monsters! My hair's standing on end just thinking about those razor-sharp teeth. Bloody hell, we came this close to not making it.' He holds up his thumb and forefinger to indicate the distance. 'If it wasn't for Peanut, we'd be goners.'

'Good point, Kenny,' Max says. 'Okay, so we might have a few hurdles, but if we stick to the plan'—she directs a steely look at Peanut—'with Ruby in our corner, we'll be okay.'

The pit men happily agree to return to the realm with the Aussies. Ruby will take care of any security issues, and the twins will remain with Edra in the passage.

Max is anxious to get to Ryker. Peanut's account of what happened in the arena has her on edge again. She shudders to think that her dream wasn't that far off the mark. She's so caught up in her thoughts, she doesn't notice Jack take her hand in his until he squeezes it. She looks at their clasped hands, then into his eyes; that same profound expression he's been wearing lately is there again. She doesn't get it— she thought they'd dealt with that already. So why the look?

'You're worried about Ryker again, aren't you?'

His question surprises her; she frowns.

Jack motions for them to step away from the others to talk. Max looks out into the open plains of the reserve. The day is coming to a close—the sun is low, blanketing everything with a tinge of gold, and a gentle breeze cools her heated cheeks. It all appears peaceful, safe to venture from the group. They walk a short distance, hand in hand.

Max hesitates—it's crunch time. Like it or not, she needs to hear this if they're to move on. 'Um, so … what's wrong?'

Jack looks into the distance, his thoughts apparently elsewhere. His hold on her hand tightens for the briefest moment before he lets go. He then shoves both hands into his jeans pockets.

Max draws in a deep breath. *This can't be good.* 'Jack?'

He says nothing.

Oh God, he's dumping me, here in the middle of

nowhere! 'Jack, you're scaring me. Is it something to do with the weird visions of Ryker? I thought you were okay with that.'

He releases a held breath and turns to face her. 'Max, the visions aren't the problem. I told you that already.' He takes a step away from her and crosses his arms.

She mirrors his posture. 'What then?'

Jack shifts from one foot to the other, struggling to look at her. 'It's this connection you've got with Ryker.'

Max frowns. *Connection?*

'I mean, you're with me, but you're dreaming about him. I need to know where I stand in all of this, Max. What's going on?'

Max blinks in surprise. Her world spins, her equilibrium derailing. She shakes her head, not quite sure what just happened. Jack waits in silence for an answer—his pain palpable. And suddenly she understands. *He's jealous of Ryker!*

And just like that, she falls a little more in love with him. She steps up to him, unfolds his rigid arms and wraps herself in them, squeezing him tight around the waist. His heart hammers against her ear. And then he softens, and the beat slows. He rests his chin on her head. Her eyes close, and she breathes him in, his familiarity calming her.

'Jack, you're my *always*. I thought you knew that.' She looks up to face him. His brown eyes suddenly deepen, and the green flecks in them sparkle. That grave look is gone. She smiles. 'And Ryker is family— the brother I never had. Knowing he's in trouble, well, it's got me freaking out. You can understand that, right?'

He pulls her into a hug, presses his lips to her hair and nods. And with a gesture as simple as that, her off-kilter world is tilting on its axis again.

51

T.K.O

It's time to go. They're just about ready to re-enter the realm. Ruby squats on her haunches at the foot of the portal with her head between her knees. She draws in a few deep breaths and takes a moment to psych herself up, her earlier bravado now debatable. *Will you quit it! They're only dogs!* But Mitchell's description of Wulf's mongrels has Ruby's heart pumping at a ridiculous pace. Absentmindedly, she rubs at the faded ten-centimetre-long scar on her leg—a permanent reminder of the dog attack twelve years ago, when she was just a child. She shakes off the memory. *I can do this! I've beaten up muscle-clad thugs with this shield, so a couple of overgrown hairy mutts aren't going to get the better of me!*

'Hey, I never noticed that before,' Peanut says,

stroking the raised pink line. 'How did ya get that? It's a beauty.'

Ruby gets to her feet, shrugs and steps away. She definitely doesn't want to talk about this. Her fear of dogs is irrational, and she knows it. Stacks of people have all sorts of fears: some of spiders, others, heights, and some even of clowns. But to Ruby, it's a sign of weakness, and one that's been an ongoing struggle to overcome.

Peanut follows, his brow raised—clearly, he's not going to drop it.

Ruby groans. 'I was bitten by a dog when I was a kid, okay? Are you satisfied?'

Peanut's hands shoot up in front of him. 'Whoa, no need to bite my head off.' He frowns. 'So what's your problem?'

She shrugs, then turns away. 'I hate dogs; that's all.'

He laughs. 'What? All dogs or just the one that bit you?'

'All dogs—it's a phobia.' There, she said it. And now she couldn't care less what he thinks of her.

Peanut laughs again.

Ruby's eyes narrow. She grits her teeth.

'That's nothing; I'm scared of moths.'

Peanut's admission jolts her out of her self-pity.

'Yeah, can ya believe it? Six-foot tall and shit-scared of moths. Can't handle them—big ones, little ones, black or white; they all freak me out.' He shudders.

Ruby can't hide a smirk.

'C'mon,' he says, pulling her into his side, 'we'll do this together. Let's go finish those dogs off once and for all.' Peanut kisses her brow, then looks at her. 'You ready?'

Ruby takes a deep breath and smiles. She's ready—it's payback time.

Hand in hand, Peanut and Ruby pass through the wispy veil, the others following behind. As expected, it's dark in the passageway. Kenny estimates it to be about three hours before dawn and, according to him, the perfect time to start their trek—less likely to come across any *unfavourables*.

Peanut and Ruby move forward to assess the situation. Ruby activates her shield; Peanut secures the night-vision goggles and magics them both invisible, then they inch closer to the exit, Peanut stopping to pick up a few stones. They listen out for any threat, but all is quiet.

At the mouth of the passage, Ruby retracts the shield, and Peanut throws a few stones into the forest, then they listen to hear if they stir a reaction. They hear a whimper. Ruby and Peanut exchange a look. Peanut points in the direction the sound came from.

No doubt it's one of Wulf's dogs, and by the sounds of the restraint in that whimper, it wouldn't surprise Ruby if Wulf was lurking in the darkness too. *Bring it on!*

Ruby releases Peanut's hand to allow him to investigate. Now visible, she sets herself up to lure the enemy out of hiding, her shield at the ready.

A thrashing sound comes from the distance, heralding the approach of another threat—guards? But they'd anticipated this. Ruby reinforces her stance.

And then Wulf commands his beasts to attack, and the air fills with menacing growls. Two massive black beasts fly through the air towards her, dark eyes gleaming, fangs luminous in the moonlight. She staggers back and swallows hard, then reminds herself that, now more than ever, she needs to stay firm—her friend's lives depend upon it. One dog pounces. Ruby stares it in the eye, fortifies the barrier and watches it slam against the shield with a tremendous thud before falling limp. Moments later the second dog comes at her and meets a similar fate. Rivulets of blood trickle from the contact site, smearing her view, but not enough to prevent her seeing Wulf's goon racing towards her wielding an axe. Ruby relaxes her shield, allowing it to temper, so when the weapon connects, it rebounds and hits the goon straight between the eyes, knocking him out for the count.

Wulf's fury is obvious, the look of revenge clear in his eyes. He's ready to attack. And just at that moment, three guards appear. They're quick to take in the situation. One pounces on Wulf, knocking him to the ground. Wulf's pathetic attempt to defend himself against the huge and well-trained guard is almost laughable. Another guard dives at Ruby but ricochets off her shield, landing head first, with a sickening crunch, on a nearby boulder. He doesn't recover. The third guard mysteriously convulses, electric sparks flying, and then falls limp. Ruby glances at the brute on Wulf and witnesses him deliver the blow to end, for good, the tyranny of the ruthless savage.

The guard turns to take on more. He sees Ruby and lunges at her. But the contents from an invisible aerosol-can put a stop to that. He doubles over in pain, clutching his face, and screams for help.

Ruby warns Peanut to move aside as she transforms her shield to take on the form of her infamous boxing glove, and with one almighty blow, she punches the helpless one-hundred-and-fifty-kilogram blubbering mass of flesh into oblivion.

Five bullies and two dogs down, none to go—the path is paved.

52

A Safe Haven

Ryker

To his relief, Ryker realises he's not as lost as he thought he was. Peanut had pushed him towards the forest, but he was so disorientated at the time, he had no idea where he was heading. But his instincts must've guided him to familiar ground. He can hear the water in the distance—the river. He knows this area like the back of his hand. Should he run to the treehouse or go to the river where he can mask his trail? The dogs are closing in on him. But are there two? *It sounds like only one.* Either way, he needs to made a decision now, and the river is his closest option. Choice made, he sprints downhill towards the water.

The devil is on his tail, its breath ragged as it exerts itself to get to him. Ryker doesn't look back.

He knows it's only a matter of seconds before he'll have to face the brute and battle for his life. He digs deeper, and the river comes into view. But what good will it do him now? It'll only slow him down. He decides to stop in the clearing by the river and take the beast head on. He stops and swings around, looking for something to defend himself with. He spots a fallen branch, lunges for it, then turns to face his attacker, weapon lifted ready to strike. But it's not one of Wulf's monsters.

The animal skids to a halt. It's Connor. His flea-bitten, scruffy friend jumps up on his hind legs, wags his tail and yowls happily.

The branch falls from Ryker's hands, and he crumples to the ground.

Connor morphs into his human self, squats by Ryker's side and rests his hand on his shoulder. 'Hey, are you all right? Man, I didn't mean to scare you.'

Ryker can't respond. He's too shaken.

Connor helps him to his feet. 'Come on, let's get you freshened up. You'll feel better with all that blood washed off.'

Ryker stumbles to the water's edge then collapses, exhausted. After a while he sits up and rubs his brow. 'I honestly thought you were one of Wulf's mutts … I thought that was it—the end.' He reaches down for some water and slowly washes the blood from his hands and forearms, then cups his hands to take a drink and splash water over his head.

Connor looks away, rueful. 'Sorry, buddy.' He scratches at his skin. 'Yeah, they came after me at first, and then, for some reason, took off in the opposite direction. But right now, I couldn't care less about them because I'm dying to jump in for a swim. You coming?'

Ryker watches Conner dive into the water with reckless abandon, then splash about like a kid at the beach on a hot summer's day. 'You've got no idea how long it's been since I've seen this much water.'

Ryker chuckles. 'Um. I think I do.'

Connor's face screws up. He sniffs his armpits. 'Geez, I must really stink. Funny how you can't tell after a while.'

Ryker thinks back to his own confinement. 'Hey, you know something? We figured it was you guys we battled in the arena all those years ago. There were four of you, right?'

Connor comes out of the water and leans against a boulder to dry. 'That was you?' He shakes his head, remembering. 'Man, you guys were all over us. We didn't know what hit us. But then again, we were pretty clueless back then. Superpowers? Who would've guessed it? The first time Mitch and I got clued up was after we were thrown down the pit. By then it was too late.'

Ryker frowns—it all makes sense now. His team annihilated Connor's team.

Ryker's team had realised their superpowers pretty much from the get-go because of the twins. Ryker smiles, remembering the first time Banji and Ulan found they were able to read each other's thoughts. And then, nothing was off limits. The twins had full access into everyone's heads, whether they wanted it or not. He laughs now, but he didn't find it so funny at the time, especially when he needed to be in his own headspace, which became increasingly more often as time went on. Anyway, it didn't take long before they each found they had superpowers. After that, they honed them, and winning battles wasn't as impossible as they'd initially thought it would be.

Ryker hadn't given Connor's team much thought after they were sent into exile. His sole focus at the time was survival. His reflection on this now leaves him with a heavy heart. Connor's friends died in the forest while he lived. 'Hey, I know it's too little, too late, but I'm really sorry about the other two guys in your group.'

Connor's shoulders slump.

They sit for a while, drying on the rocks, both lost in their own reflections. Ryker's thoughts wander to the reason for them being here—the assignment.

He curses under his breath. 'What a bloody mess!' His insides churn, knowing the mistakes he's made. 'What were we thinking coming back here? It's all been for nothing.'

Conner frowns. 'So you weren't pulling our leg— you really did find a way out of here?' His eyes widen. 'And you came back? Voluntarily?'

Hearing it put that way makes Ryker question the state of his mental health. He sighs. 'Insane, right?' He shakes his head, remembering all the kinds of stupid he's been lately. 'And you know what? The plan was solid. It would've worked if only I didn't get distracted. I'm an idiot; that's all there is to it.'

Ryker thinks about Aelianna and frowns. She wasn't at Wulf's side at the last challenge. He can only hope she escaped somehow, because he can't afford to think otherwise. Trying to factor her in the operation is why they're in this mess in the first place. *Go in, find the portal and get out. Yeah, right!* He grits his teeth, thinking how badly he's let his mother down. 'What a freaking mess!' He turns to Connor, 'Come on, let's get the hell out of here!'

Connor jumps.

'Sorry, mate. It's nothing you've done.' Ryker rubs his brow and sighs. 'You know something, if I could kick my own arse right now, I would. I should've just stuck to the plan.' Ryker stands, ready to leave. 'And because I didn't, there's some unfinished business I need to put to rights before we can go home.' The look of disappointment on Connor's face just deepens the blow. He shakes it off. 'So are you with me?'

Connor shrugs. 'I guess so. What's another couple of hours?'

And so Ryker leads them back into the forest, his mind ticking over with what needs to be done.

53

Tying up Loose Ends

Ryker

Dense cloud cover, threatening to storm, obscures the light that would normally filter through the canopy, and Ryker struggles in the near darkness to lead the way. 'So, Connor, I guess being a dog has its advantages.'

'Yeah, I suppose. But I'd rather have what Peanut has—that'd be totally wicked!'

'But as a dog you've got certain skills, right? Like seeing in the dark?'

'Sure does. Helped me stay sane while we were down in the pit. Mitch has the same power, you know?'

'What? Night vision?' Ryker reflects on this. 'I guess that makes sense now—you guys being able to see me in the pitch black.'

'Yeah, but his night vision is better than mine for

some reason. I think it's because he's only got the one power. With me, night vision's a bonus—comes with being a dog, I guess.'

Ryker smiles. 'I would've loved to have been a fly on the wall the first time you transformed.'

Connor barks out a laugh. 'Mate, you've got no idea! I didn't know what was happening to me. We almost crapped our pants. Hey, watch out!' Connor grabs Ryker to stop him from falling into a deep trough. 'Phew, that was close! How about you let me lead.'

'Thanks, buddy. I was hoping you'd offer.' Ryker points out the trail he's been following. 'Just follow this; it'll take us to where we need to go.'

Connor's brow knits. 'So where exactly are we going?'

Ryker grins, anticipating Connor's reaction. 'Okay, swear you won't freak out, but I've promised a friend that I'd bring him home with us.'

Connor's frown deepens. 'Why would I freak out? The more people we can get out of this place, the better. Right?'

Ryker considers the word *people* and chuckles.

Connor snorts. 'What's with the joke?'

Ryker considers how he's going to approach the subject. 'Well, do you remember in the battles how there were five of us?'

Connor nods, and Ryker explains how he stumbled into The Valley of Lost Souls and found Jaeger.

Connor's eyes widen. 'You've got to be kidding me. Ghosts!'

Ryker shrugs. 'I know. Weird, right?'

Connor gropes for words. 'Weird? Talk about the understatement of the century!'

Ryker runs his fingers through his hair. 'You've got no idea how much I need to do this, not just for me, but for the whole team. Jaeger's death hit us hard, especially Edra.'

Connor remains silent for a long time, then lets out a drawn breath. 'Man, are you sure you wanna do this? I mean, d'ya think that's wise? Your friend, Edra. How d'ya reckon she'd react to seeing him again—dead and all? Personally, I'd have a heart attack!' Connor rubs at his chest. 'In fact, I think I'm having one now.'

Ryker frowns. 'You've got a point, but I've promised Jae that we'll give it a go.'

Connor scratches his head. 'So how are you planning on doing this?'

Ryker shrugs. 'To tell you the truth, I've got no idea. I'm hoping it'll come to me once we get there.'

Connor snorts. 'What? Just wing it?'

Connor's reaction makes Ryker question what he's doing. They're in the middle of a forest, wandering in the near dark, following markings he'd left earlier that lead to a valley of dead people where he plans to rescue a ghost. Nothing in his years of training could've ever prepared him for anything like this.

I must be insane!

'Well,' Connor chuckles. 'I guess anything's doable. Look at me, I'm a dog, for crying out loud!'

And just like that, the seed of doubt evaporates into a cloud of mist.

They soldier on and follow the trail down the steep decline, the temperature noticeably plummeting the further they go.

'Man, did it just drop twenty degrees or what?' Conner shivers and rubs his arms to stir up some heat. 'Nah, forget this for a joke. I need a coat.' He transforms into his dog self and leads the way, his nose sniffing the ground, presumably picking up traces of Ryker's scent from when he last came this way.

Ryker pushes on, hoping Jaeger reveals himself sooner rather than later. And it's not the frigid temperature that has him shivering; this place just gives him the creeps.

54

ᏢHOLY ᏩHOSTS!

CONNOR

Wrapped in his fur coat, warmed from the chill, Connor follows Ryker's trail down the slope to The Valley of Lost Souls. And although warned, hearing about Ryker's ghost friend totally *did* freak him out. As a kid he hated ghost stories, and now he's about to meet one. As they descend deeper into the shadows, although uneasy about what's about to happen, Connor tries to keep a level head. But then suddenly the hair on the back of his neck stands on end; his base instinct tells him to watch out, and all logic flies out the window. He stops. A low, threatening growl resounds in his throat, and he bares his teeth in preparation.

Ryker pats him on the head. 'Settle down, boy. It's okay.'

Connor snorts. *So I'm back to being a dog to you, am I?*

Oblivious to his insult, Ryker points upwards, drawing Connor's attention to something floating above them. 'There they are, the lost souls I was telling you about.'

Connor gasps at the sight of so many of them, floating without effort, their wispy outlines palpable.

And then, to Connor's alarm, one of them seems to notice them. The ghostly figure breaks away from the rest, swoops down, stops before Ryker and looks, if possible, excited. 'You came back!'

Ryker chuckles. 'I said I would, didn't I? I couldn't leave you here, bro.'

The ghost moves in closer, then frowns. 'Hey, what happened to you? You look like you've gone a few rounds with Mike Tyson.'

Ryker chuckles. 'It's all good. It's not as bad as it looks.'

'So have you found the portal?'

Ryker smiles. 'We have, buddy. And we'll be out of here first thing in the morning if all goes well.'

The ghost whoops. 'So what did you tell Edra? Does she know?'

Ryker shifts uncomfortably. 'Um, no, not yet. Look, I wasn't sure how we were going to do this.'

Connor struggles to concentrate on what's

happening. His animal instinct to leap at the silhouettes above overrides his human one, so he transforms.

Ryker's friend falls back. 'Hey, wow! I didn't see you there.'

Ryker makes the introductions. 'Jaeger, this is Connor. You might not remember him, but we challenged him and his team in the arena back then.'

'No kidding!' Jaeger hovers excitedly. 'And you're working together on this?'

'Long story.' Ryker chuckles. 'I'll tell you some other time. Right now, we need to get going.'

The ghost's expression falls. 'What's going to happen next?'

Connor raises an eyebrow. *Yeah, how are we doing this, Ryker?*

Suddenly, something transparent, cold and wispy swoops past him, almost knocking him to the ground. 'What the …?' Connor spins on his heel, trying to keep the *something* in his sights. And then to his horror, the *thing* returns, stops before him, blinks a few times, then shakes its head. 'Connor, is that you?'

Another ghostly figure swoops down to investigate. It leans in a little closer to study him, then turns to the first one. 'Sebby, it *is* him!'

For a moment, the two ghosts stare at each other,

wide-eyed, then whoop at the same time.

Connor stumbles back, not quite believing what he's seeing. 'Sebastian? Eddie?'

The two bounce about, spinning in circles with excitement. It takes a good while for them to settle. 'Yeah, it's us! Man, it's good to see you!'

Connor blinks a few times. 'Now this is just *too* fricking weird!'

Sebastian and Eddie laugh.

Connor hunkers down on his haunches. 'I'm kinda spinning out here.'

Ryker squats next to him. 'Just breathe, buddy.'

'So you've come to take us home, right?' one of them asks, his expression full of hope.

Connor takes a moment to get his head around what's happening. 'Yeah, Seb, I guess something like that.'

'Eddie, did you hear that? We're going home!' The two friends holler, hoot and wrestle each other in excitement.

'So I'm guessing these are the two guys that didn't make it to the pit?' Ryker laughs.

Connor's mind reels. 'Yeah. Eddie, Sebastian, this is Ryker. He's gonna help us out of here. Hey, do you guys remember Ryker's friend, Jaeger? We battled him in the arena.'

Eddie swoops past Jaeger to take a closer look,

then shakes his head. 'But that's not saying anything, everyone kinda keeps to themselves here. Our existence is pretty empty, really—just one big, fat, boring void of nothingness.'

Ryker smiles. 'Well, we're about to change that.'

'You hope,' Connor mutters under his breath.

But Ryker's smile oozes confidence. 'You've said it before, Connor, anything's doable. Come on, let's go make this happen!'

Connor is only too happy to make tracks—all these ghosts floating about them has taken its toll on him. He doesn't think his state of mind can take much more.

But Ryker doesn't leave immediately. The furrow in his brow suggests he's carefully considering their next step. He looks from Connor to their transparent friends. 'Guys, as it stands, from here we're on course to the South African portal, but I'm not sure if that's where we should be heading.' He runs his hand through his hair. 'To tell you the truth, with or without your help, Connor, the risk of not making it there in the dark is too great. We could get lost. And I really don't think I'd survive another bout with Wulf's hounds if we were to come across them.'

Connor knows he wouldn't either.

'I don't know about you, but I need to rest,' Ryker continues, 'and I know a safe place to do it. We can recuperate there and be in better shape to face whatever Wulf might throw at us tomorrow. Come first light, we'll head to the South African portal where our friends are waiting.'

Connor nods with relief. He's exhausted. All this long-distance running has taken its toll on him too.

55

SURPRISE!

RYKER

Ryker wakes to the sound of movement beneath the treehouse. He rolls over and peers through the gaps in the floor, squinting to get a good view in the dim pre-dawn light. He relaxes when he sees Peanut. And he's not alone; Max, Jack, Ruby and Kenny are there with him.

'Oi, Ryker,' Peanut calls up in a loud whisper, 'let down the rope, will ya!'

Connor jerks from his sleep, wide-eyed and disorientated. A low growl rumbles from his throat. Looks like he's preparing to transfigure.

'Whoa, it's okay.' Ryker grins. 'The cavalry is here.'

Ryker leans over the edge and spots Mitchell with the pit-people half hidden in the bushes eyeing him.

'Hey, Ryker, is Connor up there with you?' Mitchell calls up.

Connor sticks his head out and waves down. 'All good, Mitch. And you're not gonna believe who else is up here!'

Ryker chuckles, anticipating Mitchell's reaction, then scurries down the rope to land at Jack's feet. He fist-bumps the boys and hugs the girls. Max remains by his side. He immediately feels the heat from her healing energy.

'Just a sec, I'm coming,' Connor calls down.

Mitchell looks on as he descends, a blank expression on his face. 'So who else have you got stashed up there? The Easter bunny?'

Eddie and Sebastian float down to hover before them.

In his hurry to get away, Mitchell stumbles backwards, trips and lands on his backside. Jack grabs Max's arm and tugs her behind him. Ruby spontaneously deploys her shield to encase all those that aren't fast enough to scramble away. Peanut and Kenny gape at the vision before them. The men from the pit huddle outside the dome and watch, wide-eyed and cagey, from afar.

Connor grins. 'Cool, huh?'

Sebastian laughs. 'Hey, Mitch! Long time, no see.'

Mitchell opens his mouth, then closes it again,

speechless, his finger pointing from one ghost to the other. Jaeger floats down to join them, and Mitchell, eyes bulging, scrambles even further away.

'Everyone, this is Jaeger,' Ryker announces. 'You might remember me mentioning we lost him in one of our battles. I'm hoping we can somehow take these guys home with us.'

'Say what!' Peanut takes another step back.

Their reaction doesn't surprise Ryker. He's still trying to get his head around all this *ghost* stuff himself. 'The thing is, they've been trapped in this place called The Valley of Lost Souls—'

'Hey, I've been there!' Peanut interrupts. 'And I'll tell ya somethin' for nothin'; you wouldn't catch me dead near a place like that!' He shivers. 'It's spooky!'

Ryker chuckles at Peanut's unintentional pun. 'Well, the thing is, they haven't been able to pass to the other side—not sure why, but we can't leave them here like this. I figured we'd at least try to take them back. What do you reckon?'

Going by everyone's stunned silence, he's grateful Edra and the twins aren't here too. He'll need a little more preparation for the *Jaeger reveal* when it comes to them. How he plans on doing that … well, he'll deal with it when he needs to.

'So, Jack, where did you leave the others?'

Jack blinks a few times. 'Um, yeah, right …' He

shakes his head as if trying to process his thoughts. 'The others! Shit, I nearly forgot. You'd better hurry; they're back at the passage, waiting.'

'They're what?'

Jack raises his hands to fend him off. 'Hey, I told them to stay in the reserve, but Banj insisted they wait in the passage.'

Ryker curses under his breath.

'Geez, if looks could kill!' Peanut jokes. 'Chillax, bro, they're safe. My best girl has taken care of everything—the guards won't be hassling anyone any time soon. And we'll be long gone before Herodus realises what's happened. And don't worry about Wulf and his cronies either. She's looked after those pains in the neck too.' He turns to give Ruby a wink.

Ryker frowns—it can't be that easy. He looks at Max; she reassures him with a smile. So his passage home is paved. How can he ever repay his Aussie friends for all they've done for him? Suddenly he remembers the mission. 'But what about your dad, Jack? He'll be expecting me to come back with you; we'll be blowing our cover.'

Jack laughs. 'Our cover?'

Peanut slaps Ryker's back. 'Mate, I think that horse has already bolted. You *do* realise that we've been MIA longer than expected, don't ya? Somehow, I don't think it's Jack's dad you need to be worried about.' Peanut jerks his head towards Jaeger's ghost. 'I reckon you're gonna have your hands full tackling that other little matter. Edra's gonna totally flip when you drop that bombshell.'

Ryker inwardly groans.

Max takes his hands in hers. 'Hey, we've got this. Just go look after the others.' She gives him a hug. 'And as for your mum, well, we can work out how we're going to fix it for her later. We've found the missing portal, and that's what we came for. Right?'

He's torn. Time and time again his friends have stuck their necks out for him. And only God knows what repercussions they're to face when they return. He feels he can't abandon them like this.

'Yes, you can, and you will!' Max shoves him. 'Now, go!'

'I wouldn't argue if I were you,' Peanut says with a grin. 'She can be pretty scary.'

Ryker splutters. 'Who? Max? Scary?' But Max is right. He tugs her to his side to give her a hug and then gives her another squeeze before turning to go.

And then Peanut surprises him with a slap on the back. 'Wait up, I'm coming too.' He gives him a wink. 'Just in case you run into trouble.'

'And you're to come straight back!' Ruby steps up to him with her hands fisted on her hips. 'No mucking around. No chasing dogs, no playing the hero, no straying from the plan. Just see them to the passage, then get your arse straight back. Got it?'

Peanut gives her his famous lopsided smile. 'I'll be back before you know it.' He turns to leave.

Ryker follows, a grin on his face—the forces at work between those two is beyond him. *Definitely belongs in the too-hard basket.*

With Jaeger hovering by his side—the other ghosts remaining with the Aussies—Ryker quickly sobers and turns his focus to reaching the other portal. He can't afford to drop his guard now; they're too close to completing the mission.

The woods are quiet at this hour of the morning, and the freshness in the air sharpens his senses. As they step through the dimly lit forest, he thinks of the upcoming challenge. 'So, Jae, we've got a bit of explaining to do when we get there. And I won't lie, I'm not sure how Edra's going to react. She might not handle it too well.'

Peanut stops, turns and snorts. 'Not handle it too well? Mate, tell it how it is. She's gonna freak! One hundred percent! If this doesn't tip her over the edge, I don't know what will.'

Ryker gives him a steely look.

Peanut pouts. 'Hey, don't look at me like that; I'm not saying anything we don't know already. As if she's not messed up enough.'

Ryker grits his teeth. If Peanut wasn't such a good mate, he'd flatten him.

Peanut frowns. 'All I'm saying is I'd hate to be in your shoes. All right?'

Jaeger stops, a look of unease in his eyes. 'She's not in a good place, is she?'

Ryker holds back from answering. Does he tell him the way it really is, or does he sugar-coat it? He sighs. If it was him, he'd want it straight up. 'The truth? No … no, Jae, she's not.'

Jaeger's shoulders droop. 'Ryker, this is wrong.' He stops for a long while, deep in thought. 'Look, I can't do this. I've changed my mind.' He turns to leave.

'What? No. Stop!' Ryker whips around and glares at Peanut.

Peanut shrinks back.

The glow emanating from Jaeger's form vanishes. 'I'm not going to hurt Edra, not again.'

Ryker runs his hand through his hair. 'Look, there's no easy way of doing this, but we need to do it. Okay? Neither of you deserve what's happened, not you or Edra. But we can't leave you here—not like this. I have no idea what's going to happen— maybe we can do it, maybe not—but we at least have to try. If there's a chance you can move on from this, then we should take it. Jae, Edra will always have us to lean on; we'll never let her down. We've done it before, and we'll do it again. Whatever it takes.'

Peanut sighs. 'Look, I'm sorry for letting the cat out of the bag.' He scratches his chin. 'I guess subtlety's not my thing. But it's like Ryker said, it's gonna be tough—no ifs or buts about it—but you've at least gotta give it a go.'

Jaeger remains silent.

Ryker shifts uneasily. 'So what do you think? This might just be the closure that Edra needs—a chance to say a proper goodbye.'

'I'll tell ya what *I* think,' Peanut says, his eyes darting around the forest, 'I think we need to make a decision, pronto. It'll be daybreak soon, and I need to get back to the others before they send out a search party.'

Jaeger blows out an unsteady breath. 'Okay, let's do this.'

With the issue dealt with, Peanut sets the pace, charging ahead using the night goggles to help guide them. Ryker struggles to keep up with him.

'These goggles are awesome,' Peanut says. 'Saved our butts a few times already.'

Ryker chuckles. 'Keep them.' He then realises that Peanut is following some kind of path. 'How do you know the way?'

'Oh yeah, that?' Peanut turns and grins. 'There's a

trail from one gateway to the other, so between these goggles and Mitch's freaky night vision, making our way back and forth has been a cinch.'

'A trail?'

'Yeah, it's Banji's doing,' he says, pointing down at some whitish stones on the ground. 'So you could say that making our way in the dark has been a walk in the park.' He stops to laugh at his own joke.

The sound of something stirring in the bushes up ahead has Ryker on high alert. He grabs Peanut by the arm and raises his hand to silence him. Peanut vanishes. Jaeger whooshes into the sky, and Ryker dives for cover.

Molan appears from the darkness. 'Come forth, my friends, it is I.'

Ryker's thoughts race to Aelianna. Was he too quick to think she'd escaped Wulf? Is she still in trouble? But the look on Molan's face doesn't indicate it.

'Hey, Molan, you came!' Peanut reappears, his face bright. 'It's good to see ya, but I'll tell ya what, you nearly gave me a heart attack!'

Peanut's reaction to seeing Molan shocks Ryker into forgetting to ask after Aelianna.

Molan chuckles. 'My apologies, my friend, but since our last conversation I have reconsidered your thinking and have come on your suggestion. We have anticipated you passing this way.'

Molan suddenly jumps back, his eyes wide, his finger pointing at Jaeger's ghost. 'But what is this? Make haste; save yourselves! The spirits have escaped The Valley of Lost Souls!' He turns to run.

'Molan, stop,' Ryker calls out after him. 'It's all right. He's a friend.'

Molan turns warily, and Ryker explains Jaeger's presence to him. He's just finished his explanation when he catches sight of movement out of the corner of his eye. *Aelianna?* He must be seeing things. But it *is* her, inching closer, eyeing Jaeger, hesitant to approach. Ryker goes to her and takes her hand. 'Are you all right? What are you doing here?'

Her gaze flicks to her father, but she says nothing. Ryker frowns. 'What's wrong?'

She looks down; her cheeks colour, but she remains mute.

Her silence is killing him. 'What is it? Do you need help?' He squeezes her hand to coax her to look at him, but she looks away. *What's going on?*

Ryker turns to Molan for an explanation. He and Peanut exchange a conspiring look. Ryker glares at them—they don't have time for games; there's still that matter of Edra's bombshell he needs to deal with. Beads of sweat form on his brow. That, and having Aelianna so close to him, is definitely scrambling any coherent plans he may have had.

Molan steps forward. 'Yes, my son, we do need your help. I have something to ask of you.'

The timing couldn't have been worse—they're so close to finishing this. But if the good people of the forest need his help, how can he refuse them? He sighs. 'Then ask; I'll do anything I can.'

Molan holds his hand out to Aelianna. It's then that Ryker notices the small sack she's hiding from view behind her back. 'Ryker, Aelianna deserves a life free from danger. I ask that you take her with you.'

Ryker blinks a few times—Molan's words take a moment to register.

'Although at first, her mother was unwilling to part with her, she now agrees,' he continues. 'Aelianna's impulsiveness of late will surely lead to her demise. With all that concerns you, Ryker, the girl appears to have lost her senses.' He laughs. 'To throw caution aside and traipse through the woods only to return your satchel, what must she have been thinking? Was it ever a wonder she was caught by Wulf's thug? We can only be thankful to you and your friends once again that she was returned to us, safe.'

Ryker frowns, not understanding. Molan slaps a fatherly hand on his shoulder. 'Do not fret; her mother has given her blessings. She and the children have said their farewells.'

Ryker is lost for words.

His silence confuses the older man, and he becomes agitated. 'But, Ryker, you must! Wulf will rally and come for her—of this I am certain.' Molan's grip tightens. 'And I will never forgive myself if any harm comes to her. Please take her and protect her, for I know she will be safe with you. You have my blessings.'

A million stars blind his senses, then Ryker remembers to breathe.

Aelianna's eyes fill with tears, and she takes off at a run.

Ryker jolts from his state of shock to take chase. He has her in seconds, crushing her to his chest.

'Forgive my father,' she says, choking back tears. 'Do not take pity on me; I understand your decision. Ryker, go, leave while you are able.'

He can't interpret her anguish. Is Molan forcing her to go? He needs to know. 'Aelianna, there's nothing more that I want than for you to come back with me, but if this is not what *you* want, you've got to tell me now.'

Aelianna pulls out of his hold, her eyes searching his for the sincerity in his words. Then a smile as big as the sun warms her face to melt away any confusion.

'Then, you'll come back with me?'

Aelianna lowers her head and nods.

If anyone's heart could burst from happiness, it's Ryker's. He pulls her back into his arms and places a gentle kiss on the top of her head.

'Oi!' Peanut chuckles. 'A little too much public display of affection going on there! We've got places to go, things to do, people to meet … so let's get a move on.'

Hand in hand, Ryker walks Aelianna back to her father. 'I'll protect her with my life, Molan, I promise you.' He then grabs Peanut and pulls him into a man-hug. 'You're a good mate, Peanut.'

Peanut laughs. 'Hey, maybe I've found my calling in life, *The Looove God!* What d'ya reckon?'

Ryker chuckles. 'I'm sure Ruby will be rapt. Speaking of which, you'd better get going. We'll take it from here.'

Peanut turns to go. 'You're right—can't keep the lady waiting.'

'And Peanut,' Ryker calls out after him, 'be careful.'

Peanut gives him a wink. 'No worries, you too. Oh, and if you happen to run into any guards, just use Jaeger to scare them off—that'll do the trick.' He vanishes, his laughter echoing in the distance.

Ryker shakes his head, turns and takes Aelianna by the hand. They move on, Molan and Jaeger trailing behind.

Soon the rocky outcrop is within Ryker's sights,

his stomach does a flip, and it's not the threat of coming across guards that has him in a sweat, it's knowing what's ahead of him, and what effect it will have on Edra. He takes a breath; he owes it to Jaeger to see it through. He turns to his ghostly friend. 'You ready?'

Jaeger hesitates. 'I can't explain it—I'm so ready to see where this takes me, but I'm scared shitless knowing what it'll do to Edra, especially after hearing what she's already gone through. I love her, man, and I hate myself for what I'm about to do.'

Ryker runs his hand across the top of his head. Aelianna reaches out and gives his arm a gentle squeeze, her smile reassuring. And just like that, the task doesn't seem so daunting.

As they near, Ryker scans the area for any sign of trouble, but just as Peanut had assured him, the coast is clear. He motions to move on, but Molan stops, his eyes wide, reminding Ryker of their superstitious beliefs. 'You have nothing to fear, Molan; I promise you. The stories you've been told are just that, stories.'

Molan shakes his head. 'I trust what you say, Ryker, but it does not appease the apprehension ingrained in me.' He gestures for Ryker to move on. 'There is no need for me to proceed any further. Go before I have a change of heart.'

Ryker pauses. Before him stands a father

struggling with his emotions because he may never see his daughter again. Ryker's heart breaks a little. Father and daughter embrace for the last time—sentiments exchanged, words unspoken, tears fall uninhibited. Molan swipes at his cheeks, then turns to go. 'Keep her safe, my son.'

'You have my word.'

Molan nods and disappears into the darkness.

Ryker stares after him, somehow not believing what just happened. The warmth of Aelianna's hand in his reminds him that it did. He takes her, folds her in his arms and kisses the top of her head. 'Are you ready?'

Her eyes, still red and glistening with tears, are wide with hope. She smiles.

His heart explodes.

56

THE INESCAPABLE BOMBSHELL

Ryker instructs Jaeger to remain hidden until he calls for him—he'll prepare Edra first. But how he's going to do that, he still has no idea. He rubs his sweaty brow, hoping for inspiration. Aelianna steps up, takes his hand in hers and squeezes it. He looks into her deep chocolate-coloured eyes, and his stomach does a flip, his emotions playing ping pong with his thinking. One second, he's in a mess of pain, worrying how Edra will cope with the bombshell, the next, he's flying high with the promise of a future with this goddess at his side.

Aelianna places her hand on his chest and smiles. 'Do not fret; all will come to pass. What you are doing comes straight from your generous heart. Have faith, Edra will understand.'

All of a sudden, the weight of the burden lifts—he's not alone. They'll tackle this thing together and, somehow, he knows everything will be okay. He draws in a deep breath, then they turn to enter the passageway, ready to take on this new beast.

Ulan is the first to see them, and the look of relief on her face is obvious. 'Ryker, thank God you're safe! You're lucky the guards—' She stops at the unexpected sight of Aelianna. Ryker pulls her to his side. 'Ulan, Banji, Edra, this is Aelianna. She's coming home with us.'

Ulan tugs Aelianna into a hug. 'We've heard so much about you. I'm so happy to finally meet you.'

Aelianna smiles.

Banji steps up to shake her hand. 'Hi, I'm Banj; we met briefly in the woods. Brave thing you did, bringing us Ryker's kit like that. It definitely came in handy.'

Ryker stops. Molan's earlier comment now makes sense. He turns to Aelianna and frowns. 'What were you thinking?'

Aelianna ignores him and turns her attention to Edra. She reaches out to take her hands. 'And you are Edra. I feel we all shall be good friends.'

Edra appears uncomfortable with Aelianna's

familiarity; she cuts the introductions short. 'Let's go. No point hanging around here any longer. No offence, Aelianna, it's nothing personal, but I'm done with this place.'

Edra attempts to step away, but Aelianna holds firm. 'Edra, I know of your sorrow, and I am deeply pained.'

Ryker's head whips around so fast, he gets a crick in his neck. The colour drains from Edra's face; it's clear she's far from being okay with this. Her eyes lock with his, pleading for him to step in to help.

'Ryker has told me of your friend's passing,' Aelianna continues in a soft, gentle manner. 'Forgive me, for I will venture to tell you there is a place deep within the forest where the soul of a fallen one goes to rest, a place of peace.'

Ryker splutters. *What's she doing?*

Edra recoils at the mention of such a place and yanks her hands free. She steps back, pupils dilating. Her breathing accelerates. 'So are we getting out of here, or what?'

Ulan glares at Ryker. Suddenly, she gasps. Her hand flies to her mouth, eyes widening. She communicates something with her brother, then jumps to Edra's side. Banji shakes his head in amazement, a bowled-over expression on his face. They've read Ryker's thoughts and know what's coming.

Ryker takes a deep breath. There's no turning back; he needs to finish this. He follows Aelianna's lead. 'Edra, Aelianna mentions this place because I've just come from there, and there's something you should know.'

Edra's breath hitches. Aelianna closes the distance between them and rests her hand on Edra's. 'If you had the opportunity to see your loved one again, to say a proper goodbye, would you take it?'

Edra stares ahead, frozen in place.

Ryker doesn't dare breathe. The twins remain mute.

'Is … is that even possible?' Edra says in a barely heard whisper.

Aelianna takes Edra's hands in hers again. 'Yes.'

Edra stiffens. The depth in her eyes becomes shallow. She's gone.

Ryker searches Ulan's face, silently asking what's wrong.

Ulan shrugs.

Sweat beads on Ryker's brow. He turns to Aelianna. *What now?*

Aelianna smiles and motions for him to return his gaze to Edra.

A single teardrop runs down Edra's cheek. She's back. Edra swipes at the tear. 'Then I want to go there.'

Ulan squeezes her shoulder. 'Are you sure you

want to do this?'

Edra forces a smile, draws in a deep breath and nods.

This is his cue—Ryker braces himself. 'Edra,' he begins, 'while I was in The Valley of Lost Souls, I found him … I found Jae.'

Edra wavers.

Ryker steps forward to steady her. 'Hey, you'd better sit down. There's more.' He helps her to the ground, where she places her head between her knees and draws in a few deep breaths.

Ulan squats by her side.

Ryker hesitates a moment before stepping away. Moments later he returns with Jaeger.

Banji and Ulan gasp.

Edra scrambles to her feet, grabs Ulan by the arm and clings to her.

Jaeger smiles, the earlier emptiness now gone from his eyes. He looks at Edra. 'Hello, beautiful. God, I've missed you.'

Edra collapses, out cold, but Ryker is there to break her fall. He lays her on the ground. 'I guess that went as well as could be expected.'

'Ryker! What the hell!' Banji yells.

'Hey, Banj, don't blame Ryker; it's my fault.' Jaeger whooshes to Edra's side, presses his lips to her brow, then strokes her hair. 'Man, that was tough.'

Ulan snorts. 'You think!'

Edra stirs, and Ryker looks about them uneasily. 'Come on, we need to get her out of here before someone comes. We can deal with this on the other side.'

The twins help Edra to her feet and through the portal.

At the sight of them vanishing, Aelianna gasps and steps back.

Ryker takes her hand, squeezes it and waits for the shock to pass.

Her gaze darts back and forth from him to the diaphanous veil. He can't expect any of this to be easy for her. He'll give her the time she needs.

He turns to Jaeger. 'You ready?'

Jaeger steps up to the wispy curtain and pauses. His eyes close, and his chin lowers in silent prayer. Ryker takes a deep breath and prays with him—only God knows how this will pan out.

Jaeger takes a deep breath, turns to Ryker and grins. 'Whatever happens, happens, right?'

Ryker shrugs. 'We won't know until you take that step.'

'So here's hoping.' Jaeger takes one step, then two, closes his eyes and disappears through the formidable barrier to whatever lies on the other side for him.

Ryker waits, his breath held, half expecting the

portal to spit him back out, but nothing happens; the diaphanous barrier remains tranquil.

He takes Aelianna by the hand. 'Are you ready?' She pulls back, but he tightens his grip. 'Do you trust me?'

She hesitates, then nods.

'Then close your eyes, and I'll take you home.'

At first, her eyes scrunch tight, but then they soften, and she smiles the biggest smile.

Ryker's breath catches. With his hand secured around hers, they step forward together, and then they're gone.

57

Out of the Frypan & Into the Fire

Jack

There's no sign of Peanut, and time is running out. Jack chews his lower lip and tugs at his hair, wondering what's taking him so long. As was the plan, they've made their way to the periphery of the gateway and are lying low, waiting before going any further. They're behind the shield only metres from the portal, ready for any guard encounter. The stillness of the morning doesn't fool them—anything could still happen. Max is by his side. He's sticking to her like glue—there's no way he's going to risk leaving her behind again. Ruby and Kenny are on the lookout at ground level, while Eddie and Sebastian hover in the treetops. The guys from the pit remain silent and huddle together close by.

But too much time has passed and dawn is approaching. *Where the hell is he?* Jack can't help but think the worst. 'He's in trouble; I know it. I'm going back.' He dives into one of the backpacks to retrieve a can of pepper spray.

'What? No!' Max grabs his shirt to stop him racing off, her eyes narrow. 'We've got to trust him. We stick to the plan. We wait!'

Just then, Eddie swoops down to warn them that guards are approaching. 'I don't know how many, but we'll know soon enough. Seb's having a closer look.'

'We should go through now while we've got the chance,' Kenny tells them.

Jack hesitates; he looks from Kenny to the portal and groans. 'Not without Peanut!'

Ruby grits her teeth. 'I'm not going anywhere either.'

Max rests her hand on Ruby's shoulder. 'We'll stick it out together.'

The group bunch closer together. Ruby reinforces her shield.

Sebastian returns after a few minutes. 'There are three guards, and if I'm not wrong, Herodus has one of the Invincibles with him. I distracted them for a while, but then I noticed a heap of people coming out of the forest from the other direction. I had to come back to warn you. We're outnumbered. They're closing in on us.'

Jack starts to panic, but then realises that the people Sebastian is talking about could be the good people of the forest coming to help. And just as he thinks it, their friends appear.

Medwin leads, waving his baton in the air in excitement. 'Prepare yourselves. The enemy approaches!' The other dozen or so forest men who follow hold up their weapons and cheer.

Jack smiles. *Who's outnumbered now?*

Within moments, a group of warriors emerge from the forest. And sure enough, just as Sebastian had guessed, Herodus is among them with Shant. Jack takes a deep breath in preparation. Of all the remaining Champions, Shant was the one he was most dreading meeting again—his ability to conjure a tornado out of thin air had, in the past, been their greatest challenge.

Suddenly there's pandemonium. Medwin and his men charge, and they don't hold back, battling with a daring Jack can hardly believe. A few of them appear to be actually enjoying themselves.

Jack reinforces his hold on the spray can. 'Ruby, let me out. I can't just stand here and watch.'

At that moment, Shant frees himself from the grips of two assailants and raises his arms ready to create havoc. But before Jack has a chance to react, the realm's hero is thrown to the ground by an invisible force. To Jack's relief, several forest men come to Peanut's aid, and between them they soon have that threat well and truly snuffed.

Herodus growls, his fury obvious. He prepares to pounce on one of the forest men. Jack sees it and runs at him hard, knocking him to the ground, then blasts him with the full force of the pepper spray. Herodus claws at his face, screaming, oblivious to what comes next. A weighty boulder smashes down on him with a sickening crunch, ending his oppression once and for all.

With the threat of Herodus and Shant gone, they only have the guards to take care of, but the gatekeepers are fighting a losing battle. One is on the ground struggling to fend off three attackers, and another is just about to get whacked in the gut by a floating tree branch. Connor and Mitchell have broken from Ruby's protection, clearly eager to throw themselves into the thick of things. In full rage, they attack the final guard, taking turns to deliver blows to his head, one with a mallet, the other with a club—courtesy of the forest dwellers.

Then Ruby bursts forward to put her unrelenting shield to work. One by one, the guards cop her fury. Sebastian and Eddie look at each other, smile mischievously and join the attack. The guards take off screaming.

The team's way home is now clear.

Jack searches for Max. She and Kenny appear from the woods, the pit men close behind. 'Hey, are you okay?'

Max checks him over. 'Yeah. You?'

Just then Molan emerges from the forest, out of breath. 'I heard the commotion from afar and came as quickly as I could.' He looks about them and smiles. 'But I see I have arrived too late.'

Jack surveys the battle field. Several forest men stagger to their feet, bloodied and wounded but pleased with their efforts. He grins at their triumph and wonders how well they would have managed without them.

Jack sees Mitchell and Connor at the foot of the portal, both with their mouths gaping. 'After all these years, we've finally made it,' Mitchell says in a whisper. He turns to Connor. 'Mate, we're going home!' But his exhaustion prevails; he falls to his knees.

Connor collapses in a heap next to him, and together they stare at the wispy veil, mesmerised.

Jack takes Max by the hand. 'Come on, let's get out of here.' He searches for Sebastian and Eddie. 'Hey, are you guys ready?'

The ghosts look at each other. 'What'll happen to

us now?' Eddie asks.

Jack scratches his head. He hadn't given it much thought. He turns to Molan, who exchanges a questioning look with Medwin.

Medwin frowns. 'I cannot say, for I have no experience in such things, but my senses remain positive. I can only tell you I have no ill premonition.'

Eddie shrugs. 'Well, anything's better than what we've had to put up with these last few years. Right, Seb?'

'Too right, I'm out of here. See you lot on the other side.' Sebastian vanishes through the floating portal, and Eddie follows close behind.

Having witnessed this bizarre phenomenon for the first time, Flavius and the other men from the pit take a few steps back.

'Are you guys coming with us?' Jack asks.

'Jack, if it is their will, they can remain with us,' Medwin tells him. 'We will take them in as our own or help them find their families. But now, you must make haste, for the guards that fled will return with others.'

And just as Medwin predicts this, Jack hears the sound of a horn in the distance, signalling an impending attack.

'But you've got to come with us,' Max says.

Medwin sighs. 'We have considered this, young

Max. Perhaps one day our paths will cross again, and the opportunity will present itself, but until then, we will remain—our new friends need our support.'

Jack shakes the men's hands, thankful for everything they've done. 'We couldn't have done this without you.'

'Go now, return to your loved ones.' Molan turns to seek Peanut. 'And Peanut, I thank you for your hand in securing Aelianna's happiness. She and Ryker are well suited, and I am confident in my decision in letting her go.'

Jack's head whips around. *Say what?'*

Peanut grins and waggles his eyebrows. 'Hey, no worries, Molan; she's in good hands. You can bet Ryker will treat her like a princess.' He turns to Jack, who watches on numbly. 'I guess there are a few things I need to explain, huh? But later, 'cause right now we need to get the hell out of here.'

Before Jack knows what's happening, Peanut shoves him through the portal, where he lands with a thud. Having the wind knocked out of him, he takes a moment to collect himself. And when he does, he freezes, eyes wide. A dozen hostile-looking military officers surround him, pointing their firearms at him. He lifts his hands in surrender.

The ruckus behind him as the others fall through the portal doesn't divert his gaze, but to the other side of him, he spots something that does. He needs to blink a few times to trust what he's seeing. Suddenly the presence of these soldiers is nothing compared to what's before him. His two no-longer-transparent and very-much-alive new friends, Eddie and Sebastian, stand petrified on the spot also with their hands up before them.

What the …!

'FREEZE!'

58

Edra's Dream

Edra

A warmth, like nothing she's ever felt before, wraps around Edra's heart. *If this is heaven, let me stay here. Let me sleep forever.* But then she feels someone poke her, trying to arouse her. She moans and rolls over. The gentle prodding persists. She ignores it—she's way too happy to wake from the dream she's having. She tries to hold onto the image of Jaeger standing before her, full of life, teasing her with a mischievous look in his eyes. A smile curls on her lips.

Edra hears him, clear as day, asking her to wake. *But I am awake, aren't I? I'm here, with you.* She snuggles into a tight ball. *And I never want to be anywhere without you again.*

She feels his gentle kiss on her brow.

God, I've missed you.

And now she can smell him, that all-so-familiar scent she's missed. Her smile widens. A delicious tingle runs down her spine. She nestles a little tighter.

'Babe, you need to wake. We need to keep moving.' Jaeger's voice is deep and smooth, like melted dark chocolate.

'Mmm. No, I don't want to,' she mumbles. 'Just a few more minutes.'

'Then I'll go without you,' he threatens.

'No,' she says with a pout.

'Then wake up so we can leave together.'

Yes, together. Her smile widens; she hugs herself closer.

But then in her dream, Jaeger turns to leave. 'No! Jae!' He doesn't stop. *No! I'm not letting you go again!* 'Come back!' In a panic she stirs awake, but her eyes won't open. She swipes at them, but they won't budge. A profound dread envelopes her, threatening suffocation. 'Jae! JAE!'

'Hey, it's okay; I'm here.' He shushes her, pressing her firmly against his chest.

The sound of his pounding heart beats against her ear. She relaxes.

'I've got you,' he whispers softly, 'and I'll never let you go again.'

Tears prickle at her senses. *No, never again.*

But she needs to see him, to look into his eyes to know he's not lying. She looks up.

He caresses away the moisture from her cheek and smiles. 'Hi there, beautiful.'

Suddenly reality hits. She jerks out of his hold and scrambles away.

Ulan dives to her side. 'It's okay, Edra. You're safe. We're home.'

In a panic she looks around and realises where they are. They're by the jeep, concealed in the scrub, in the reserve. Banji hovers nearby, and Ryker methodically scours the area, Aelianna close by his side. She chances a look back at Jaeger, questioning her sanity. But he's there, real and alive. 'What the hell?' Edra jumps to her feet, ready to run. The motion makes her head spin. She stumbles but Jaeger is quick to catch her.

'I'm sorry, babe. I know this is way too much. I'm struggling to get my head around it myself.'

'Bloody hell, we all are!' Banji approaches, scratching his head.

'B …but … you're …' Edra struggles to put two words together.

Jaeger smiles a crooked smile. 'Yeah, I know. Weird, right?'

'You were dead, and now you're …'

'Alive.' Jaeger shakes his head again. 'Go figure!'

Her head starts to swim. And then Ryker is in her

face. 'Edra, breathe. Don't try to understand it, just take it for what it is, because right now, we need to get out of here.'

Jaeger stands and offers her his hand. 'I want to go home. Are you coming?'

Numbly she allows him to help her up and onto the jeep. He jumps in next to her and pulls her into his side. She closes her eyes and nestles into him, savouring the moment. If she wakes up and realises it's all been a dream, so be it. She's clinging to that right now, and it's all that's keeping her sane.

59

ONE WEEK LATER

MAX

The night sky sparkles with twinkling stars. The moon, according to Kenny, is in its fourth phase—the waxing gibbous phase—a perfect night for a campfire, albeit in Max's backyard. Max snuggles a little closer to Jack to warm herself against the cold. He throws his arm across her shoulders and smiles down at her, then hands her the marshmallow he's been toasting. She laughs at Peanut's shenanigans. *Once again* they're hearing Peanut's version of Jack's blindside—when Molan revealed that Aelianna was going home with Ryker.

Ruby groans.

'That was gold! Mate, ya should've seen the look on your face!'

Jack shakes his head. 'Why was I even surprised?

433

When was the last time you stuck to a plan?'

'*Me* not stick to a plan? Let me tell ya somethin' for nothin', *buddy*, I *did* stick to a plan—it just wasn't *your* plan.' He nudges him. 'Anyway, I reckon Ryker can wear *that* crown; he's the *king of stuff-ups!* Look at the bloody mess he got us into! And in the end, we didn't even finish what we set out to do!' He shakes his head. 'Man, I feel bad for his mum, though.'

'Okay, you two, quit it!' Ruby plonks herself between the two boys. 'You're just lucky things turned out the way they did.' She turns to Max. 'Have you spoken to Ryker lately? How *is* Isebel?'

'We skyped last night. She's not so good, but they're keeping positive.' Max looks at Jack and gives him a wink.

'And how's Edra coping?' Ruby continues. 'Talk about the shock of the century! I can't even begin to imagine going through what she just did.'

'Well, the whole "the dead coming back to life" thing is pretty creepy if you ask me,' Peanut says. 'I nearly had a heart attack when I saw Seb and Eddie standing there with a pulse again.'

Jack chuckles. 'Same.'

Peanut turns to Kenny. 'So, Kenny, what's the go? How come that happened?'

Kenny shrugs. 'I don't get it either.'

Peanut snorts. 'No offence, Kenny, but it's so

weird, you not knowing. We're kinda used to you having all the answers.'

Kenny shakes his head. 'Look, my best guess is that our dimensions weren't ever supposed to intersect—like we were never meant to be there. So things go back to the way they're supposed to be—no superpowers, no death, no nothing.'

'What! No way!' Peanut jumps up in a state. 'Hang on a sec!' He fumbles to undo the fly of his jeans, then drops them in search of something on his leg.

'Peanut!' Max yells, her face warming. 'What the hell are you doing?' She looks at Ruby, and they both burst into fits of giggles.

Oblivious to everyone's amusement, Peanut clicks his fingers. 'Quick! Someone, give me a light!'

Jack hands him the torch on his smartphone.

Max nudges Ruby with her knee. 'He's your boyfriend, do something!'

Ruby covers her eyes and turns away. 'Nope. I don't know him, never seen him before, don't *want* to know him.'

'Arghh! You're kidding me. They're almost gone!' In a panic, Peanut looks closer. 'This is *so* not fair. I can't believe it; you can hardly see them!'

'See what?' Max turns to look.

His shoulders slump. 'My scars!'

Max moans. '*Your scars?* Is that all?'

'IS THAT ALL? Max, that's all I've got to show the guys!'

Ruby groans. 'You twit. Will you pull your pants up? No one wants to see your scrawny arse.'

'Well, that's one way of proving Kenny's theory.' Jack laughs, then reaches over to high-five Kenny.

'Hey, Max, how's Aelianna coping with her new life?' Ruby asks. 'I've got to laugh. Is she still freaking out with the TV?'

'You know, I'd be freaking out too if I thought someone was trapped in a five-centimetre-thick box mounted on the wall.' Kenny chuckles. 'I can't even begin to imagine how her head's dealing with all this technology.'

'She's been a good distraction for Ryker, that's for sure,' Max says. And she's been a great support to Isebel too. In fact, it's the reason Annie isn't over there yet.'

Peanut stops short. 'What? She's not still going, is she? What about us?'

Ruby glares at him. 'What *about* us?'

He pouts. 'We need Annie too!'

'Vhat you like, Peanut?' Annie calls from the open kitchen window. 'You hungry again? Maybe I make it some Dobos cake?'

That earns him a punch in the arm from Ruby.

'Ow! That hurt!'

'Good, maybe it'll teach you to think of others instead of yourself for a change.'

Max giggles, then calls up to the house. 'It's okay, Annie, we're all good here.'

'I wonder how Mitch and the boys are doing,' Jack says. 'They've left the hospital already, right?'

'Yeah, I caught up with them yesterday,' Peanut tells them. 'I thought they might need a friend. You know, someone to talk to.'

Ruby softens hearing this. 'Aw, Peanut, that's so sweet.'

Peanut pouts, then crosses his arms. 'Oh, so now I'm sweet, am I? Two seconds ago, you didn't think so.'

Ruby soothes the spot on his arm where she hit him. 'Aw, poor Charlie. So tell us, how are they?'

With the dispute forgotten, Peanut launches into telling them. 'Well, you remember how overprotective *our* folks were after we went missing, well, you can imagine *their* families. After so many years lost, they've all had to make some pretty major adjustments.'

'We've been pretty lucky, you know,' Jack says. 'Okay, so it's been tough, but we've dodged a few bullets and have somehow come out the other end in one piece.'

Max nods. 'If not clued up and stronger.'

'And we're lucky the media painted us to be heroes in all of this,' Kenny says. 'Thanks to Max's quick thinking, they believed that we went back to save those kids. If only they knew what really happened, hey?'

They all laugh.

'So how did the olds cotton on, anyway?' Peanut asks.

'Well, you remember how we switched numbers in my dad's phone,' Max begins, 'the next day, he tried ringing Deputy Thompson again and got Ruby's voice mail. He knew then that we were up to something, so he rang Jack's dad, and from there, he found out that Ryker was here. It didn't take them long to figure out the rest. You know we're lucky that we came back when we did, because Ryker's dad was ready to come charging over here with an army of his own men.'

Jack laughs. 'Now *he's* what you call scary! You should've seen him that first time he came, Max. I nearly crapped my pants.'

Peanut jumps up to impersonate Ryker's dad. He's got his accent and mannerisms down pat. They all laugh. Everyone, that is, except for Kenny. Max notices. 'Hey, Kenny, is everything okay?'

Kenny's smile vanishes.

'Hey, what's up, buddy?' Jack gets up and plonks

himself next to him.

Kenny shrugs. 'It's nothing.'

Jack nudges him. 'C'mon, spill.'

Kenny fidgets in his seat. 'Well, you all know how strict my parents are, and that we kind of lied to them about me going back into the realm?'

'Yeah, Kenny, they think you were just guarding the portal and nothing more,' Max says. 'Dad's asked Deputy Thompson to cover for you too, so neither of them will be saying anything.'

Kenny lowers his gaze. 'And your dad's okay with all of this?'

'Sure, he is. Why wouldn't he be? Don't worry, Kenny, you can trust Dad.'

Kenny brightens hearing this. 'Seriously, Max, you've got no idea how tense my parents have been. If they ever find out what I really got up to, I'll be grounded until I'm fifty.'

Max laughs. 'Trust me, Kenny, your secret's safe.'

Jack smiles at her, then gives her a wink. Ruby catches the exchange, her eyes narrow. 'Hang on a sec; what's going on?'

Max's lips clamp shut in a cheeky grin.

Ruby and Peanut exchange a look, and before they know it, Max and Jack are cornered in an interrogation. 'Hey, what gives?' Peanut takes turns in scrutinising them. 'You two are keeping something from us, so out with it!'

He waggles his eyebrows in a way that makes Max laugh. 'You can waggle as much as you like, Peanut, but it's not happening—I promised not to say a word.' Max crosses her arms, presses her lips together and grins.

Peanut draws back. 'Hey, you can't do that! Jack, make her tell us!'

Jack clamps his lips tight too.

'No way! You too?' He turns his attention back to Max. 'How come he gets to know?'

Max shrugs.

'Hang on a minute,' Peanut says suspiciously, 'you're not thinking of going back, are you?'

'Going back!' Ruby cries out. She pushes Peanut out of the way to look Max in the eye. 'Tell me, now! You're NOT going back, are you?'

Max can't lie to her; she turns away.

Ruby dusts her hands in triumph. 'And there's your answer. Looks like they are.'

'I knew it!' Peanut jumps up. 'Great work, Rubes.' They high-five each other.

Peanut dives back to Max's side. 'Now, back to the grilling. So we've established that you're going back in, but why?' he asks himself as though working out a complex riddle.

Kenny laughs. 'Isn't it obvious? They're re-entering with Ryker's mum to get rid of her cancer.'

Peanut's eyes widen. 'Genius!' He leans over to high-five Kenny. 'So is he right? Are you going back for Isebel?'

Jack nudges Max. 'You may as well tell them.'

Max can't bring herself to open her mouth to say the words—she had promised her father not to tell. But then on the other hand, them guessing is another story. 'You've kinda got it right; Dad will be returning with Isebel. Jack and I are staying put.'

Kenny's face screws up like he's not quite getting something. 'But what about my theory? Even if you get rid of the cancer, won't it come back once she returns?'

Max whips around to look at Jack. That right there, that one unchallenged theory, asked so innocently, is like a kick to the gut.

Jack frowns thoughtfully, and then his eyes widen. 'Hey, this might work. Your dad can get rid of the cancer while they're there, so when they start her treatment back home, she won't need so much of it because the cancer won't have got to the stage it is now. It might give her a head-start. Kenny, what d'ya reckon?'

Max jumps to her feet. 'Of course! I can't believe I didn't think of that myself.'

Peanut rolls his eyes. 'Geez, someone's sure got

tickets on themselves.'

Kenny grins. 'Sounds like a win-win situation.'

Peanut grabs Max in a head-lock and messes up her hair. 'Sure does. Isebel wins and so does Kenny.'

Kenny frowns. 'I don't get it. How do I win?'

'Duh! For someone so smart, sometimes I wonder. The doc's just about to do something he's not supposed to be doing, so I reckon that little secret of yours is pretty safe with him.' He looks at Max. 'Am I right?'

Max pulls out of Peanut's hold and grins. 'I guess you could say that.'

'Too bad we can't make the most of what the realm has to offer,' Kenny says in all seriousness. 'Your dad could potentially change the future of medicine.'

'Try getting "the powers that be" to come on board with that!' Max says. 'Look at how they reacted to us "going back to rescue the boys"?'

Peanut snorts. 'You're not wrong. But you know what…' He shifts in his seat, suddenly serious. 'I reckon there's heaps of kids out there that've stumbled across what we have and never found their way back. And I think it's up to us to do something about it.'

There's a distinctive gleam in Peanut's eyes that makes Max wonder what's put it there. 'What are you getting at?'

Peanut sits taller. 'Now hear me out before you

shoot me down. We know for a fact that two portals exist already, and I'm guessing there are heaps more out there …'

Kenny jumps up, excited. 'Peanut, I know where you're going with this, and I reckon you're onto something—I've been thinking the same thing. And since we've been back, I've been paying attention to the news and keeping tabs on anything suspicious— you know, things that might be realm-related, like people mysteriously vanishing.'

Peanut's eyes widen. 'No way! Hey, great minds think alike.'

Kenny paces before them. 'I figure there's got to be a way to investigate this further. Knowing what we know could help find these missing people.'

Peanut's face lights up. 'Hey, we could all become private eyes. It'll be just like we're back in the realm, snooping around for clues. We could get Ryker and the gang in on it too. They could keep an eye out for stuff in their neck of the woods, and we could cover places around here.'

'Settle down, Sherlock,' Ruby says to him grimly. 'There's no way in the world I'm going back in there, so count me out.'

'Think about it, Rubes, we won't need to go back. We could just keep our ear to the ground and report to Deputy Thompson. Hey, maybe they can set up a task force that deals with what we find. Whoa! Hold your horses'—he stops mid-thought—'maybe we can call ourselves something cool, something like … like *The Triple C*.'

Jack laughs. 'The Triple C?'

'Yeah. The Central Communications Co-operative! What d'ya reckon?'

The smirk on Jack's face vanishes; his eyes widen with unexpected interest. Max can see the same look on Kenny's face and realises that Peanut's suggestion suddenly doesn't sound so lame. Her excitement escalates as she envisages them tracking down a heap of portals all over the world. There must be hundreds of them; thousands in fact. Her mind races with the possibilities. It's genius.

'Man, who's hungry?' Peanut cries out suddenly. 'All this thinking's got me starving. Hey, Annie,' he calls up to the house, 'have ya got any of your awesome apple strudel left?'

And just like that, Peanut's one defining moment of brilliance disintegrates into thin air.

GLOSSARY OF AUSTRALIAN SLANG

Arvo: informal/slang for afternoon detention.

Bloke: informal for a man.

Buckley's chance: informal/slang for no chance (phrase source from the improbable survival of convict William Buckley).

Crack: as in give it a crack—informal; try your best.

Dead set: informal; term used to confirm when you're serious.

Dirty: informal, used to emphasise one's disgust for someone or something.

Dob/dobbing: informal for inform against someone.

G'day: informal, shortening of good day. Used when meeting or greeting someone.

Gobsmacked: informal, dumbfounded/utterly astounded.

Gunning: informal, trying to get something, for example a prize.

Gurgler: informal for a drain.

Larrikin: informal for a harmless prankster.

Mate: informal for good friend.

MIA: missing in action.

Mobile: short for mobile/cell phone.

Mug: informal for ugly face.

No-brainer: informal; something requiring little mental effort.

Noggin: informal for head.

One up: informal; having an advantage.

Shenanigans: informal for silly or high-spirited behaviour; mischief.

Stacks: informal, a heap of/plenty.

Stoked: informal, being in an enthusiastic or exhilarated state.

T.K.O: term used in boxing; a technical knockout.

Vegemite: a thick brown Australian food-spread made from yeast.

A Note From the Author

If you enjoyed this book, I would be very grateful if you could write a review and publish it at your point of purchase. Your review, even a brief one, will help other readers to decide if they'll enjoy my work.

If you want to be notified of new releases from myself and other AIA Publishing authors, please **sign up to the AIA Publishing email list**. You'll find the sign-up button on the right-hand side under the photo at www.aiapublishing.com. Of course, your information will never be shared, and the publisher won't inundate you with emails, just let you know of new releases.